"WE'RE NOT KIDS ANYMORE," TUCKER SAID IN A DANGEROUSLY QUIET VOICE. "You're a woman and I'm a man, and you know damn well what's between us. It's time to settle this, once and for all."

"If only we could!" Emma said desperately, looking into his steel-blue eyes. "How? Just tell me how we can forget about this!"

"We'll let ourselves go all the way, as far as we want. Right here on this cot. And then it'll be over. Over forever," he repeated, as if reassuring himself, as he tore his gaze from her lips.

He didn't want any misunderstandings.

"Listen, Malloy, there's something you need to understand. I'm not looking to saddle myself with a wife. And Lord knows you'd be the last one I'd pick if I were—"

"I'd sooner marry a skunk as marry you!" she cried indignantly.

"Good, Malloy, that's real good. So we're safe. I'm not the marrying kind anyway—never have been and don't ever expect to be." He shrugged. "But sometimes a woman gets in your blood. . . ."

WHEN THE HEART BECKONS

"A WONDERFULLY EXCITING ROMANCE from the Old West. The plot twists in this novel are handled expertly. . . . It's great from start to finish."
—*Rendezvous*

"Jill Gregory combines all the drama of a gritty western with the aura of a homespun romance in this beautifully rendered tale. The wonderful characters are sure to win readers' hearts." —*Romantic Times*

DAISIES IN THE WIND

"*Daisies in the Wind* is a fast-paced Western romance novel that will keep readers' attention throughout. Both the hero and heroine are charming characters."
—*Affaire de Coeur*

FOREVER AFTER

"A CHARMING TALE of dreams come true. It combines a heartwarming love story with an intriguing mystery." —*Gothic Journal*

Dell Books by Jill Gregory

Always You
Cherished
Daisies in the Wind
Forever After
Just This Once
Never Love a Cowboy
When the Heart Beckons

Never Love a Cowboy

Jill Gregory

A Dell Book

Published by
Dell Publishing
a division of
Bantam Doubleday Dell Publishing Group, Inc.
1540 Broadway
New York, New York 10036

The trademark Dell® is registered in the U.S. Patent and Trademark Office.

ISBN: 0-440-22439-X

Printed in the United States of America

Published simultaneously in Canada

July 1998

10 9 8 7 6 5 4 3 2

OPM

For Rachel,
With love and admiration and boundless
happy wishes for the future—
Happy Graduation, honey!

Chapter 1

"WELCOME HOME, HONEY."

For a moment Emma Malloy couldn't reply to her father's huskily spoken words. As she stepped across the threshold of the beloved two-story ranch house where she had grown up, her throat closed up, aching with emotion.

She was home. *Home.* With lavender dusk gathering behind her across the great mountain-scalloped Montana skyline, the house of her childhood, of countless precious memories, welcomed her as no other place ever could. Cheerily lit, cozy, beckoning, the house invited her with the aroma of fresh-baked bread, the glow of a fire to banish the coolness of the night, and the warmth of the people who meant the most to her in the world.

After five long years at school in the east, she was back at Echo Ranch, back where she belonged.

And there was only one thing in the world that could possibly spoil it.

But she wouldn't think about that—about *him.* Not now.

She wouldn't let anything ruin this moment, least of all Tucker Garrettson.

Her face shone as she turned in a slow circle and took in the familiar comfortable furnishings of her home.

"Just as I remember," she breathed.

Her father set down her trunk and smiled. He had seemed somewhat quiet on the ride home from town, and even though he had insisted nothing was wrong, she still wondered. But now there was no mistaking the joy that lit his handsome, craggy face.

"It's good to have you back, Emma. Real good." His eyes grew wet as she suddenly launched herself into his arms. "Ah ha, little girl," he chuckled hoarsely, stroking her hair, "you haven't changed so much after all. I see you still cry only when you're happy, never sad, eh?"

"True," she gasped, dashing away the tears. "And Papa, I *am* happy—so happy to be home. I've missed you more than I could say. And I've missed the ranch and Whisper Valley. And . . . " she took a deep, emotion-laden breath, "and all of Montana," she acknowledged with a fierce little laugh. "Philadelphia is splendid, but it isn't home."

"Never will be?"

"Never will be."

She hugged him tight, this big bear of a man who had raised her since her mother died when she was seven. He had sent her east to school, as he'd promised her mother he would, to give her a taste of life outside Whisper Valley and Echo Ranch. And she'd missed him every day. She'd missed the way he'd tousled her hair when he greeted her in the morning, missed the low easy timbre of his voice as he gave instructions to the ranch hands at the start of each day, missed the quiet evenings they'd spent together in his study. During these evenings, Emma would have been curled in the armchair with a novel, and her father would have been at his desk, working, always working on the ranch books, with a cup of whisky-laced coffee at his elbow and the rich aroma of his cigar breathing masculine life and character into each corner of that sturdy, handsome room.

She'd come back home the first summer, but not since, and though Winthrop Malloy had visited Emma several times a year back east, it hadn't been the same as being together here, where they both belonged.

Relief flickered in Win's keen brown eyes as he heard her words and realized that her years at a fancy girls' school among rich easterners hadn't changed her. Oh, she was taller all right, and as shapely as a beautiful young woman ought to be, and her rich silky black hair—which had almost always been either clamped in braids or left to fly in wild disarray in her youth—was now prettily curled and kept in place with a rose-colored velvet ribbon which matched her traveling dress. But she was still his darling bright-eyed Em, the girl with more spunk than any ten cowhands, the girl who could outride anyone this side of the Rockies, who could shoot a rifle as well as he could himself, and who loved Whisper Valley every bit as much as he did.

"Corinne, look who's back. Corinne! Hell, where are you, woman?"

Before Emma even had time to take three steps into the large, high-beamed parlor, footsteps pounded through the hall from the kitchen and she was enveloped in cushiony arms that squeezed tight.

"Wal, now, look at you. All grown up and pretty as a picture. What happened to that scrape-kneed little monkey who used to steal chocolate cake when my back was turned?"

"Guess she grew up." Emma grinned as she leaned back in the embrace of the plump little gray-haired woman whose bright green eyes were no larger than peas. *I won't cry again,* she thought fiercely, blinking back tears as she kissed the housekeeper's leathery cheek, and nearly overcome by affection for this plainspoken woman who had cared for her ever since her mother had died.

"She sure did. Now hold still, and let me look at you. Turn around, Emma. My, my, what a dress. Made in Philadelphia, I'll wager?"

"Actually, Paris." Emma waited patiently as Corinne inspected her from head to toe, her head tilted, bird-like, to one side. She seemed fascinated by the delicate black lace trim and elegant train of Emma's rose silk traveling dress. And by the intricate beadwork on her matching rose shoes. Corinne also studied her face, the way she held her shoulders, and the line of her figure.

Finally, the housekeeper's face broke into a wide grin. "You're sure every inch the lady." She chuckled, then shook her head wonderingly. "Who would've guessed that my wild little monkey would've turned into such a high falutin' fancy-looking gal?'' She said it with love and rich pleasure, and looked ready to burst with pride.

''Well, fancy . . . maybe. The clothes are, at least.'' Emma laughed. ''But I feel it only fair to warn you—even now, I wouldn't turn my back on a fresh-baked chocolate cake, Corinne, if I were you.''

''Which you ain't, that's for sure. If you was me, you'd be plumb tuckered out. I've been cooking your homecoming meal all afternoon, and now it's going to burn if I don't get back in that kitchen and tend to it.''

This was the Corinne she remembered. Always muttering, grumbling, her bark far worse than her bite.

''Ummm,'' Emma sniffed the air appreciatively. ''Don't tell me you fixed roasted chicken?''

''And beef stew. *And* them potatoes fried with onions you always had a hankering for.''

''And chocolate cake,'' Win Malloy added, winking at Emma as Corinne sent him a scowl before bustling back toward the kitchen.

He hefted Emma's trunk and started toward the curving oak staircase. ''Corinne's been fussing in the kitchen for days. And polishing floors and lamps as if royalty was coming to stay.''

''Everything looks wonderful, Papa.''

''You'll find that nothing much has changed since you've been away.'' He turned right at the head of the stairs and led the way to her bedroom. ''I've kept your room as it was. Thought you might want to add some new things, pick out what you want. I expect you'll want some fancy female knickknacks. Maybe some new curtains. Whatever you like, Em. Change whatever you want in the house, too. This is your home, and it should suit you now that you're all grown up.''

"As a matter of fact, I do have a few ideas about that. I brought some things with me from Philadelphia, from Aunt Loretta's house. But oh . . . '' She broke off as she reached her doorway. Warmth and pleasure and a thousand happy memories flooded through her.

It was all just as she remembered. The room was large and simply furnished, with a wide featherbed covered by the same green and blue patterned quilt she'd had since she was a child, and with the same rag doll cradled on a pillow in the center. The green cotton curtains at the window were somewhat faded now, as was the rag rug across the polished wood floor, but the bedside table and lamp, the bookshelves, and the big oak dresser with the gold-framed photograph of her mother sitting atop it, beside a white china pitcher and basin, were as sturdy and solid as ever.

"It does feel *wonderful* to be home,'' she said softly, glancing over at her father with satisfaction. But with a sinking of her heart, she saw that he looked distracted again. His brows were knit, his eyes shadowed with worry, and it was obvious his mind had wandered to something other than her homecoming, something that deeply troubled him.

"What's wrong, Papa? Please tell me.''

He stiffened, and his attention sharpened on her, even as a flush came over his face. "Nothing, honey.

Nothing worth speaking of. Don't you worry about a thing.''

"Is there something I *should* be worried about?''

"Yep, sure is.'' He moved toward her and pinched her cheek, a glint of warm humor suddenly lighting his eyes. "How you're going to beat off all the young cowpokes for miles around once they hear you're home. And once they see what a looker my little girl's grown into. Why, I'll have to fight 'em off night and day—''

"Papa,'' she scolded him. "You're changing the subject.''

He grinned at her.

"See you downstairs, honey. I reckon you'll want to rest for a while after your trip.''

Then Emma was alone in the room of her childhood, surrounded by the familiar sights and smells— the dancing fragments of memory.

Papa's probably only concerned about some minor problem with the ranch, she told herself as she set her small silk handbag on the table. She made up her mind to coax him into telling her about it at supper.

Then, with light, eager steps she crossed to the window and lifted the curtain, hoping to catch the final glow of sunset. But she was too late. Mysterious gray darkness draped the land. But pure Montana air wafted like cool silk over her, and she knew that the glorious mountains and canyons, the grass-rich plains, and the singing waterfalls were out there and would be there in the morning, as they had been a thousand mornings before.

She could wait.

For now, all she could see were the shadowy forms of the ranch outbuildings and in the distance, the indistinct jaggedness of black looming peaks.

Whisper Valley—the most beautiful place on earth.

"I won't leave you again," she whispered.

She thought of the letter inside her handbag, the letter from Derek Carleton tucked alongside her lace handkerchief and velvet money pouch.

It was a marriage proposal, written in Derek's flawless black script, and it was eloquent and heartfelt. She'd memorized every word of it.

But she had yet to answer it.

First, I guess I need to decide if I'm in love with him, Emma thought ruefully, tracing a finger across the windowpane.

Love. That was something she hadn't yet figured out. How *did* one know when one was in love? She enjoyed Derek's company when he'd escorted her to balls and parties and operas. She liked him, she enjoyed kissing him—but she didn't feel anything like the raging passion she'd always associated with being in love.

And, even if she did love him, Emma had made up her mind that she would only marry him if he would agree to live here in Montana, preferably at Echo Ranch.

And that was one very big "if." Derek was headstrong and ambitious, and the son of a powerful railroad magnate. He had plans of his own. And she wasn't sure if he loved her enough to meet the one condition she would impose if she did decide to accept his proposal. She wanted to live in Montana. Period.

Her gaze fixed again on the darkness beyond her window and shifted, without her being aware of it, to the south, to where the Garrettson ranch straddled a huge chunk of the valley.

Emma's turquoise eyes narrowed. Why was she thinking about the Garrettsons?

None of them are worth a plug nickel, she reflected, letting the curtain drop. They were the only part of Whisper Valley she hadn't missed at all—especially Tucker Garrettson.

With any luck at all, he'd have left home by now and she'd never see him again. That would suit her just fine.

Luck? Emma deliberately turned away from the window. She kicked off her shoes and sank down on the bed to rub her feet.

It was luck that had started the feud between the Malloys and the Garrettsons sixteen years ago. Her father's luck.

True to his name, Win Malloy had beaten Jed Garrettson at poker one fateful night—and in a flash had gone from being a rancher of modest means and aspirations to one of the biggest stockmen in the valley. On that one last hand, he'd won half of the Garrettson spread—the biggest spread in the valley.

And had made himself an enemy for life.

Three enemies, actually. Jed and his two sons, Beau and Tucker. Grimacing to herself, Emma whipped the ribbon from her hair, shook it loose, and lay back against the pillows of her bed.

Against her will, the image of the younger son, Tucker, swam into her mind. Her nemesis, her enemy. Since their childhoods, the feud had enveloped them, hardened them, one against the other.

Except for that one day . . . that terrible, humiliating, unforgettable day . . .

It had happened just days before she'd gone away to school. She'd been almost fourteen then, teetering oh-so-awkwardly on the brink of womanhood. He had just passed his eighteenth birthday.

But with a strangely vivid intensity she remembered the breadth of his shoulders, and, even at that young age, the promise of raw, rough handsomeness he'd exuded. She could still see the sunlight gilding his sandy hair that day he'd "rescued" her, the mocking glint in eyes that were stunningly, devastatingly blue . . .

It had been warm and humid that day in May— warm enough so that the flowers drooped in their grassy beds and gave off a sweet scent that lingered in the air, and warm enough so that Emma had coiled her hair high on her head that morning, leaving her neck bare to catch whatever coolness the breeze might offer. She'd stepped down wrong on the rough track that ran along a belt of trees and had gone down hard. The ferocious bite of pain had actually made her feel faint for a moment.

But then she'd recovered and had tried to stand, only to gasp at the wrenching pain that shot through her ankle.

She couldn't get up.

She was half a mile from home, she'd realized.

And nearly the same distance from the schoolhouse. Her books and papers had scattered when she'd fallen, and the little sketch she'd made of a barn kitten was streaked with dirt.

Now what am I going to do, Emma had wondered in dismay as the sun beat down on her shoulders and her ankle throbbed.

But she hadn't cried. She'd crawled on her hands and knees to gather up her sketch and her books, then had forced herself to stand. Gritting her teeth, she'd hobbled forward. Each step was agony. But she had to get home and she refused to crawl.

By the time she'd made it to the bottom of a knoll, with another rise curving before her, she'd been ready to weep. But she took another step. And another. And then suddenly, with the next, the pain intensified, everything blurred, and she went down again with a cry of sheer frustration.

That's when Tucker had appeared. Sneering at her. Through a blur of hot tears, which she'd angrily swiped at with the back of her hand, she'd looked up to find him towering over her.

"What do *you* want?" she'd demanded, her voice shaking as much with wrath as with pain.

"Question is, what do you want? Do you want to get home?"

"No, you idiot, I want to go to Timbuktu. Now get out of my way."

She'd clutched at her books then and stumbled up, determined to walk away from him without so much as a wince. But the pain was almost more than she could bear, and the moment her foot touched the ground fresh agony splintered through her—and then Tucker moved forward so fast she thought he was going to knock her over, but instead he scooped her up.

She might have weighed no more than one of the flowers crushed beneath his booted feet as he grabbed her and hoisted her into his arms with a grunt.

Of course she'd hit him. With her books. She'd slammed them against his shoulder. "Let me go. Damn you, Garrettson, get your hands off me. I can walk."

"The hell you can."

"The day I need help from anyone named Garrettson is the day I'll shoot myself."

"Then go home and shoot yourself. See what I care."

"I'll shoot you if you don't set me down. Or my Pa will. If he finds out you touched me . . . "

"As if I'm scared of your Pa." He'd snorted then, and continued walking, breathing a bit hard, but holding her tight, and Emma had been so shocked by this turn of events that she'd forgotten to keep hitting him and instead had clutched at her books and thought that never in a million years would she have expected a Garrettson—especially Tucker Garrettson—to come to her aid.

Not that she had needed him to, not at all. She could have made it home herself, it just would have taken a while longer. But it seemed like an eternity with him trudging along carrying her, and she tried hard not to move, not even to breathe, for it was the strangest feeling to be held this tight and this close by her enemy.

It was easy to hate him—his being a Garrettson was enough. Added to that was his undeniable good looks, and the fact that for years he'd been the only boy in school as quick as she was at learning arithmetic and facts and spelling.

Of course, he was older. But every time he'd shown her up over the past years, Emma had resented him a little more. Just as she resented the smug smile on his face when he reached the first outbuildings of Echo Ranch. He halted.

"Guess this is the end of the road, Sunshine."

"So what are you waiting for? Set me down."

He did. He dropped her on her rump in a pile of hay behind the corral. It was Emma's turn to grunt.

Tucker dropped down on one knee beside her. There was laughter in his eyes now, infuriating laughter which made hot color rush into Emma's already flushed cheeks. Her turquoise eyes flashed like a sky caught in storm.

"Next time maybe you'll say thank you and I won't have to drop you on your butt," he told her, grinning.

"You've got the manners of a mongrel, Garrettson! Get off my land!"

"Your land?" His silver-blue eyes looked as icy cold as a glacier. "Only because your pa cheated at cards."

She slapped his face, her hand leaving a red mark on his left cheek.

For a moment, deathly stillness gripped the summer air. From the corrals came the muted sounds of horses whickering, of cowhands whistling or calling to one another. She could hear her father's hound dog, Blue, barking in the distance. But she might have been alone on the ranch, for she was isolated here beyond the far corral, half hidden by the stables. Isolated on the fringes of the ranch—with Tucker Garrettson.

"Go on," Emma challenged, her chin rising as she gazed into his eyes. "Hit me back, I dare you!"

"I should." When Tucker had leaned in closer, looming over her, it was all she could do not to flinch. "I damn well should, Malloy. You ought to have thanked me, 'stead of hitting me. The coyotes could have gobbled you up for supper before you crawled home on your own. A simple thank-you would have been enough, but I guess it's too much to expect. From a Malloy."

He grabbed her up by the front of her plaid shirt then, yanking her halfway off the ground. "I never should have bothered with you."

"Who asked you to?" She pried at his fingers trying to loosen them, but he only held on tighter.

"Let me go, or I'll hit you again! Or scream!" she gasped, frightened and uncertain, suddenly aware that their faces were only inches apart. The blaze of his eyes sent a strange heat coursing through her, and suddenly she couldn't breathe.

"The hell you will."

"I will . . . I . . . "

What happened then surprised both of them. Tucker stared at her furiously and then he kissed her—just pulled her close and *kissed* her. Before either one of them realized it.

He let her go just as suddenly, expelling his breath

in a rush, shock showing on his face, and for a moment Emma couldn't remember where she was. She couldn't even remember *who* she was.

Then it all came flooding back. Especially the fact that Tucker Garrettson's lips had touched her own.

She scrubbed furiously at her mouth. "Get out!" she yelled. "Get away from me!"

Tucker stepped back, looking stunned. He raked a hand through his hair, knocking his hat off, then he stooped quickly to pick it up, but not before she'd seen that his face was every bit as flushed as her own.

"I just did it to shut you up." He sounded dazed, his gruff voice filled with a hollow disbelief. He seemed to be speaking almost to himself. "It didn't mean a thing."

"Damn right it didn't!" Emma yelled.

Before she could shout at him again, he turned on his heel and walked away, back the way he had come. Not fast, not as if he was scared that she would call out for one of the hands, or her father. His gait was steady, sure, and deliberately unhurried.

Emma couldn't take her eyes off him until he vanished over a rise.

Then she'd hauled herself up, hobbled the rest of the way to the house—and had spent the next five years trying to wipe that kiss from her mind as she'd wiped it from her lips.

Emma sat up abruptly, restless and irritated with herself. *Why on earth was she thinking about Tucker Garrettson when she ought to be thinking of nothing except the pleasure of being home?*

Damn him. Damn his entire family for all the

trouble they'd caused. If not for the Garrettsons sharing the valley, coming into town, *inhabiting the earth,* life would be far sweeter.

Deliberately, she banished his image from her mind.

She refused to let Tucker Garrettson—or any of the Garrettsons—spoil her homecoming. Not for a minute.

She swung her legs off the bed. She could already smell the heavenly aroma of Corinne's roasted chicken wafting through the house.

Time to change for dinner.

CORINNE JOINED EMMA AND WIN FOR THE MEAL AND AFterward they sat together on the porch, the three of them, drinking hot coffee from mugs, gazing at the night while a cool Montana breeze slid over them and stars twinkled like fairy lights in the purple sky.

Emma had regaled them with stories of school, of Aunt Loretta's house in Philadelphia, of tea parties and dances and nights at the opera, picnics and boat rides and grand balls in the city.

But when she'd asked about how things were in the valley, her father had seemed evasive. "Things are fine," he'd said, a bit too heartily. "Just fine."

She'd shot him a quizzical look, her brows lifting. "Papa, the ranch . . . it's doing well?"

"Booming."

"Are we shorthanded?"

"Nope. Got all the men we need to take care of business."

"What about the books? Do you need me to do some work on them? My teacher, Miss Donahue, said I've got a knack for figures. I'd be glad—"

"Everything's in order, honey. There's not a thing for you to worry about."

Now, on the porch, Emma sat up straighter in her chair and slanted him a considering look. "You know, Papa, I'm not a child," she began slowly. "I'm not weak and I'm not easily upset. If something's wrong, you can tell me about it."

He forced a smile. "Know what, Corinne? I think my little girl has had her imagination overdeveloped back east."

"Hmmmph." Corinne shot him a darkling look.

"I'm telling you, Emma," Win said stubbornly, "nothing's wrong."

But Emma clearly saw the tension in his shoulders, in the heavy set of his jaw. At just over six feet tall, Win Malloy was a striking man, handsome with his thick salt and pepper hair and his trimmed mustache. There was good humor in his square face, and kindness and warmth in his eyes beneath their shaggy brows. His voice was as strong and sure and friendly as the easy stride of his walk. But though the years she'd been gone hadn't physically changed him much, she knew that he was different than she'd ever seen him before.

Besides the tension, his chin looked sharper, more stubborn, even the harsh slope of his nose and jawline appeared more obstinate. And there were deep lines etched beneath his eyes as if he hadn't been sleeping well.

She glanced over at Corinne who met her eyes. "Is there something I should know?"

But Win threw the housekeeper a keen glance, and Corinne merely pinched her lips together and shrugged her rounded shoulders. "He'll fire me if I say one word to upset you on your first night back, so I reckon I'll keep my tongue inside my head."

"Fire you? Papa would never—"

Emma broke off at the sound of hoofbeats in the darkness. Her father was already on his feet, his gun drawn as she and Corinne peered through the night, trying to discern the single rider approaching.

"It's me, Win," Sheriff Wesley Gill called out.

Gill slowed his horse to a halt and dismounted with the natural movement of those who've spent countless years in the saddle. Bowlegged, he ambled up the steps as Winthrop Malloy sank back into his chair.

"Evening, Win. Corinne."

"Howdy, Wes," the rancher and housekeeper murmured together.

The sheriff cleared his throat and flashed a quick hesitant glance at the dark-haired girl who was still standing, looking so surprised to see him.

Well, he was none too happy to be here himself. The last thing he wanted was to disrupt Emma Malloy's homecoming with upsetting news, but this had to be done.

He studied her in the space of a second, this slender young woman with the cascade of night-black hair, this girl who'd shared his family's table for many Sunday suppers; who'd sat at his knee amidst his four sons while he told tall tales; who'd taught his youngest boy, Seth, how to play checkers when he was six; who'd learned from his wife Sue Ellen how to bake a boysenberry pie; and who'd once, when she was nine, nearly set the house on fire.

"Glad to have you back, Emma. Dang, haven't you turned out pretty? Remind me a bit of your ma. Next to my Sue Ellen, and Corinne here, of course," he added with a gallant smile, "she was the loveliest woman I ever did see."

"Thank you, Sheriff Gill. Won't you have a seat? May I get you some coffee?" Emma couldn't imagine what would bring him to Echo Ranch at this time of night, but the gracious cordiality she'd learned in Aunt Loretta's home sprang automatically to her lips. Wesley Gill was her father's longtime friend, and next to Ross McQuaid, he was his closest friend. Still . . .

Had he come all the way from town so late at night merely to welcome her home?

It seemed doubtful.

"No, thanks, Emma." Shuffling his feet, the sheriff declined the chair she gestured him toward. "I can't be staying. Uh, a word with you, Win?"

"Sure, Wes. Inside."

And Emma watched with a sinking heart as her father and the sheriff disappeared inside the ranch house, the door thudding shut firmly behind them. Their voices dwindled away as they headed toward the study near the rear of the house.

Emma resumed her seat, her lips pursed thoughtfully. After a moment she set her mug down on the porch rail and turned to Corinne.

"All right, you may as well tell me everything. There's trouble, that's plain. But what kind of trouble would involve Sheriff Gill?"

"Garrettson trouble." The housekeeper sighed, then swore under her breath. "Didn't mean to let that out," she muttered.

Garrettson trouble. Of course. She should have known.

Eyes darkening, Emma sat up straighter. Tension shot through her, tautening the delicate bones of her cheeks and churning her stomach.

"What have they done now?" she demanded. "You may as well tell me all of it, Corinne. I won't give you a moment's peace until you do."

"You always were a stubborn thing. You might look like your ma, but you've got your pa's mulish nature."

Emma managed a tight smile. "I'll take that as a compliment." She gritted her teeth. "Out with it. I'll explode with worry if you don't tell me quickly."

Despite Emma's firm tone, the housekeeper could see the strain in her face. She nodded in defeat.

"Your pa can tell you the whole of it tomorrow, but I'll just say that things have been bad lately— worse than ever before between the Malloys and the Garrettsons."

With her fingers laced tightly together in her lap, Emma kept her voice calm with an effort. "What have they done now?"

"Lots of things. None of it's been proved though. Some Echo cattle turned up missing on the north range, maybe fifty head. Our foreman got jumped in town one night—roughed up pretty good. Your pa is sure Jed Garrettson and his boys are behind it all."

"Those no-good, low down—" Emma jumped up and began to pace around the porch. "So that's why Sheriff Gill is here. He's investigating the Garrettsons, trying to prove that they're behind these things?"

"Not exactly."

Something in the woman's tone made the flesh prickle behind Emma's ears. "Then why?" she asked very quietly. She suddenly became aware of an owl hooting from a nearby branch, of the wind nipping lightly at her cheeks and rustling the new summer leaves. But her gaze was fixed on Corinne's face, which looked mighty grim.

Corinne held her coffee cup between gnarled hands, staring down at it.

"Beau Garrettson was found shot in the back day before yesterday," she said flatly. "Shot dead—on Malloy land."

"What?"

Corinne nodded, her face as somber as Emma had ever seen it. "That's right, sorry to say."

"How horrible! Who did it?"

"Jed and Tucker both blame your pa. They think he gave orders for Beau to be killed, or else that he just killed him outright himself." She shook her head disgustedly. "They've vowed revenge."

Beau Garrettson. Dead. Emma shivered. Then as the full implications of what Corinne had been saying sunk in, her chin jerked up and she clenched her hands into fists.

"That's absurd! Papa would never shoot anyone in the back!"

"Try telling that to Jed. And to Tucker. That boy's even fiercer than his pa, if that's possible," Corinne added, frowning. "They're insisting Sheriff Gill lock your father up for murder!"

"How dare they!"

Emma felt a knot tightening, tightening inside her. She felt cold all over, as cold as if it were January and not June, as if she were sitting here in the thick of winter without a coat or gloves.

Her father didn't want to worry her—that's why he'd told her nothing of this trouble during the ride home from town or during dinner, or after. That knowledge made love vibrate all the more deeply through her.

And with it came tension and worry and fear.

Damn the Garrettsons—damn all of them! She was sorry about Beau. She didn't have anything against him personally—nothing other than that he was a Garrettson. She didn't even remember him all that well. He was about ten years older than she—tall, broad-shouldered, like all the Garrettsons, and his hair was darker than Tucker's, nearly brown. He'd never spoken a word to her when their paths had crossed. Never even glanced her way.

Unlike Tucker, who had delighted in making her life miserable.

Nonetheless, she was sorry for Tucker Garrettson and his father. But knowing what she did about the Garrettsons, Beau had probably gotten himself into some kind of trouble. Some gambler he'd cheated at cards or some man whose wife he'd slept with had put a bullet in him . . .

On Malloy land.

She swallowed hard.

She *wouldn't* feel sorry for the Garrettsons.

She *did* feel sorry for her father, for having this ridiculous accusation laid at his door. Anyone with a grain of common sense would know that Win Malloy would never stoop to murder, would never under any circumstances shoot a man—even his worst enemy—in the back.

"Well, Corinne, I wouldn't worry," she said, more to reassure herself than the housekeeper who continued to rock slowly in her chair. There was a forced conviction in her tone. "I'm sure Sheriff Gill will clear up this entire ridiculous matter—"

"Don't be so sure."

The hard masculine voice emanating from the darkness shattered the peace of the night. Emma spun around, a hand at her heart. Corinne's gray head flew up, the rocking motion of the chair ceasing abruptly.

Tucker Garrettson stepped out of the shadows smooth as the devil himself and set a booted foot upon the bottom step of the Malloy porch.

Chapter 2

IT WAS THE CLOSEST ANY GARRETTSON HAD ever come to the Malloy ranch house, an insolent intrusion beyond any other.

"Where did you come from?" Emma demanded, her hand still over her pounding heart.

"Oh, hell. It's you again," Tucker Garrettson's deep voice drawled as he ignored her question.

The night seemed to stop. Everything, the dazzle of stars, the hooting of the owl, the creak of the rocking chair. It all stopped. She stared at the lean, wide-shouldered man looming less than three feet away from her and the world jolted to a heart-slamming, sickening halt.

"G—get out," she managed at last to sputter. "Get off my property while you're still in one piece."

He laughed derisively in reply.

Damn you! Emma thought as rage swept through her. Yet she couldn't stop staring at him, taking in all that was the same, and all that was different since the last time she'd seen his face.

He'd changed a great deal, a very great deal. Gone was the boy with the promise of rough-hewn handsomeness and powerful strength. That promise had been fulfilled in the extraordinary man who stood before her. Even through the darkness of a night lit only by moon and stars, and the feeble light spilling out from the windows of the house, she could see that this man was as sleek and dangerous as a tiger. At six foot four, he was all muscle and brawn, a sinewy, steely cowboy with a pair of shoulders that could have been carved of granite, hair that glinted gold beneath crystal starlight, and an attitude of arrogant cynicism that could only come from hard-living, hard-bitten experience, and a hardened soul.

His eyes. Those incredible razor-blue eyes. She remembered their vivid color, but there was a cool cynical quality about them now that hadn't been there when he was younger. She felt caught in their mesmerizing pull as she stood gawking. Beside her, Corinne pushed herself up from her chair.

"You're not wanted here," the housekeeper snapped at Tucker.

But he gave no sign of having heard her. His gaze remained rivetted upon Emma's face.

"You," he said, his eyes so chilly it nearly froze her blood, "never should have come back here."

"You," Emma deliberately echoed him, "better get the hell off my land."

His eyes glinted then with some emotion she couldn't read, and for an instant she wondered if he was remembering the last time she'd said those words to him, out by the corral. But before he could reply,

Corinne stepped hastily forward and put a hand on Emma's arm.

"Go inside now, Emma, and fetch your pa and the sheriff. They'll know how to run him off."

She might not have spoken. Neither Tucker nor Emma took their eyes from each other to pay her the slightest heed.

"So. Your father's inside?" Tucker sprang up the steps. "Good, he's the one I want to see."

Just as adroitly, Emma blocked his path. "He's busy."

"Right. With Sheriff Gill." It was more a statement than a question, for obviously he had seen Gill's horse. With a taunting smile, he looked Emma over, clearly contemptuous of her intention to hold him back. "It'll take more than you to stop me, little girl," he said softly. "I came to watch Gill haul your Pop off to jail. And I'm not going to miss a minute of it."

"Over my dead body." Enraged, Emma shoved at his chest, trying to knock him backward, but he stayed where he was. In frustration, she clenched her fists and half raised them, but Tucker moved faster, seizing her wrists and clamping her hands back at her sides with an easy strength that made her gasp.

"Let me go!" she cried furiously. "I'm not going to let you upset my father with your hogwash. Now I'm sorry about your brother . . ."

"Like hell you are."

"I am. Truly . . ."

"You? Win Malloy's daughter? Hell, Sunshine, you don't give a damn about Beau and you know it. Now step aside. My business is with your father."

They'd been so engrossed in their anger, neither of them had heard the front door open or the quick footsteps coming outside. But they both heard Win's voice whip through the air.

"Take your filthy paws off my daughter, Garrettson, or I'll blow so many holes through you your own pa won't recognize your corpse."

Win had his gun aimed right between Tucker Garrettson's eyes.

Beside him, Sheriff Gill looked grim as death and Corinne was fit to be tied.

"Win, you damn fool, put down the gun," Gill ordered. "Put it down, I said!"

Emma felt Tucker's fingers digging into her flesh. If anything, they'd tightened at the ultimatum. He obviously had no intention of releasing her until he was good and ready.

"Papa." She tried to keep her tone steady. "Do what Sheriff Gill says. There's no need—"

"Hands off her *now!*" Win boomed, and Emma peered fearfully up into Tucker's face. Her father was a crack shot. He wouldn't hesitate to shoot, she knew, because he had absolute confidence in his ability to blow Garrettson's head off without mussing a hair on her head.

"He'll do it." Her voice was urgent and low. "You'd better do as he says."

Tucker met her eyes for just a moment. The deep rage she saw there, rage held under rigid control, rocked her. And she saw something else, too, something flickering beneath the anger. Grief. Grief for his brother.

For a moment she almost couldn't blame him for coming here, for daring to confront her father. He truly believed that Win had something to do with it. He was wrong, but he didn't know that. Something akin to sympathy stabbed briefly through her heart.

She held her breath as he hesitated, and no one spoke. The darkness nearly sang with tension. Then Tucker loosed his grip.

Emma sighed with relief and stepped back out of his reach.

"Papa, please." She spoke without taking her gaze from the lean, muscular man before her. "I hate him every bit as much as you do, but after all, you can hardly shoot him for—"

"For setting foot on my property and manhandling my daughter?" Win demanded. "The hell I can't and there isn't a jury in this territory who won't honor my right to do it."

"So you're admitting it. You killed Beau. Because you found him on your property." Tucker's voice was low and cold. Colder than the blasts of wind that gusted down from the Big Belt mountains during the heart of winter.

"He admitted nothing!" Corinne spat, and Tucker flicked an arctic glance over her.

"Hiding behind your womenfolk, eh, Malloy?" Contempt rolled off each word. "I should've known."

"Now that's enough." Sheriff Gill grabbed Win's arm as he started toward Tucker, the gun still levelled. "Enough out of you, Garrettson, and out of you, too, Win. The law will handle this—and that's me. Anyone gets any other ideas, they're going to be the one landing in jail. Savvy, Tucker?''

"Why aren't you arresting him, sheriff?" Tucker strode forward now, brushing past Emma as if she were invisible. "Could it be because he's your friend?"

"Your pa's my friend, too, Tucker. And so was your brother. And I've never had a bone to pick with you, neither—up until now. But I'll haul your butt into a cell if you don't get out of here pronto and stay off Malloy property. I'm going to investigate Beau's death, and I'm going to find out what happened. And when the person responsible is found, he'll pay. That good enough for you?"

"Don't have much of a choice, do I? For now." The last two words held a world of ominous meaning. Emma glanced from Tucker's tough, implacable face to her father's flushed and angry one.

"That better not be a threat," she told Tucker, her hands on her hips.

He merely shot her a scornful glance. Without another word, he turned on his heel and stalked back into the darkness from where he'd come. In the silence that followed, they heard the gentle whicker of a horse some distance off, then the pounding of hoofbeats which gradually diminished into the velvet hush of the night.

Taking a deep breath, Emma hurried over to Win and touched his arm. "Papa, are you all right?"

"Me? I'm fine, Emma, just fine. Though I'd like to teach that boy some manners. He had no right to come here and spoil your homecoming. I didn't want you to know anything about this until you'd had a chance to settle in.''

''I told you, I'm not a child, Papa. And even when I was, you never treated me like one, at least, not usually.'' She smiled gently, and as he searched her face, his own harsh expression softened. Reaching out to touch her hair, he smiled back, calmed by his beautiful daughter's loving manner.

''Sheriff Gill.'' Emma turned toward the other man. ''You don't take what that fool said seriously, do you? You know Papa would never have killed Beau Garrettson for trespassing. No matter how much we despise the Garrettsons, he wouldn't do that.''

''I know your father's a good man, Emma. He's one of the best friends I've ever had. And I promise you that I'm going to clear this up before we have any more fool bloodshed.''

''That sounds good enough for me,'' Corinne put in. She threw Win a challenging look, her brows raised. ''What about you, boss?''

''Sure, so long as the Garrettsons steer clear. But if they start any more trouble . . . ''

''Don't say it, Win.'' Gill shook his head wearily. ''I don't want to hear any more threats from either side. There's been enough for one day.''

Where had the wonderful sense of peace gone? Emma searched for it later as she readied herself for bed. Her insides were churning. Trouble was brewing, bad trouble. It had been underway for some time now—while she'd been enjoying herself at Aunt Loretta's and gallivanting around Philadelphia with

Derek. Her father had been under siege, dealing with all the problems caused by the Garrettsons alone.

But she was back now. She was here to stay, and she'd help him get through all of this. Together they'd find a way to stop the Garrettson raids on their cattle—and put a stop to the accusations regarding Beau's death.

"You're not alone any more, Papa," she whispered as she slid the brush through her hair, then set it down on the bureau and moved toward her bed. She slipped wearily between the sheets.

As she turned her cheek on the pillow, an image of Tucker Garrettson setting his boot on the porch step whisked unbidden into her mind.

The churning inside her increased. "I hate that man," she muttered. "Even more than I hate that sore-loser of a father of his."

Jed Garrettson had never gotten over losing a portion of his land to Win Malloy. He'd never been able to accept that Win had built his share of the land into a ranch every bit as impressive and profitable as the Garrettson's Tall Trees spread. Or that her father's opinions and good judgment were valued as much as Garrettson's by the other stockmen in the valley. It had been eating away at Jed all these years, contaminating his heart, his sons, his men—and now the feud between the families was far more dangerous than ever.

She remembered the expression in Tucker's eyes when he'd stared at her father on the porch tonight. So cold, so determined. There was very little resemblance between the hardened man who'd shown up here and the boy she'd once known at the school-house. *He's become a hundred times worse,* she told herself as she tossed restlessly in her bed.

And a hundred times more handsome.

It was a relief that he had scarcely even glanced at her, that even when he *had* looked at her there had been not the slightest trace of interest in his gaze. He couldn't have remembered that day he'd carried her home, much less the kiss. Thank heaven for that.

She couldn't understand why, with all that had happened to her in the intervening years, with the challenges and amusements of Philadelphia, *she* still remembered.

Now if only I could remember how to fall asleep, she reflected grumpily as she flipped over onto her back. Then she sighed a sigh which seemed to bounce off the quiet walls of her room, and from outside, as if in a distant, wild echo, she heard the call of a wolf—lonely, mournful—and then another and another.

Yes, she was home. Emma closed her eyes and snuggled deeper beneath the blanket. She imagined the huge, gray-black mountains to the west standing guard over her. The sky stretching endlessly above. And with the song of the wolves filling her ears, and the comforting whisper of the wind at her window, she at last found sleep.

Chapter 3

EMMA AWOKE TO A COOL, PALE DAWN AND THE staggering view from her window that she remembered. She bounded out of bed full of energy and never stopped for a moment to even think about the Garrettsons until the day was done.

She spent the day getting reacquainted with the ranch, the horses, the men. It felt so good to be home she could scarcely believe it. Despite whatever trouble there had been, the ranch appeared to be thriving. It bustled with activity, from the corrals to the barns to all the sheds and outbuildings. There were several new hands and a new foreman; the corrals were in good shape, and several outbuildings had been added since her last visit. Her father had acquired a perfectly beautiful sorrel mare named Angel whom Emma fell in love with and instantly claimed for her own.

"Guests coming tonight, honey." Her father appeared suddenly behind her in Angel's stall late that afternoon as she rubbed down the mare. They'd gone for a brisk ride into the foothills, and Emma had concluded that Angel was a dream. The mare was quick and spirited, and Emma patted her as she finished the rubdown and added fresh oats to the mare's food bin.

"Thought we'd have sort of a little welcome home party," Win continued, eyeing with approval the way Emma cared for the horse. His little girl hadn't lost her touch. "Wes and Sue Ellen Gill will be joining us for supper, so will Doc Carson, and Ross McQuaid and Tara."

"Tara!" Emma's smile lit her face at the thought of her longtime friend with the brown braids and quiet smile.

"Thought you'd like that," Win chuckled. "Tara's all grown up, too, honey, just like you. And quite a fine young lady. She's our schoolteacher now."

"I'll bet the children love her, and she must be a far better teacher than that old worm, Mr. Huet." She made a face at the thought of her former teacher, then grinned. "Oh, it will be wonderful to see her again."

Delighted, Emma fell into step with her father as they headed toward the house.

The McQuaids owned a small ranch on the other side of the stream that meandered along Echo's northern boundary. Ross and her father went way back: he'd been at the table during that fateful poker game all those years ago when Win had trounced Jed Garrettson and won his land. And Tara had been her friend since the first Sunday school picnic Emma could remember. The two of them had teamed up to win the potato sack race when they were seven, beating Elizabeth Miller and Jane Brownellen by a nose.

She and Tara had exchanged a few letters when she'd first left Whisper Valley, but after that they'd mainly kept in touch with each other's news through their fathers. Eager to see her childhood friend again, she hummed a little tune as she freshened up and dressed for dinner. She'd have to learn from Tara what had happened to their other classmates at the two-room schoolhouse—the boys and girls with whom she'd spent so many hours, and what had befallen their former teacher, Mr. Huet, the stern humorless man who had delighted in publicly humiliating any student who didn't know his or her lessons.

She remembered the one time she had approved of Tucker Garrettson. He had knocked Mr. Huet to the ground with one punch when the teacher had ridiculed poor slow-witted Harvey Wells for missing every single word on the spelling test.

Mr. Huet had threatened to take the stick to him. Tucker had broken it in two. Standing over the teacher, Tucker had told him that if he ever heard a word about him picking on Harvey again, he'd come back and break *him* in two.

Mr. Huet had just lain there, trembling. The schoolroom had grown quiet as a tomb. Then, with a snort of contempt, Tucker had turned and walked out and he'd never come back to school again.

Why was she thinking about that at a moment like this, when she should be fixing her hair and going downstairs to help Corinne with supper? Up until this moment she'd managed to avoid thinking about Tucker Garrettson for the entire day.

As if drawn by some invisible hand, she moved to

the window and drew back the curtains. A soft orchid dusk draped the land. She found herself staring through the shadows toward the rolling grassland that lay west of Echo Ranch, that rich grazing land where the cattle bore the Garrettson brand, where the big rough log house which she'd never even seen up close and certainly had never entered dominated a majestic clearing, and where the forbidding Garrettson men lived.

There were only two of them now. With Beau laid to rest, she guessed the house would feel empty and bereft. Tucker's and Beau's mother was dead, like her own, so there would be no soft step or comforting smile to be found there. Just Tucker and Jed, alone with their anger and their grief.

A shiver ran up her spine. For a moment she almost pitied Tucker, shut up there in that house with Jed Garrettson, who had to be one of the moodiest, most cantankerous men ever to have lived. *Perhaps if I'd grown up on Tall Trees with him for a father instead of here at Echo Ranch with Papa, I'd be rude and insufferable, too,* she reflected, then gave her head a toss.

Why was she making excuses for Tucker Garrettson?

She knew why. Because she couldn't help feeling sorry for him over the loss of his brother. But no doubt Beau Garrettson had brought trouble on himself. The day she fell to worrying about the Garrettsons, Emma decided, her fingers tightening on the curtain, was the day she ought to pack up and leave Montana for good.

And that wasn't going to happen. She was back, and every part of her thrilled to the coming dark that wrapped the mountains, to the wide open space of country so huge and breathtaking one could live there a hundred years and never tire of gazing at it.

As the first stars popped into the sky, she turned from the window, feeling peace and happiness settle over her. She slipped on her lavender muslin dress and matching kid boots, secured tiny dangling pearl earrings in her ears, added a dainty amethyst heart necklace, and went down to the warm glow of the lamplit parlor.

Tara and Ross McQuaid had just arrived.

"Tara, my goodness! You haven't changed a bit!" She hugged the petite, dark-haired girl warmly, then stepped back to grin at her. "Well, I mean, you're even prettier now, if that's possible, but I'd have recognized you anywhere," she declared.

Tara smiled, small dimples showing in her freckled cheeks. Her soft brown eyes grew wide as she studied the stunning, slender young woman greeting her.

"You're the one who's beautiful," she exclaimed, and her pretty heart-shaped face sparkled with pleasure. "Oh, Emma, it *is* good to see you again. I want to hear all about Philadelphia. You must have gone to the opera. And to fancy balls. And done all sorts of wonderful things. I'm dying to hear all about it."

"And so you will, but if I start rattling on forever, you must promise to interrupt me and tell me I've become a bore," Emma laughed. She ushered Tara and Ross into the parlor, her father following behind.

"Mr. McQuaid, you're looking well."

"Oh, can't complain," Ross sighed, and Emma hid a grin because complaining was the one thing Ross McQuaid was known to do. A spare, leather-skinned man, he was several years older than Win, with a long, sallow face and stone-gray hair that was thinning on top. He'd spent much of his youth panning for gold or silver, working in the mines, on the railroad, drifting—until he married Tara's mother, settled in Whisper Valley, and started the Empire Ranch. It was a small spread, which had never grown as large or prosperous as its ambitious-sounding name, and operated on a far smaller scale than Echo Ranch or Tall Trees. McQuaid was a respected stockman in the community, and though he was always grumbling about the weather, or market prices, or shipping rates, he was an avid card player, a good fishing companion to her father, and a doting father to Tara. He counted Jed Garrettson among his many old friends and had never taken up sides between the two ranchers.

"Please," Tara said, as Win poured elderberry wine for the two young women, and brandy for Ross and himself, "tell me—what was it like living in Philadelphia? It must have been so exciting."

"Not nearly as exciting as teaching school to the children of Whisper Valley, I'll wager. I hope no one's put snakes or spiders in your desk, as they did to Mr. Huet."

"They tried it once. With a dead mouse." Tara's lips curved upward. "As a matter of fact, Beau happened by that day and . . . "

She broke off suddenly, chagrined.

"Beau?" Emma glanced from Tara to Ross to her father. "Do you mean Beau Garrettson?"

There was a tense silence.

At last Ross McQuaid cleared his throat. "That's right. He'd been courting Tara for some time before he . . . he . . . "

"Before he got himself shot," Win finished evenly.

Tara swallowed. "Please, I'd rather not talk about it," she whispered.

Studying her in her sober navy gown with its prim collar, her head drooping, Win's stony expression softened. "Sure, Tara, honey. I'm sorry. I know you cared for that . . . well, never mind what he was."

"I think our other guests have arrived," Emma murmured, grateful for the interruption. But as she greeted old Doc Carson and Wesley and Sue Ellen Gill, her mind was racing.

Tara had been seeing Beau Garrettson.

It seemed that even tonight, the Garrettsons were proving themselves unwanted guests in her home. Beau's ghost had now cast a pall over the evening.

But not for long. Emma refused to let anything get in the way of the festive meal Corinne had worked so hard to prepare, and set about making all of her guests feel welcome and comfortable, banishing all vestiges of the Garrettsons.

It worked. For a while.

"So, Miss Emma," gray-whiskered Doc Carson said later at the big oak table as he passed around a plate of corn muffins fresh from the oven, then reached for a second helping of Corinne's special country fried steak. "I've got me a feeling you're going to have yourself lots of company once these cowpokes around here get wind that you're back." He winked at her father. "You'd better load up that rifle, Win," he chuckled. "You'll have to fight the boys off—they'll all be loco in love with Emma and begging her to marry them."

"Well, now, that's up to Emma," her father returned with an answering grin. But he gazed proudly down the table at the girl who was regarding him with a faint blush and raised brows. "She had plenty of beaus in Philadelphia, from what Loretta told me, but she keeps her own counsel about that. I reckon she can make up her mind about who to marry just as she makes up her mind about everything else. So long as she doesn't take too long. I've got a hankering to bounce a grandchild or two on my knee before I'm done with this world."

"We're going to Bozeman to see our grandson and granddaughter day after tomorrow," Sheriff Gill put in. "Those young 'uns are a handful. But there's nothin' like it, nothin' at all. You'll see," he grinned, waving his fork at Win Malloy. "I'll wager one of these cowpokes around here will sweep Emma off her feet by the end of summer, and you'll have yourself a grandchild by this time next year."

Emma choked on her elderberry wine. "Whoa!" she gasped between coughs. "Can we slow all this down a bit, please? Papa? Next thing I know you'll tell me there's a wedding gown upstairs on the bed and all I have to do is put it on and show up at the church!"

"Now, Emma, honey, I only meant—"

"We know what you meant, Win," Sue Ellen Gill chuckled. Then she wagged her finger at him. "Land sakes, won't you men let this girl catch her breath before you start walking her down the aisle? She's only been home a day!" She helped herself to more of Corinne's string beans and, earning Emma's ardent gratitude, adroitly changed the subject. "Emma, honey, your father told me you studied music with a highly regarded instructor in Philadelphia. Will you play something for us after supper?"

"I'd be happy to. But only if Tara will sing along with me." Emma folded her napkin and threw Tara a hopeful smile across the table. "I remember you always had the most heavenly voice. And you could draw so beautifully, too," she exclaimed, her eyes growing vivid with the memory. "You used to copy famous paintings from books and they always looked exactly the same. I used to try to sketch animals and flowers the way you did, but I could never get the hang of it." She laughed. "My rabbits looked like prairie dogs!"

"Oh, no, Emma, you just needed practice!"

"I needed much more than practice," Emma retorted, still laughing. "Come, say you'll sing along with me."

"But this is *your* night," Tara demurred. She shook her head. "We're here to celebrate your coming back to the valley. And we want an exhibition of all your accomplishments."

"All of them? Hmmm. Does that mean you wish to see me walk across the room with a book on my head? A great big heavy one? That was one of the things we had to learn in deportment class.'' Emma's eyes danced. ''Now *there's* an achievement. You'll all be most impressed.''

They laughed and then Tara turned to her father. ''Didn't you say you had something important to tell Mr. Malloy tonight?''

Ross paused with his glass halfway to his mouth. He frowned and set it down. ''Yep, but . . . I wasn't going to do it at the supper table, honey. Doesn't seem quite right—''

''An announcement, Mr. McQuaid?'' Emma leaned forward eagerly. She was anticipating something festive, something to celebrate. But that apparently wasn't the case, since Ross looked plainly reluctant and a bit peeved at Tara for bringing the matter up.

''Later,'' he muttered. ''After supper.''

Win Malloy was watching him shrewdly. ''I'm about finished eating, Ross. And so's most everyone else. You won't put us off our supper. If you've got something to say, say it.''

''Oh, dear, I didn't realize.'' Tara bit her lip. Distress was etched across her heart-shaped face. ''I shouldn't have . . . forgive me, please,'' she murmured to Ross.

He sighed and ran a hand through his thinning hair. ''Well, honey, that's all right.'' He looked at the others assembled around the table and straightened his shoulders. ''It's just that I've been thinking,'' he said quietly. His gaze shifted to Win, watching him intently. ''Maybe we should offer a reward—for information about who was behind Beau Garrettson's murder.''

Everyone at the table went dead quiet. Win Malloy's usually warm brown eyes flickered coldly over his old friend's face. "Had a feeling it had something to do with that business," he grunted curtly.

Emma found herself clenching the edges of the white lace tablecloth and deliberately dropped her hands into her lap. "Now Mr. McQuaid, why would any of us want to do *that?*''

"Because all this rumor and suspicion isn't good for anyone—least of all your father, Emma. Why, everyone in town is buzzing."

"So what?" Corinne asked sharply.

"So, the sooner we get to the bottom of this, the sooner we can start cooling off this war that's brewing between the Malloys and the Garrettsons. And the sooner everything in Echo Valley can get back to normal, or as normal as it can be."

"Let Jed Garrettson offer a reward if he wants to." Win's eyes blazed.

"He has." Sheriff Gill cleared his throat. "He's offered a thousand dollars to anyone who can help pin the murder on you, Win."

"My God." Emma pushed back her chair and jumped up. Her gaze flew to her father's face and the tight rage she saw reflected there sent her own anger spilling out.

"How dare he! Sheriff Gill, this is ridiculous! Are you going to let the Garrettsons get away with making these terrible accusations?''

"Not much I can do about it except find the real killer."

"Any idea who that might be?"

"Not a clue." He shrugged, his thin mouth turning down with regret. "That's why I'm thinking that Ross's idea might not be so bad. If Beau was mixed up with any dirty business, the folks who might know about it wouldn't exactly work on the side of the law. If it's someone who usually runs from the law, they might come forward only if it's worth their while."

"And what makes you think Beau might have been involved in something crooked?" Emma persisted.

"Not a damn thing." When Sue Ellen clucked her tongue, Wesley Gill corrected himself. "Excuse me for cussing, ladies. But it's mighty frustrating. Aside from your pa, Emma, Beau didn't have an enemy in the world that we know about. He seemed to be a fine, upstanding young man."

"He was." Tara looked at each person in turn. Her voice was low, intense. "He was honest and good."

The sheriff nodded. "So it seemed. We all know how hard he and Tucker worked that ranch. Especially now that Jed's heart is going bad and he can't handle as much as he used to. So who'd want to murder him? And what was he doing on Malloy land anyway?"

Win's mouth was grim. "That's what I'd like to know."

"So would I," Emma added darkly.

It was Corinne who broke the silence that followed by rising and beginning to gather up the plates.

"I reckon we've all had enough talk about murder and the Garrettsons for one night," she said firmly. "This is supposed to be a celebration. We should be showing Emma how glad we are to have her home, not fretting over troubles that will just as soon wait to be settled."

"I couldn't agree more," said Tara, rising. "Here, Corinne, let me help you clear the table."

"No, dear, I'll do that." Sue Ellen reached for the empty meat platter Corinne had picked up. "You girls, you go ahead now, shoo. Take a walk, catch up on all the news and gossip. You can come back for dessert. I reckon Corinne and I can handle the kitchen chores between us."

Thankful for the chance to chat together, and with the men retiring to Win's study for cigars and whisky, Emma and Tara strolled out onto the porch.

It was a cool, crystal clear night. Stars winked in the sky, and there was a little breeze, just the faintest stirring that brought with it the scent of pine. Companionably, the girls sat side by side and spoke of all their common acquaintances, what had become of this one and that, who had married whom, who had left town, who had given birth to twins, all the deep and ordinary dramas of life in an isolated ranching community. But all the while that she listened to Tara's lively accounting and her stories of the children now in her class, Emma was thinking about the grim expression on her father's face when Ross had made his announcement about the Garrettsons' reward.

Her heart ached for him and she couldn't stop it. *How long had things been this bad?* she wondered.

She'd stayed away too long. Papa had needed her

and where had she been? Sitting in an opera box beside Derek, or waltzing with him or one of his friends at some stupid party where the talk was all of the Carnegies and the Althorpes and the Vanderbilts—and of course, the Carletons. Derek's family was among the wealthiest and most socially prominent in the city.

Her stomach knotted. She should have come home sooner. Even though her father had never told her there was trouble, she should have *known*.

Well, there must be something I can do now to help lift this damned burden of suspicion the Garrettsons are hefting onto him, she thought. When Tara paused for breath, she broke in abruptly.

"What do you know about Beau Garrettson's death?"

"I . . . beg your pardon?" Tara blinked. "What do you mean?"

"I mean, where exactly did it happen? And when—what time of day? I don't wish to force you to talk about something that's painful," she added quickly, "but if you can, Tara, please tell me every detail you can think of. I must know."

"He was in your south pasture." Tara spoke softly, sorrow shimmering in her eyes. "About half a mile from the stream. He was found early in the morning, by one of your hands. Red Peterson, I think it was. Red had gone there to check on some sick calves."

Tara glanced down with a small, barely perceptible shudder.

"And he was shot in the back?" Emma persisted, as gently as she could.

"Yes," Tara was still staring down, her voice low. "In the back."

"Well, Tara, that's it, don't you see? That's proof right there. Any person with a grain of sense would know that Win Malloy is incapable of shooting anyone in the back, even his worst enemy—or his worst enemy's eldest son. Only a coward would do something like that."

"Oh, Emma, I know as well as you do that your papa didn't do it. So does my father. And I believe most folks around here are pretty certain there must be another explanation. Why, your father is respected by everyone in town, everyone clear across the whole valley," Tara exclaimed.

"No thanks to Jed Garrettson." Emma could scarcely keep the bitterness from her voice.

"You mean because Jed still, to this day, claims that Win cheated him at poker that night?"

"Yes. But he didn't! My father would never cheat at anything!"

"Of course not." Tara reached over and squeezed Emma's arm. She spoke softly. "My father told me about that night. All about it. And he said that Jed simply couldn't accept losing so much of his land. It devastated him. And he's never gotten over it and probably never will."

"But things were never this bad before," Emma whispered. She stared into the darkened heavens as if she might find some answer there. "I've heard about everything that's been going on the past few months. And I keep wondering, what has happened to bring things to this pass?"

"I wish I could tell you," Tara said softly.

Emma glanced at her face. Tara was watching her with intent concern, her eyes glistening in the night. Suddenly she felt a flood of gratitude for this friend who was still so steadfast after all these years. Tara was worth ten of so many of the girls she'd met back east, girls who only cared for clothes and jewels and for a person's pedigree.

"Thank you for trying to help," Emma forced a smile. "I know this isn't an easy time for you either."

"No." For a moment, Tara averted her face. Then she straightened her shoulders and turned back with determination.

"Let's talk about something more pleasant."

How brave of her to try to cheer me up, despite her own loss—and I've been behaving selfishly, Emma reflected in chagrin. *If Aunt Loretta were here, she would scold me for hours.*

She cast about in her mind for a happier topic of conversation, but before she could find one, Corinne stomped to the porch door and summoned both girls inside for dessert. Emma found the aroma of coffee and fresh-baked apple pie far too tempting to resist.

"You know," Tara exclaimed as they rejoined the others in the dining room, "it seems to me I've been doing almost all the talking, Emma Malloy. And meanwhile, I'm dying to know about the grand people you met in Philadelphia and all the wonderful things you did and saw."

"Oh, we can talk about that anytime," Emma replied. But she knew she wouldn't be able to escape the evening without relating some dazzling stories of city life.

And she didn't. But all the while she was regaling her guests with details of the entertainments and wonders available in the city, she knew that what she was saying was only skimming the surface of what she'd found among her aunt's wealthy and sophisticated circle.

And it was the unspoken parts that had made her all the more determined to return to Montana where she belonged.

She loved Aunt Loretta dearly, and many of her aunt's friends were kind and warmhearted people. But too many of those she'd encountered lived in a world where money and social status mattered far more than a man or woman's character. This had always irritated her to no end; she hadn't realized how much she cherished the code of the West, where men or women were whatever they made of themselves. A good, honest, hardworking cowhand was treated by everyone with the same respect accorded her own father or Jed Garrettson, the two wealthiest men in the territory. That was a concept Derek couldn't seem to comprehend, and he was as guilty as anyone of judging people by who their parents were, how much money they possessed, what kind of home they owned with how many servants, and how lavishly they traveled and entertained.

Those things mattered to him, and they didn't matter a bit to Emma. It was one of the reasons she had doubts about marrying Derek. He claimed to have fallen in love with her despite the fact that she had grown up on a ranch, that her father didn't own and control a large ranching syndicate, but actually *worked* his own ranch, each and every day of his life.

And if he saw me here drying dishes after dessert and sweeping the floor and washing the table, he'd faint, Emma thought later, when the guests had gone, and she'd shooed Corinne and her father off to bed while she finished tidying the kitchen.

And that's probably why we'll never get married, no matter how kind and amusing Derek is, no matter how many times he insists that he could make me happy.

They were different in too many ways. Ways that were too important to ignore. And besides, Emma reflected as she surveyed the spotless kitchen with satisfaction, there had always been something lacking between them. She felt so little emotion when he kissed her. And she was certain that if she loved him, she should feel more.

Oh, Derek was handsome enough. With his lean jaw, wavy chestnut hair and teasing blue eyes, he'd set hearts fluttering among all the girls at school. His manners were perfect, his voice low-pitched and attractive. He had a fine set of shoulders, a firm chin, a pleasant laugh. His lips were nice, too, warm and giving when he kissed her. He held her close and whispered compliments in her ear. But his kiss aroused only a faint stirring inside her. Nothing at all like . . .

She stiffened in the kitchen, gripping the back of a chair. With all of her will, she blocked the thought.

She'd been about to think: *nothing at all like when Tucker Garrettson kissed me so many years ago.*

Idiot, she chided herself as she snuffed the light and headed up to bed. Thinking about a man who is your enemy—and your papa's enemy. Just because he's handsome as sin and exudes that air of confident power and is so purely powerfully male he takes your breath away. He's also arrogant as the devil, mean as a coyote, and just plain bad news. *Very bad news.*

It made no sense. There could never ever be another kiss between them—not that she'd want there to be—so she'd best forget that one ever happened.

You can well believe Tucker has, Emma told herself as she closed the door of her room.

He probably forgot about it the very next day.

But this thought, instead of giving her peace and reassurance, had the totally opposite effect.

As she changed into a white lawn nightgown and brushed her hair until it fell in black shimmering waves, Emma tried to picture Derek, tried to remember his kiss, one of the *many* kisses he'd given her, and drew a blank.

Damn Tucker Garrettson. Damn him to hell.

Chapter 4

THE NEXT MORNING, THE WIDE CLEAN PLAINS beckoned her. After that first invigorating ride on Angel yesterday, Emma was eager to take the mare out again and let her stretch her legs—or her wings, she corrected, remembering that beautiful, airy stride. But there were chores to finish first.

She bounded out of bed, more than ready for the work at hand, and donned a blue-and-yellow plaid blouse and a denim riding skirt, feeling more at home than ever as she upswept her hair into a ponytail and tied it with a yellow ribbon.

If only Derek could see me now, she thought and smothered a laugh as she threw one last glance in the mirror. She looked nothing at all like the girl who had arrived with him in a swirl of pink organza at the Vanderbilt's New Year's Eve ball.

The next few hours were busy ones. As the sun peeked over the horizon, she helped Corinne fix and serve breakfast for the ranch hands. Win Malloy insisted on this daily meal for his men—scrambled eggs

and ham, sausage, thick slices of toasted bread
slathered with strawberry preserves, a heaping bowl
of canned peaches, and hot strong coffee. Then there
was the kitchen to clean, pots to wash, and the house
to tidy and dust. And Emma took over what she called
"chicken duty" and spent time in the henhouse,
which left Corinne more time for laundry and mending.

At noon Emma fixed herself a sandwich and set
about baking a pie for dessert that night.

It was mid-afternoon before she finally allowed
herself to slip away from the house and saddle Angel.

The air whistled over her, hot and dry, as she and
the mare flew along the trail that dipped through the
foothills. Lilac mountains loomed ahead as she swept
past stands of larches and hemlocks. Glorying in the
day, she drank in the scent of summer and sun. Here
and there bluebells peeked out from behind crags and
rocks, while bold poppies and asters brightened the
prairies.

Emma clung to Angel and urged her ever faster as
the vista surrounding her became a blur of blue grama
grass studded with cacti, majestic mountains stretching like giants against the horizon.

She glimpsed the silver splash of distant streams
gliding down among the rocks. High up, the glitter of
a waterfall caught her eye, so far away she couldn't
hear the roar of water. Only the wind and the thud of
Angel's hooves pounded in her ears.

And then there was the sky. Dominating everything else, the sky. It soared heartshakingly blue and

brilliant above the dwarfed land below—bigger, wider, deeper than a hundred seas.

Blue . . . so blue.

Sky and grass and trees.

Freedom.

She laughed aloud with the sheer joy of being alive . . .

The shot rang out of nowhere. It zinged past and ripped through the wall of rock beside her. It lodged with a *crack* in the mountain wall.

Emma whipped around in the saddle. She saw nothing, no one. Then she spotted a rise crested by a stand of cedars to her left and had a glimpse, no more than that, of a mounted figure riding away. To her frustration, she was too far away to see his face, his height, build, or much of anything.

"Oh, no, you don't," she muttered, fury and fear mingling. "Come on Angel, this way, girl."

With swift determination, she turned the horse toward the rise. One quick yank brought her .45 from the pocket of her riding skirt. She was clicking off the safety even as Angel's hooves ate up the distance between the trail and the rise.

But the figure had vanished. Completely disappeared. There were no clear footprints; the ground here was strewn with rocks, wildflowers, dirt, and twigs. No prints, no trail.

Where had he gone? She felt the danger in the air. Her neck prickled as she pulled Angel to a halt, hesitating. After a moment she dismounted, thinking that if she searched the ground more closely she might find at least one clear boot print, or something else that might give her a clue. Before she knelt, she glanced around again, but she could see no one. And she heard nothing, nothing but a bird flitting through the leaves overhead, chirping in the sunshine. A squirrel darted past, startling her, quickening her heartbeat. And then she thought she heard . . .

Something.

Hoofbeats.

Emma's heart leaped into her throat. Someone was riding fast through the trees, and she braced herself, gripping the gun. Then there was a whoosh and a great bay horse was bearing down on her and Tucker Garrettson was leaning low in the saddle.

For an instant she was sure he meant to run her down. She couldn't move. The bay thundered close, then swerved aside and came to a scrambling halt no more than ten feet away.

Tucker vaulted from the saddle. It was only as he sprang toward her that Emma remembered she was holding a gun.

She jerked it up and pointed it at his chest. It didn't matter that her hands were shaking. Her finger was poised, however tremblingly, upon the trigger.

"Don't come any closer!" she gasped.

For all the good it did. Tucker ignored her order. All strapping six feet four of him clad in a denim shirt and dusty Levi's came on at her like a charging ox.

"Stop!"

He must be crazy, Emma thought helplessly, and then there was no more time to think because he reached her in one agile lunge and wrenched the gun from her grip. Contemptuously he tossed it down in the grass, then gripped her hard by the shoulders and shook.

"What the hell do you think you're doing?" The roughness of his deep voice roused her from mute shock, like spurs driven into horseflesh. "What are you, Malloy, a damned fool?"

Emma tried to break free, but she might as well have tried to free herself from a bear trap. She kicked at his shin and felt joy when he winced. But when his eyes frosted over like a lake in December, she had to fight a white hot flash of fear that sliced through her.

Her voice quavered only a little as she yelled, "Take your hands off me, Garrettson!"

"The hell I will."

Emma vaguely realized that she could have pulled the trigger while he was coming at her and killed him on the spot.

She could have, but she hadn't. She refused to ponder why. She only knew that now Tucker Garrettson's incredibly strong hands were digging into her shoulders. He was towering over her, scowling at her as if at any moment he would strangle her with his bare hands. She was all alone here in the middle of nowhere, miles from the ranch, from the nearest house, from any of her father's men, with only the tall grass and the cedars and the sweet scattered wildflowers to witness what would happen.

She pushed against his chest with all her might.

It didn't budge him. He didn't even blink.

He changed his tactics though, seizing her by the arms, and backing her up until she was pinned against the trunk of a tree. With his legs planted apart, hemming her in, he loomed over her. He was far too close for comfort. The bark of the tree scratched right through her shirt into her back. She was damned uncomfortable and damned helpless.

"Damn you, Garrettson." She struggled futilely, sweat filming her cheeks. She hated feeling vulnerable and weak, hating being bested by anyone—especially him.

Then just as suddenly as she'd started fighting him, she stopped. Struggling wouldn't help, Emma realized savagely. And she refused to give him the satisfaction of beating her at a contest of strength she couldn't possibly win.

Her chin came up. She stood perfectly still, except for the uncontrollable quivering. To her frustration several strands of her hair had tumbled loose from her ponytail and were straggling any which way about her face. Tucker, on the other hand, looked cool and in control, his straight thick sandy hair glinting beneath his hat, his eyes cooler, bluer than the Montana sky.

Damn you, Tucker Garrettson, she thought yet again.

She was breathing hard, but her eyes, glaring up into his hardened face, blazed with defiance.

"So, Garrettson, now that you've got me, what are you going to do with me? Stake me out in the sun? Shoot me in cold blood? Or don't you have the courage to do it while I'm watching you?"

Tucker's eyes glittered like ice shards. So far he was managing to keep his temper in check, but just barely. He studied her in furious silence, this she-wolf dressed up like an earthly angel, this passionate glowing beauty with hair the color of midnight and large, sensuous eyes that shimmered up at him, their shade a dazzling combination of blue and green. Lord help the man who didn't know better than to fall for the outward loveliness of her—dark satiny hair a man wanted to bury his hands in; sculpted cheeks; a full, poutily ripe mouth so beautifully shaped and inviting it looked as if it had been made solely for kissing; and a complexion as fresh and delicate as the creamy skin of a peach.

Just looking at her made him feel as if he'd been gut-punched.

Then he noticed that his long, intent stare was making her angrier and every moment more uneasy. She was squirming again, just a little, beneath his grip. *Good.*

Enjoying the fact that he was making her uncomfortable, he let his gaze travel leisurely downward. He surveyed her slowly, thoroughly, and with mounting irritation that any woman so sharp-tongued and icy should possess a body that was so inviting and voluptuous, a body that ignited heat and wanting in a man.

Damn, Emma Malloy could get under his skin deeper and faster than any woman he'd ever met.

Only part of it was her exquisite beauty. The other part was her attitude. For a woman whose father was a cheat and a fraud, who only had acquired her fancy clothes and fancy education because of stolen land and cattle, she was mighty sure of herself and mighty stuck-up. She thought she was better than everyone else, Tucker reflected grimly. *No, that wasn't true,* he had to acknowledge as his fingers tightened around her slender wrists, *she only thought she was better than the Garrettsons*. To everyone else, Emma Malloy was a sweet, smiling princess, a caring neighbor, a young woman of charm and graciousness, who just happened to be lovelier to look at than any other woman he'd ever seen.

He was damned if he'd let her get to him.

Her breath was coming quickly. There was fear beneath the defiance in her eyes, beneath the furious trembling of her mouth, but she was struggling hard to hide it. He admired that. In spite of everything, he had to hand it to her. She might be a Malloy—and that meant a liar and a cheat—but she was no coward.

"Take it easy," he told her and gave her one last shake.

"Take it easy? With you using me for target practice?" she demanded, sweeping him a savage look from beneath those sooty lashes. "You tried to kill me!"

"If I wanted you dead, you'd be dead."

"You think so?"

"Yeah, I think so. And if you'd stop to think about it for a minute, and not go off half-cocked, you'd know that I didn't shoot at you."

"And why is that?" she bit out scathingly.

"I don't shoot women. Not even you."

She kicked him in the shin again. The same shin. He let out a grunt and an oath that shocked her as he let her go. Emma grabbed her momentary advantage and ran with it. She bolted out of reach and started toward Angel, but Tucker tackled her and rolled her over, pinning her to the ground.

Emma screamed. She fought and kicked. But she found herself lying beneath him deep in the tall grass. His weight upon her left no doubt that she wouldn't be going anywhere without his permission.

"You bastard, let me go!"

"Not a chance. But kick me again, and I'll kick you back," he warned tightly and shifted his body, subduing her flailing legs beneath his own powerfully muscled calves.

"Damn you, Garrettson!"

He grinned, a slow, mocking, infuriating grin that made the blood pound in her head.

"Curse all you like, Malloy," he told her coolly, "but the fact remains that you're an idiot. And so's your father. He has no business letting you roam around alone when you have no more sense than an infant."

Her jaw dropped. "What is that supposed to mean?"

"Someone just shot at you—I heard it *and* I saw it from down by the gulch. And what did you do? Get down behind the rocks? Take cover? No, not you. You went after him!"

"Wouldn't you?" Incensed, she glared up into his implacable, infuriating face. His eyes were so icy they chilled her, even with the sunshine beating into her face. "Don't tell me the Garrettsons are cowards . . . ."

"What I would do and what you should do are two very different things."

"Why?" Her mouth twisted scathingly. "Because I'm a woman?"

He gripped her chin, not gently, between his thumb and forefinger. "Damn it, yes."

"Really! I didn't think you'd noticed!"

The moment she said the words, Emma wanted to snatch them back. What on earth had made her say them? Somehow, they'd just tumbled out.

Tucker started to say something and Emma braced herself for some insulting remark, but suddenly a twig snapped, and Tucker moved like lightning. He covered her body with his own and went for his gun.

But it was only a fox slinking through the brush. He expelled his breath and let his heartbeat slow. All was quiet, peaceful. They were alone. Giving his head a shake, he raised himself up enough to holster his gun and stare down at the girl lying helplessly beneath him.

Emma's eyes locked on his as unspeakable tension flowed between them. It seemed to fill up the air, eating all the oxygen, making breathing impossible. She felt perspiration sheening on her upper lip and nervously licked it. A sweet, sharp sensation coiled through her belly.

Tucker Garrettson had protected her. He'd shielded her with his own body, doing so without hesitation when he thought there was danger.

Heavens, what is happening? How did I get here? she wondered dizzily. *In a damned meadow underneath Tucker Garrettson?*

She shifted slightly beneath him, all too aware of every place where the powerful muscles of his body radiated against her.

"I had a gun," she managed to say breathlessly,

desperate to get the conversation back on track and convince him to let her up. "I went after whoever shot me because I was going to stop him, with my gun, if necessary. Until you knocked it out of my hand."

"Right. And you think you'd have shot him?"

"Yes!"

"The way you shot me?"

"I would have shot you," she cried.

But Tucker was relentless. "You thought I did it, didn't you? When you saw me? So why didn't you shoot me?"

Why indeed, she wondered. She had believed, for that one fleeting instant, that he was the one who had shot at her. It had filled her mind, exploding through her with a sickening shock. So why hadn't she fired?

She closed her eyes against both the glare of the sun and the intense heat of his gaze. She couldn't bear looking into that ruggedly handsome face another moment. The image of the young Tucker—lean and muscular, fair hair tumbling forward over his brows, eyes gleaming—was already burned into her memory. But this man, the rugged hardened giant he had become, the one whose breath now warmed her cheek and whose muscled arms now held her down, was even more dangerously handsome than the boy whose unexpected kiss had stayed with her over so many years.

Tucker stared down in doubt and alarm at her closed eyes and still form.

"Malloy?" He felt panic shooting through him. "Malloy? Malloy! Hey, are you all right?"

Had she fainted? Fear shot through him, and Tucker scrambled off her and lifted her up, cradling her fearfully against him, but just as suddenly as she had closed her eyes, Emma Malloy opened them.

"Don't flatter yourself, Garrettson. I'm fine. Though you might think women are weak creatures who swoon every time you look at them, who run scared when someone shoots at them, you obviously don't know beans about women and you don't know beans about me!"

"Can't say as I want to either," he retorted, his jaw tightening.

But the feel of her in his arms was playing havoc with his concentration. Why did she have to feel so good? Soft, delicate. Womanly. And a honeysuckle perfume clung to her hair, her skin. His loins grew heavy as he breathed in the fragrance of her.

For a moment, looking down at her, his memory flashed back to the ornery girl he'd carried home years ago against her will. A stubborn, gawky, dark-haired girl with a sprained ankle who'd tried like hell to walk.

This girl—this woman—was all grown up now. She was graceful and lovely, the budding hint of beauty that had been there before now fully, dazzlingly bloomed. But there was something about her that still spoke of that spunky kid who'd hit him and shouted at him, and never once thanked him for helping her get home. Maybe it was the willful tilt of her chin, the energy and courage that drove her, or the intense loyalty with which she'd defended her father last night.

The same way he would have defended his.

Drawn as if by a magnet, his gaze shifted once

more to the sweet, petal-pink curve of her mouth. He felt something coil in his gut, felt a tightness in his loins that made him shift back, lest she feel it, too.

Perhaps she already had. "Don't," she breathed. He saw her catch her breath, saw her eyes widen with fear.

"Don't even think about it, Garrettson." Desperately she began to wriggle in his arms, frantic to break free.

Tucker's grip tightened around her. He knew he should let her go, but suddenly he couldn't. Wouldn't.

"Don't think about what, Malloy?"

"About . . . about . . . " She groped for words, her face burning. "You know," she grated out.

"Tell me," he challenged, leaning closer, his breath ruffling her hair as she struggled.

Fury surged through her. "No! Let me go!"

"Don't think about kissing you?" he persisted, a mocking glint in his eye. "Isn't that what you wanted to say?"

"No!" she burst out. And then, under his penetrating, taunting blue gaze, as he leaned slowly, deliberately closer, she cried, "Yes!"

"Let me get this straight. You *want* me to kiss you?"

In a shaking voice, Emma gasped, "You know I don't!"

Tucker gave a short hard laugh. "Seems to me you're remembering a certain afternoon. An afternoon when a bratty little girl hurt her ankle and . . . "

"I don't know what you're talking about. I don't remember any such afternoon—"

"The hell you don't. You kissed me that afternoon."

"What? I kissed *you*?" Outrage brought vivid color flooding into her cheeks. "I kissed *you*?" she squeaked again. "No, Garrettson, you kissed *me*. Against my will. Totally, completely against my—"

"The lady doth protest too much, methinks." he murmured.

"Shakespeare? You're quoting Shakespeare?" If she hadn't been so stunned, and so appalled to be held firmly enfolded in his arms, she might have fallen prey to hysterical laughter. "I didn't even know you could *read*."

"There's a lot you don't know, Malloy."

"I do know that you kissed me that day and it was . . . it was the worst . . . moment of my life. I blocked it from my mind and never thought about it again because it was so horrible. And then I had to see you again when I came home—the very day I came home—"

"Guess I spoiled your homecoming . . . "

"You certainly did your best! But I'll be damned if I let you spoil anything for me—or for my father. And let me just tell you—*warn* you—that if you ever dare to try to kiss me again, to even think about trying to kiss me . . . "

"I won't."

He shifted her away from him abruptly, setting her down with a thump in the grass. For a moment she just sat there, looking so adorably stunned and confused, and so much like that younger, less sophisticated Emma he had kissed before, that he was struck by the sudden ridiculous impulse to take her in his arms and kiss the daylights out of her.

Whoa, boy.

Tucker checked himself and reclaimed his senses with a frown. Taking a deep breath, he dragged his gaze away from her bewitching face. What the hell had he been thinking?

That was the problem. He wasn't thinking, he was only reacting, reacting to a beautiful woman with gorgeous turquoise eyes that could hypnotize a snake. Reacting to a beautiful woman who could make him forget everything—who he was, who she was, and all that stood between them.

He sprang up, then reached down, and jerked her to her feet. He'd gotten a little too close to Emma Malloy. No, a *lot* too close. But it wouldn't happen again.

"Go home." He picked up his hat, which had fallen off when he'd tackled her. Setting it back on his head, he turned away from her. "You don't know what's been going on here lately. If you're smart, you'll go back where you came from."

"Do you mean Philadelphia? Forget it. I'm home to stay."

He swung back, his jaw taut. "Don't be stupid. You think you know what you're in for, but you don't."

"The hell I don't." Now it was Emma's turn to advance upon him, and she was shouting without even realizing it. "Our foreman was beaten. Our cattle have disappeared. The Garrettsons have been on the warpath."

Tucker shook his head. "Why waste my breath?" he muttered, half to himself.

"Are you denying that you and your brother and father were behind those things?"

"Damn right I am."

"The same way you're denying that you shot at me?"

His eyes narrowed dangerously. "Get out of Whisper Valley, Malloy. Philadelphia's a lot safer."

"You'd like that, wouldn't you? You'd like me to leave my father here alone to deal with you and your father and your . . . "

She stopped herself on a little gasp of horror. For just a moment, in her anger, she'd forgotten that Beau was dead. She'd been about to say "with you and your father and your brother."

Tucker's mouth was a thin, harsh line. "Montana's not safe for you," he warned, his tone as hard as the planes of his face. "If you're smart, you'll leave—pronto."

"That sounds like a threat," she said quietly, holding her breath and searching his face.

He held her gaze for a long moment. The June heat poured down in the silence that followed, a silence broken only by the chatter of a meadowlark.

"Take it however you want," Tucker told her evenly.

He moved abruptly then, so abruptly that Emma flinched before she could stop herself. He only bent down and retrieved her gun from the grass.

"Take this. You might need it."

His tone was cool, impersonal, but as she took it

from him, her fingers brushed his hand, and his skin felt wonderfully warm and alive.

Her own skin burned in response, all the way up her arm into her neck and her cheeks.

Hastily, Emma dropped the gun into her pocket and turned away, suddenly needing to be gone from there, to put much more than a few feet of distance between them.

"And by the way." He spoke to her back as she stalked toward Angel, who had meandered around the trees to graze.

"You're on my land."

She froze. Then she spun about, staring at him in mingled contempt and hauteur. "You're wrong. This is Malloy land. Don't think I don't know my own . . ."

But her voice trailed off because she suddenly became aware that she *was* on his land. Damn, that slope of trees there was the dividing line between the Malloy and Garrettson property. In chasing the man who'd shot at her, she'd been so absorbed in catching up to him that she *had* ridden onto Garrettson soil.

Her spine stiffened. "You're right. But don't worry. It won't happen again."

"See that it doesn't."

Her shoulders taut, her head high, Emma led Angel to a rock, and mounted. She glanced over at Tucker as he headed for his horse and couldn't resist one final jab.

"By the way," she called airily over her shoulder as she rode past him. "Don't hold your breath waiting for me to leave town. As a matter of fact, my fiancé will be arriving in time for the Fourth of July dance. Since we're both going to be settling here, I'm eager for him to get to know all my friends. *You* needn't bother to attend.''

And with this parting shot she rode off at a gallop and spared him not even a single backward glance.

Chapter 5

TUCKER FOUND HIS FATHER FIVE MILES NORTH OF the ranch, working with two of the men to gather up strays.

It took only one swift glance at his father's face to see that he'd come at the right time. Jed's ruddy skin was flushed, perspiration was pouring down his temples and soaking his red neckerchief, and Tucker could hear his raspy breathing in the hot thick air.

"Are you all right? You look like hell." Because he was alarmed, his words came out sharper than he'd meant them to and louder. One of the hands, old Nebrasky, who'd been with them for more than a dozen years, glanced over, brows raised. But all he did was lift a hand in greeting before spurring his mount toward one of the cows that had scrambled down a gully, leaving the father and son alone.

Jed Garrettson spat and then glared at his son. There was a blistering fire in his shrewd blue eyes. " 'Course I'm all right. Why the hell wouldn't I be?"

"It's hot. You look tired." Tucker met his father's

glare with unflinching toughness. He could be just as ornery, just as stubborn as his father, especially when he had reason to be riled. Which he did now. The day was hot, too hot for a man with a bad heart to be out in, doing this kind of work. And Jed knew it. He had simply ignored that fact and his doctor's warnings to take it easy. "Why don't you head back to the house and take a few spoonfuls of that tonic Doc Carson gave you? I can finish up here."

"Who do you think you're talking to, boy?" Jed's flush deepened and he snapped each word out like bullets. "I'm in every bit as fine shape as you are. So don't tell me I look sickly when I don't, and don't *ever* tell me what to do."

"Ahuh. Well, maybe I should just mosey on into town then and put a down payment on your coffin right now. You keep this up, you're going to need one before the week's out."

"Did you come up here just to be a burr under my saddle or was there something I can do for you?"

Man to man, they glowered at each other. And suddenly Tucker found himself biting back a laugh. Yep, no one was more irascible than his father, no one more bullheaded. Except maybe he, himself. A crooked grin began at the corners of his lips, but there was no answering humor in his father's square, angry face.

"What's so damned funny? Well?" Jed's hands tightened on his horse's reins. "Tucker, are you going to answer me or just sit there snickering all day?"

Nebrasky rode up, interrupting before Tucker

could respond. "That's the last of 'em, boss. Les and me'll head 'em back to pasture."

"I'm going to check back behind Hidden Rock," Jed barked as Nebrasky wheeled his horse toward the other cowhand and the straggling cows.

"No, Pa, that can wait," Tucker interrupted, clamping a restraining hand on his father's arm before Jed could ride off.

"For what? I don't have all day. Thanks to that murdering bastard Malloy we're short a man."

Tucker's hand dropped. Ice seemed to fill his body and poured out of his eyes. Was that all Beau's death meant to his father? One less hand to pitch in and work the ranch?

He knew it wasn't. But he also knew that Jed would never admit how much he missed Beau, how much he was hurting.

In fact, he'd probably never speak about him again. Just like he never talked about the woman who had been his wife, Beau and Tucker's mother.

Dorothea Garrettson had died giving birth to Tucker, and he wasn't sure his father had ever forgiven him for that.

Nor that he'd ever gotten over her sudden, heartbreaking death.

"Someone took a shot at the Malloy girl today."

That got his father's attention. Jed's gaze sharpened on Tucker's face and for a long moment he sat completely still in the saddle.

"Who?" he asked at last, gruffly.

"Don't know. I was too far away, couldn't get a

good look at him. Only thing I saw was black clothes and a dark horse.''

He noted then that his father was wearing black, and his gelding was a bay.

"Is she dead?"

The cold sound of his father's voice filled him with anger. Anger he didn't understand, but somehow managed to contain.

"Whoever it was, missed," Tucker replied, his own tone cool and unemotional. "I reckon they were just trying to scare her."

"So what does this have to do with me? Or with you, for that matter?"

Tucker met Jed's raised brows and impatient stare with a show of easy calm, but his nerves were rattled more than he knew. His father asking if Emma was dead had chilled him to the bone. He'd never for a moment thought that his father could have been the one to shoot at her, even only to scare her, but for Jed to ask if an innocent girl, even if she was a Malloy, was dead with such icy indifference, filled Tucker with a grim realization and an ominous foreboding. Things were going from bad to worse—and fast.

"It has nothing to do with us—unless one of our men did it, thinking to pay Malloy back for Beau's death."

"You're loco, boy." Jed Garrettson snatched off his hat and swatted it at a fly that had landed on his horse's twitching ears. "We've got good men working for us. They're a loyal bunch, that's true, but none of 'em would shoot at a woman. Even if she is Malloy's kid.''

"You're probably right." Tucker tended to agree with his father's assessment, but he was too disturbed by the shooting to let the matter rest without making certain. "Still, think I'll have a little visit down to the bunkhouse tonight."

"Suit yourself," Jed shrugged. His face now shone with sweat, and his dark shirt front was soaked with it. "But I'll tell you one thing, if Gill doesn't lock Win Malloy up pretty soon, I'm going to be the one doing some shooting. And not in the back, either."

Tucker met his father's hard gaze with one of equal steel. "Just don't do anything stupid. Give Gill a chance to handle this. If he doesn't, I promise you, I will. Malloy is finally going to pay for everything he's done to this family, one way or another. I give you my word."

Their eyes locked in unspoken agreement. Jed nodded, satisfied. Their dislike of Win Malloy united them as much as their devotion to the Tall Trees ranch did. And underneath it all was the shared sorrow over Beau. Neither of them felt capable of speaking of this, or expressing it in any way, but it was there, strong and deep as a river current, flowing sure and true. Beau would be avenged. And Malloy would pay.

And the feud that had gone on all these years would finally end. The Garrettsons would come out victorious at last.

"You know," Jed said slowly, pulling his hat low over his eyes so Tucker could no longer see how weary they looked, "think I will head back to the house and let you check Hidden Rock, after all. I've got plenty to do trying to balance the books. Don't have time to go riding here and there after these fool strays all day. Why not let you earn your keep, eh?''

"Sure, why not?" Tucker swung his horse around. "And don't forget your tonic, old man. It's in the desk drawer."

"Damn it, boy, if I want my tonic I know where to find it! I've got a feeble heart, not a feeble brain!''

"Coulda fooled me," Tucker retorted, and turned his horse toward the hills before his father could say another word.

Silence filled the deepening dusk as several hours later Tucker strode from the barn toward the ranch house. All the hands were eating supper in the bunkhouse, the sun was sinking over the mountains in a final splash of blood-red and heavenly gold, and he hated the idea of another night sitting at the table with his father, enduring yet another silent meal as the shadows fell across the floor.

A chill touched his shoulder blades as he entered the huge split-log ranch house. Despite the June heat, the house always had a cold feel to it. Maybe because it was too large just for the three of them—no, the *two* of them, he corrected himself grimly. Or maybe because there was no woman there to add warmth, laughter, softness.

There were no rugs on the handsome oak floors, no comfortable cushions on the chairs or sofa, nothing but an old Indian blanket draped across the black horsehair couch, some bottles of gin and whisky on

the sideboard. There were no white lace curtains at the
windows as he'd observed at the Malloy ranch and
others; there was only heavy brown burlap to keep out
the night, a rocker and wooden chair set before the
fireplace, and then the worn brown leather chair that
was his father's exclusively, placed near the window
and the desk.

The supper table wasn't laid with a pretty cloth, as
he'd seen in other homes where he'd been invited to
dine. It was just a bare oak table upon which were set
out some old mismatched plates and mugs and eating
utensils. Cookie, the hunch-shouldered, red-mus-
tached, garrulous old coot who prepared the meals for
the ranch hands and the owners of Tall Trees, would
lumber in any minute now and just set a platter of beef
in the center of the table, next to a bowl of potatoes
and maybe another of string beans, and that was that.

Nothing fancy. Certainly nothing pretty.

But who needed fancy and who needed pretty?
Tucker asked himself in amusement as he climbed the
stairs to his room at the end of the hall. He sure as hell
didn't. Pa didn't. And Beau never had.

Now Emma Malloy, she would need pretty. No
doubt she liked all kinds of nice things, things she'd
learned about in Philadelphia.

Why the hell was he thinking about her at a time
like this when his stomach was growling and his
throat was parched, and he had a damned mess to
figure out?

But he hadn't been able to stop thinking about her
all day. Hell, for two days now. Not since he saw her
that night on the porch, a delicate raven-haired vision

in that soft, clinging dress, defending her father with all the spunk in the world. And certainly not since this afternoon when she'd lain beneath him in the grass, her skin glowing, her eyes sparking with rage, frustration, and, at one point, for just a moment, he'd swear with a trace of longing.

Longing? For what? For you to kiss her again? he asked himself.

He'd heard what she'd said. She didn't even remember that first time. But he didn't believe her for a moment. A smile flitted briefly across his face as he washed up and then paced the confines of his narrow, spartan room.

He wasn't gloating over his power over women—Lord knew, that was something he could never figure out and sure couldn't take credit for. He merely felt an immense satisfaction that Emma Malloy had been as affected by that day as he'd been.

If *he* still thought about that kiss, for some reason he couldn't fathom, it damn well was fitting that *she* did, too.

But hell. He'd never been able to figure out why.

How many times had he thought of her since that day when he was barely eighteen, a boy, nearly ignorant of women except for what he'd picked up in Susan Mae Jensen's barn—and in an upstairs bedroom of the town saloon on his sixteenth birthday, when Beau had treated him to a night alone with a voluptuous whore named Polly Dee?

Too many times to count. Emma Malloy would pop into his head at odd moments, sometimes when he rode past the schoolhouse, or other times when he passed near where he'd found her struggling along the day she'd hurt her ankle. Sometimes even when he was on a trail drive, lying in his bedroll, staring up at the stars.

Hell, she'd been fourteen. It had been one kiss. One damn little kiss.

A kiss he'd shared with the daughter of his enemy.

He didn't even know to this day why the hell he had wanted to kiss her at all.

Now was a different story. She was eminently kissable—and more untouchable than ever.

But damn it, those vibrant, thick-lashed eyes could haunt the devil himself, Tucker reflected, pacing. And it seemed particularly ironic and unfair that a woman as stubborn as a stuck door should have features as delicate as crystal.

Suddenly he remembered something and stopped short. Downstairs, in the parlor, there *was* something pretty, something nice, after all. Two things, actually. The photograph of his mother in a silver frame upon the mantel, and right alongside it a dainty glass figurine of a woman playing a harp. The figurine had belonged to his mother, one of the few possessions of hers his father had kept out in plain sight.

For some reason that delicate cut-glass statue, all smooth flowing lines and elegant perfection, reminded him of Emma Malloy with her small, proud chin and classic profile. Maybe because the figurine was fragile, breakable, breathtakingly beautiful. And so was she.

Get her out of your blood, he advised himself as he raked a hand through his hair and then stomped downstairs to the supper table. He refused to glance toward the figurine when he passed by the parlor.

Too bad he wasn't already married and settled down, that would remove any temptation. He'd thought about it now and then, about marrying someone, thought that it would be nice to come home to a woman's smile and a woman's touch—someone to share his life with and maybe fill this house with something besides intermittent arguments over ranch business, male silence, and late night gulps of whisky to keep the loneliness at bay. But he'd never quite been able to bring himself to pop the question.

Tucker knew there were several women in town and daughters of neighboring ranchers who, according to the quaint way Sue Ellen Gill put it, had "set their cap for him."

But he enjoyed his freedom too much to get caught. *Trapped,* was the way he saw it. Marriage seemed too much like a cage, and Tucker hated even fences. He couldn't imagine giving up his late-night visits—hell, *all-night* visits—to the girls who worked at the Jezebel Saloon. Or giving up gambling, drinking, and working as hard as he pleased. He was set in his ways and liked not having to answer to anyone, not having to be tied down to anyone or anything other than the business of the Tall Trees ranch.

Hell, there wasn't a woman he knew worth giving up his freedom for.

Tucker had concluded that he wasn't a marrying man.

Now Beau, he'd had his heart broken at twenty when Patricia Stockton up and married Henry Daniels and they'd moved to Wichita. It was years before he got over Patricia and took up with Tara McQuaid and that had seemed like it was going to work out.

Until Win Malloy got in the way with a gun and a heart full of hate.

And no doubt underneath that gorgeous feminine exterior, Emma Malloy had a heart full of hate, too. She was probably as ugly inside as she was beautiful outside. A snake hidden inside the petals of a flower.

Yep, get her out of your blood and out of your head, Garrettson. Concentrate on nailing Beau's murder on her no-good father.

But he couldn't stop thinking about the fact that someone had taken a shot at her today. Right on the edge of Tall Trees land. Right after supper he'd have a few words in the bunkhouse with his men.

"You're not eating much," he commented to Jed a short time later. They were seated across from each other, up until now silently attacking their supper. The sun had vanished over the slate-blue mountains. Gray ghostlike shadows shrouded the rolling land beyond the window.

"Not hungry."

Jed Garrettson frowned at his plate of beef and beans and potatoes and slowly speared another forkful. His heavy-lidded eyes grew thoughtful as he brought the food to his lips without enthusiasm or interest, eating apparently out of a sense of duty.

"Thinking about Beau?" Tucker spoke without glancing at his father, concentrating on his own nearly empty plate of food.

"Hmph. Why would I be? That won't bring him back," Jed snapped.

Coolly, Tucker's gaze lifted to meet his eyes. Jed Garrettson's once-thick mahogany hair was thinning now and streaked with gray. He was about the same height as Win Malloy and he looked robust, but Tucker and Doc Carson knew that appearances could be deceiving. He was able to do far less around the ranch now without wearing himself out than he'd been able to do only six months ago. Tucker knew his father would also rather eat his boots than admit it. Or admit any kind of weakness, even sorrow over his wife's death, or his elder son's.

"If he hadn't died, things might have been different around here in the not so distant future," Tucker heard himself musing. "He might have married Tara McQuaid. They might have settled down, had a couple of kids. This house would have come alive again."

"No use talking about what might have been!"

Tucker's eyes narrowed. "Fine. You want to talk about hiring another man?"

"Nope." Jed speared his meat as if it were an enemy. "I'll take up the slack. Always could do the work of three hands and still can." His graying brows drew together challengingly.

"Sure you can. If you want to land in an early grave."

The fork hit Jed's plate with a clatter. Next came the thump of his fist on the table, a thump so forceful it rattled both drinking glasses. "Don't tell me what I can and can't do, boy! I was running this ranch when you were a peanut and your brother could barely sit a horse.''

''I'm not a peanut anymore, Pa,'' Tucker pointed out with what he considered remarkable patience. ''And we're partners. We do what's best for the ranch—and for each other.''

''Who lets you decide what's best? Well?''

''Damn it, for once in your life, old man, give in. You're not going to win this one.''

''Give in?'' Jed snorted. ''The hell I will. Never learned how.'' He suddenly yanked two cigars out of his vest pocket and tossed one across the table to his son. Tucker caught it one-handed and they lit up in silence, a strangely companionable silence despite the growling words exchanged only a moment before.

Nothing was said for a long time as they smoked and the only sound was the rustle and cry of night creatures prowling the brush beyond the open window. Then Jed removed the cigar from between his lips and spoke in an offhand tone.

''I s'pose if you've got it in your head to hire another man, we could probably use the help.''

''Fine.''

''But I'm not agreeing for the reason you think. Not because I can't do the job.''

The considering glint in his father's eyes had already signalled to Tucker that his father had something else up his sleeve.

He cocked an eyebrow. ''You going to tell me what's on your mind, Pa, or do I have to guess?''

''Reckon I just find it interesting about that girl coming back here now.''

"You mean the Malloy girl."

"They say she's a looker. Haven't seen her in years—never paid much attention before."

With a touch of impatience, Tucker stuck the cigar between his teeth. "What does she have to do with our hiring on more men?"

A thin smile played about Jed's lips as he leaned forward. "Think about it, Tucker. When Malloy hangs for killing your brother, that girl will be left with the ranch. It's a mighty big place. A lot of work. Anyone can see it'll be too much for her to handle." His smile widened to a grin of delight. "What do you want to bet we can get her to sell?"

In his mind's eye, Tucker saw again that stubborn little chin lifted so proudly, the flash of turquoise eyes. "Don't count on it," he said dryly.

"I am counting on it. We're going to persuade her, one way or another."

In a way, Tucker realized, his father's plan made sense. It could happen. First they'd watch the old man hang, then send Emma packing—back east where she'd come from. Hell, why would she want to stick around in a town that had just hanged her father for murder? Why would she want to burden herself with a ranch when she could be in Philadelphia, being courted by a bunch of rich easterners, going to parties, pouring tea for her hoity-toity friends?

The day could be coming, and soon, when Whisper Valley would be free of the Malloys, once and for all—for good.

And the land that had been stolen from the Garrettsons would be theirs again—for good.

"You might be right, Pa. It *could* happen that way," Tucker acknowledged slowly. He blew out smoke and shifted back in his chair, stretching his long legs out before him. It occurred to him that all this could come about sooner rather than later, if anyone came forward with information to pin Beau's murder on Malloy. "The reward should help." He met his father's eyes over the curling smoke of the cigars. "Malloy might find himself behind bars right soon."

"That's what I was thinking. So you see to hiring that new man pronto. I've a hunch we'll need more wranglers before the summer's out, what with buying up their cattle and all, adding it to our herd. Hell, we'll need half a dozen more hands."

Jed's deep-set eyes lit with something very close to glee.

Tucker felt only a grim eagerness to be done with the matter once and for all. He wanted justice for his brother. And an end to the feud before anyone else got hurt. Neither would happen until Malloy was hanged.

He pushed back his chair. "Think I'll head into town tonight and let the word out that we're looking to hire."

"You do that, boy. You do that."

By the time Tucker left the house a short time later his father was hunched over his desk, poring over the ranch books. The silence of the house melted into the silence of the night as Tucker strode through the darkness to the bunkhouse.

Unlike many ranches which provided only the most rudimentary lodgings for their wranglers, the

Tall Trees bunkhouse was a long, rambling building solidly built of logs, like the main house. It had a fireplace and a stove, and bunks lined the mostly bare walls, which were adorned here and there by pictures the wranglers had cut out of magazines or the Sears Roebuck Catalogue and tacked up near their beds, pictures of women in bathing costumes and fancy ball gowns, in walking dresses and feather-plumed hats.

Nebrasky and Linc Tanner were playing cards, while Les read a dime novel, and Bill Rayburn whittled a block of wood. He had carved himself a collection of rabbits, chipmunks, and squirrels. The wood block he was working on now would be a bird, Tucker saw. It was taking shape nicely.

Some of the men had already turned in for the night and were asleep, others were writing letters, or flipping through catalogues or books. They looked up when he knocked and entered, greeted him with casual respect, waited expectantly. For a moment Tucker let his gaze hold each of theirs, taking a swift, hard survey.

Would any of them have shot at Emma—even just to scare her? It seemed hard to believe. They were all good men, had all worked for the Tall Trees ranch for years. None of them had ever been known even to cuss in front of a woman.

"Someone took a shot at Win Malloy's daughter today," Tucker said quietly.

Heads jerked up, eyes fastened on him with searing attention, the men who had been lying down swung upward to a sitting position.

Bill Rayburn, who'd gone to school with Emma,

froze with his knife in mid-air. Tucker saw his Adam's apple bob. "Is Emma all right?" Bill asked quickly.

"She's fine. Whoever it was, missed."

Some of the men nodded with relief, others relaxed back against the bunks, but all of their gazes still remained fixed on Tucker's grim face.

"Nobody here saw or heard anything? Anyone come across any strangers?"

There were mumblings, head shakings. Their faces showed only the surprise and dismay he would expect at the news that someone had tried to kill a woman.

"Just because we all know what Win Malloy did to Beau is no reason to take anything out on his daughter. She wasn't even here when Beau was shot. And she's a woman."

"Hell, Tucker, we know *that.*" Les jumped up, scraping a hand through his shoulder-length black hair, his squinty royal blue eyes alight. "Anyone can see she's a woman—quite a woman. You seriously think we'd shoot at Emma?"

"I've known her since she was no bigger'n a kitten," Nebrasky grumbled.

"And if I was goin' to do something to her, it sure wouldn't be shoot her," Bill muttered, a wistfulness in his eyes even as he gave Tucker a sheepish smile.

Tucker noted each man's face and reaction—some of them bristling at his veiled suggestion and others just shaking their heads in disbelief.

"All right—just so we're clear," Tucker said, his

voice calm, even, full of understated meaning. "Our feud is with Win Malloy and only him. We're going to gather in town to watch him hang for murder one of these days. But let's remember that his daughter wasn't even here when Beau was killed. In every way, she's out of it."

He heard the muttered assents, saw every head nod, before he turned and left the bunkhouse, stalking toward the stables.

But instead of being able to put what had happened today out of his mind, he found, as he rode to town, that Emma Malloy was still preying on his thoughts.

Why? The danger was over, he told himself in irritation. And it wasn't anything to do with him anyway.

Let her damn fiancé look out for her.

Fiancé.

His chest tightened, remembering how lightly she'd shot that parting arrow at him. Of course she'd have a fiancé. A beautiful woman like that. She had a way of walking which made a man sweat, a way of smiling which made a man want to taste the sweet heat of her lips. Emma Malloy no doubt had had scores of men buzzing around her in Philadelphia, Tucker thought, his lip curling in a sneer. He sure felt damned sorry for whichever poor sucker she'd managed to get her hooks into.

And that poor sucker would be here soon enough. She obviously wanted to parade him around by the nose at the Fourth of July dance. It was only two weeks away.

So let him look after her, keep her from getting her fool head blown off, he thought roughly, scowling beneath the sheen of the moon.

He spurred his mount faster through the night, suddenly thirsty for a bottle of whisky and the attentions of one of the girls working in the Jezebel Saloon. He didn't care which girl it was, so long as she didn't have black hair or turquoise eyes. So long as she didn't have a sweet laugh or a stubborn little chin. So long as she could make him forget for a few brief hours that the night was hard and lonely, that a feud was consuming the land like a fire, that his brother was dead—and that a lovely woman was his enemy.

A tall order.

He had little hope any of the girls in the Jezebel would be able to fill it. But maybe enough whisky would do the job.

Chapter 6

IT WAS SEVERAL DAYS LATER THAT EMMA DROVE the buggy into town to attend to some errands at the bank and general store—and to discover if she had received a letter from Derek.

But the first thing she discovered, to her dismay, was that she wasn't the only one who'd left ranch work behind to come to town that day. Tucker Garrettson was also in town, standing by a horse trough in front of the Jezebel Saloon. He wore a blue chambray shirt and black pants that molded to his powerful thighs, and a blue silk bandanna around his neck. He was deep in conversation with Mary Lou Kent, whose father owned Kent's Mercantile. Emma noticed that Mary Lou was gazing up at him from beneath her lashes, smiling with open coquettishness. She had her hand on Tucker's arm, and as Emma watched, Mary Lou tossed her dainty red head and began to talk with great animation.

What's she telling him, about the rising cost of feed? About a new shipment of hair ribbons?

Tucker's head was bent, his hat in his hand, and he was listening attentively to every word she said.

Without Emma realizing it, a grimace settled over her mouth. She suddenly remembered that she'd always despised Mary Lou Kent.

She turned away from them, toward the bank, thinking that Tucker and Mary Lou, two of her least favorite people in the world, undoubtedly deserved one another, but as she did so she ran straight into Mabel Barnes.

"Heavens, child, do watch your step," Mabel chided as Emma bounced off her ample bosom and dropped her handbag on the boardwalk.

"Excuse me, Mrs. Barnes." Flustered, Emma scooped her handbag up and draped it over her arm, then straightened her bonnet and the skirt of her gingham dress.

"No harm done, dear, no harm done." Mabel peered at her and smiled. She and her husband owned the Whisper Valley Grand Hotel—Whisper Valley's *only* hotel. And both she and Mr. Barnes were immensely proud of it. Along with Sue Ellen Gill, she was the leader of Whisper Valley's social committee and responsible for all the festivities to take place during the July Fourth fireworks display and celebration, including the dance.

"I'm glad I ran into you, Emma, dear, or that *you* ran into *me,* if you know what I mean." She chuckled at her own joke, and dabbed a handkerchief across her thick perspiring neck as the hot June sun beat down.

"Sue Ellen told me you were back in town—just

in time for the celebration! You are coming to our Fourth of July dance, aren't you, dear?''

Through waxen lips, Emma forced a bright smile. ''I wouldn't miss it, Mrs. Barnes. Please tell me what I can bring. Tara told me that you're in charge of refreshments.''

''Indeed I am. Now let's see, you could bring a lemon pie if you'd like. Or perhaps a spice cake. Or . . . '' She pursed her lips, her bulging brown eyes closing a moment in concentration, then opening abruptly, ''I know—those ginger snap cookies Corinne is famous for. They were so delicious at the May Day dance last year, my James couldn't stop talking about them for days. Or else . . . oh, dear,'' Mabel fretted, twisting the handkerchief in her plump, damp hands, and peering at Emma from beneath her gray frizz of hair with mounting dismay. ''Such decisions. It really is so difficult being *in charge.*''

''Yes, I'm sure it is,'' Emma said soothingly, wondering how soon she could escape. ''I'll bring the lemon pie *and* the ginger snap cookies,'' she suggested, beginning to edge away.

''Oh, my, what a *good* idea,'' Mabel bestowed on her a delighted smile and snagged her arm companionably, half turning her. ''Now, see Mary Lou over there. She's bringing a rhubarb pie,'' she said slyly. ''I understand it's Tucker's favorite.'' She chuckled, her gaze shifting with keen speculation to the couple behind Emma. ''She's had her cap set on that young man for quite a while, let me tell you—but she's not the only one, you know, for Delores Thompson has had him come to dinner for a month of Sundays. And then there's Elizabeth Miller . . . ''

''I'm sure I don't care *who* sets their cap for Tucker Garrettson,'' Emma interrupted sharply, then froze in consternation at her curt tone, and rushed on apologetically, ''I'm sorry, Mrs. Barnes, I don't wish to be rude, but . . . ''

''Yes, yes, dear, it's quite all right.'' Mabel Barnes nodded understandingly and sighed. ''Land sakes, I was forgetting the feud. Forgive me, Emma. I know how things are between you and the Garrettsons, indeed I do, and I'm sure the last thing you want to hear about is any of them.''

''It's not only that . . . I must get to the bank . . . I have so much to do.''

''Well, then, heavens, dear, run along.'' Mabel patted her arm. ''I'll see you at the dance!'' she called out gaily as Emma hurried on her way. ''And don't forget about the pie and the cookies!''

She continued calling as the distance between them grew. ''It's all going to be downright festive. Fireworks, you know, and balloons. Fiddlers and dancing. You won't lack for partners, I reckon,'' she added, her clarion voice trumpeting up and down Main Street. ''I hear all the young men from miles around have been calling at Echo Ranch! You're bound to be the belle of the ball!''

Emma stiffened, then kept walking, but a flush began at the base of her throat and spread in warm gentle waves up to the roots of her hair.

She knew that Tucker and Mary Lou could not have helped but hear what Mabel had shouted through the center of town. And she knew that Tucker was bound to wonder why an engaged woman would have young men calling on her from miles around, why anyone would expect a woman who was about to be married to be the belle of any ball.

Tucker Garrettson might be a lot of things—arrogant, irritating, and overbearing all came to mind—but he wasn't stupid. He was sure to realize that she wasn't really engaged at all and that she didn't have a fiancé as she'd told him or else she wouldn't be entertaining suitors.

Why, oh, why, had she told him that stupid lie in the first place?

But Derek is real, she thought miserably. *His proposal is real. It's only that I haven't accepted it—not yet.*

So why had she told Tucker about it and pretended that the matter was all settled?

To irk him, to bring him down a peg, she reflected in annoyance. Just in case he thought she really was interested in having him kiss her again. To show him that with a fiancé coming to Montana in the imminent future, she certainly wasn't the least bit interested in any attention from *him.*

And she wasn't.

Which was why, after being stopped yet again on the way to the bank by some other acquaintances who welcomed her home, she found it completely galling that Tucker had apparently finished his conversation with Mary Lou and headed to the bank as well. In fact, he had beaten her to the entrance.

And now he had paused and was watching her

approach through narrowed eyes. As she came up toward the door, her head held high, he moved lazily forward to block her way.

"What do you think you're doing?" Emma demanded.

"Talking to you."

"Well, I'm not the least bit interested in talking to you."

"Care to explain why you told me that whopper the other day?" he asked nonchalantly, ignoring the impatient stamp of her foot as he continued to impede her progress into the bank.

"I don't know what you're talking about. Kindly get out of my way."

"You know exactly what I'm talking about." Infuriatingly, Tucker folded his arms across his chest. "You don't have a fiancé, Malloy. Fact is, you're fancy free. Entertaining young men from all over the territory. Preparing to be the belle of the ball."

"I didn't say that. Mabel Barnes did."

"Uh-huh. But if you're about to be married, why didn't you tell her? Why don't you tell the rest of the town, too, so all these poor, loco, love-sick cowboys can quit moonin' over you and concentrate on a woman who's actually available." He studied her with insolent amusement gleaming from his eyes. "Why the hell did you only tell *me?*"

Vivid pink color flooded her cheeks as Emma struggled to frame some kind of explanation. She felt her face growing hotter as an answer eluded her. And it was obvious Tucker Garrettson noticed her embarrassment—he had the nerve to smile, a mocking, lazy smile that made her want to hit him!

"If you must know," she bit out at last with all the hauteur she could muster, trying to sound like Aunt Loretta when she was lecturing an indolent or bungling servant. "Everything is not . . . exactly official between my fian—between Derek and me. *Yet.* Not that it's any of your business."

He ignored the part about it not being his business. "What does that mean, 'not official?' " His eyes, if anything, gleamed even more intently.

"It means that Derek's made me an offer, a proposal, but I haven't given him an answer yet—oooh, *why* am I telling *you* this?"

She was losing her mind, that was the only explanation. "Let me pass!" she demanded in vexation.

He laughed then, and Emma had to clench her nails into her palms to keep from scratching at him.

"After you, ma'am," he drawled with exaggerated politeness and shoved open the door.

With a little hiss of breath, she brushed past him. Red dots of rage flared before her eyes and for a moment she didn't even hear her old friend Patsy Feather speaking to her as she took her place in line.

"My goodness, Emma. It's good to see you, but don't you look flushed. Are you feverish?" Patsy glanced down for a moment at her young son, Billy, as he jumped up and down in little circles, humming to himself, then she turned back to study Emma's flushed face with concern. "You look like you're going to burst with apoplexy."

"Well, I'm not. And I'm not feverish, either."

"Well, honey, whatever is the matter?" Patsy asked in a low tone.

"Uncouth, ill-mannered varmints, that's what's the matter." Emma raised her own voice deliberately. "One in particular."

Patsy's gaze followed hers to Tucker. He merely tipped his hat to her as he took his place in line behind Emma.

"Ah. I see." Patsy, who well remembered one particular spelling bee in school where Tucker and Emma had dueled to the finish and eventually tied, gave a sigh. "The feud."

"This has nothing to do with a feud," Emma announced clearly as she saw several people she knew turn and notice she and Tucker right beside each other in line. "It has to do with a certain person who falls far short of being a gentleman."

"Aw, Emma, hope you don't mean me," said big, freckle-faced Pete Sugar, one of the hands from the Triple Bar Ranch, and everyone laughed.

"Never you, Pete," she fairly purred and sent him a brilliant smile which made him gulp and grin and stutter. Behind her, she sensed rather than saw Tucker stiffen.

But at that moment a shout from the rear of the bank drew her attention—and that of everyone else.

"Nobody move! This is a stick-up!"

All heads swiveled at once to stare at the three men fanned out at the rear of the bank. Bandannas masked their faces and only their eyes were visible above the strips of cloth. Their guns were drawn and pointed with grim purpose at the suddenly hushed array of bank customers.

Emma saw that poor wobbly old Mr. Perkins, the bankteller, tried to reach under the counter for his gun, but a shot rang out, and his thin, badly shaking arm froze in mid-air. The leanest of the outlaws stalked forward, blue smoke rising from his gun.

"Don't try it, old-timer! The next shot puts a bullet between your eyes."

Little Billy Feather, clinging to Patsy's skirts, began to cry. Patsy quickly scooped him up and pressed his head against her shoulder, stroking his hair with small, frantic strokes. "Hush, Billy, honey, hush."

"D—don't shoot," Mr. Perkins quavered, and the outlaw, obviously the leader, gave a harsh bark of laughter.

"Reckon we'll have to shoot you, old-timer, if you don't move quick enough. Now open the vault." He waved his gun for emphasis and Mr. Perkins hastened to obey.

Emma held her breath, wondering what the chances were that she could reach the pearl-handled derringer in her pocket. She'd never said a word to her father about someone taking a shot at her the other day, figuring that he had enough on his mind, but ever since then she'd taken care to arm herself anytime she went out. She almost slipped her hand into her pocket to grip the gun as the outlaw leader leveled his weapon at the teller. But she quickly realized that would be foolhardy. There were too many people at risk—it was no time for taking chances. From the looks of the outlaws, their rough clothes and hard, glinting eyes, they wouldn't hesitate to spray bullets around the bank at the slightest provocation.

Emma quickly noted several things about the leader. He was young, sallow-skinned, almost vibrating with nervous energy—a reed-thin, whippy figure in his dusty gray trousers, dirt-covered boots, a black shirt and vest, and a black bandanna hiding the lower part of his face. Above it, icy blue eyes darted around the room. His lashes were thick and dark, like his shoulder-length hair. Rapidly he surveyed the bank customers as if just waiting for somebody to make a move so he could shoot them.

But fear and an acute awareness of their danger held everyone motionless, watching and waiting. Behind her, she could hear Tucker's angry indrawn breath and remembered the famous Garrettson temper.

The stubborn fool will probably do something stupid any moment now and get himself and every one of us killed.

"Don't you dare try anything," she whispered fiercely over her shoulder, turning her head only slightly.

But instantly, the blue-eyed outlaw pointed his gun at her.

"You. Stop talking."

Her heart leaped with fear as he advanced toward her. Emma forced herself to meet those mean pale eyes with a show of composure.

"Not that I don't like to hear from a pretty lady, but I can't afford to be distracted. We got ourselves serious business to conduct here."

"Then I suggest you get on with it."

The outlaw blinked at her, obviously not expecting such an icy, contemptuous response from the slender beauty with the cascading sable hair. Then his eyes narrowed. The gal looked soft as peach fuzz, but her tone was pure flint, reminding him of the grayheaded old-maid schoolmarm back home who'd tanned his hide with a hickory stick nearly every week of his boyhood.

Emma was watching his eyes and saw them start to glisten. She also saw his knuckles whitening as he gripped the gun tighter. Fear flicked through her as he snapped out his next words.

"You backtalkin' me, missy?"

"N—no." She hated the tiny quaver that crept unbidden into her voice, and with iron resolve, stiffened both her spine and her tone. She was a Malloy and wouldn't cower before anyone. "I'm just advising you to finish taking the money and get out. Unless you enjoy frightening innocent people and children?"

"You *are* backtalking me! I oughta teach you to talk to me that way . . . "

The outlaw raised his arm to strike her, but suddenly in one swift movement Tucker Garrettson shoved Emma back, then stepped in front of her, positioning himself between her and the outlaw leader.

"You don't want to do that," he warned and the quiet command in his voice made the outlaw check his blow.

Instead of a woman he now faced a tall, muscular man with eyes hard as granite. Something about those electrifying eyes made him restrain himself.

Emma gritted her teeth. "There's no need . . . to speak up . . . on my behalf," she managed a bit breathlessly over Tucker's shoulder. "I can speak for myself."

"And get yourself killed. Or knocked cold." Tucker didn't bother glancing back at her. He locked gazes with the outlaw leader, staring him down with steely authority, even as the outlaw at the back of the bank trained his gun on him and shouted for him not to move.

"If I were you, I'd finish my business and get out of here pronto, before the sheriff gets wind what's going on," Tucker said softly.

The outlaw's pale eyes flickered, perhaps with uncertainty, perhaps with fear. Then his muscles tensed with anger, and his gun hand quivered.

"What's holding things up?" he shouted roughly to his companions. "Get the money from that old-timer and get it fast."

"I got it!" The burly outlaw with the bushy black brows wheeled away from the teller's window, gripping a gunnysack that bulged with money. His free hand still held a gun pointed at Mr. Perkins.

"Then let's get the hell out," shouted the outlaw in back, whose face was shielded by a green bandanna. But just then the bank door opened and Harriet Tanner, the blacksmith's wife, stepped in, with her two pigtailed granddaughters in matching calico dresses skipping at her knees. "Why, mercy me, what in the world—"

The outlaw with the green bandanna yanked her inside and shoved her forward into the line of people.

The little girls shrieked. And little Billy let out an answering wail in Patsy's arms.

"Shut that kid up!" the outlaw leader roared as his companion with the money began backing fast toward the door. Whirling, the leader aimed his gun at the screeching child.

"No—don't shoot!" Patsy screamed. And at the sight of the gun pointed at the crying child, Emma acted on instinct, without thought or plan. She lunged sideways past Tucker and went for the outlaw's gun hand.

Taken by surprise and knocked backward by her weight, the bank robber grabbed at Emma and yanked her with him as he tumbled. They struck the floor together, locked in a life and death struggle for the gun that lasted less than the blink of an eye. The outlaw belted her with his fist. For a moment, that was all she knew, that and the blinding flash of pain that enveloped her.

She was only faintly aware of Tucker descending on the bank robber with swinging fists, only dimly heard the man's sharp groans. From somewhere above she heard shots, screams, shouts, as the bank exploded with frantic activity.

Then everything was a blur of noise and pain and confusion.

She had no idea how much time passed before her head cleared. The pain throbbing through her jaw and both temples made it difficult to sit up, but she did, and tried dazedly to peer around.

At that moment, Patsy and Pete Sugar knelt beside her and started helping her to her feet.

"What happened . . . "

"Two got away," Pete told her disgustedly, slipping an arm around Emma's waist as her knees wobbled. "Tucker shot the one with the money, and I missed the one in back. He and the leader somehow hightailed it out when folks started jumping all over the place trying to get out of the way. They just grabbed the money and rode off—those sons-of-bitches."

"Don't look, Emma," Patsy cried, steering her away from the bloodied form in the center of the floor. It was the outlaw with the black eyebrows. "You don't need to see that, you just need to get out and get yourself some fresh air."

Other than old Mr. Perkins, leaning with both hands on the counter and looking as if he was going to faint, Emma saw dimly that they were the only people left in the bank.

"Billy's outside with the Tanner girls and Harriet. I didn't want him in here with that dead man on the floor, but I had to come back and see to you," Patsy rushed on. "What you did—Emma, that was the bravest thing I ever saw."

"Me, too." Pete was holding tight to her elbow.

"The hell it was. It was damn stupid." Tucker spoke from the entrance of the bank.

Everyone stared at him.

But he looked only at Emma, dazed, with a bruise on her cheek, just barely managing to stand under her own power.

"We're organizing a posse. Gill's away, visiting his grandkids in Bozeman today, but Clem's got a group riding out to follow the robbers. They headed north.'' He spoke to Emma then, his tone as cold and steady as before.

''You got an uncontrollable hankering to get yourself killed?''

''Now, Tucker, don't start in on her,'' Patsy exclaimed. ''If not for Emma, the Lord knows what might have happened to my Billy. I shudder to think about it—''

''Then don't.'' Tucker strode forward, his jaw tight. ''Go home, Patsy, and see to your boy.''

He spoke more roughly than he'd intended but the sight of the beginnings of what would no doubt become an ugly bruise on Emma's face, and the pallor of her skin made him furious to the depths of his soul. ''You're lucky that rascal didn't shoot you,'' he told her harshly.

''What . . . was I supposed to do? Let him shoot Billy?''

She swayed forward suddenly, and it was Tucker who caught her.

''Let me . . . go.''

Tucker pushed her into Pete's arms. ''Here, Pete, take her. Before she falls down and cracks that thick skull of hers.''

''I'm fine.''

''Sure you are. Better take her home, Pete.''

''I said I'm fine!''

''But Emma, you don't look so good.'' Pete blushed, correcting himself quickly. ''I mean you look right pretty and all, like always, but that bruise . . .

and you damn near fainted. How about it, if I take you home . . . ''

She shook her head, fighting off the dizziness with sheer willpower. "I can . . . take myself.''

"Stubborn as a mule," Tucker muttered. He turned abruptly and headed out the door.

Emma let Pete and Patsy help her outside, but when Pete offered to fetch her buggy, she refused. She still had errands to do, and she wasn't about to go home empty-handed, and have to tell her father that she'd let a bank robbery keep her from getting the supplies and mail she'd come for.

Trying to ignore the pain in her cheek, the clinging dizziness, the memory of the gunshots and screams, she somehow managed to make all her purchases and to collect the mail. When she saw the letter from Derek, she could only stare at it numbly. She'd read it later at the ranch. Instead of feeling better, what was left of her will was dissolving as the hour wore on and she wanted only to get home, throw herself down in her bed, and shut out the disturbing violence of this day.

But Doc Carson stopped her on her way to her buggy, venting his anger about the outlaw who had struck her and telling her that Clem Tray, Sheriff Gill's deputy, would want to ask her a few questions if he and the posse didn't catch up to the outlaws.

"He's planning to talk to everyone who was in the bank. Only a few questions—to see if you can add anything to the descriptions we got." Scrutinizing her more closely from beneath his scraggly brows, he shook his head angrily and muttered, "Those bastards! Excuse me for being blunt, Emma, but you're not looking any too well. Why don't you come into my office and let me put some ice and some salve on that bruise before it swells up and turns black and blue.''

Emma shook her head. ''There's no need. It's not . . . too bad.''

He frowned as he surveyed her pallor, the strain tautening her cheeks. ''Looks bad to me. But I reckon most of all you need quiet and bed rest,'' he decided, nodding more to himself than to her. ''At least until tomorrow. Want me to take you home?''

Again she shook her head and declined. ''I'll come back to town tomorrow and answer all the questions I can for Clem. I think maybe you're right about that bed rest. I'm headed home now—but I can certainly get there myself,'' she added with a wan smile meant to reassure him.

''Well, if you say so. I'm so sorry that scoundrel took a swing at you.'' Doc Carson tipped his head to one side and continued to regard her in concern. ''You're white as a sheet, little girl.''

''I'm perfectly all right.'' She let him help her set her bundles in the buggy and then climbed into the seat. The sun was hot and bright overhead as she bade him good-bye and steered the horses up Main Street.

Why did everyone think she needed help getting home? Just because of the bank robbery. It was over. All over. And she was fine. Her cheek hurt like hell, but she wasn't about to faint or anything . . .

She was going to faint.

Emma reached this conclusion half a mile out of

town. The crystal blue sky and imperious mountains looked on silently as she felt the heat and the emotion of the day stripping away the last remnants of her composure. Her throat was dry, her eyes ached beneath the brim of her bonnet, and the wave of dizziness that assailed her was so strong that she pulled the horses to a halt, and dropped her head into her hands, willing it away.

"You're not going to faint, you're not going to faint, you're not going to faint," she whispered over and over as she closed her eyes to shield them from the dazzle of the sun.

"I knew you were going to faint," a hard voice behind her said, and she recognized it dimly.

But even that voice couldn't rouse her as the beating sun drained the last of her strength from her body, and she slipped sideways on the seat and fell into a mist of blackness.

Chapter 7

"DAMNED STUBBORN WOMAN," TUCKER MUT-
tered as he lowered Emma to the ground.
He'd caught her just in time before she tumbled right
out of the buggy. She'd fainted all right, fainted dead
away, just as he'd guessed she would.

Still muttering a string of curses without even being aware he was doing so, he laid her carefully in the
tall grass and hunkered down beside her.

Fear pumped through him. She looked whiter than
a lily—a dew-frosted lily, since her skin was sheened
with perspiration. Against all that white, the bruise
stood out like a beetle on an angel food cake.

Tucker cursed himself for not having prevented
the outlaw from striking her. He ought to have
guessed she'd do some damn fool thing like going for
that gun. She had to be the plumb stubbornest woman
he'd ever met. With a swift movement, he untied the
ribbons of her bonnet, which had fallen askew. He
removed it and began fanning her face with it, hoping

the breeze would help revive her. With his other hand, he smoothed back the dark satin strands of her hair.

She moaned and stirred a little. Tucker noticed the high, tight collar of her blue and white gingham gown, buttoned clear up to her throat. Swearing, he set his fingers to the task of unfastening the topmost delicate button, then the second.

"Emma. Emma, wake up."

Even as he anxiously watched her face, her eyelids began to flutter.

Relief made his voice gruff. "That's it. Wake up."

She opened her eyes. At first she stared unseeingly up at him, then the turquoise depths suddenly cleared and focused. Her eyes widened and she lurched upward with a suddenness that made Tucker curse.

"Damn it, woman, no, you don't. Don't you move." Grasping her shoulders he gently but firmly pushed her back. "Don't even think about trying to sit up."

Sit up? For one horrible moment, Emma was afraid she was going to *throw* up. The world was spinning dreadfully. Tucker's face was going round and round, and his features were blurred and indistinct. She clutched at her wayward stomach, uncertain what was worse, her queasiness or the brutal ache in her head.

"Go away," was all she had the strength to whisper as she hastily closed her eyes again to block out the whirling.

"And leave you for the buzzards? I just might."

But his hands were on her shoulders, holding tight. A strangely reassuring feeling. He wasn't going anywhere.

She struggled to clear her head. What had happened? Oh, the robbery. That bullying outlaw. Driving home in the buggy.

She remembered driving home, the ache in her head, the dizziness. How she'd felt herself slipping away.

"Did I fall out of the buggy?"

"You deserved to," he told her brutally. "But lucky for you, Malloy, I came along in time to catch you. Reckon that makes me wonder what you ever did in Philadelphia without me around to look after you."

That did it. Her eyes flew open again. This time, to her relief, the spinning had stopped.

"I'm perfectly able to look after myself," she whispered between clenched teeth. "What did you do with my buggy?"

"Chopped it up for firewood. Cooked your horse over an open flame. Calm down, Malloy," he added as she tried to sit up yet again and he had to push her back down once more. "It's right over there."

He was half-amused, half-alarmed by her feeble struggles to push herself up when he was trying, as gently as he could, to hold her down.

"Fine. Then . . . let me up . . . Garrettson. There's nothing wrong with me . . . "

"Nothing that a good spanking wouldn't fix."

In horror she stared up at him, suddenly wary of the hard set to his jaw, the dark glint in his eye. "You—you wouldn't dare—"

"Don't bet on it." But at the panic that swept across her face, he suddenly let out an exasperated oath.

"Damn you, Malloy, I'm not going to turn you over my knee—not right now, anyway. I'm trying to get you to settle for a minute. Rest, get your strength back before we head for home—"

"We? *We?*" She nearly choked on the words *"We* are not going anywhere!"

"That's what you think. Now hold it—*damn,* you are the most ornery woman!" He seized her roughly as she tried to lurch up again. "I let you have your way in town and look where it got you, Sunshine. From now on we do things my way."

"Like hell we do!" she gasped.

He threw back his head and laughed. Emma felt anger flooding through her. "What is so damned funny?"

"You. The elegant lady fresh from the best Philadelphia ballrooms—who cusses just like her old man."

"Only when there's something—or someone— worth cussing at!" Suddenly, Emma flinched in alarm. His grip had shifted. He was reaching for her, and she didn't trust at all the grim light in his eyes. "What . . . are you doing?"

"What I should have done in the first place, Malloy. I'm seeing you to your door. Personally."

Despite her protestations, her attempts to wriggle free, Tucker scooped her up in his arms as if she were as light as a thimble and strode toward the buggy. Though she wanted to beat at him, to force him to set her down, her head ached too much, and each step he took jolted through her. "What's the matter?" he asked, seeing the strain in her eyes.

Wordlessly, she shook her head.

A wave of alarm washed over him. "You're not going to faint again, are you?"

"Of . . . course not. But my head hurts . . . that's all."

What if she needed a doctor? He had just decided to bring her to town so Doc Carson could have a look at her when he heard horses approaching.

Tucker spun toward the sound, his grip on Emma tightening.

He saw Win Malloy and his foreman, that son-of-a-bitch Curt Slade, heading toward him with all the fury of riled buffalo.

He watched them come. The expression on Malloy's face when he saw his daughter in Tucker's arms was almost laughable.

But there was nothing amusing about his words as he spurred his horse to an even faster gallop and roared, "Garrettson, you're a dead man!"

"P—papa . . . n—no!"

"Put my daughter down, Garrettson. *Now.* Get your filthy paws off her!"

Malloy and Slade yanked their horses to a halt in a skitter of dust. Before Emma could speak again, her father had vaulted from the saddle.

"Emma, honey, what happened? What did he do to you?" He sucked in his breath and turned a mottled red as he got close enough to see the bruise on her face. "Garrettson, I'll kill you!"

Tucker held his ground, as calm as if he were out for a Sunday stroll. "Back off, Malloy."

From the corner of her eye Emma saw Curt Slade dismount, his burly form moving with surprising agility. His narrow black eyes seemed to shine like polished coal in the sunlight as he drew his gun. Her father advanced on Tucker, wrath blazing from his face.

"Tucker didn't hurt me, Papa!" she cried out and lifted a hand beseechingly.

Win stared from her to the tall, powerfully muscled man still carrying her in his arms. His shaggy brows drew together in an uncertain frown.

"Well, then, honey, who did?"

"I'll explain it all later. I just want to go home."

"You heard her," Win barked. He glowered at Tucker, who was every bit as tall as he was and younger and stronger. "Hand over my daughter, Garrettson—or else!"

Steady as granite, Tucker eased Emma into Win's outstretched arms.

"No, Papa, I can walk," she protested. But somehow the thrumming in her head weakened her voice, making it sound feeble and shaky.

Win held her tightly, his tone full of concern. "Hush, honey, don't fret now. I've got you. We're going home."

Tucker found himself staring after them as Win Malloy carried his daughter to the buggy and gently placed her inside. Strange feelings churned through him as he saw the tenderness with which Malloy lifted his hand and brushed it against Emma's pale face, the way she tried to smile at him though she was obviously in pain. There was a sweet father-daughter accord there that struck him powerfully, though he hated to admit it. It was so unlike the rough, argumentative indifference with which he and his own father communicated.

What was wrong with him? Why the hell did he care about all this family love between the Malloys? He'd wasted enough time on Emma Malloy for one day—hell, Tucker decided darkly, for a lifetime.

He turned away to get his horse and felt a fist slam into his jaw.

Curt Slade smiled as Tucker Garrettson went down.

"That's what you get, Garrettson, for daring to touch the boss's daughter. You're not fit to lay a finger on Miss Emma Malloy. So here's more."

Slade, his black eyes glinting, aimed a hard kick at the fallen man's temple.

Win had just started back to get his horse and tie it to the buggy, when both he and Emma saw Slade's sucker punch.

As he aimed that vicious kick, Emma screamed.

But the kick never connected. Tucker had been stunned for one precarious moment by the unexpected punch, but he regained his wits with alacrity and rolled aside, out of the way of Slade's boot. Like lightning he grabbed Slade's foot and yanked.

It was the burly, black-haired foreman's turn to go down in the grass with a sickening thunk.

Then the fight was on. Emma, feeling more faint

than ever, watched with her heart in her throat as the two men punched, kicked, wrestled.

Slade was big, and though not as tall and sinewy as Tucker, he was built like an ox. Each time he swung a massive fist and his face twisted into a vicious mask, her heart stopped, but she soon noticed that few of his blows connected. Tucker was swift, sure of himself, and every bit as brutal as the ranch foreman.

He slammed a right hook into Slade's jaw that sent the other man reeling, followed it up with a left to the stomach that had Slade doubled over, gasping. Tucker hit him again, and Slade went down. This time Tucker was on him, his fists striking again. And again.

"Enough!" Win Malloy shouted, but Tucker appeared not to hear. The black Garrettson temper had seized him and nothing else got through.

"Stop! Stop!" Emma was pleading faintly, sickened by what she saw. And whether it was her words and soft voice which finally penetrated the haze of his fury, or the fact that Slade wasn't putting up a fight anymore, Tucker at last leaned back, wiped the sweat from his eyes with his shirt sleeve, and let his fists drop.

A hideous silence hung in the June air.

Then Win Malloy strode forward, his own fists clenched. "If you've killed him—"

"He's alive. Which is more than I can say for my brother." Tucker got to his feet, but he looked ready to fight again if Malloy moved a muscle.

Emma held her breath, wondering if she had the strength to stumble out of the buggy and intervene if they came to blows, but her father, though enraged, held himself in check.

"I think you've done enough for one day, Garrettson. Damn your hide. All I want is to see to my daughter, but if you think I'm going to drive off and leave you to finish Slade—"

"I'm finished with him right now. And with you, too, Malloy. And you, too, Sunshine," he called to her, his lean face taut with contempt.

His jaw throbbed. How had he let that bastard Slade sucker punch him? No one had done that to him since he was ten. Must've been the girl's fault, he'd been so worried about her needing a doctor he'd forgotten to keep his wits about him for just a moment, and wham.

That'd teach him.

He swung up into the saddle, paying no attention to the sight of Win Malloy helping a groaning Slade to his feet. But as he turned Pike toward home he couldn't resist one final glance toward Emma Malloy.

She was watching him. Her face wore a frightened expression.

Good. She ought to be frightened. He was glad she was frightened.

He gripped the reins, ready to spur Pike to a gallop. But suddenly he yanked the bay to a halt.

"Get her to a doctor, Malloy. To hell with Slade. Your daughter needs a doctor."

Gritting his teeth, he rode off without waiting for an answer, wondering why in the hell he had bothered.

Emma was wondering, too. Even as she noted that Slade was all right—despite the blood dripping from his nose and the two bruises already swelling around his eyes—she gazed after Tucker Garrettson in awe, fear, and bewilderment.

Awe because of the emotions he aroused in her. Fear because of his toughness. He was a hard man capable of unmerciful violence, the violence she'd seen unleashed with such cold competence on Curt Slade today. And bewilderment, because he had once again this afternoon come to her rescue, helped her when no one else had been there to do it, and even after that terrible fight, he'd still taken time to tell her father she needed a doctor.

She slumped back against the seat, too weary and filled with pain to reflect further. To her relief, a moment later her father clambered into the buggy.

"I'm taking you home now, Emma. Slade's all right. He's going to ride to town and fetch Doc Carson out to the ranch. Come on now, take it easy, and we'll be home before you know it. Don't try to talk yet, but later I want to hear exactly what happened to you."

She nodded and wondered what he would say when he found out.

Chapter 8

TARA RODE OVER TO VISIT EMMA LATER THAT evening and sat by her bed in the softly lit room. Doc Carson had been there earlier and had prescribed rest and quiet, so Corinne had brought her dinner up on a tray, and everyone was tiptoeing around lest they disturb her.

"I'm really fine," Emma assured her friend quietly, but the truth was she still did have a headache, and she was not unhappy to be propped up on pillows in her bed, sipping lemon tea, snug and safe from the world. "How did you know that I'm an invalid—at least until tomorrow?" she asked Tara with an attempt at a smile.

"Tucker told me."

Emma nearly choked on her tea, but managed to swallow it with only one tiny cough. "He did, did he?" She spoke with what she hoped was remarkable self-control.

"I rode over to Tall Trees to see him and Jed before supper tonight. I'd baked them an apple pie—

just thought they might like it. They have no women-folk to fuss over them, you know.''

Emma stared at her.

''I'm fond of them, Emma,'' Tara explained quietly, her velvet brown eyes fixed on Emma's face, pleading with her to understand. ''It's no disloyalty to you or to your father, it's only because of Beau. I got to know the Garrettsons better when Beau and I were courting. I feel sorry for them—two men shut up in that big house and all . . . ''

''It was nice of you to bring them the pie.'' Emma set her teacup down on the table beside her bed. She pushed a stray black curl behind her ear. ''So,'' she said casually, ''just what did Tucker tell you about today?''

''Not much, you know how he is. Tucker barely says two words unless he's riled or something.'' Tara offered a glimmer of a smile. ''He did say that you were a stubborn fool, that you were hurt during the bank robbery, and that even though you did a brave thing, it was a damned stupid brave thing, and you deserved to get conked on the head.''

''I'd like to conk *him* on the head,'' Emma fumed. ''Never have I met a more unlikeable man!''

Tara studied her, then leaned back against her chair.

''He seems to feel the same way about you.''

''Good. Then we're even.''

''Before Doc Carson told me I could come up, he filled me and your father in about everything that happened in the bank today. You were so brave, Emma. Standing up to that outlaw—''

"Anyone would have done the same if they'd seen the man pointing a gun at little Billy Feather," Emma exclaimed. Suddenly a sharp pain wafted through her head. She sank against the pillows and closed her eyes. "I don't think I want to talk about it anymore . . . " she said softly. "Or think about it. I never meant to have such an exciting day, believe me. I just wanted to go to town and see if I had a letter . . . "

The letter! Her eyes flew open. "Tara, I think my father set a letter on the table there. Do you see it?"

Tara went to the table and picked up a cream colored envelope with firm black script across the front of it. "Is this the one?"

"Yes, oh yes. Would you read it to me?" she asked. "I'm still a bit dizzy, though Doc Carson said that and my headache should go away in a day or two, but it will make my head hurt to try to read right now."

Tara returned to her chair and broke the seal. "Who is it from?" she asked, unfolding a length of fine cream paper.

"Derek Carleton." Emma found herself grinning as Tara raised her delicate brows, her gaze fixed expectantly on Emma's face, her eyes dancing.

"A suitor, I presume?"

"You might presume that." Her grin widened. "He asked me to marry him," Emma confided. "And I just might." Suddenly all of Derek's ardent devotion to her came rushing back in a flood of happy memories—his kindness, his compliments, his care for her comfort—and her cheeks flushed with warmth. Particularly when she compared his exquisite solicitousness to Tucker Garrettson's rude treatment.

"If he sweet-talks me prettily in this letter and agrees to come to Whisper Valley for the Fourth of July Dance," she added contemplatively, then chuckled as Tara let out a smothered laugh.

"Are you sure you want me to read this? It might be personal."

"You're my dearest friend." Emma reached out and touched Tara's hand. "I'd never keep any secrets from you. Besides, I must know what Derek has to say, and since I can't read it myself and I won't ask my father to read it to me," she giggled, "you're elected!"

"Dearest Emma," Tara began, and at the salutation, she paused a moment and smiled at Emma, before continuing.

"How I miss you. The sun seems dim in Philadelphia since you left and the moon glimmers far less brilliantly than when you and I gazed at it together."

Tara broke off, beaming. "I must say, he sounds terribly romantic!"

"Oh, he is. Derek is devoted to me." Emma was picturing him in the stately drawing room of his father's grand house, writing this letter as he best pondered how to woo her. Derek Carleton knew exactly how to touch a woman's heart, and he was certainly doing his best to capture hers at this very moment.

"Go on," she urged, her smile widening.

"Nothing could keep me from coming to Montana for your town's little Fourth of July dance. Nothing could keep me from seeing you. I'll be arriving on the 3rd. May I see you then? I don't wish to wait a moment longer than necessary to see your enchanting face again.

"And when I do, I'll be expecting an answer to my question. I trust I know what it will be. You wouldn't disappoint a man who cherishes you as much as I do, would you, my sweet beautiful Emma?

"As always,

"Derek"

Tara leaned back in the chair, letting the letter drop into her lap. Her face wore a startled expression. "My," was all she seemed capable of saying.

"Yes, Derek is always certain of his own feelings," Emma spoke slowly. No longer amused, she felt the impact of the letter, of Derek's strong feelings for her, and was embarrassed by her own cavalier attitude. "If only I were as sure of mine," she told Tara quietly.

"Do you mean that you really don't know yet if you want to marry him? What's he like?"

Emma began to twirl a strand of her heavy dark hair around her finger. How to describe an elegant, dashing young man with a laugh that made everyone near him feel like laughing, too?

"Derek is everything one would hope for in a husband," she said slowly. "Tall. Handsome. Aunt Loretta says he cuts an elegant figure and it's true.

He's charming—always quick with a joke—and he's generous with compliments to those he cares for. He's also very kind and considerate and is considered smart as a whip.''

"He sounds perfect. And I suppose he's also very rich?'' Tara prompted. Emma was surprised by the wistfulness of her voice, the faint tinge of envy. Then Tara gave her head a shake and a rich blush tinted her cheeks. "I'm sorry—that was a thoughtless question. It really doesn't matter, does it?''

"To some people it might. But not to me.'' Emma waved a hand that encompassed her room, the ranch, the vast splendid land beyond. "I have everything I want right here. Echo Ranch is quite enough for me. But yes, Derek's family is wealthy—and quite powerful in his circles back east.''

"And he's in love with you!''

"So he says.''

"Then Emma, what's wrong? Why wouldn't you jump at the chance to marry him?''

Emma drew a hand absently across the blanket that draped her from the night chill. "For one thing,'' she murmured thoughtfully, "I want to stay in Montana and Derek has every intention of remaining in Philadelphia. If he moves anywhere, it will be to New York, to pursue business opportunities.''

"New York. Philadelphia. I would think you'd want to live in such exciting places.''

"I did live there. For five years,'' Emma reminded her. She sighed. "And I missed Whisper Valley every single day.''

"So there's no possibility that you would accept his offer and move away?"

"None. But I may *accept* his offer and convince him to stay." A mischievous smile flitted across Emma's face. "After all, if Derek loved me enough he would do that for me, don't you think?"

"I don't know. No one's ever loved me that much."

Emma stared at the sorrow in her friend's face. She sat up straighter in the bed and spoke softly. "What about Beau Garrettson?"

Tara flushed and shifted in her chair so suddenly the letter dropped on the floor. She bent hastily to retrieve it.

"I'm sorry." Emma could have bitten off her tongue. "It must be terribly painful for you to talk about him. Let's talk about something else—"

"No, it's all right." Tara shook her head. She was studying the letter clasped in her hands, running her fingers along the smooth paper, but she continued quietly. "Beau and I *were* in love—at least I think we were—but he died before he ever had the chance to really tell me how he felt."

"I'm sorry about Beau. I really am. But . . ." Emma cast around for the right words. There was no bringing Beau Garrettson back and she was suddenly fearful that Tara would spend the rest of her life mourning him. "But there will be someone else . . . in time. Your heart will heal, Tara, and then . . ."

"Beau was special. *Special,* do you hear me?" Tara said vehemently, her voice shaking, her eyes brimming with sparkling tears. "There aren't many men with what he had . . . damned few . . . "

She suddenly buried her face in her hands and wept.

Horrified, Emma swung her legs off the bed and then lurched a bit unsteadily to Tara's chair. Her stomach was churning with dismay. She leaned down and wrapped her arms tightly around the weeping girl.

"Tara, forgive me, honey. That was tactless and stupid. It's too soon, the hurt is too raw. Forgive me, please."

"It's . . . okay." Tara struggled to regain her composure. With Emma's arms around her, consoling her, her sobs gradually subsided. "It's not your fault. It's just that whenever I think of Beau, of what might have been, it nearly splits me in two."

"I envy you," Emma whispered, smiling into that sad, spent face. "You had a love that was true. Strong and true. Not everyone finds that, not even if they search their whole lives."

"Maybe you'll find that with D—Derek." Tara gave her a hopeful smile and took a long shuddering breath. "I want you to try, Emma. I really do. I would like to see you happy."

"I am happy." Emma gave Tara one last hug, and eased herself back toward the bed. "Being at Echo Ranch with Papa makes me happy. But . . . " She winced slightly as she sank back against her pillows once more. "Having my head hurt this way does *not*. I hope it's better by morning. And I hope the posse catches those damned outlaws who robbed the bank before they hurt anyone else."

But they didn't catch them. The posse came back weary and defeated and when Sheriff Gill returned, he was informed that over two thousand dollars had been stolen from the citizens of Whisper Valley.

Yet even this sobering news didn't dampen the spirits of the townsfolk and ranch families who were gearing up for the Fourth of July celebration. And Emma was particularly looking forward to it.

ON THE DAY OF DEREK'S ARRIVAL, HER FATHER DROVE HER to town in the buggy and they awaited the stagecoach together.

When it arrived at midday beneath a sky of pure china blue, her pulse quickened with anticipation. And when Derek Carleton stepped down into the sunlit street, she felt a rush of pleasure at seeing him.

"So that's your young man," her father said approvingly. He spoke in an undertone as Derek approached with his smooth, confident stride. Emma could see why her father was pleased. Derek cut a dashing figure but didn't have an overly citified air about him. The sun gleamed upon his wavy black hair, his black wool suit was expensively cut but not overly fussy, and his deep mahogany eyes were gazing at her with unabated delight.

"He's not exactly my young man, Papa," Emma said softly, feeling compelled to correct him, but then she held out her hand to Derek and a smile lit up her face as he brought her fingers to his lips.

"Emma." After kissing her hand, he kept it clasped firmly within his own, showing no intention at all of releasing it. "You're as beautiful as ever! No, even more beautiful. You're positively radiant! You can't imagine how I've missed you. And this must be your father. Sir." At last, he released her hand to shake her father's. "A great pleasure to meet you."

It was just like Derek to take control of the situation, not to wait for her to introduce him. He was aggressive in business as well as in his personal relationships, just like his father. Perhaps that was the key to their incredible success.

"Did you have a pleasant journey?" she asked when the formalities were done.

"Most pleasant. I thought of you during the entire trip. It passed the time delightfully." He grinned then, and Emma found herself caught up as always in the dazzling Carleton charm.

"Which way is the hotel?" he asked as he retrieved a handsome suitcase from the baggage the stagecoach driver had set down on the street.

"You're not staying at a hotel, young man. You're staying at Echo Ranch," her father informed him genially.

"Haven't you ever heard of western hospitality?" Emma asked, tucking an arm through Derek's.

"Yes, but I didn't expect you to go to such trouble."

"Oh, it's no trouble. There's plenty of room. Besides, we wouldn't see each other nearly as much if you stayed in town."

"Now that *would* be a shame. After all, you're the reason I came here in the first place, Emma—all the way out to this godforsaken part of the country. Only for you, Emma. You know that, don't you?''

"Godforsaken?" she asked with a toss of her head, her eyes narrowing. "I'd call it blessed."

But just as she was challenging him, unable to subdue her resentment about what he'd said about her beloved Montana, she caught a glimpse of Tucker Garrettson from the corner of her eye. He was just emerging from the saloon, and he was arm in arm with one of the saloon girls, a buxom redhead who was hanging onto his arm as if she'd fall on her face without its support.

"I think I'm going to be sick," she muttered, before she realized she'd spoken aloud. She gave a little gasp as her father and Derek both stared at her.

"Honey, what's wrong? Is that headache back again?" Win Malloy asked anxiously. "I thought it was gone for good."

"Papa, it's not that." But the last thing she wanted was for her father to see Tucker and for them to get into an argument—or worse, a fistfight—right in front of Derek.

"Is it the sun?" Derek frowned worriedly down at her. "Emma, here, let me help you into the buggy."

"I'm fine, Derek, truly I am. I just meant that I'm sick to death of people thinking Montana is at the end of the earth. Which is what you just implied." But her eyes were no longer narrowed at him. She gave him a dazzling smile and slid her hand up his arm. "Only look at the sky, the land," she urged sweetly, hoping Tucker could see her rapt expression as she gazed at Derek Carleton. "Is there anything as magnificent?

Oh, Derek, admit it, you've never seen such a slice of heaven on earth.''

"You're the only slice of heaven I need to see," he whispered, leaning down and speaking so softly her father couldn't hear. Win Malloy had already seated himself in the buggy, and smilingly, Derek helped Emma into it with practiced grace.

She risked one swift glance over her shoulder as the horses trotted up the street and saw Tucker scowling after the buggy. At least she thought that's what he was scowling at. She couldn't be certain, because she turned her head quickly away lest *he* see that she was trying to see *him*.

That wouldn't do at all.

And just why was she trying to see him? Emma asked herself in irritation. She had her two favorite men right here in this buggy with her. So why should she possibly want to bother looking at Tucker Garrettson? Especially since Derek had come all the way to Whisper Valley just to see her and get her answer to his proposal?

Suddenly Emma realized that the first moment they were alone he would try to get the answer from her. Why hadn't she thought of that before? She'd been too busy hoping that he would be able to help her stop thinking about so many other things in her life. Things like Beau Garrettson's death, the cloud of suspicion hanging over her father, the shot that had been fired at her, the bank robbery and—Tucker Garrettson.

His very presence in Whisper Valley irked her to no end.

If the Garrettsons would only leave, go somewhere else, anywhere else, her life would be perfect.

But she had counted on Derek helping her to forget her troubles. So far, she reflected as the buggy rolled past clumps of cedar and aspen toward home, it wasn't working.

Tucker Garrettson remained on her mind as much as ever.

That evening she and Derek took a stroll. As dusky shadows fell over the Rockies to the north, she showed him around the ranch grounds, took him past the corrals, to the edge of the creek where cottonwoods dotted the bank and delicate pink bitterroot grew in glorious profusion.

There, as the sun set over the indigo mountains and the sky glowed rose and shimmered with streaks of incandescent opal, Derek kissed her.

He kissed her slowly, thoroughly. His arms drew her close to him. He smelled of expensive cologne, rich and spicy. There was expertise in the way his mouth moved over hers and a flattering tinge of longing. He tipped her chin up and told her she was beautiful.

And Emma wrapped her arms around his neck and kissed him back.

And even as she touched her lips to his and stroked her fingers through his hair, she nearly cried.

For she felt nothing.

Nothing.

And it was all Tucker Garrettson's fault.

Chapter 9

FOR THE PAST THREE YEARS THE FOURTH OF July dance had been held in the lobby and dining room of the Whisper Valley Grand Hotel. And so it was again this year. But everyone agreed that the Whisper Valley social committee had outdone themselves in decorating the narrow simple lobby with its pine furniture and threadbare rugs, transforming it into a festive place of glowing lanterns, patriotic streamers, and vases of flowers. There were clusters of red, white, and blue balloons tied around the stairway railing. The rugs had been rolled up to leave the floor cleared for dancing, and most of the furniture, including the tables and chairs in the dining room had been removed to make room for the throng of townspeople, ranchers, and their families who flocked to town for the celebration.

And everyone was there—Doc Carson, his gray whiskers neatly combed, Sue Ellen and Wesley Gill strolling arm in arm, Patsy Feather and her husband Ed, with little Billy clinging to her skirts. All the cowhands from Echo Ranch had spiffed themselves up in their Sunday best, slicked their hair and shined their boots to a dazzling gloss. Clem Tray, the deputy, had brought his harmonica and was standing on a crate next to Wilbur Kent, who owned the mercantile and played the banjo. On another crate beside them was Harvey Wells, the soft-spoken, slow-witted young man the former schoolteacher had ridiculed. Harvey worked in Kent's Mercantile now and played the fiddle like nobody else. Together the three musicians brought their instruments to life with a zest and energy that infused everyone dancing with a fierce, joyful vigor.

Emma swept through the front door in a swirl of turquoise silk, accompanied by her father and Derek, both sharply handsome in their dark suits, white linen shirts, and black string ties. She had taken extra care with her hair tonight, arranging it in a cluster of jet curls that cascaded down one side of her face and swirled in a riotous tangle over her shoulder. Dainty jet earrings dangled from her earlobes and around her throat she wore a jet and turquoise choker which served to accentuate the creamy whiteness of her skin and the low-cut neckline of her gown. The bodice caressed her firm, lush breasts, while the skirt flared out from her hips just enough to make dancing easy. As she stood with her father and Derek in the lobby of the hotel and gazed about, it was all Emma could do not to tap her slippered feet to the music.

Harvey Wells grinned and waved to her and Emma waved back. He began to play "Turkey in the Straw," his sweet, wide, clean-shaven face glistening with perspiration in the lantern light. Clem and Wilbur joined in and people began to clap and stomp.

"May I claim the first dance, Miss Malloy?" Derek bowed formally, his eyes twinkling. He held out his hand and Emma laid hers in it.

"I'd love to, Mr. Carleton." She laughed. Just then she saw Tucker Garrettson and the laughter died on her lips. Tucker was dancing with Mary Lou Kent and having a fine time from the looks of it.

Suddenly the festive colorfulness of the room dimmed, the lanterns lost their magical glow. She became aware of the smoke from cigars, the mingling scents of hair pomade, perfume, tobacco, and whisky. And the noise. The music that had seemed so appealing suddenly blared in her ears.

"Emma." Derek bent his head toward her, anxiously studying her face. "You're frowning. What's wrong?"

"Wrong?" She gritted her teeth and pasted on a brilliant diamond-hard smile. "Whatever gives you the impression something is wrong?"

"You look . . . you look like you could shoot someone, Emma. That's what. Didn't I compliment you sufficiently on your gown?" He was teasing now, trying to coax a real smile from her as they joined the throng of dancers. "It's lovely. *You're* lovely."

Feeling ashamed, Emma mustered up what she hoped was a dazzling smile.

"You were quite complimentary enough, Derek. You made me blush."

"And a most attractive blush it was, too."

"Derek . . . " she said, then broke off, her heart

sinking as she saw Tucker and Mary Lou swing by right in front of them on the dance floor, swaying in time to the music.

My, Tucker is holding her close. In Philadelphia, that would be considered scandalous. Everyone would be talking.

"Emma?"

"Um, what?"

"You were saying. Derek. You said, 'Derek.' "

"Oh. Yes. Derek." Guiltily she flashed him another smile and staring up into his handsome, somewhat confused face as they spun to the music, she reminded herself just how attractive and eligible he was. And patient, too. She had been evading giving him an answer about his proposal, and so far, he hadn't pushed her. "I was about to say that you don't need to compliment me quite so much. I'm not vain. And I'm not angry with you."

"Well, you seem rather distracted."

The music came to a halt, and for a moment, Emma's feet kept moving. She nearly tripped, then stopped herself in time. Distracted, yes, that's exactly what she was, she decided as Derek firmly gripped her arm.

"I keep thinking about the cookies," she said suddenly, by way of explanation.

"What cookies?"

"My spice cookies. I gave the batch of them to Mrs. Barnes and I'm wondering if she set them out on the table yet. I don't want her to forget—then no one will have a chance to enjoy them. They're quite delicious."

''If you made them, darling Emma, I'm sure they are.''

She bit her tongue to keep from snapping an impatient reply, but Emma was certain that if he didn't stop shoving compliments at her the way one fed carrots to a horse, she would scream. Derek had never been quite so tiresomely complimentary in Philadelphia, and she guessed he was trying to insure her acceptance of his marriage proposal through flattery. He couldn't know that he was also grating on her nerves.

She smiled again, rather forcedly, and said, ''Excuse me, Derek, I'm just going to check on the cookies and then I'll be right back.''

She escaped before he could protest, slipping through the throng of people, waving and chatting briefly with those who greeted her—and that meant nearly everyone. As she neared the refreshment table, she collided with a man who turned abruptly away from the table, and as she bumped into him, the punch he'd been raising to his lips sloshed over onto his plaid shirt sleeve.

''Oh, I'm terribly . . . ''

Emma broke off as she saw herself staring into the shrewd blue eyes of Jed Garrettson.

She'd throw herself in front of a herd of stampeding cattle before she'd apologize to *him*.

''Now look what you've done.'' His frown made the seamed lines in his leathery face appear even deeper, more weathered. His eyes were colder than a Montana January. ''And not even a pardon me. 'Course, who expects manners from a Malloy, eh, missy?''

"It was an accident," Emma said icily. "Excuse me . . . "

"Hand me a damned—uh, a danged napkin— that's the least you could do, girl," he grumbled, seeming to forget the neckerchief around his throat which, in Emma's opinion, would have served as well. But she knew that Garrettson or no, it behooved her to fetch him a napkin with which to wipe his dripping sleeve.

"Here."

"Don't expect me to thank you, girl."

"I don't expect anything of a Garrettson, sir," she replied with dignity and turned away, but she found herself colliding with an iron chest, and before she could dart aside, strong arms gripped hers.

"Not so fast, Malloy."

Emma gazed up into Tucker's face, rugged and handsome and somehow, tonight, amidst the festive decorations and fancy duds, strikingly dangerous. He was wearing a black shirt with a black string tie, a blue vest, dark pants, and gleaming boots. His fair hair was slicked back, he was clean-shaven, and he smelled of soap and water and a hint of pine. There was a hard glint in his razor-blue eyes and an electricity to his touch which made her heart beat faster. Not from fear, but from some other dark forbidden emotion Emma tremblingly sought to quell.

How lucky could she get? Before her stood Tucker, tall, lean, lethal—and behind her stood Jed, garrulous and fierce. *This must be what it's like to land in a rattlesnake pit,* she thought grimly.

Well, Emma decided with a slight, rebellious toss

of her head, if either of them thought they could intimidate her, they were wrong.

"Excuse me, I was just leaving."

"Off to bat those pretty eyes of yours at your
would-be fiancé?"

Pretty eyes? Did Tucker think she had pretty eyes?

Momentarily disconcerted, Emma blinked up at
him.

"Don't try batting them at *me*," he warned, his
hands tightening on her arms. "It won't work."

Emma tried to jerk her arms free and failed.
"You're hurting me."

He started, glanced down as if he hadn't realized
he was holding onto her, and let her go. He even had
the grace to look embarrassed. "Didn't mean to."

"Don't you apologize to her, boy. Not for one
damned thing. She's a Malloy. What have I always
told you? Never apologize to a Malloy, they're lower
than dirt and they—"

"Pop!" Tucker spoke sharply. "That's enough."

"And for another," Jed went on as if his son
hadn't spoken. "She just dumped a glass of punch all
over me and never so much as begged my pardon.
How's that for manners, eh? No upbringing. But then
what can I expect from Win Malloy's daughter?"

"How dare you!" Emma was trembling now,
trembling with rage that started in her heart and
surged clear down to her toes. "Don't you even mention my father's name. You're not good enough to lick
his boots—"

"I'll handle this, honey." Win Malloy gently

eased Emma behind him then stood before both Tucker and Jed, feet planted apart, fire in his eyes.

"Which one of you yellow-bellied cowards was picking a fight with my daughter?"

"Back off, Malloy." Tucker gave him a warning glance. "Before you regret it."

"Any man who shoots an innocent boy in the back has no business calling anyone else a coward!" Jed Garrettson shouted and swung his fist at Win.

Win Malloy ducked, and threw a punch in return, but Tucker blocked it. At that moment, Emma sprang forward and clutched Tucker's arm.

"Let my father go!" she cried. Tucker could have shaken her off like a bear shaking off a mosquito, but he didn't.

However, Derek Carleton, who had spied the growing commotion at the refreshment table and had seen that Emma was smack dab in the center of it, had reached the scene. Seeing that the two men there were obviously trying to cause an altercation with Emma's father, Derek spoke briskly.

"Get out of the way, Emma." He then took a swing at the younger man, the big tall one with eyes like blue granite.

He hit Tucker square in the jaw.

"Derek! No!" Emma's voice rose in dismay.

By then everyone had scattered out of the way of the brewing fracas, everyone except Sheriff Gill and Ross McQuaid.

They barged in, getting in between all the men, but it was Tara McQuaid who instantly grabbed

Tucker's other arm and stopped him from beating the city slicker to a pulp.

The expression on his face made it clear that that was exactly what he would do if he didn't have a woman hanging desperately on each of his powerful arms.

"Whoa, boys, that'll be about enough," Gill ordered. "This is a town dance, not a saloon alley, and I won't have no fisticuffs getting in the way of everyone's good time."

"What about my good time, sheriff?" Tucker grimaced as he shook himself free of both women. He took care not to shove either of them while he did so, but the glare he sent Derek Carleton was not so gentle. Some might have called it downright deadly, and Derek himself took an involuntary step backward.

"I'd say taking a few swings at Win Malloy and this tenderfoot would be my idea of a good time."

"Tucker, no!" Tara cried. He threw a look at her distressed face.

"Don't," she whispered. She reached out again and gingerly touched his sleeve. She offered him a sweet, half-cajoling smile. "Come on. Let's go dance. Please."

He hesitated. His father was arguing with Gill, and so was Win Malloy, both at the same time. Emma stood silent, beautiful as a sunrise. Carleton had slipped an arm around her shoulders and she was leaning against him, her fingers clutching his arm. She looked fragile, exquisitely feminine and elegant as Irish lace.

And she looked just right beside that slickly handsome city dude with his fancy clothes and suave air.

He turned away in disgust. "If you want to dance, Tara, we'll dance," he muttered as gallantly as possible under the circumstances.

Emma watched with a twisting knot of jealousy in her stomach as her worst enemy and her best friend slipped off to the dance floor together. The silence that had followed the altercation ended abruptly. Everyone began chattering at once, drinking punch, dancing, swarming around the table laden with food.

Music filled the hotel again, louder than ever.

"You okay, honey?" Her father squeezed her shoulders as Gill and Ross McQuaid walked Jed Garrettson to the other end of the room, trying to calm him down.

"I'm fine, Papa." She smiled reassuringly up at him. "But I wasn't about to let either of those Garrettsons get away with insulting you. With insulting *us.*"

"And neither was I, sir," Derek jumped in. He tossed a contemptuous glance in Jed Garrettson's way. "How dare those men treat you and Emma that way. Barbarous miscreants." He rubbed his fist. His knuckles were red and bruised. "I only wish they hadn't stepped in quite so quickly. I would have relished the opportunity to teach that fellow in the black shirt a lesson."

Emma shuddered, knowing that if the sheriff and Ross hadn't intervened when they had, it was Derek who would have learned a lesson. His boxing skills, well-honed in Philadelphia under the tutorship of the excellent Mr. Xander, would be no match for the brutal power of Tucker's fists if Tucker had decided to hit him back. She'd seen what he'd done to Curt Slade and Slade was by no means a tenderfoot.

Thank heavens he hadn't unleashed that savage skill on Derek.

But Emma was under no illusions about who had stopped Tucker from giving Derek the thrashing of his life.

It was Tara's quiet plea that had checked Tucker from retaliatory violence.

The knowledge gave her a strangely unpleasant jolt.

"My goodness." Sue Ellen Gill made a tsking sound as she and Corinne joined the three of them. "That was mighty exciting, Win, but I want your word we won't have any more shenanigans tonight— nothing that would spoil the festivities."

"That varmint isn't worth it," Corinne declared, folding her puffy arms across her chest. Her small green eyes snapped. "And neither is that son of his. I don't care how handsome he is, how many fool women in this town are in love with him—that boy is nothing but trouble."

Sue Ellen shook her head. "Oh, Corinne, you know as well as I that Tucker is quite a fine young man, steady as they come even if he is a bit wild when it comes to wom—" She broke off. "That's neither here nor there," she conceded as Emma and Win both regarded her through narrowed eyes, and Corinne clucked her tongue. "Mabel Barnes and I would like your word, Win," she hurried on, "that you won't go picking any more fights with Jed Garrettson."

"He picked a fight with me," Win retorted. "Actually with my daughter. But," he agreed, holding up a hand and offering Sue Ellen a genial smile, "I'll steer clear of him for the night, as much as I can."

"Well, thanks be to heaven for that." She patted Emma's arm. "You look lovely, honey. And your spice cookies are going fast. Pete Sugar's eaten half the pie already, I'll wager. Oh, here he comes. Reckon he wants a dance with you." And she winked companionably at Derek as she moved off toward the end of the room where her husband and Ross had Jed Garrettson cornered, no doubt bent on wringing a promise from him as well.

"Emma," Derek said hurriedly, taking note that the gangly cowboy Mrs. Gill had called Pete Sugar was indeed bearing down upon Emma with a besotted expression on his face. "May I have . . ."

"Howdy, Emma. Can you spare a poor cowboy a dance that'll be the bright spot of his life for many lonely nights to come?" Pete bowed to her and grinned up into her eyes so beseechingly that she laughed out loud, a delightful musical sound that made both men want to grab hold and kiss her.

"Come on, you handsome devil," she teased, and as she accepted the calloused hand he held out to her she threw a half-smile over her shoulder at Derek.

He looked so crestfallen she was immediately sorry she'd said yes to Pete, but on the other hand, maybe it would help soften the blow when she told Derek later that she couldn't accept his proposal. She dreaded doing it but unless she began to feel something more for him than fondness and affection, she didn't see how she could pledge to spend the rest of her life with him, every single day—every single night.

And from the disparaging comments he'd been making about Whisper Valley ever since he'd arrived in town, she wondered if he'd even consider her wishes about remaining in Montana. Emma knew she would never change her mind about that.

Just as she wouldn't change her mind about the Garrettsons. They were the most ungracious, ornery, obnoxious family she'd ever had the displeasure to know.

She was amazed that Tara willingly visited the Garrettsons from time to time, that she could endure spending time in Tucker's company, as she was doing right now. In fact, Emma noted, as Pete spun her with more vigor than grace around the dance floor, Tucker was leading Tara out onto the dance floor at that moment, and to her amazement, poor Tara actually looked pleased.

She's just being kind. Because of Beau. They both lost him, all three of them lost him, she told herself. *It was a bond they shared, nothing more.*

But she wondered if she ought to warn Tara about Tucker's very potent charm. Like a snake, that man could hypnotize. If Tara wasn't careful, she might wind up . . .

Like me, Emma thought, filled with a mixture of despair and rage. *Haunted by a stupid kiss from a man who's nothing but trouble.*

Not that Tucker would ever kiss Tara.

"Emma, something wrong?" Pete peered into her face as they whirled across the floor.

"No, of course not."

"You looked like you were thinking about something bad. Like the bank robbery. Or maybe like you were sucking on a lemon."

"Pete, I promise I'm as happy as a butterfly in spring." Emma summoned up her brightest smile and was determined to keep it glued in place. She managed to do it, too, until much later, when, after she'd danced with her old friend Bill Rayburn and Doc Carson and Red Peterson—and most of the cowboys in the valley—she found herself waltzing with Curt Slade. Suddenly, he whisked her clear off the dance floor, around the corner of the lobby, into a tiny hallway of the hotel that led to the kitchen.

No one else was around.

"Mr. Slade?" Emma glanced up at him in astonishment as he stopped dancing and wedged her up against the wall. The smile he gave her made her blood boil—it was filled with self-satisfaction, smugness, and a banked excitement.

"Is there something you have to say to me that can't be said in the company of others?"

"No, ma'am."

Despite his respectful words and tone, there was nothing respectful in the way he was looking at her. Inspecting her, actually. Emma didn't appreciate the way his black eyes skimmed across her face, then shifted downward to fasten upon the swell of her bosom. If he wasn't picturing her naked, she was a two-tailed cat.

"Then why are we here, instead of dancing? I would like to go back." Emma pushed away from the wall and started past him, but he grabbed her wrist and locked his fingers around it.

"I just want to warn you, ma'am."

"Warn me?"

"Stay away from Tucker Garrettson. He's bad news."

"I know that, Mr. Slade. Come to think of it, you know it too, don't you?" Because she resented what he'd said, and his cornering her here, trying to intimidate her for some reason she didn't understand, she added smoothly, "He certainly got the better of you that day you picked a fight with him. I trust you've recovered from your injuries?"

His eyes flashed then and she saw rage in them. And something else—menace. It was gone as quickly as it appeared, but Emma caught her breath and took a step backward.

Slade smiled again, pleased to see that she was frightened. A woman should be frightened of a man; it helped her to remember her place. But it wouldn't do to scare her off before he had time to put his plan into action. Like a wild, high-spirited filly, she needed gentling first. Then later, there would be all the time in the world to break her and dig in his heels for the ride.

Because Curt Slade had plans. Big plans. And Emma Malloy was an important part of them.

As the boss's daughter Emma was not only the prettiest thing he'd ever seen, she was also rich. And just snooty enough to suit him. No one else in the whole territory of Montana would have a woman like her. Such women were rare as rubies. And after he courted her, he'd marry her, and share in all the lovely land and cattle her papa would leave behind when he was gone.

Slade had toyed with this idea before Emma Malloy had ever come home, and then when he'd seen her, though she'd never given him more than a passing glance, he'd made up his mind the way things were going to be.

He'd thought to impress her that day she fainted, when he and Malloy found her with Tucker Garrettson, but Garrettson had turned the tables on him. Damn him—he'd pay for that. He surely would. And Emma Malloy would pay for what she'd said just now, throwing it in his face.

But not yet.

Slade didn't know a hell of a lot about women who weren't whores or dancing girls, but he knew that soft young things raised in the east liked to be treated nice, pampered, fussed over. So he forced himself to smile wider as he reached out and brushed a hand across her pretty pale cheek.

"That hombre didn't hurt me, ma'am. Don't you worry about that. He got in a few lucky punches, but his luck won't hold. I'm tougher than Garrettson, tougher than any man you've ever met." He smiled as she pushed his hand away. When she would have edged around him, he sidestepped, blocking her.

"I can protect you. From the Garrettsons, from anyone who might come along. And with all this trouble that's going on, you need someone to protect you, ma'am. It really isn't safe, the way you're always riding out alone on that mare—''

"What I do is my concern. If my father has no objection, surely you have no right to say a word to me about how I go about my own business. Now if you'll excuse me—''

"Oh, your father." He snorted. It wasn't entirely complimentary, and Emma's back stiffened. "He indulges you, ma'am. I've seen it with my own eyes. And I can't rightly say I blame him." Slade stroked his chin thoughtfully, his eyes gliding over her again with rich approval. "You're a mighty pretty woman, ma'am. And real sweet, when you want to be. Your father can't be blamed for spoiling you and giving you your head too much. But it's not always the best thing for a pretty lady to go about so free. Not unless everyone around knows she has a strong man looking after her, a man who won't put up with being crossed—''

"Mr. Slade, I think I've had quite enough of this conversation."

"Me, too, ma'am. Enough talk." He nodded, his eyes glinting with amusement. "Time to show you what I mean. How I feel." And before she could do more than blink at him in astonishment he yanked her forward into his arms, enclosed her in a suffocating embrace that crushed her ribs, and pressed his wet, slack mouth to hers.

It was a sucking, demanding kiss that hurt her teeth. And he tasted of gin and tobacco. Revulsion surged through her and instantly Emma stepped down hard on his foot. She followed this up with a kick to the shin, and at the same time, pushed at his chest with all her might.

"Let me go, Slade! Right now!"

To her fury, all he did was grunt, lift his head long enough to grin down at her and say, "I like a woman with spirit, Miss Emma," and then he swiftly bent his head to hers again and squashed his heavy lips against her mouth.

With all her strength, Emma shoved him away. She raised her arm and slapped him as hard as she could.

There was a sharp thwacking sound and Slade froze, gaping at her. His black eyes narrowed to slits and an ugly red fury mottled his cheeks.

"That wasn't smart, Miss Emma." He advanced a step, breathing hard. "You almost make me think you don't want me to kiss you—"

"I don't! If you touch me again, I'll scream until every single person in this hotel comes running out here to find you manhandling me. And my father will fire you on the spot. No, he'll whip you within an inch of your life. In fact, if you don't leave right now and let me return to the dance, I'm going to tell him exactly what you did, and you'll be booted off Echo Ranch so fast your head will spin!"

"You think so?" His coarse laugh was like a rusty knife scratching along her spine. "Your father needs me, girl. I'm the best foreman in the territory and he can't afford—"

A new voice broke in from around the corner of the hall. "Emma?"

Slade cursed softly.

It was Derek, Emma realized in dazed relief. He must have been looking for her and heard her voice.

"I'm here," she called out, and then he swung around the corner, stopped short, and stared in astonishment back and forth between her and Slade.

"Emma, are you all right? What the devil is going on?"

Chapter 10

 DEREK TOOK ONE LOOK AT HER FACE AND HIS jaw tightened.

"Has this man been bothering you?"

"It's okay, Derek, I'm all right." Emma slipped past Slade, whose cheek still showed the imprint of her fingers. "Let's just go back to the dance."

"But if he . . . did he . . . Emma, let me teach him a lesson." Derek's voice throbbed with anger, but Emma grabbed his arm and dragged him with her.

Slade's belly laugh followed them, but she ignored him, her eyes fixed frantically on Derek's flushed, angry face. She didn't want Derek tangling with Slade any more than she wanted him tangling with Tucker Garrettson.

"I'd really love to go outside for some fresh air," she pleaded. "The last thing I want is another scene."

"But if he . . . "

"Please, Derek, I need a few moments of quiet."

"Very well," he agreed reluctantly, then took her hand. "Perhaps we both could use some fresh air."

Emma fairly tumbled out the side door with Derek right beside her. She immediately struck out toward the alleyway around the corner and leaned against the hotel's back wall, taking deep breaths of the crystal night air. The sight of the sky swimming with pearl-white stars soothed her.

She never got as far as the other doorway, several feet away and just around the corner—never saw Tucker Garrettson leaning up against it, having a smoke, no more than ten feet from where she and Derek stood.

I'll have to decide whether to tell Papa about Slade, she thought dully, torn between the urge to get the foreman fired and the urge to protect her father from having to cut loose one of his most valued employees. Considering all the troubles besieging the ranch thanks to the Garrettsons, she hated to add one more problem to her father's pile. She knew that if she even hinted at the way Slade had behaved toward her tonight, Win Malloy would run him clear out of the valley.

"Oh, I wish I knew what to do." She blew out a breath of frustration, then abruptly remembered Derek right there beside her in the alleyway.

He was staring at her, watching her with a worried, intent expression that tore at her heart. Derek might be a bit of a snob, and a hardened businessman, and a sophisticated man about town, but he was sweet. And he cared for her. She didn't know what to do about Derek, either.

"*You* don't know what to do, Emma?" His tone was gently teasing. "You? The same woman famous

in Philadelphia for her unfailing calm and self-posses-
sion? The unflappable Miss Malloy?''

''A sorry state of affairs, isn't it, Derek?'' She
shook her head ruefully.

''Tell me what's troubling you, darling. Let me
help.''

Around the corner, Tucker Garrettson's lips
twisted into a sardonic smile. *Poor dumb bastard,* he
thought, *Carleton is a goner.* She sure did have him
twisted around her dainty little finger. Tucker had to
restrain himself from laughing out loud. The poor fool
was obviously head over heels in love with Emma
Malloy and once she roped him in, he'd suffer for it.
He'd suffer for the rest of his days. *Good luck to you,
tenderfoot,* he jeered silently, and wondered if he
should stroll out now and make his presence known.

Wouldn't that annoy Miss Hifalutin' Emma Malloy?

But the moment passed as he heard Emma begin
to relate what had happened between her and Slade.
Tucker's smile vanished and his eyes narrowed in the
darkness. White-hot anger coiled within him.

He stayed where he was, though, listening with
growing fury to her account of having been cornered
and insulted by Slade. He couldn't tell exactly what
had passed between them due to the light way Emma
spoke of it, without specific details, but he heard
enough to know the man had surpassed the bounds of
polite conduct.

And in the darkness of the alley, Tucker's expression grew downright ugly. And downright frightening.

He found himself wishing he'd been there to

catch Slade bothering her so he could teach him a
lesson about respecting women. But Carleton had obviously shown up in time to come to her aid. And if
the easterner was going to marry her, that was his
responsibility, wasn't it?

So why didn't that make Tucker feel any more at
ease?

"And after Slade's behavior—you know, Derek,
he actually made my skin crawl," she admitted with a
shudder, "I would dearly love to tell my father to fire
him. I don't want someone like him working on the
ranch."

"So tell your father what he did and—"

"It's more complicated than you realize, though.
You don't understand the situation here in Whisper
Valley. My father needs Slade; he's been telling me
since I arrived home what a fine foreman Slade is, the
best in the territory. And with the Garrettsons stirring
up trouble and our not knowing what they'll do
next—"

"Emma." Derek reached out and tilted her chin
up. She grew quiet and gazed into his eyes.

"Why don't you make things simple for yourself?" He smoothed a stray curl from her cheek,
brushing her face with infinite tenderness. "Marry me
and come to live in Philadelphia. You belong there,
not here among riffraff like Slade and the Garrettsons.
No, listen," he insisted urgently when she tried to
interrupt. "If you were with me in Philadelphia, mis-
tress of your own house, with as many servants as you
wished to do your bidding, with all the luxuries and
amusements of the world at your fingertips, and with

me by your side, doing everything in my power to make you happy, your father would be free to run Echo Ranch any way he saw fit. Slade could stay on and you wouldn't be bothered by him, or by anyone or anything ever again. I give you my word.''

''That's a lovely idea, Derek, but you don't understand.'' Emma was trying to choose her words with care, trying desperately not to hurt him. But she had to make him see. ''I belong here. Montana is my home. Whisper Valley is my—my heart.''

''Don't say that!'' He grasped her by the shoulders. There was a ferocity in his voice that hadn't been there before. And a tinge of impatience.

''I want to marry you, Emma, and I want to spend the rest of my life taking care of you and making you happy—happier than you ever dreamed. But I want to do it in Philadelphia. I *must* do it in Philadelphia! My business interests are there. As well as in New York,'' he added, his eyes alight with excitement. ''All of the important people, those building this nation, building empires and dynasties, are there. And I need you by my side, with your beauty, your elegance, your vivacity, and your exquisite calm that is so marvelously refreshing, so full of tranquility. You are exactly what I need in every way, Emma. You'll be the perfect helpmate, the most dazzling, admired hostess—''

''Let me get this straight, Derek,'' Emma interrupted, staring at him. ''Do you want a wife—or a helpmate, a hostess? Do you want someone to love, someone to share your life with, or someone who will impress your friends and business associates, who will be an asset to your business aspirations?''

"Both! They go hand in hand, darling Emma, and you are the perfect woman for each of those positions." He beamed at her. "With you by my side, I can do anything. Except live in Montana," he added, his smile widening, as if that were an impossible joke.

"Are you sure about that?"

"I'm absolutely certain."

"Then," she murmured, "my dear Derek, we have a problem. An insoluble problem."

His smile faded. There was a determined set to her chin that he didn't at all like. And a most definite glint in her beautiful turquoise eyes. His brows drew together.

"Oh, now, come on, Emma, you don't mean to refuse me—" He broke off and swallowed hard as her chin rose.

"By God, you are the stubbornest woman I know!" he exclaimed, and Tucker Garrettson, dragging on his cigarette around the corner, silently agreed.

Emma told herself she didn't mind Derek saying that to her. Because he said it lovingly, not at all the way Tucker Garrettson had said it. So she could forgive him, because she knew he was right: she *was* stubborn. But only about the important things in life.

"Well, perhaps I could work something out," he conceded slowly, reluctantly. He bit his lip. "It's possible we could live part of the time here in Montana, and I could travel back and forth between here and New York. Especially if my father and I explore some of the mining and ranching interests we've been considering." He broke off abruptly and cleared his throat. "But I'd want you in New York and Philadelphia with me a good part of the time." Suddenly, his arms shot out and gripped hers. "Emma, my love, does this mean that you're considering saying yes? You *will* marry me?"

In the light of the half moon and a thousand stars, Emma gazed at him, wishing with all of her heart that she could say yes to Derek, that she could make him happy, give him what he wanted. She didn't think she could. But somehow, at this moment, she couldn't bear to break his heart. Everything he wished and hoped for, all of his dreams for a future with her, were in his eyes.

"Perhaps," she ventured cautiously, hoping he wouldn't notice her lack of enthusiasm.

But he did. "Perhaps?" Some of the hope died out of his face.

Around the corner, Tucker Garrettson contemplated the glowing tip of his cigarette. Only the rigidity of his jaw showed the tension that gripped him as if he were caught in the talons of a hawk.

"What does that mean—'perhaps?' "

"I need more time to decide."

Tucker let out his breath. He didn't know why, but her words filled him with a surging relief. And damned if he could understand it. Or figure out why in hell he was still standing here, listening to Emma Malloy and her besotted suitor. And why he was so damned relieved that she'd not yet agreed to marry the fool.

He heard her sigh and then continue speaking in that soft low voice of hers which he found so alluring.

"Derek, I'm fond of you, *very* fond of you, you must know that. But I don't know if I . . . if I love you."

He burst out laughing. "Of course you do. You must. Darling Emma, let me help you figure it out. I know exactly how to clarify things in your mind."

Emma caught her breath as with great self-confidence, bordering on arrogance, Derek bent his head to hers. He covered her mouth with his and kissed her. Not violently as Curt Slade had done, but firmly, caressingly. His arms slid around her waist with a smooth fluidity perfected in the manicured parks, plush carriages, and most elegant salons of Philadelphia.

Scowling in the darkness, Tucker eased forward without making a sound. He glanced around the corner of the building and every muscle tensed at the sight of that tenderfoot kissing Emma, holding her in his arms.

Damn him.

And damn her. She was kissing him back.

Emma pressed her body up against Derek's and kissed him with all of the fervor she could summon. She tried, she really tried, to feel something other than a mildly pleasant, but unexciting sensation that fluttered and then . . . died.

Desperately, she kissed him again, harder this time. Deeper.

Rocked by a seething anger, Tucker Garrettson ducked back into the doorway, cursing himself for being here, in the wrong place at the wrong time. And cursing Emma Malloy for causing him so many churning, unpleasant, unfamiliar emotions, emotions he was in no mood to try to sort out.

When Derek lifted his head a moment later, he was smiling, his expression filled with satisfaction. "There, you see?" He brushed his fingertips along the whiteness of her throat.

"You can't possibly have any more doubts."

"No." Emma swallowed down her disappointment. "I don't have any more doubts."

Derek was already tightening his arms around her waist for another soul-searching kiss. "Then we'll make it official right now?"

"In an alley?" Stalling, Emma pretended to be appalled. "It's not terribly romantic, Derek."

"No, it's not." He laughed. "And normally I wouldn't do anything quite so idiotic as pressing you for an answer here, but Emma, you confuse me."

"I do?"

"More than I care to admit." He pressed a quick kiss to the tip of her nose. "Tell you what. Tomorrow I'll take you on a picnic and we'll find the perfect time and the perfect place to settle everything between us officially."

He made it sound like a business contract, Emma thought, but she jumped at the reprieve. Tomorrow sounded like a long way off. Surely by then she'd be able to think of a gentle way to tell Derek that much as she liked him, she didn't come anywhere near to loving him.

"Mr. Carleton."

She nearly screamed at the deep voice that broke the quiet of the darkened alleyway. *Tucker Garrettson.*

Emma felt herself turning crimson as he approached with soundless, catlike strides. As he threw the glowing butt of a cigarette down on the ground, and stomped on it, she wondered just how long he'd been there in the alley, and if he had seen Derek kissing her.

"You!" Derek's arms dropped from around her and he jerked around to face Tucker. "Garrettson, isn't it?" he demanded, and to Emma's dismay, assumed a boxing stance. "Come back for more of what I gave you before?" Smiling tightly, Derek clenched his fists and raised them in readiness.

But Tucker stared him down with calm amusement. "Whoa, fella," he drawled. "Don't get your britches all knotted up. I just came out here to tell you that a telegram came for you. They're looking for you all over the hotel. Something about some business deal in New York . . . "

"Oh, good Lord, the Webbings deal!" Every vestige of animosity disappeared from Derek's face, replaced by an expression of unbridled excitement—the kind a miner would wear, Emma supposed, if he discovered gold in a creek bed. "Where is the telegram? Who has it? Quick!"

"Jeb Hathaway's your man. Miss Malloy . . . " Tucker at last shifted his gaze to Emma. If he noticed how fetching she looked in the luster of starlight, her turquoise gown clinging to her curves, her midnight hair tumbling with artless grace over her shoulder, he gave no sign of it. "Reckon I'd like a word with you."

Now what, he thought an instant later, *had made*

*him say that? And what had made him invent that tall
tale about a telegram for the easterner beside her?*

Could it be the way she filled out the soft folds of
that gown? Or the way her eyes were wide on his,
bright as jewels?

"She's coming with me," Derek said and
grabbed Emma's arm, but Emma was meeting
Tucker's challenging gaze. And she thought she read a
dare in it. The man was daring her to stay here in this
alley with him. He thought she was afraid of him!

"Go ahead, Derek. I'll be there in a moment. If
he has something to say to me, I want to hear it."

Derek frowned. "But, Emma, are you certain?"

She offered him a sweet smile and squeezed his
hand. "I'll be fine."

But the moment Derek disappeared up the alley
and around the corner leading to the hotel and she
found herself alone with Tucker Garrettson, she wondered if she was loco.

Bad enough she'd had to deal with Slade's insults
tonight. And with Jed and Tucker trying to pick a fight
with her and Papa. Now she was stuck here having to
fend off more of Tucker Garrettson's arrogance.

A sliver of moonlight beamed down, illuminating
the hard planes of his face. It touched those razor-blue
eyes and Emma saw just how hard and vivid they
were, like blue granite carved from the most formida-
ble mountain. The alley seemed darker with Derek
gone. Quieter. And more isolated from the festivities
going on inside the hotel. The fiddle, banjo, and harmonica music sounded faint and far away.

"I didn't think you'd stay," Tucker said. He moved a step forward.

"Think again." Emma's chin jutted up. But beneath the cool bravado her heart began to race as she saw the amusement and admiration soften his gaze and without realizing why, she stepped toward him in the darkness. Then she caught herself in dismay and stopped short.

Chapter 11

TUCKER CLOSED THE DISTANCE BETWEEN THEM then with one swift stride. "I reckon you're all worn out," he said softly and Emma lifted her eyes to his, trying to concentrate on something other than how devastatingly handsome he looked, with his thick gold hair and eyes bluer than steel. The lean, rangy toughness of him took her breath away. She tried to ignore the breadth of his shoulders, the easy air of grace and command he exuded, the way he smelled so good, of soap and leather and pure Montana pine.

"Now why would you think that?" she asked as nonchalantly as she could when her knees were trembling beneath her gown.

"For one thing, you've danced with most every man in the territory tonight."

So he'd noticed. Triumph fluttered through her—a purely feminine, exultant triumph. It heated her blood like wine. "You were keeping track? Why, Mr. Garrettson, I didn't know you cared."

"I don't. Don't flatter yourself, Malloy." Tucker

stuck his hands in his pockets and gave his big shoulders a careless shrug. "Reckon I just couldn't help but notice, that's all. Every time I looked out at that dance floor, there you were, spinning around in some man's arms. Your would-be fiancé must not have cared for it much."

"Derek is very understanding. Besides, I didn't dance with *everyone,*" Emma pointed out, then smiled sweetly. "I didn't dance with *you.*"

"I didn't ask you."

"If you had, I'd have turned you down flat."

"Is that so?"

"That's so." She nodded with the regality of a princess.

But there was an amused glint in his eyes that set her teeth on edge. If he thought she had *wanted* him to ask her to dance, he was wrong. Dead wrong. She never should have brought that up, Emma realized with chagrin.

To her consternation he edged even closer. She wasn't sure why it made her so uncomfortable. Probably because he was unpredictable, she told herself. She was accustomed to men like Derek and the other suitors she'd known in Philadelphia, men who behaved properly, respectfully, and kept within the bounds of propriety and decorum. There was a dangerous restlessness about Tucker Garrettson, and always had been, which suggested he would not. He had his own code of conduct, his own way of thinking, and he did just as he pleased, and damned the consequences.

But there was something else that made her uneasy. The man was just too impossibly good-looking.

In his dark shirt, string tie, with his fair hair combed and tidy, his was a compelling handsomeness lethally enhanced by the dangerous gleam of his eyes, by the indomitable line of his jaw. Even dressed up and spiffy, Tucker Garrettson looked rugged. He was like some sleek dangerous animal full of leashed energy. Barely leashed energy. The kind of energy every woman is instinctively drawn to and wary of at the same time.

And at the moment, she felt herself very drawn— even as she wanted to run away!

She needed to get Tucker out of her system. Ever since she was fourteen, she'd been thinking about him. *Well, not him, really,* she told herself. *About the kiss.* Maybe, if she just did kiss him again, she'd see that it was all something she'd built up out of nothing, a schoolgirl's fantasy. That it hadn't ever been as stupendous or earth-shattering as she'd remembered it all these years.

Yes, Emma thought suddenly, light dawning with beautiful swiftness, all she had to do was kiss him again. That would break the spell. And she'd be free of these ridiculous thoughts concerning Tucker Garrettson forever.

"You know, Malloy," Tucker was saying and Emma suddenly realized that while she'd been blathering about him in her mind, he'd gotten even closer. The man was standing right before her, close enough so that she could feel the heat and strength of him burning right through her clothes. She jerked her head up so that instead of gazing at that hard muscular chest she was staring into his face. At his mouth. Wondering . . .

No, she realized suddenly, *I mustn't kiss him. That would be wrong. It would be a betrayal of Papa, of every single Malloy who ever lived.*

Giving herself a tiny shake, she remembered he was talking to her. His voice was gritty and low, drawling. "I might have asked you to dance, Sunshine, seeing as you look so pretty and all, but I just knew it wouldn't be fitting."

"F—fitting?" Emma tried frantically to summon her scattered thoughts. His nearness was wreaking havoc on her brain. And her heart. It was beating crazily. This had never happened in Philadelphia.

What is the matter with me?

"You know what I mean. A Garrettson and a Malloy? What would people say?"

"I didn't know you cared what people said. Personally, the only person whose opinion I care about is my father. And under the circumstances, he would hardly be pleased if he saw me dancing with you, but then I wouldn't be, either! In fact," she found herself rallying, "I'd be certain I was quite mad!"

He grinned at her then, a slow, lazy grin that nearly melted her toes. Dear Lord, she mustn't—she really mustn't—ever kiss him again, not ever. Clenching the folds of her skirt in fingers that weren't at all steady, she began to turn away. "Now if that's all you had to say to me—"

"It isn't." His hand shot out and gripped her arm. He turned her back toward him. But as she swung around to face him with that midnight cluster of curls billowing over her shoulder, Tucker was damned if he could think of what else there might be to say. Damned if she didn't blow every thought out of his mind.

Except that he didn't want her to go.

"Well? If you have something to say, say it. I really have to get back to my . . . my . . . "

"Fiancé?" Mockery flickered deep within his eyes. "I don't think he's exactly that yet. You're no more going to marry that poor son-of-a-gun than you're going to run through Main Street naked as a calf."

"How dare you!" Without thinking, Emma tried to slap him, but he easily caught her wrist and yanked her closer.

"So I'm wrong? You're going to marry him?" he taunted.

"What I decide to do is none of your business. Now let go of my arm or I'll scream." It occurred to her that she'd been manhandled quite enough tonight—first by Slade and now by Garrettson and she was damned tired of it. Even though his hold on her wrist was surprisingly gentle.

"Very well—I warned you." She opened her mouth to shout, but Tucker quickly covered it with his free hand.

"Don't do that. You'll break up the dance. The whole town will rush out here and then you know there's bound to be a fight between your pop and mine and someone's going to get hurt . . . "

Emma tore his hand from her lips. "Fine, I won't scream, but you let me go, Garrettson. Right now!"

Tucker released her. Once again she started past him. "I remembered what I was going to ask you," he said abruptly.

Emma spun back. "What?" she snapped.

"How're you feeling?"

"How am I—" She stared at him blankly.

"Last time I saw you, you'd just fainted. And I heard Doc Carson paid you a visit. So, how are you feeling?"

"Fine. I couldn't be better. I needed to rest for a day or two. It was nothing serious. But . . . " Emma bit her lip. "I suppose I ought to thank you," she muttered reluctantly.

"Don't bother."

"I'll bother if I want to," she retorted and stepped toward him with renewed ire. "Unlike the Garrettsons, the Malloys do have manners. I'm not ashamed to say thank-you when it's called for. And you did," she forced herself to speak the words, "help me that day."

"What about that other day? That long-ago day?"

"I don't have the faintest idea what you're talking about!" Her glorious eyes sparked fire and Tucker threw back his head and laughed.

"Oh, hell, Malloy, why don't we just get it over with. I'll kiss you again and then we can both forget about it."

"What are you talking about? You are out of your—what are you *doing?*"

He had put his hands on her waist, drawing her close to him, much too close.

"If you don't want me to, say so now." Tucker's voice was low and rough. "Because I'm going to do it and get it over with once and for all."

"How dare you . . . " She started to struggle against him, but he swiftly pinned her arms to her sides and clamped her to him with single-minded determination.

"Shut up, Malloy."

The next thing she knew his lips were descending toward hers. Slowly, oh, so slowly. Inexorably, as if nothing could or should stop them.

Emma couldn't breathe, couldn't think. She knew she should struggle. She should scream. But as if hypnotized, she stared into his gleaming eyes, braced herself for what was to come, told herself it wouldn't matter, it would be over in a twinkling.

Then his mouth laid claim to hers. His lips were hot, demanding. They sought and held. They were as hard and implacable, as ruthless as his body. As his arms tightened around her, Emma was sure she could feel every muscle in his body. A dizzying ache filled her. She closed her eyes against the rough heat that swamped her as his mouth captured hers, but she could not protect herself against the devastating impact of the kiss. It had the jolt of lightning, hot and powerful. She moaned with delight as a delicious, uncontrollable thrill fired through her.

This is a mistake, she thought in panic, *a horrible mistake. I never should have let him . . .*

Let him? Had she truly let him? Somehow his will

and hers had melded together and she wasn't sure who had wanted it more, she only knew there was no stopping him now, no stopping any of it now. A wonderful dazzling pleasure swept through her as Tucker kissed her again, and again, at first gently, testing and tasting, then with increasing intensity and need. His mouth searched and devoured her hungrily, taking, and yet, at the same time, mysteriously giving.

This was not the sweet wild kiss of that boy from long ago, Emma realized with shock. It was even more powerful, more glorious and somehow dangerous—the kiss of a *man,* an experienced, thoroughly determined man, one who knew exactly what he wanted and how to get it. It was tender and demanding all at the same time. It made her feel as if nothing else mattered to this man than the fact that he was kissing her, holding her, and for one crazed moment she felt a burst of triumph that it was *her* he wanted. *Her*—no one else at that party tonight.

She kissed him back, ardently pressing against him, her mouth molding to the shape of his lips, her heart thundering against his chest until her entire body quaked with a need she didn't understand.

Then he deepened the kiss still further, his tongue hot and wild as it waged a battle with hers, his arms crushing her in an embrace that robbed her of breath and filled her with exultation unlike any she had ever known. His kisses were devastating her, drawing every remnant of resistance from her. As his hand slid up her slender back to curve around her nape, Emma felt herself sinking deeper into the spell of his touch. Slowly, he trailed kisses across her cheek, around the delicate shell of her ear, and down her throat until she thought she would go mad. Then he brought his lips to claim hers again. The yearning and hunger she sensed in that long, slow, deep kiss left her limp and gasping for more. An intense frustration knotted in her chest and throbbed outward through her entire body when Tucker lifted his head at last.

His breathing was rapid and harsh. Emma, clinging to his shoulders, saw with dazed pleasure that he looked as shaken as she felt. She could feel his heartbeat pounding in his chest and the whipcord tension of his broad muscled frame.

And she could feel the treacherous weakness of her own knees as Tucker muttered, "Damn it all to hell," and bent toward her to kiss her again.

Emma felt naked, positively naked, despite the fact that she was wearing this exquisite gown, jewels, hairpins, and shoes. Her curls were tumbling down, her heart was soaring, her whole body felt as if it were on fire. She reached for him and her mouth sought his with a fervency born of sweet desperation.

Nothing mattered, only this. Only him. Not the ranch, the land, the feud, only this. . . .

But even as these thoughts raced through her, reality rushed back. She gasped, shuddered, and her arms slipped from around his neck to his shoulders. She pushed at him, weakly at first, then with a desperate strength.

"Stop. Tucker—*stop.*" Her voice sounded tinny and far away. "Please. Please, stop. This is *wrong.*"

He went still. Her words flailed at him. He still had her wrapped snug in his arms and the summer-sun scent of her drowned his senses, washing him with freshness and light. She was so soft. She felt so right. Her beauty was intensified by the passion flushing her cheeks. Never had Tucker seen her eyes so dark and vivid, like a heat-infused storm. He'd rather be thrown from a horse into an icy cold pond than let her go at this moment.

"You're right," he whispered huskily, one of his hands reaching up to capture one of her cascading curls. "We should stop, but I've never been much for doing what I ought to do."

But as he leaned down to kiss her again, hungry to taste the sweetness of her, she pushed frantically at his chest and cried out, "No!"

Tucker stiffened. Her beautiful face was filled with panic. Tears shimmered in her eyes. He let her go, stepping back a pace.

Distance, he needed distance from her.

"Is this really what you want?"

"No! Yes! Oh, damn you, I don't know what I want. I want *not* to want . . . this. That." Distractedly, she waved a hand, as if that encompassed all that had passed between them.

"Then maybe you'd best go back inside now." He hadn't meant his voice to sound so rough, so unfeeling. He was feeling far more than he ought, far more than he ever remembered feeling before with any other woman. But he couldn't let her see that.

Or guess at it.

"I should have gone in before," she whispered despairingly. "Don't you . . . ever do that again."

"You wanted me to do it, Malloy. At least you can admit that."

"Only . . . to see—"

"To see what?"

"Oh, damn you to hell, Garrettson!" Emma cried and whirled around. She gathered up her skirts and ran around the corner as if a wolf pursued her, leaving Tucker alone in the alley.

Derek was just coming out of the hotel in search of her.

"There was no telegram for me, Emma. That scoundrel lied. He sent me on a wild goose chase! What did he do to you? You look upset."

"He . . . oh, never mind, Derek, it doesn't matter. Dance with me. I want you to dance with me!" Emma nearly dragged him back into the hotel.

The bright lanterns, gay banners, laughter, and music assaulted her, but she winced only a little and hurried onto the dance floor.

The first person she saw as Derek clapped an arm around her waist was Jed Garrettson. She averted her eyes as they spun around in time with the music, but then she saw her father standing beside Corinne. He waved heartily at her.

She groaned.

"Emma?"

"I'm fine, Derek. Just fine. Everything is fine."

But she had a sinking feeling that nothing would ever be fine again.

Chapter 12

 TUCKER PUSHED OPEN THE DOOR OF SHERIFF Gill's office and stepped inside.

"Gill!"

No one answered. The office looked deserted. He walked past the big oak desk strewn with piles of wanted posters and papers, past the row of bookcases and the green-shuttered window, and glanced down the corridor where the two small jail cells in back were both empty.

Tucker swore under his breath.

He'd had business in town and had stopped by Gill's office to demand an explanation. He wanted to know when the sheriff was going to get around to arresting Win Malloy for his brother's murder. But he didn't have time to wait for his return. There was branding to be done this afternoon and he couldn't afford to fritter away half the day trying to track down Wesley Gill.

He went to the desk and reached beneath a folder

for a sheet of paper, planning to leave a note demanding action.

But then his gaze fell upon the folder itself and he sucked in his breath. It was labeled "Garrettson Murder Case."

Tucker pulled up the desk chair, opened the folder, and sat down. Inside he found a sheet of paper containing a list of facts about the case, obviously written by Gill. It gave the date, place, and form of death of his brother Beau. It described who had found him, the circumstances, and the suspects.

Win Malloy was the only name written in that column.

But there was something else inside that folder, lying beneath the sheet of paper. A bandanna. It was yellow silk, neatly folded, and there were grass stains on it.

But before Tucker had time to ponder what this had to do with the case, the door rattled opened and Gill stomped in.

"What the hell are you doing, Garrettson?" the sheriff asked angrily. "Get away from that desk. Who in tarnation gave you the right to interfere with an official investigation—"

"My brother's being dead gives me the right." Tucker stood. His eyes held the same cold deadly look Gill had seen in the eyes of many gunfighters over the years. Despite the sheriff's age and experience and famous steadiness under fire, the younger man's expression sent a chill clear to his bones.

"What's this bandanna have to do with the case?" Tucker demanded.

"That's none of your business." Gill strode forward, grabbed the bandanna from him, and stuffed it back into the folder. He closed the folder and set a heavy law book upon it with a thump.

"Get out of here, Garrettson, before I arrest you for meddling in official business."

"Try it," Tucker invited, his jaw clenched.

Gill grimaced. Damned if that young man's eyes didn't scald his flesh.

No, he didn't want to tangle with Tucker Garrettson, not now, with so much on his mind. There was still the matter of the bank robbery, and not a single lead in that case, and now the Garrettson murder was pointing more and more toward his oldest friend.

Hell, he wouldn't be able to keep a lid on any of this much longer, friendship or no.

"I think you'd better tell me what that bandanna has to do with my brother's murder. I'm not leaving here, Gill, until you do."

"All right, keep your hat on." Wearily, the sheriff scratched his neck. When Tucker stalked to the opposite side of the desk and glared at him, the sheriff took his place and sank into his chair. He rubbed his hands over eyes that suddenly felt old and tired. "I found the bandanna in the south pasture of the Malloy land, near Dead Dog Tree, not far from where Beau's body was discovered."

"Know who it belongs to?"

Gill gave him a bleak look. "Win Malloy."

Scalding fury rushed over Tucker. He had a memory of his brother's lifeless body, covered with blood, and then he thought of Win Malloy at the Fourth of

July dance, drinking whisky and doing the two-step with his daughter, with Corinne, with Tara, and numerous other ladies of the town. Tucker wanted to put a single bullet between the man's eyes.

He swung toward the door, but Gill was already halfway across the office, grabbing his arm.

"Now, hold on! I'm the law here and I say—"

"The law!" Tucker shoved Gill away from him, sent him spinning back against the desk. "How long, Mr. Lawman, have you known about this bandanna?"

The sheriff straightened and from his throat came a nervous cough. "From the beginning. I thought I recognized it as belonging to Win, but I didn't know for sure until that night Emma came home, the night you showed up. Remember?"

How could he forget? Setting eyes on Emma Malloy again had left a vivid impression on him. An impression that had been haunting his days and his nights, especially the past two days, since the Fourth of July dance.

But this wasn't about Emma, he told himself harshly. He thrust her from his mind as he had a hundred times in the past few weeks. This was about her father. And his brother. And a man being shot in the back.

"Did Malloy admit that it was his? Did he?"

"Yes, he did. While you were out there stirring up trouble on the porch with Emma, me and Win had a little talk. He told me the bandanna was his, but— damn it, Garrettson, listen to me! He claims he doesn't know how it got into that pasture. He gave me his word he never was out there that morning, and that he didn't shoot Beau."

"What the hell do you expect him to say? Did you really expect him to confess?" There was no mirth in Tucker's curt laugh, only contempt and a frightening icy rage. "You're old and you're soft, Gill. The man's your friend. You want to believe him, but you know as well as I do that he did it."

"That's not true. Someone else might have shot Beau and planted the bandanna there—just to shift suspicion away from himself," Gill fired back. "Hell, Tucker, half the territory knows about the bad blood between the Malloys and the Garrettsons. It makes sense that the real killer might try to frame Win Malloy—"

"The real killer *is* Win Malloy. No one else would have it in for my brother. Beau didn't have an enemy in the world. And you know it, Gill."

There was a short silence.

"I'm proceeding with my investigation," the sheriff said at last. "It's possible I might be arresting Win Malloy within a matter of days. That good enough for you?"

"I want him behind bars now."

Gill's face tightened. "Listen, Tucker. Listen good. Nobody—not you, not your pa—tells me how to conduct my duties. I'll do what needs to be done, when I have enough proof and a case that will stand up in court."

"Yeah, and he'll probably buy off the judge, too." Contempt roiled through Tucker's voice as he stalked to the door and slammed it behind him.

He rode home hard and fast and spent the rest of the day in the branding corral working in grim furious silence, working until sunset when everyone else had long gone into supper, working until his bones and mind were weary and numb. But when he joined his father at last in the dining room, he said nothing about what he'd learned at Gill's office.

It was better that he keep it to himself for now. If Jed heard about the bandanna, he would only get himself worked up into an uncontrollable rage. He'd either storm Gill's office and raise hell or ride straight to Echo Ranch and go gunning for Malloy.

Tucker knew neither scenario would be too healthy for his father. He wasn't sure how much strain Jed's heart could take, especially now in the midst of the summer heat.

So he made a decision. He'd hold off. Give Gill a few more days. And then . . .

Then, if the sheriff didn't do what needed to be done, he'd take matters into his own hands.

SHORTY BROWN RODE HARD FOR THE RANCH HOUSE, WITH Red Peterson right behind him. "Boss!" Shorty hollered, standing up in the stirrups. "Boss—trouble! Come quick!"

Win had lingered over his morning coffee, immersed in conversation with Emma and Derek. But at the sound of the commotion he jumped up with alacrity and shoved back his chair.

"What's happened now?" He frowned and started for the door.

Emma's heart began to pound. She and Derek followed Win as he charged onto the porch just as the riders pulled up in a cloud of dust.

"Cattle—poisoned. Fifty head. They're dead, boss. Down by the creek. Another ten of 'em look sick—"

Fury twisted Win Malloy's features as he started toward the stables. "Mark my word, they've gone too far this time. If they want a fight, by God, I'll give them one!"

Emma's heart chilled at his words. "Papa, what can I do?" she called after him.

"Stay put. Keep young Carleton company. This is going to get ugly, honey, real ugly, and I don't want you getting caught in the middle. If the Garrettsons insist on starting a range war, damn it, I'll give them what they want in spades."

Emma stared after him, sick with dismay. Range war. The Garrettsons had poisoned their cattle and touched off a full-scale range war. She'd never seen such a thing, but they were legendary across the west. There would be killing now. Men would die, perhaps by the dozens.

An image of Tucker burst into her mind and fear made her sit down hard in the porch chair. But not fear of him. It was fear *for* him that made her legs wobble.

Tucker.

She'd been trying desperately *not* to think about him ever since the Fourth of July dance. Ever since he'd turned her world upside down with his kiss, held her in his arms, made her forget Derek, the feud, her own notion of right and wrong . . . everything.

Everything but the feel and taste and strength of him, the savage intimacy that she'd never known with another human being.

"Personally," Derek was saying, jolting her out of her reverie, "I prefer the more sophisticated methods of fighting employed by the financial giants back east. They can be brutal, but no one resorts to poisoning animals or shooting at their fellow man."

"Oh, shut up, Derek," Emma cried, vexed with his constant subtle and not-so-subtle criticisms of life in Montana.

As he stared at her open-mouthed, she jumped up and ran to the stables. She couldn't bear to sit idly by in the midst of this crisis. She was going to the creek to see for herself.

The sight of the poisoned cattle sprawled in the grass sickened her.

Who could do such a thing?

Not Tucker, she told herself, remembering how he'd protected her that day she'd been shot at, and during the bank robbery, how gently he'd carried her to the buggy after she'd fainted. How he'd stood up for Harvey Wells to Mr. Huet even as a boy, and how he had restrained himself when he'd had every right to fight back when Derek had punched him at the dance.

For all his toughness and sinewy strength, there wasn't a cruel or malicious bone in Tucker's body.

It couldn't have been him.

But she wouldn't put it past Jed Garrettson, not for a moment. And nor would her father.

So she felt no surprise when Win framed his battle plans that evening. He ordered her from that time on to stay close to the ranch house. She could no longer take Angel for rides beyond the boundaries of Echo Ranch until further notice.

"But Papa, no one is going to shoot at me," she protested, then fell silent as she recalled once more what had happened the day after she'd come home.

She'd never told him about that, and now she threw him a furtive glance, wondering if he could see by her face that his precautions were too late.

But Win Malloy was a man driven, and he charged on without noticing his daughter's sudden silence.

"You never know. I'm taking no chances. And that brings me to another thing—and don't argue with me about this, honey. It's for your own good. I can't fight the Garrettsons and fight you, too."

"You don't have to fight me, Papa. I'm here, I'm on your side. I'll help however I can."

He nodded. For a moment a brief approving smile lit up his eyes, then it vanished, and his frown of concentration returned. "It's imperative that until this fight is finished, you don't go to town alone. Take at least one of the hands with you anytime you go beyond our land. And keep the rifle handy at all times."

"No need to worry about Emma, sir. I'll look after her."

Derek moved closer to Emma on the sofa and took her hand in his.

"See that you do, Carleton. I'm counting on you."

Then Win had gone out to the bunkhouse to confer with Curt Slade and issue his orders to the ranch hands. There would be border patrols every night and day around the clock. Slade was in charge of setting up the schedule. He was to hire more hands, as many as needed. The cattle and every inch of Malloy land would be guarded. Trespassers were to be shot.

And if any Garrettson cattle were to wander onto Malloy land, they were to be rounded up and branded immediately. The Garrettsons owed him more than sixty head to compensate for the cattle they'd poisoned. He'd get it back from them one way or the other.

And Sheriff Gill had been summoned to investigate the poisoning.

"Emma," Derek said to her later that evening as they sat together on the sofa, mulling over the tumultuous events of the day. Her father and Corinne had gone to bed and they were alone in the ranch house, with only the hum of a thousand night creatures outside to keep them company.

"Don't you think it's time that you stopped playing these games and gave me a proper answer?"

Emma looked at him, guilt washing over her. He was right. Derek had traveled all this way to woo her and get the answer he sought. She'd let him come and had kept him dangling, hoping against hope she would find it in her heart to accept his proposal—that Cupid's arrow would somehow pierce her heart and they could begin to plan a future together.

It hadn't happened. In fact, here in Montana, she felt even less for Derek than she had in Philadelphia.

There he had been in his own milieu and he'd shone. Here . . .

He rode passably well, but he just didn't seem to fit in with this rugged land or to be comfortable with the men and women who populated it. Even Corinne, who treated him with careful respect, seemed distant and reserved toward him, a sure sign to Emma of her disapproval. And though her father liked Derek because he admired his business acumen—business was nearly all they ever discussed, the stock market, the spread of the railroads, the future of the country—she knew her father would never want her to leave Montana, not when he'd spent the past sixteen years building a cattle empire, every inch of which he loved, and hoped to pass down to Emma.

In the end, though, Emma knew hers was the only opinion that mattered. And though she liked Derek, and enjoyed his company, she knew more than ever that she didn't love him. She'd realized that for certain at the Fourth of July dance when he'd kissed her. A kiss that had fizzled before it had even started.

And she'd known it with even more certainty when Tucker Garrettson had kissed her. The delicious sensations that had been ignited inside her when Tucker's lips had captured hers had left her electrified and shaken and hungry for more.

Which was impossible. Because she knew it would only lead to disaster if she should ever let Tucker Garrettson kiss her again.

Which she wouldn't. She just wouldn't.

She'd previously believed that if he kissed her again, the magic would evaporate, the spell would be broken, and all of her foolish memories would dwindle to ash. And instead, he'd shown her that the memories were *real,* the magic was *potent,* and the emotions stirred up by his touch were too dangerous and powerful to tangle with.

She had to steer clear of Tucker Garrettson.

And that was that.

"Emma." Derek put his finger beneath her chin and tilted her head so that she was forced to meet his eyes.

"I'm waiting."

She took a deep breath. "I'm sorry, Derek," she whispered as gently as she could. "I can't marry you. I don't love you the way I should."

His sharply indrawn breath and the pain etched across his face told her her words had hurt him.

"You're being silly. Is this because of my refusal to live in Montana? I told you we can talk about some arrangement."

"It's not that, Derek. It's me. I don't feel the way I should about you. It wouldn't be fair."

"Fair. Fair? I came all this way to see you, to hear your answer, I put up with that stupid primitive celebration you called a Fourth of July dance, when I could have been at the Cummings' ball in Philadelphia, and now you tell me *no?*"

The Cummings' ball. Oh yes, she remembered that. An annual affair, she'd gone with him last year for the Fourth. Private fireworks over their private lake. Oyster patties and champagne, a lavish picnic with snowy linen cloths spread upon the grass, and men and women decked out in silk and lace ordered all the way from Paris. And then dancing in the Cummings' great ballroom, festooned with exotic flowers, fountains, and the finest European musicians.

"I'm sorry."

His lips tightened. He dropped his hand from her chin. "I don't understand you, Emma. I don't understand any of this. Why you would prefer to live in the wilderness instead of in the east with cultivated people instead of barbarians who fight and spit and chew tobacco and—"

"Derek, I think you've said quite enough." She rose, carefully containing her anger. Why waste it on Derek when she had the Garrettsons? It was the trouble they were causing that really mattered.

"I assume you'll want to leave Whisper Valley as soon as possible?"

"There's no reason to stay, is there?" he countered bitterly. Then he stood up and caught her hand. "Emma, I'd hoped it would turn out differently. I care for you. I thought you cared for me."

"I do care about you, Derek, but not in the way that I ought to if I were going to become your wife. Good night."

She withdrew her hand from his and gave him a wan smile that had more to do with her own guilt and a sense of politeness than with any real warmth. He turned stiffly away.

"Good night then."

There was a note of resigned formality in his tone that made her feel sad, but nothing more.

She waited until Derek had gone upstairs before moving to extinguish the lamps. But as the darkness and quiet of the house enfolded her, she wondered what the new day would bring.

Conflict, violence. Death?

She wished suddenly that Tucker would appear at her door, right at this very moment, that he would push his way inside, tell her he had nothing to do with the poisoning of the cattle, and then . . .

Then take her in his arms and just hold her. Hold her tight and close and safe.

Safe from the impending doom she had a feeling was about to crash down upon them all.

But when she looked out the window, the night was black and empty. The moon gleamed in lonely silence. And with a heart that weighed heavy in her breast, Emma turned away and climbed the stairs to her bed.

Chapter 13

DEREK CARLETON WASN'T ABLE TO LEAVE Whisper Valley as quickly as he would have liked. The eastward bound stagecoach wasn't due for two more days, so he bought a ticket in advance and told Emma he would stay at the hotel.

"Are you sure, Derek? You're welcome at the ranch."

"What's the point? You're not going to change your mind." He sounded so petulant that Emma was reminded of a small boy being denied an ice cream treat.

She tried hard not to grin as she gazed up at him as they stood together on the boardwalk. It appeared to her that Derek's pride was hurt far more than his heart. She was relieved to know that and offered him a smile.

"No, I won't change my mind, but you might be more comfortable out at the ranch."

"I'll be fine at the hotel. Do you think it's easy for me to see you, Emma, to be in the same house with you, knowing that you've just rejected me?'' He shifted his bags from one hand to the next. ''I assure you, I'll be far more comfortable at the hotel.''

''Then I'd best be getting back.'' She glanced at the gray sky streaked with dingy clouds. The air smelled of rain, and an ominous heat hung heavy as damp wool in the thick atmosphere. There was a peculiar quiet, a foreboding energy that sizzled on the horizon.

Shorty had driven her and Derek to town, per her father's orders that she always be accompanied by at least one of the hands. The tall stringy cowboy with hair the color of sun-bleached straw had already picked up a half dozen sacks of supplies, loaded them in the wagon, and now hung back a respectful distance while she bade Derek farewell.

''I hope we can remain friends. I wish you a safe journey home, Derek. It's possible I won't return to town again before you leave.''

''Good-bye, Emma.'' Derek leaned forward as if to kiss her, then he checked himself, frowning, and straightened. He sighed. ''I wish you well, too,'' he told her stiffly. ''Though what you see in this wild, isolated country I cannot begin to fathom—''

He broke off as she pursed her lips in silent annoyance and shook his head with a bitter smile. ''Perhaps you're right. We wouldn't have been suited after all.''

Impulsively, she stretched up on tiptoe to kiss his cheek. ''You'll find a girl who deserves you, someone who can love you with all her heart. You'll see.''

He looked surprised for a moment, then squared

his shoulders and gave her a jaunty grin. "You'd better believe I will," he agreed, with the crisp cockiness she'd always found charming in him. "But I won't forget *you, Emma.*" With that he turned and headed toward the hotel with his usual brisk and confident stride.

Derek will be fine, Emma realized as she crossed the street to join Shorty. *He already seems half-relieved that he can return to the life he loves without ever having to think about setting foot in Montana again.*

But she suddenly stopped in the middle of the street as she realized that Shorty had vanished. He was no longer standing by the wagon outside the feed store; he was nowhere in sight. As she stared around the center of town in bewilderment, he suddenly came running from Doc Carson's office.

"Sorry, Emma. I just had to speak to Doc Carson a minute. It's about Abigail. She took sick this morning—I just heard."

Abigail Porter was the young freckle-faced widow who owned the boardinghouse on the edge of town. She and Shorty were engaged to be married within the next few weeks.

"Shorty, that's too bad. Is there something I can do?"

"Doc Carson's already seen her. He said she's got a fever, maybe influenza. Lizzie, who helps out with cookin' and cleanin' for the boarders, went to Livingston a few days ago to visit her sister. She's supposed to be back by suppertime, but right now,

Abigail's all alone. I'd like real bad to stay with her, just 'til Lizzie gets back.''

"Of course. What can I do to help?" Emma asked quickly, falling into step beside him as they hurried toward the boardinghouse.

"Well, that's real nice of you, but I can sit with her for a few hours. I just don't want to leave her all alone. Would you mind waiting 'til suppertime for me to take you back home?"

Emma cast a doubtful glance at the sky. The storm that was brewing, racing down from the mountains, looked to be a bad one. It could prevent Lizzie from getting back at all—and make it impossible for her and Shorty to make the trip to Echo Ranch until morning, if they didn't head out right away. She bit her lip, thinking how her father would worry if she wasn't back home in time for supper.

Besides, she was anxious to make certain that he was all right. With tensions running so high in the valley, anything could be happening out on the range today.

"Listen, Shorty, I'll drive myself home. You stay with Abigail."

"No, ma'am, can't do that." Adamantly, the cowboy shook his head. "Your pa would skin me alive."

"He won't because I won't let him. Come on, Shorty, do you seriously think the Garrettsons are going to come after me? I've got the rifle and I'm probably a better shot than you are. I just want to get home before the storm because if I don't, my father will be sending out a search party for both of us. Everyone will be worried." She touched his long, wiry arm.

"Besides, this way, if the storm's bad, you can stay here and take care of Abigail the whole evening, and I'll explain everything to my father."

He hesitated, his tongue nervously circling his lips. "Your pa won't like it."

"He'll like it less if he has to come searching for me through thunder and lightning and if he misses out on one of Corinne's fried chicken dinners," she told him with a laugh. "Now, go, Shorty. Go see to Abigail."

She gave him a little push, and with a grateful glance back at her, Shorty took off, bounding toward the trim, white-shingled boardinghouse.

Emma headed out of town at a brisk pace. She didn't like the looks of the sky and hoped her father and his men would come in off the range before the storm broke. Of course, not all the men would be able to seek shelter from the storm. Some would be left on patrol, with only their slickers, bandannas, and Stetsons to protect them from the elements.

She heard the first low growl of thunder just as she was heading through the lower pasture not far from the creekbed. It was still another five miles to home. She urged the team faster and wondered if she'd get soaked before she got them to the stables.

Then she heard a low whoop and the whinny of a horse and she reined in, forgetting all about the storm.

The sounds had come from a belt of trees beyond a small rise to her left. She reached down and grabbed hold of the rifle. Some sixth sense made her heart start to thud.

It could be her father's men, in which case there

was nothing to fear. Or it could be Garrettson riders, up to no good.

She had to find out. And if it was the Garrettsons. . . . Her fingers tightened around the rifle.

But as she cleared the rise and gazed down into the stretch of open grassland flanked by spruce and hemlock, her blood froze.

Not thirty feet away, Curt Slade, Red Peterson, Ace Whitlock, and four other Echo Ranch hands were taking turns kicking a man on the ground. As she watched, the man made an effort to get up, and Slade grabbed him by the shirt, lifted him off the ground, and slammed his fist into his face.

Then Ace kicked him. Red aimed another kick as the man attempted to roll aside, but he never executed it.

The sound of rifle fire made him freeze. Slade and all the cowboys went for their guns and spun around toward the lone figure on the rise.

"Get away from him," Emma shouted.

Shaking with fury, she snapped the reins and drove the wagon straight toward the knot of men. A dizzying horror swept over her as she stared down at the battered form of Tucker Garrettson at Slade's feet.

"Put your guns away and get back!" They were still shuffling and muttering among themselves when she leaped from the wagon and ran toward Tucker.

Eyes downcast, they made room for her.

"Miss Emma, you shouldn't concern yourself with him. Go on home," Red began, but she pushed him aside and dropped to her knees beside Tucker.

Sick fear clawed at her. He was alive, but just

barely, as far as she could tell. His head lolled back; he gazed up at her without recognition.

There was blood all over his face, all over his shirt.

"Help me," she gasped. "Help me get him into the wagon."

But when Ace and Red stepped forward, Curt Slade blocked their path. He stood directly over Tucker and stared down at Emma, his black eyes narrowed.

"There's no cause to get yourself all dirtied up with this varmint's blood, ma'am. He was trespassing. And we have our orders."

"You get out of the way!" Emma shouted at him, rage thickening her voice. "Red, Ace! Help me with him right now—I can't lift him alone."

The cowboys all shuffled their feet, threw her worried glances, scratched their heads, but none of them came forward or answered her as the foreman glared warningly at each man in turn.

"Damn you—you're all cowards," she cried, and slipped an arm beneath Tucker's neck.

"Miss Emma." Slade's mouth was a thin, hard slash in a face that was coldly vicious. "This is no place for a lady. You shouldn't see such things, shouldn't worry your head about them. You don't understand."

"Oh, I understand just fine." Her eyes bored into his, brilliant with rage. "I understand that you've all nearly beat a man to death. That you started this, Slade—and I'll tell you something. I'm finishing it. Right here, right now. You're fired."

He gave a start and wiped the back of his hand across his mouth. "Now look here, you'd better watch what you say—"

"Don't threaten me. Get out before I shoot you like the dog you are, Slade. Get your gear from the bunkhouse and go. My father won't want you anymore after I'm done talking to him."

She saw the incredulity, then the flash of murderous fury in the foreman's eyes, and if she hadn't been so consumed with terror for Tucker, she might have flinched. But she merely shifted her gaze from Slade's, and rivetted it upon Red Peterson.

"Red, you and Ace lift him into the wagon *now!* Or I'll fire both of you, too!"

They sprang to obey her, ignoring Slade, who stood stiff and furious, his jaw clenched so tightly he looked like he'd be frozen in that position for eternity. Jagged lightning danced across the sky as the cowboys lifted Tucker into the back of the wagon. Emma hastily unrolled the blanket folded in the corner and threw it over him. He had passed out, she noticed in alarm. He looked like a man with one foot in the grave.

"Now get back. Don't you touch him again. Don't any of you touch him!" she cried and jumped back up on the wagon seat.

Red and Ace fell back in grim silence.

Picking up the reins, Emma spoke desperately over her shoulder in a voice only she could hear. "It's all right," she whispered. "Hang on. You're going to be just fine."

But as she steered the team back over the rise, the

skies opened and the rain came in a hard silver torrent.

"Hang on, Tucker," she pleaded, biting back a sob as the wagon careened through a grassy field which had turned almost instantly into a sea of mud.

The sky was an eerie, frightening green. Thunder boomed so loudly the horses reared and almost bolted and icy rain pellets that were hard as glass bombarded them. Emma was forced to slow the horses for fear of overturning the wagon.

"Easy!" she called to the team but she herself jumped at the next slash of gold lightning.

She couldn't see farther than ten yards before her, but she pressed doggedly on. Then, as the wind whipped the leaves and the tall grass into a frenzy, and the rain soaked her clothes and streamed down her face, she knew she had to get Tucker to shelter immediately.

That was when she remembered the line shack. The one tucked away amidst the high brush near Three Rocks Canyon.

It was only half a mile west of here. Home was at least three miles distant.

But even as hope rose and she sought to turn the team, lightning struck a tree no more than a stone's throw from her. Screaming in panic, the horses reared up and Emma fought to get them under control.

"Just a few more minutes," she muttered through clenched teeth as she used all her strength to head the frightened horses west.

Through slashing rain and the punishing roar of thunder, they raced for the shack.

* * *

"TUCKER? TUCKER, YOU HAVE TO HELP ME. I CAN'T . . . do this . . . alone."

Panting and sobbing, she pulled at the tall, rangy man sprawled across the wagon. The rain pelted her cheeks which were already wet from her tears. Watery blood flowed down Tucker's battered face, and his shirt was sodden with it.

He was too heavy for her to lift and as thunder boomed close by, she cast a frantic glance at the shack only twenty feet away. It might as well have been miles away.

"Tucker, please. *Please,*" she whispered desperately, and she heard a low grunt. His eyes half opened.

"Keep your . . . hat on . . . Malloy. Get out of the . . . way. I . . . can walk."

It hurt him to speak, she could see that. His eyes closed again, then opened with obvious effort. But instead of letting go of him, Emma grabbed his arm firmly and began to ease him over the side of the wagon.

"Move . . . out of the way." His muscles bunched, his lips clamped together as he pushed himself over the side of the wagon.

"Let me help you."

"Don't want . . . fall on you . . . "

"You wouldn't dare." She bit back a groan under his weight as he half-fell out of the wagon, but she kept him from tumbling to the ground.

He sagged against her, breathing hard, but he was on his feet, though none too steadily.

With her arm around him, supporting him, Emma stared at the shack's door.

"Almost there," she gasped. "Lean on me."

The rain nearly blinded them but they made it at last, pummeled by a wind that tore howling through the brush. Emma kicked the door open, using all of her strength to keep Tucker from pitching forward into the blackness.

Then they were inside the shack where it was blessedly warm and dry. Emma had never been so glad to see four walls in her life.

Through the dimness she saw the outline of a cot in the corner. Moments later, she had Tucker lying across it, a thin straw-filled pillow beneath his head. Aside from a grunt, he hadn't said another word.

Emma didn't speak, either. She wondered what to do first: tend to his wounds, build a fire, or see to the horses.

She'd gotten the kerosene lamp on the three-legged table burning. Its strong amber glow illuminated even the gloomy far corners of the shack. The place was rough and small, but it was dry—and she knew there would be food and supplies in the barrels set against the wall.

But first she knelt beside Tucker, staring in horror at the damage that had been inflicted on his body. It must hurt him unbearably, she thought, pain twisting through her heart. Gently, without thinking, she reached out and smoothed a sodden lock of dark gold hair back from his brow.

Her fingers trembled at the touch of his hair. She felt tears stinging her eyes and blinked. When her vision cleared, she saw that Tucker's eyes were open and he was staring at her.

"Don't . . . cry over me, Malloy. I'm already . . . half-drowned."

"I'm not crying. It's only the rain."

"Yeah, right."

They became aware at the same time that her fingers were still lightly stroking his hair. She withdrew her hand.

"Are you all right?" she asked quietly.

"I've been . . . a sight better, Malloy."

"I'll get some water to clean you up, then we'll put some salve on your wounds."

"First . . . the horses."

"But—"

"Damn it, woman. The *horses.*" His tone was firm, as if he were the one who was in charge, not she.

Emma shook her head. "You're a cowman to the core, aren't you?" Every cowman knew the value of good horseflesh. Tucker had been raised with the same creed her father had instilled in her—always feed and care for your horse before yourself.

"There's a lean-to out back. I'll get them inside." She stood up, brushing dripping tendrils of hair away from her eyes. "Don't go anywhere, Garrettson. I'll be right back."

Bracing herself, she pushed the door open and dashed out once more into the deluge. But as she unhitched the horses from the wagon and started to lead them toward the lean-to, another crash of thunder drove them beyond skittishness to downright panic. They both reared up, and Emma had to drop the reins and jump aside to escape the flailing hooves as they came down hard.

Then the animals bolted. The reins whipped through her hands as the team tore off into the raging storm.

Now we're really stranded.

The mountains, awash in nature's fury, seemed to mock her, while the vast Montana sky drenched her in an onslaught of tears.

They'll probably go home, she realized as she plunged back toward the shack. Her father would no doubt be frantic when they returned without her.

But she couldn't help that now. She had Tucker to care for.

He was sitting up when she stumbled back into the shack, tossing her streaming hair back from her eyes. Something broke inside her as she stared at his bruised and bloody face. The wicked cut across his chin tore at her heart, and the raw welt oozing over his left eye made her ache.

"What happened?" he asked.

"They bolted."

He started to swing his legs over the side of the cot, frowning. "Are you hurt?"

"Only my pride. Now stay put, Garrettson. Don't you dare get up from that cot."

To her relief he made no effort to get up. In fact, he slumped back against the wall, and his eyes drifted closed.

Anxiety drove her as she found salve and bandages in a wood box on the shelf and put a kettle of water on to boil. But when she was ready with all her supplies and hurried toward him, he roused himself and fixed her with a remarkably stern gaze for a man who'd been beaten and kicked and stomped.

"See to yourself first, Malloy. Get out of those wet clothes." He was sounding more exhausted now. The strain in his eyes frightened her.

"And put on what clothes instead?" She forced herself to smile cheerfully, hiding her concern for him. "I forgot to bring my traveling valise."

"Gotta be a blanket somewhere. Build a fire, wrap yourself in the blanket, and set your clothes out to dry."

"I'll think about it. After I get you fixed up, and set *your* clothes out to dry."

To her surprise, he didn't argue with her. Then she looked at him and saw why.

He was staring at her. Not at her face, but at her chest. At her breasts, to be exact, which were clearly outlined by her clinging wet cotton shirt, which may as well not have been there at all.

Emma fought the urge to cross her arms over her breasts. But she couldn't fight the color that rushed into her cheeks.

Then Tucker's gaze lifted to her face. And what she saw in his expression made the color in her cheeks flame hotter. Desire flared in his vivid blue gaze. The sparks in his eyes seared her, and their intensity took her breath away.

She tore her gaze from his. *Tend to his wounds. Think about nothing but that.*

Hastily, she unknotted her bandanna, slipped it off, and dipped it into the kettle of hot water. A bit more energetically than was necessary, she began to dab at the blood and the bruises.

"Ouch. Damn it, can't you be more gentle than that? You've got the touch of a rampaging coyote."

"Serves you right," Emma murmured, but she eased up and began to dab more delicately at the ugly cut across his chin. When she began to apply the salve to his wounds, Tucker winced once, then scowled at her.

"Liniment," he said suddenly.

"That's what this is—hold still."

"No—spell it."

Emma stopped and leaned back, staring at him. Her eyes narrowed. "I know how to spell liniment," she informed him icily.

"Maybe you do and maybe you don't. I remember a certain spelling bee—ouch!" He grabbed her hand. "You did that on purpose."

She had. Because she remembered the same spelling bee. She'd spelled liniment "linament." And Tucker, taking his turn after her, had spelled it correctly and won first place.

"You're still a sore loser," he said softly, his fingers closing tightly around her hand.

"That's not true." Emma tossed her head. "If I still carried a grudge, I would have left you where I found you today instead of going to all this trouble for a man who—who doesn't appreciate me."

"I appreciate you, Malloy."

Emma took a deep breath. She fastened her gaze on the welt above his eye. "Hold still," she commanded and slipped her hand from his grip. Carefully, she began to daub the salve across the welt, then applied a bit more to the scratch on his neck, all the while intensely aware of his gaze, which had not left her face for a moment.

"I need to get you out of this shirt," she said. Because she'd covered him with the blanket in the wagon, his clothes were not as soaked as hers, but his shirt was damp and bloody.

"Yes, ma'am." His eyes glinted as he watched her bite her lip, then slowly reach for the top button of his shirt. The storm raged outside, but as Tucker watched the beautiful, slender woman who had saved his life fumble with the buttons of his shirt, he felt a heat in his blood that no rain or wind could touch.

Emma cursed her own fingers for their unsteadiness. His nearness, the solid strength and masculinity of him, assailed her and seemed to make breathing more difficult for her. As she opened his shirt, she steeled herself against the sight of his wide chest matted with dark gold hair. But she couldn't breathe for a moment and found herself staring.

"As bad as all that?" he asked dryly, and she shook herself in mortification.

"There's a . . . bad bruise or two," she said with what she hoped was nurse-like crispness. The bruise on his shoulder and forearm were not all that bad, she saw to her relief.

Her gaze traveled lower, down the length of his lean, sun-bronzed torso. Oh, my, she thought, her heart fluttering uncomfortably. He was magnificent, all muscle and sinew and curling golden hair.

"Do you . . . think your ribs are broken?" she

asked uncertainly, trying not to let him see how unsettled she was by his hard, masculine body.

"One way to find out," Tucker murmured.

She bit her lip, then caught the amused gleam in his eyes and swallowed back her hesitation. "This might hurt," she warned, then slowly reached forward. Her fingers trembled as ever so carefully she touched his abdomen. He didn't flinch, but she felt his muscles tighten. Gently, she pressed and probed his warm, taut flesh, her palm and fingers tingling.

As her hand slid along his skin, she saw the amusement vanish from his eyes, replaced by a smoldering intensity.

It wasn't pain he was experiencing, she realized. It was something quite different. Heat suffused her cheeks and quickly she drew her hand away.

"Nothing appears to be broken," she said a bit breathlessly. "You're lucky."

"Yeah," he answered slowly. "I'm lucky you came along when you did."

For a long moment their eyes met and held. A strong current of sensual awareness sizzled between them, and Emma felt strangely lightheaded.

She took a deep breath and pulled her gaze away from his intent, watchful eyes. "I'd better tend to those bruises," she told him as steadily as she could. Tucker nodded.

While the wind whipped at the walls of the shack, she braced herself to touch him again.

His eyes seemed to burn into her when she leaned closer. As she gingerly applied the salve, she tried not to think about the hard, masculine flesh she was rubbing with her fingertips.

But it was a good thing she was wearing wet clothes and her teeth were chattering because beneath her sodden skin, her blood was growing ever more uncomfortably hot.

And Tucker Garrettson, with his cool, shrewd eyes, was sure to notice, whether he was injured or not. She had the feeling he could see right through her sometimes—nearly all of the time—and it was dreadfully disconcerting.

She glanced at him, bracing herself to hide the feelings swirling inside her, but then she saw that for this one moment at least, she was safe from Tucker's intently perceptive gaze.

He had passed out.

Chapter 14

AS THE RAIN PELTED THE ROOF OF THE ROUGH little shack, Emma sat by Tucker's side and watched him sleep. She had found a blanket under the cot and had draped it over him. But she couldn't stop looking at him, studying him in the lantern's glow, pondering the mysteries of her own heart.

She didn't want to deal with the things she was thinking, the things she was feeling. She didn't want to confront what was happening to her or admit that when she looked at him lying there, tenderness welled up in her until she thought her heart would break.

Finally, when her skin was clammy and her lips nearly blue, she rose and went about the business of making a fire.

The woodbox was full, and there was flint and matches, and it was easy enough. The roaring blaze was a wonder and a joy. Basking in the warmth, she stripped off her white cotton shirt and navy riding skirt and spread them before the flames. Though her petticoat was damp, she knew it would dry soon enough before the fire, so she kept it on. She unbound her hair from its blue ribbon and its pins and combed the damp tendrils with her fingers, letting them spill over her shoulders. Then she turned her attention to the barrels near the wall and found rations—hardtack and jerky and coffee.

As she made the coffee she wondered if the delicious hot smell of it would waken Tucker, but it didn't. He was out cold.

So she sat on the floor before the fire and gulped the black liquid, more to warm herself than anything else. The memory of what Slade and the others had done to Tucker made her burn with anger and with fear.

What would have happened if she hadn't come by, if she hadn't noticed or heard the men?

Her throat closed up. She ached all over at the thought of what had happened to him, and she gulped down the rest of the coffee with desperate urgency. She needed to be strong now, to take care of Tucker until this storm was over and she could get him home or to Doc Carson.

She wouldn't even let herself think about what she would have to deal with once her father learned that she had interfered with his men and taken Tucker's side.

She wondered what time it was. It was so dark outside she couldn't tell. Surely by now it was past suppertime. But she wasn't hungry. She felt empty inside and afraid. She was terrified of Slade's and the other men's violence and she was terrified of herself, of her own wildly uncontrollable emotions.

What had happened to that self-possessed young woman who was so in command of herself, who had cultivated a knack for remaining in control?

Tucker Garrettson had happened.

As lightning split the sky, raging in fury over the blackened mountains, Emma stood up, trembling. The shack felt as if it were trembling, too, shaking like a leaf in the wind as she tiptoed across the floor and gazed at the battered man asleep on the cot.

My enemy, she thought. *My father's enemy.*

This infatuation—for that's what it was, a crazy infatuation, nothing more—must end, she told herself firmly. *Now. Tonight.*

She lifted a second blanket from under the cot and moved wearily to the opposite side of the shack. Slumping down in a corner as far from Tucker Garrettson as she could get, she wrapped the moth-eaten blanket around her and sat with hunched up knees and bleary eyes, recounting to herself all the reasons she had to keep her distance from Tucker Garrettson.

And at last she fell asleep, with her enemy's name drifting upon her lips and floating through her mind and embedding in her heart.

She didn't know what awakened her. She'd heard nothing—the first warning she had was of a strange sensation, that of being lifted up from the bottom of a murky midnight sea. She swam out of sleep, pushed through the fog of exhaustion and confusion, and realized that she was being carried across the shack.

"Tucker, put me down! What are you doing?"

"That's a first." He ignored her questions, her

demands, and gave a slight groan as he set her down on the cot with a gentle thump.

"What's a first?" Emma shot up and would have jumped off the cot if he hadn't pushed her firmly back down. Obviously, she realized, the beating he'd suffered hadn't affected his strength—or his purely male stubbornness.

"You calling me by my first name. Tucker." He studied her, his long-lashed eyes lingering on her face until she felt her mouth go dry. "I reckon I like it."

"Don't get used to it. It won't happen again. I was just confused because you woke me up when I was sleeping so soundly. Now, are you going to let me up off this cot or not?"

"Not," he replied steadily and sat down beside her.

There was a faint amused smile touching his lips and Emma wondered why he was smiling and how he was managing to do it. It had to hurt.

"But you're the one who should be lying here," she protested. "Why did you get up?"

"I woke up," he explained patiently. And gave her a push backward down onto the mattress, a push that was half-playful, half-business. "Saw you all scrunched up in the corner and realized that's no way for a lady to catch some shut-eye."

"How very chivalrous of you, but you're the one who's hurt, who needs to recover, who is under *my* care, at least until this storm ends and we can ride out of here . . . "

He jerked a thumb toward the window and she saw what she hadn't noticed before. The rain had ceased. Pale gray light shone outside, with a hint of luminous opal crowning it. Dawn was coming, slow and fresh and clean.

"Ohhh."

"It'll be daylight soon. Your clothes should be dry by then."

For the first time, she remembered that she was only wearing her petticoat. Her mouth dropped open. At the glint of amusement in his eyes, she snapped it shut again, but stiffened with mortification as she remembered the intimacy of Tucker's arms around her as he'd carried her here. She snatched up the blanket on the cot and held it up across her breasts, flushing when she saw his surprisingly appealing smile, which disappeared as quickly as it had come.

"Soon as you're ready, I'll walk you home, Miss Malloy."

"Miss Malloy?" Emma was certain she'd heard him wrong.

Tucker had all he could do not to scoop her into his arms as she tilted her head to one side, studying him warily. She couldn't possibly know how adorable she looked with her dark hair tumbling like a cloud over her bare creamy shoulders, her eyes soft and still dreamy with sleep. He had to fight the urge to bury his fingers deep in her luscious hair, lower himself over her, and take her right there on the cot.

He kept a tight lid on the feelings clamoring inside him though and reminded himself that he owed her.

Yeah, he owed her. He owed her respect. And

gratitude. If she hadn't come by and stepped in when she did, he'd be dead.

Slade would have seen to it.

"I'm not sure I can handle all this courtesy," Emma said slowly. "Careful, Garrettson, or I'll start to suspect that a true gentleman lurks somewhere beneath that cold, rough exterior of yours."

"Aw, shucks, Malloy, it's not all that cold."

Despite his lighthearted words, Emma saw the sudden tension in his shoulders and felt a blast of shock as she saw his gaze on her, watching her with a searching gentleness.

Suddenly it took all the desperate strength she possessed to keep from leaning forward, throwing her arms around him, and tasting that strong, sensuous mouth once again. But she knew that if she gave in to the emotions flooding through her now, she would be lost.

Why did he have to look so—so handsome? Even with the bruises and the cuts, even with little sleep and a bandage above one eye, he looked remarkably fit, amazingly competent, dangerously attractive.

Face it, you fool, she told herself despairingly—he looked downright splendid. Even as he sat perfectly still on the edge of the cot, not touching her at all, except with his eyes.

She sprang up and off the cot, but he caught her wrist and tugged her down again so that she plopped down beside him. The blanket slipped away from her grasp, whispered to the floor.

Tucker ignored it, staring down at her wrist, snagged within the circle of his strong fingers.

"We can fight this thing," he said quietly, "or we can give in to it. And get it over with."

"What . . . thing? I don't know what you're talking about."

But she knew, even as she breathed the words. And he knew she knew. She saw the glint of determination darken those mesmerizing steel-blue eyes.

"Us, Malloy. The thing that's going on between us. What's been going on ever since that day when we were kids and I carried you home. No more games," he told her roughly as she started to protest and tried abruptly to wrench free.

"We're not kids anymore. You're a woman and I'm a man, and you know damn well what's between us."

"They must have hurt your brain when they were kicking you today. You're not making sense—"

"None of this makes sense." His voice was sharp as he interrupted her. He reached out, cupped her chin, and tipped her head up so that she was forced to meet his eyes. His gaze locked on hers with a fierceness that knocked the breath from her.

"Not a damned bit of sense," he added and leaned toward her.

Dear heaven, he was going to kiss her.

Panicked, Emma jerked back. A quaver throbbed through her voice. "Don't!"

The quaver made him stop. He was rigid, on fire, holding on to reason by the skin of his teeth. "Give me one good reason not to kiss you, Malloy," he grated out.

"You poisoned our cattle."

"Like hell."

"You trespassed on our land today, planning to do heaven knows what—"

"That's a damned lie. Slade and your men attacked me on *my* land. Roped me, dragged me onto Malloy land, and then proceeded to try to beat the living daylights out of me."

"No!" She recoiled in horror. *"No."*

He said nothing, just met her gaze with a hard, unwavering stare.

Emma's hands flew to her throat as the truth rocked her. She saw it in his eyes, knew that it had happened exactly as he'd said. Stricken, her gaze swept over that handsome, bruised face, the mouth so firm, the lean planes so strong, filled with a combination of toughness and assurance, the eyes so devastatingly, brutally hard and yet alive, alight . . . searching.

Searching for what?

For what was inside of her. He was trying to read her, to see what she felt.

He mustn't find out about that. She felt too much. Far too much.

"That's terrible." Genuine horror and dismay brought the glitter of tears to her eyes. "I'm . . . sorry."

When Tucker saw the pain shining in her beautiful eyes, something deep inside of him tightened like a fist. Her lips were trembling. Her hands shook. Was her distress all for him? For what he'd gone through?

His gut clenched. Damn, how he wanted her. She was so damn sweet. He hadn't ever expected that.

Tough as nails, yes—he'd seen that side of her—but her heart was as big as Montana and as soft as duck down, and he wanted nothing more than to wrap her in his arms and press all that delectable softness and sweetness against him.

Wanting her was an agony. It hurt worse than anything those bastards had done to him yesterday. Every muscle throbbed with the need to hold her against him, to take her, taste her, know her in the most intimate, thorough way a man can know a woman.

"Emma, we've got to settle this thing. I want you—you want me—"

"I don't!"

"Now who's lying?"

He asked the question quietly, but there was steel beneath it. Emma thought she'd melt from the intensity with which his gaze pinned her. She jerked back on the cot, surprised when he made no move to stop her. Then she scrambled backward still farther, lengthening the distance between them.

"I want you to move away from me, Tucker Garrettson. Now. Go over there."

She pointed toward the corner.

Tucker's mouth twisted up in a grin that was so roguishly boyish it made her heart flip over. But the narrow-eyed look he gave her the next instant was pure grown-up male. "Even old Huet couldn't send me to the corner when I didn't want to go."

"I want you as far away from me as possible."

"Prove it."

He edged closer.

"Get back!" she ordered and retreated farther.

To her consternation, he came closer.

"Back!"

"What are you so afraid of, Malloy?"

"Not you, Garrettson!"

"Maybe you're afraid of yourself. Of what you might do if you kissed me again, if you'd let yourself go—"

"You are plain crazy! I've no desire to kiss you ever again. How many times do I have to tell you! Oh, what are you doing? I said to get away!"

But he was following her. Maddeningly, deliberately moving ever closer as she inched farther back. Emma scurried all the way to the wall and then was trapped there with her back against the unyielding wood, and Tucker advancing bit by bit. She didn't at all trust that determined expression on his face. He touched her outstretched foot and she yanked it back, tucked it beneath her. His hand reached out and slid up her arm. Slowly, caressingly, deliciously.

"I liked you better when you were passed out. How did you recover so quickly anyway?"

"I had tender loving care."

"It's nearly daylight. It's time to go back!"

"It's time to settle this, Malloy—once and for all."

She didn't want to settle anything. She wanted to run, from him, from herself. From the emotions swamping her, drowning her in thoughts and needs she wanted to know nothing about.

But as he continued to stroke his hand up her arm, she found herself captured by the gleam in his eyes. She tore her gaze away from their compelling blue depths. Unfortunately, her glance next fell upon his mouth. And she remembered all too well the hot firmness of his lips, their sensuous shape and texture, the feel of them on her own lips, on her skin, against her hair. . . .

Her heart began to hammer. She dropped her gaze again, confused and desperate, fighting panic. Only to find herself staring at his magnificent broad chest, bare and bronzed, rippling with muscles.

"Oh, good Lord," she whispered frantically. It was close to a prayer. And then Tucker reached out, grasped her arms, and drew her forward with a swift easy motion that left her gasping.

He pulled her to him, down across his lap, cradling her in his arms as she stared dizzily up at him.

"Emma. This can't go on. We've got to get this out of our systems. You're torturing me—"

"I'm torturing you?" she gasped, and he nodded, one of his hands coming up to stroke her hair. The silken waves flowed through his fingers. So rich, Tucker thought, so soft.

Torture.

"It's worse than what those bastards did back there. A lot worse." His hand touched her cheek, traced the delicate outline of the face that had burned in his dreams. The fragility of her both frightened and compelled him.

He forced himself to speak calmly, though he felt far from calm. Churning need and desire whipped through him, held in check by every ounce of will-power he possessed. Only the most rigid shreds of control kept him sane as the beautiful girl in his arms looked up at him through wide, brilliant eyes filled with confusion, and, he thought in wonder, with longing.

"We'll both be better off if we finish this and then forget about it," he said, dragging in a deep steadying breath.

"If only we could!" Emma squirmed up to a sitting position on his lap, feeling heat pervade every inch of her. His nearness, the sinewy muscles and iron strength of him, the dangerous tension she sensed just beneath the surface, nearly undid her. She wanted to throw her arms around his neck. She wanted to press herself to him and be held, kissed, and . . . she knew not what.

But she should run, run for her honor, if not her life.

Instead she regarded him like a dying woman seeking deliverance.

"How?" she breathed. "Just tell me how we can forget about this!"

He took a deep breath, hanging on to control as he tried not to stare at her in her petticoat, her creamy breasts swelling delectably above a scoop of white lace, her hair swirling like velvet. "We'll let ourselves go—just this once," he said more harshly than he intended. It was costing him not to seize her in his arms and take what he wanted—hell, what he sensed they both wanted.

"We'll let ourselves go all the way, as far as we want. Right here on this cot. And then, it'll be over. Over forever," he repeated, as if reassuring himself. He tore his gaze from her lips, those glorious rosebud lips, and met her eyes with more sternness than he intended.

He didn't want any misunderstandings.

"Listen, Malloy, there's something you need to understand. I'm not looking to saddle myself with a wife. And Lord knows you'd be the last one I'd pick if I were," he went on grimly, determined to be completely, ruthlessly honest. "Don't mean any offense, but both of our fathers would shoot us and rightly so if we ever—"

"I'd sooner marry a skunk as marry you!" she cried.

"I feel the same way." He let out his breath in relief. "Good, Malloy, that's real good. So we're safe. I'm not the marrying kind anyway, never have been and don't ever expect to be." He shrugged. "But sometimes a woman gets in your blood. . . . "

His voice trailed off. It had never happened before, not to him, not like this, not with the fevered potency with which this woman was in his blood. But in the past there'd been a time or two when only by bedding a woman he'd taken a fancy to had he been able to forget about her. He reckoned this would turn out the same—it would have to. And then he could move on.

"So if we agree to get this all over with, right here and now, we'll both be better off."

Eagerly she grasped him by the shoulders, her slim fingers burning into his flesh. "I want that. I can't bear to keep thinking about you, imagining—"

So she'd been doing that, too. Tucker felt a surge of desire so powerful he nearly groaned. It took all of his self-control to fight it back. He was sore as hell all over but wanting her hurt far worse than anything Slade and the others had done to him. Yet he held back.

Not yet. When we have everything plain and settled between us.

"Well, this should take care of it," he assured her. Then he added in a low tone, "I think."

"You *think?*" Uneasily, Emma sought to understand what he meant. Doubt flickered across her face.

"I'm almost sure." Tucker's voice roughened. "It's never been this bad before."

Then he could have kicked himself. Damn, why had he admitted that? Her eyes flashed with something, and he could have bitten off his tongue for possibly giving her hopes of—of what? Snagging him?

"This one time . . . we'll let things go," he said again, firmly. "Then . . . that's it. It's finished. Over. No matter what. You got that, Malloy?"

"No matter what," she repeated, nodding her head, but her eyes were fixed once more on his mouth. Longing consumed her.

She ached. Being this close to him made her ache.

"Garrettson . . ."

"What, Malloy?"

"Will you please kiss me now? I can't wait any longer. I feel like I'm sick with something, something strange and unpredictable and—and I just want to be cured."

He nearly laughed out loud, then groaned, both charmed and tortured by her innocence, her sweet desperate passion. His need for her flared within him, catching like a prairie fire.

But she was right in what she said about a cure. That's what he wanted, too. And when they'd finished making love, they'd both be cured. Once and for all.

"It'll be my pleasure to kiss you, Sunshine," Tucker said softly. Every muscle in his body throbbed with the wanting of her. But gently, carefully, he drew her trembling body close. "Come here."

The sensuous softness of her on his lap was unbearably delightful. Intoxicating. Almost as intoxicating as the fragrance of her, the way she tasted, as he remembered . . .

And then it was no longer a memory. He was kissing her, tasting her again, his lips devouring her sweetness even as he willed himself to go slowly.

But there was no slowing or stopping them now.

The impact of their mouths as they clung together stunned them both. An explosion of gentleness rocked Emma, then changed to something darker, deeper as Tucker's mouth claimed her own with a driving hunger that burned clear through to her tongue.

"This'll do it," he murmured against her mouth. He caught her hair in his hands, his fingers tangling, holding on tight. At the same time she thrust against him, her body locking to his, and her breasts pressed against his naked chest with such sweet ardor he wanted to die. But not before he'd had her, all of her. Right here on this cot.

She dragged her head up, breaking the kiss, her eyes glazed. "You're sure this is going to work?"

It was a low, ragged whisper. Sexy as hell.

"Yeah."

"I won't ever want to kiss you again?"

"No." He was inhaling the summer soft woman-scent of her, trying to command himself to go slow, to be gentle. Fighting the urge to tear off her petticoat and toss her down on the bed without further ado.

"And I . . . " His lips drew on hers, nibbling, drinking. She tasted like a wild sun-drenched rose. "I won't want to kiss you again, either."

"Yes, that's what I want. We'll go back . . . to being enemies." Emma's mouth parted and she felt a delicious fire as his tongue invaded her mouth, flicking, exploring, expertly teasing.

"We'll start remembering whose side we're on, it will be so much easier."

"Easy as pie." He lifted his head, stunned by the vibrant beauty of her, by a honeyed freshness so overwhelming he thought for one blinding moment he would never get his fill. "If you ever see me being beaten by Slade and your father's men again, you'll ride right straight on in the other direction."

Her arms locked around his neck, her fingers sliding up to weave through his hair. "Umm-hmm. That's . . . what I want."

She kissed him again. It was a warm, fervent kiss that went on for a very long time, leaving her panting for more, clinging to him. "Do you . . . swear to it?"

"So help me God."

She wondered if all this kissing, holding, and touching was hurting him. He'd been badly beaten. He must be sore. His lips had been bruised. But if he was in pain, he gave no sign of it. He was so strong and so surprisingly gentle as he held her and caressed her nape, her hair, the length of her back.

Excitement shot through her when he began to lower her beneath him on the cot. With a groan, he braced himself above her. "You're in pain," she protested. But he shook his head.

"Less pain than I'd be in if you pushed me away now, Sunshine." Grinning, he kissed her again. Then his mouth and tongue became even bolder, and Emma felt her senses start to reel. When Tucker's hand slid down her throat, across her shoulders, and to her breast, she gave a tiny gasp of shock, but it quickly turned to a sigh of pleasure.

His thumb stroked her nipple through the thin cotton of her petticoat, rubbing and teasing, even as his hand kneaded her breast. Dazzling sensations swept through her and she gave a moan of pure soaring bliss.

His splendid body pressed down against her, warmth meeting warmth. His thighs were strong and muscled, his stomach hard and flat as a plank. How delicious it felt to have him atop her, Emma thought in dazed wonder, then she caught her breath as she felt his hardness between her thighs, knew his desire was every bit as great as hers. Joy swept through her and she writhed beneath him with agonizing desperation that intensified as Tucker touched her, kissed her, tenderly tormenting every inch of her.

She reached for him, holding him gently against her. She wanted to feel all of him, know all of him.

Emma never knew how their clothes landed in a heap on the floor of the dawn-lit shack. She only knew that the new sun brushed his shoulders with gold as he nibbled her naked breasts, one after the other, and drove her wild. She only knew that the cot rocked and groaned beneath their straining bodies, that the beautiful corded muscles of Tucker's body bunched and shone with perspiration as they rolled and thrashed and twisted, as she inhaled the scent of horses and leather and musky male sweat. She only knew that having grown up on a ranch, she had thought she knew all about the mating process, had thought herself beyond surprise, beyond trepidation. And she knew that everything she'd ever thought before was nothing, nothing compared to the wondrous earthy truth of making love with Tucker.

She found herself lost—lost in a hot, seething whirlwind where only she and Tucker existed. Their bodies, their needs, their hearts. His hands touched her breasts, her belly, stroking her so gently she wanted to cry, and his whispered words, caressing her soul, were so sweet she wanted to cry again. Each touch made her want him more. Need him more.

Then everything began to happen so quickly, she knew she was hurtling toward some marvelous place even higher, more dazzling, more overwhelming than where they were—she and Tucker together. When he eased inside her, the thrust tore her maidenhead with a sharp pain and tears pricked her eyes.

But she bit back a cry.

Tucker went still, frowning, his eyes gleaming into hers. "Are you all right, Emma?"

Emma. He'd called her Emma. His tone was so tender she could only nod. She felt the throbbing need in him, pulsing through the powerful length of his body with an intensity as feverish as her own. "Ye—es. I've just never done this before. But if you stop now, Garrettson, I'll k—kill you," she quavered on a husky, tear-filled laugh.

He combed her hair back from her face and kissed her eyelashes, her cheeks, her mouth. "The U.S. Cavalry and a thousand war-painted Indians couldn't stop me now, Malloy."

He moved inside of her again and saw the pain flash momentarily through her eyes. Then it was gone and a wondering pleasure glowed deep inside the turquoise depths as Tucker pushed inside her again, slowly. This time he slid in deeper.

Her eyes were locked on his. Wide. Trusting. So trusting. Her beauty sliced him keener than a knife. With her skin flushed the delicate pink of a mountain sunrise, she was exquisite. She smelled like the freshest, sweetest wildflowers and kissed him with swollen red lips that intoxicated more than any spirits he'd ever imbibed. And her body was full of soft delectable curves and hollows that fit like magic with his. He'd never forget the round firmness of her breasts, or the way her nipples had crested hard as pebbles beneath his fingers.

"Come with me, Sunshine," he whispered and pierced deep inside her, filling himself with her. He groaned and sweat filmed his skin as she responded with an ardor so beautiful and natural it took his breath away.

Need roared through his blood, intensifying with every movement of her hips. Desperation drove them both. She answered his every thrust, responded to every touch, lick and kiss, demanding more, taking all he had to offer . . . and giving. Giving with a light, open lovingness Tucker had never known.

Then the passion enveloped them and they raced beyond thought, to a place of hope and need and heat—a place of wild pleasure. Emma was flying, flying on love and elation and joy, a joy so complete it seemed it must stay with her forever. And as a luminous lavender dawn kissed the world, she and Tucker careened through a starlit heaven—and far beyond.

Chapter 15

EMMA AWOKE IN BLISSFUL DREAMY PEACE. SHE felt light as air, and at the same time sated, as if she'd feasted upon a delicious five-course banquet. But the sweet sense of contentment faded the moment she opened her eyes and realized where she was. Daylight flooded through the small window of the shack and illuminated every dusty inch of the rough shelter. It streamed across the cot upon two entwined bodies—hers and Tucker's.

Her heart lurching, she suddenly recalled everything that had happened between them in the magic waning hours of the night. Each kiss, each touch, each word. She grew hot all over, then cold seeped through her, and she shoved her hair back from her face. Trembling, she pushed herself up to a sitting position and stared down at the golden-haired man sleeping alongside her.

She knew then that the reason she'd been sleeping so peacefully was because she'd been curled up in Tucker's arms. One of his legs was still thrown across both of hers. And one bronzed, muscled arm still clasped her waist.

Inching herself carefully away, she extricated herself from his embrace and sat there with her knees drawn up, staring at the lean hard lines of his face, the tawny stubble along his jaw and above his upper lip, and the way his hair tumbled forward over his brows. Her breath caught in her throat. He was so handsome. So terribly handsome and strong, and yet he had been so gentle with her, so careful and heartbreakingly tender.

As she stared down at him, she felt herself begin to shake like a dandelion puff caught in an autumn gust. Those long-lashed eyes, closed in sleep, would open any moment and hit her like twin flares. She couldn't face him.

Not after what they'd done.

Her nakedness which had seemed so gloriously natural and beautiful to her last night now filled her with shame. Even as she stared hungrily at Tucker's bronzed chest and the rigid muscled plank of his stomach, at the sculpted gorgeous length of him sprawled on the cot with such ease and splendor, she knew that she had made a terrible, terrible mistake.

She wasn't over him.

She wasn't cured.

She yearned for him every bit as much as she had yesterday—no, more. More!

Panic whipped through her. Perhaps the fire in Tucker would be doused when he awoke, as he'd predicted, and he would no longer want to have anything to do with her, much less kiss her or make love to her, but she . . .

She hadn't gotten over him. Not by a long shot.

On the contrary, when she looked at him now, remembering the rough sweetness of his kisses, the enthralling feel of his body against her, within hers, she knew that she would never get over him.

Not as long as she lived.

A sob nearly broke from her throat, and she choked it back with supreme effort. Slowly she rose from the bed, reached for her petticoat in a white lacy puddle on the floor.

She had to get away.

She almost made it.

She was dressed, once more neat and proper in her blouse and skirt and shoes, her hair finger-combed and loose, her hand on the door of the shack when Tucker sat up on the cot.

"Going somewhere, Sunshine?"

His voice was low, raspy with sleep. That and the name he had used during their lovemaking brought a tremble to her shoulders. She thought her knees would buckle and gripped the door for support.

Stop it, she ordered herself, trying to get herself under control before she turned around. Trying to brace herself for the sight of him, for the piercing fire of his eyes.

He's probably had dozens of women and none of them woke up the next morning ready to die for wanting him, ready to throw away family pride, loyalty, everything, just to be held by him again.

Grow up, she pleaded silently. *Show some grit.*

Her feet felt like lead as she forced herself to turn and meet his gaze.

She hates me, Tucker realized, the moment he saw Emma's face. She was white as a lily, and her lovely, delicately sculpted features were taut and drawn. There was a wariness in her eyes that he'd seen when he'd found her lying on the ground with a twisted ankle when she was fourteen years old. As if she expected the worst from him. The trust, openness, and vibrant giving of that incredible hour before dawn might have existed only in his imagination.

"My father . . . will be looking for me." Her own voice sounded stiff and cold to her ears. She was glad of it, glad that she was hiding the pain that seared her soul. It would only have taken one word from him, one smile or gesture, to have her flying across the room and into his arms again, but he gave her no such encouragement.

He nodded. His face was grim and shuttered.

"I'll take you home if you'll give me a minute."

"That won't be necessary. I'm perfectly safe. This is Echo land, remember?"

He leaned back against the wall, his eyes narrowing. "So it is."

"I suggest you leave then as soon as possible— before my father's men come across you and think that you're trespassing. Unless . . . " She faltered suddenly, studying him with concern. "Unless you're too badly hurt to walk home? I could bring you back a horse."

"You're not worried about me, are you, Malloy?" He said it lightly, half-teasing, hoping he might coax

one of those breathtaking smiles from her. And for a
moment, he thought he would. She stared at him, hesitating, her eyes softening as she gazed at his face, at
his bruised shoulders and chest, at the cot where they
had lain together through the small hours of the dawn.
Her lips parted and for an instant Tucker thought he'd
gotten through to her. Their eyes met, and he swore
she was remembering, as he was, all the passion and
sweetness they had shared.

But then she drew a deep, shuddering breath and
the frosty distant look returned to her eyes. She shut
him out cold. "No, Garrettson, I'm not worried about
you. I have better things to do than worry about you."

Her tone made it clear—abundantly clear—that
the hours they'd spent together in this shack, in each
other's arms, didn't matter a speck to her. The feud
continued full force.

So much for last night, Tucker thought grimly.
From the expression in her eyes, it might never have
happened.

All right, so she felt nothing for him now. They'd
both gotten that damned loco passion for each other
out of their blood and now it was over. She was done
with him for good, just the way he'd promised her she
would be.

There was only one trouble.

He wasn't done with her.

Not by a long shot.

Tucker swung his legs over the side of the cot and
bit back a groan. Hell, he was sore from what those
bastards had done to him yesterday. But that didn't
matter now. What mattered now was that Emma was

about to leave and he had no idea when he would see her again.

"Maybe I'll drop by and pay you a visit sometime," he said and immediately felt like the biggest fool in the territory.

"Now why would you want to do that?" Her tone was tight and frigid as a wintry blast. Yet as he regarded her, he thought for a moment that he saw uncertainty in her eyes again, a touch of longing. Then it was gone, and the turquoise eyes were hard as jewels.

"We're finished with each other, remember? We made a deal."

How she wanted him to surge toward her, take her in his arms, kiss away the hurt and doubt and emptiness inside. To tell her that he would never be finished with her.

But he merely watched her with that unreadable expression in his eyes, saying nothing.

And then he reached for his trousers and began tugging them on.

Emma hastily turned back toward the door. "Good-bye," she murmured, fighting the tears that welled up in her eyes, but he stopped her with his next words.

"Maybe we should talk about that deal."

She glanced back. He was standing beside the cot, watching her speculatively and somewhat warily. He had his trousers on, but nothing else. How glorious he was, she thought, her heart hammering painfully. The sunlight gilded his chest and the tousled silk of his hair. His eyes were bluer than the rain-washed sky, harder, more like ignited flint. She remembered the way he had gazed at her last night as they'd rolled together upon the cot—tangled, tussled, entwined as if they belonged that way. She'd wanted to drown in his eyes, in his arms, in his love.

Emma knew she was grasping at straws. She wanted to read something more into his comment and his scrutinizing look than what he meant—something that would indicate he had doubts, too, about whether or not their bout of lovemaking had rid them for good of the senseless passion they'd both been suffering from.

Such as maybe a hope that their passion wasn't so senseless.

But if he felt that way, wouldn't he just say so? Wouldn't she be able to see something, something other than a distant questioning wariness in his eyes?

"I can't see that there's anything much to talk about," she replied carefully, with a little shrug. "But go ahead, if you have something to say."

"I don't. Far as I'm concerned, it's finished." Tucker could tell she was dying to get out of there. She didn't look like a woman seeking love, or passion, or reassurance, only like one who wanted to run like hell.

And why not? This morning, with the sun shining bright and clear and hot, she must see how utterly insane they had been last night. The feud between the Malloys and Garrettsons was too long-standing, too intense. There could be nothing between them but enmity. Whatever crazy passion had exploded between them last night, triggered long ago when they'd been too young to know better, had been extinguished once and for all after burning itself out in that inferno.

Today it was only ash.

That was all that was left.

So why did he have this urge to pull her into his arms and kiss her lips until she came alive again and bloomed like the most precious flower in the world?

That would be disaster for both of them. He knew it. Knew that beyond this shack there was no future for them—hell, there was no *them*.

"So long, Sunshine." Tucker spoke softly. He kept his tone even with an effort. He searched desperately for something else to say, some parting words that would be right under the circumstances. "You're a hell of a woman."

And the moment he said it, he knew it was all wrong.

She winced, then her eyes frosted over. He wanted to snatch the words back. They made him sound like a son-of-a-bitch, made her sound like she was some sporting woman who'd satisfied his needs and would soon be forgotten. But hell, he'd never slept with his enemy before and didn't have much practice in making small talk while she was headed out the door. He'd wanted to say she was beautiful, desirable, unforgettable . . .

"Get the hell off my land, Garrettson." Emma marveled at how cold and controlled her voice sounded when her mind and heart were in chaos. "The truce is over. As of now, you're trespassing."

Without another glance, she slammed the door behind her and stalked away. But as she strode toward home beneath the brilliant shimmer of the sun, she felt that she was walking through a maze of icy darkness.

The tears began as she moved across the tall grass, past brush and bramble. They poured down her face and she couldn't stop them. She didn't even have the will to try.

"If I never see Tucker Garrettson again, it will be too soon," she gasped, stumbling once over a twig as the agony in her heart took hold and squeezed the breath from her lungs.

And if he doesn't come after me and stop me and tell me he feels something for me, something even remotely like what I'm feeling for him, I'm going to die.

No, you won't, she corrected herself as she descended a rocky knoll, then began running until she reached a rolling section of flower-dotted pasture that wound toward the ranch. *You're a Malloy, you're strong. A survivor. You can live without Tucker Garrettson. You don't need him, he's the last man that you need, the very last man.*

But she glanced back over her shoulder, unable to contain the flicker of hope. It died quickly though at the empty horizon, the grand sweep of land, mountains, and sky.

Tucker wasn't coming after her.

Why should he, after all? He'd gotten all he wanted.

The tears flowed. Blind and heartsick, Emma stumbled home.

Chapter 16

SHE MADE IT NEARLY TO THE GATE WITH THE sign proclaiming ECHO RANCH written in big black letters before she heard a rider approaching from the south. The last thing Emma wanted was to see anyone. She'd been hoping to ask Corinne to let her father know she was home and safe, then dash upstairs to her room without having to face him and answer questions, but there was no mistaking the sound of hooves galloping her way.

Whoever it was had seen her and was in a big hurry to reach her.

She drew a deep breath, tried to compose herself, and turned.

Jed Garrettson was bearing down upon her.

When he reined in his big bay before her, he sat in silence, breathing hard as he studied her. Lacy clouds skimmed overhead in an azure sky, a beautiful sight. There was nothing beautiful about the harsh ruddy face of the man glaring at her, one gloved hand resting on the pommel of his saddle.

"What the hell's the matter with you, missy?" he demanded, his fierce brows swooping together in a frown.

Emma started. She'd been so amazed to see Jed Garrettson here, nearly at her front door, that she'd forgotten about the tears still trickling down her cheeks. She scrubbed at them with the back of her hand.

"Hey, there, girl, speak up. Something happen to you?"

Ask your son! she wanted to scream at him, but instead she squared her shoulders, ignored his questions, and asked one of her own.

"What are you doing here, Mr. Garrettson? If my father catches you on our land he'll—"

"He'll what? Shoot me, like he shot my boy Beau?" Garrettson shouted.

Emma forced herself to take two deep breaths before answering him. "Get out before there's real trouble, Mr. Garrettson. That's all I have to say to you."

She turned away, started toward the path that led home. But he spurred his horse forward, blocking her way. "Damn it, missy, not so fast. I'm looking for my boy. For Tucker."

She hesitated. Though she wanted to sidestep him and continue on her way, to ignore the worry creasing Garrettson's face, the throbbing fear beneath his harsh tone tore at her. Before she could decide what to say, he went on quickly.

"Tucker didn't show up for supper last night. Didn't come home at all. Now sometimes he goes to town and stays the night—but I don't think that's where he was. You see . . . " Jed Garrettson's voice cracked and he rushed on, trying to conceal the anguish consuming him, "his horse came back without him. So I know something happened to him, something bad." He was breathing harder now, his face growing redder by the moment. A muscle worked convulsively in his jaw. "By God, missy, if your father has killed both of my sons—"

"There's no need to make threats, Mr. Garrettson. Or to worry yourself into a stew. Tucker isn't dead— he's fine. My father hasn't done anything to harm him."

"I'll kill him," Garrettson rasped, as if she hadn't spoken. "I swear I'll kill him! Like I should have done years ago . . . "

Suddenly, he gave a gasp, and the reins slipped through his fingers. Alarmed, Emma saw his eyes widen and glaze over. He clutched at his chest then slumped forward over the pommel, a choking wheeze dribbling from his lips. The next instant, even as Emma sprang toward him, he was sliding toward the ground.

"What is it—what's wrong?" she cried, frightened by the ashen shade of his skin beneath its leathery tan. "Mr. Garrettson, can you hear me?"

His eyes bored into hers, glittering with pain. "Saddlebag. Tonic . . . "

She flew to the bay and tore open the saddlebag. "Is this it?" she cried, kneeling beside him with the amber bottle half-filled with liquid.

Soundlessly he reached for it. Emma held her breath as she watched him gulp down the contents.

For one heartstopping moment, he closed his eyes and his color drained away, then the puffy redness seeped back into his cheeks.

"Lie still—don't try to get up yet." Emma eased him back as he struggled up on one elbow. His breath came out in harsh, painful rasps.

"Got to find . . . Tucker . . . "

"There's no need to worry about Tucker. He's fine. I saw him just a little while ago. He had some trouble, but he's well and he should be on his way home by now."

Jed Garrettson stared at her. "Just what kind of trouble . . . did he have?"

Emma shivered in the sun, remembering the sight of Tucker being kicked and beaten by Slade and her father's other men. She swallowed down the bile in her throat. "He'll explain it to you. Wait—no! Mr. Garrettson, where do you think you're going?"

"Gotta see my boy . . . he's all . . . I have left." Jed Garrettson staggered to his feet, glowering when she stepped forward to help him. As he stood there, shaken, weak, but proud as an old oak tree that's endured countless droughts, blizzards, and wind storms, Emma saw him for the first time not as her enemy, her father's enemy, but as a weary old man terrified of losing all he had left in the world.

She wondered if Tucker knew how important he was to his father.

"I think you should rest for a while first."

"And let Win Malloy catch me on his land? He'd shoot first and ask questions later, just as he did with Beau."

"He didn't shoot Beau."

"Hmph. You want to believe the best of him, girl, that's understandable. It's not a bad thing to stand by your kin. I'd admire you for it, if you weren't a Malloy. And if your pa weren't a cheating, yellow-bellied murderer."

Jed Garrettson staggered to his horse, stuffed the tonic back in his saddlebag, and mounted. He wavered a bit in the saddle. Then he glowered over at the young woman who stood silent before him. She looked miserable.

He wondered why.

Then he remembered she'd been crying when he'd first come upon her. And he wondered if that had anything to do with Tucker. Maybe she and the boy had had words. Maybe he'd been trying to make her see she was living with a devil.

For a moment, he almost felt sorry for her. She wasn't all bad. She'd helped him when he was down, brought him his tonic. And she'd told him about Tucker.

Too bad she was a Malloy. She was lovely and she had a fine elegant air about her. Reminded him a bit of his wife, who'd come from a good Southern family, a real lady. If this gal's name had been anything other than Malloy, he'd have thanked her for what she'd done, maybe even tipped his hat to her.

But he wouldn't thank a Malloy or show courtesy.

He gave her a curt nod, clucked his tongue at the bay, and turned the horse toward Tall Trees.

Emma watched him until he disappeared through

the hemlocks, then she trudged past the gate and went home.

WIN MALLOY DIDN'T LIKE IT ONE BIT. HIS DAUGHTER HAD fired his foreman for carrying out Win's own orders to stop all trespassers? He couldn't believe it—and more, wouldn't stand for it.

He was a man who rarely lost his temper with Emma, but on this occasion, he raged at her, stalking up and down the length of the parlor, not even letting her get a word in edgewise. While the breakfast grew cold on the sideboard in the dining room, and Corinne hovered with pursed lips in the hall, listening and fretting, Emma watched him pace and shout and lecture, her face stony and set as he had rarely seen it.

"And when it comes to handling the men, Emma, you have got to stay out of it. Is that clear? I can't have you giving them orders different from mine. The men have to respect me and know who's boss, and they won't know that if you keep telling them the opposite of what I say!"

"Papa, if you'll just listen to me—"

"No, Emma, you listen to me!" She recoiled when he shouted at her, and Win raked a hand through his hair, searching for some vestige of patience. "Look, honey," he began again, keeping his voice even with an effort. "You've been out east for a long time and you've grown soft, softer than if you'd stayed here all your life. You used to know that if you let someone get away with stealing your horse just once, or your cattle, you'd just as well lay down and die because you're as good as dead. In these parts, toughness answers. Nothing else."

"Papa, that doesn't excuse—"

"Slade was following my orders," Win shouted. "And I *won't* fire a man for following my orders!"

He drew a deep breath, frowned at her, then stomped to the fireplace and back again, struggling for some degree of control. He'd spent a sleepless night terrified about her—he hadn't yet even changed out of yesterday's clothes or eaten a bite of food since yesterday's noon meal. He'd ridden through much of the storm, searching, calling, relentlessly combing the valley and the nearby hills. Finally he'd returned to the ranch, soaked, shivering, desperate—praying with every fiber of his being that she'd found shelter and was waiting out the storm.

He'd cursed Slade and the others for not making sure she got home all right, but he knew it wasn't really their fault. Emma could be plumb pigheaded. She'd put that no-good Tucker Garrettson in the wagon and gone—and who the hell knew where?

He'd even ridden right up to the Garrettson ranch, in case she'd taken Tucker there. But Jed Garrettson had fired his damned rifle at him before he could do more than yell he was searching for Emma. The bastard had driven him off with a volley of shots, and Win had been so furious he hadn't even told Garrettson that Emma and Tucker had last been seen together.

"Too bad I didn't think of that line shack yesterday," he muttered now, glancing over at his daughter's stubbornly set face. "We don't use it much anymore. But if I'd gone there, you wouldn't have had to be shut up alone all night with Garrettson.'' The frown between his brows deepened. He hated the thought of Emma being trapped for even a moment with that hombre, much less spending the entire night holed up with him in that shack.

''He didn't give you any trouble, did he?'' he demanded, his jaw clenched.

She shook her head, totally at a loss how to answer. *Trouble? Tucker Garrettson? He'd given her nothing* but *trouble since she'd known him.*

But what had happened between them last night was hardly her father's business or anyone else's. No one must ever find out.

The very thought made her shudder.

''He wasn't . . . in very good shape.'' This was mostly true. At first. But later . . .

She'd better not think about later, Emma decided, thrusting away the memories that kept trying to flood back.

''Papa, this isn't about Tucker. It's about Curt Slade.'' She followed Win to the mantel and stood before him, staring directly into his eyes. ''He's bad news. He's not the kind of man you want working for Echo Ranch.''

Win slammed his fist against the mantel, his anger exploding. ''Damn it, Emma, he's *exactly* the kind of man I want working for Echo Ranch!''

''But he lied, Papa! Tucker Garrettson wasn't trespassing! Slade and the men roped him on his own land and brought him onto ours! They dragged him—

they were beating him savagely when I got there—
they would have killed him!''

Win Malloy stared at her as if she'd lost her mind.
"Who told you that?" he demanded. "Garrettson?"
He shook his head in disgust. "And you'd believe him
over our own foreman?"

"Yes, Papa, I would." Emma's voice rose angrily
to match his. "Because in my opinion Curt Slade is
one of the most unsavory, untrustworthy, unprinci-
pled . . . "

She broke off in chagrin as at that moment, Slade
himself appeared in the doorway.

He held his hat in his hand as he rapped respectfully on the door to summon their attention.

"Ace said you want to see me, boss? Oh, Miss
Emma, you're back." A grin wreathed his face, he
came forward quickly. "Can't tell you how glad I am
to see you safe and sound, ma'am."

Emma glared at him, too stunned by the man's
nerve to reply.

"Slade, we've got to settle this trouble between
you and my daughter. I don't like what happened yesterday." Win paced to his desk, sat on the corner of it,
and surveyed the foreman steadily. "It seems Emma
is under the impression that Garrettson wasn't trespassing at all. She says he told her that you and the
men dragged him from his own land onto ours and
proceeded to beat him without mercy. Any truth to
that?"

"No, sir, that's a lot of hogwash." He glanced at
Emma and bowed his head for a moment, apologetically. "Beggin' your pardon, ma'am." He turned

back to Win Malloy, looking him straight in the eye. "Why would we waste our time doing something like that? We were patrolling our borders, just as we've been doing for days and we caught him red-handed."

Emma took an angry step forward. "You're lying."

He turned to her once more, and for a moment she glimpsed the blaze of anger in his black eyes, then he wiped clean all traces of emotion. There was no anger, no bluster, none of the smugness and swagger she had seen that night at the dance.

You should have been an actor in a traveling show, Emma thought with furious contempt as the foreman regarded her with every appearance of humble respect.

"Ma'am, that dirty son-of-a-gun Garrettson lied to *you.* Being a lady and all, and gently raised, I know it was upsetting for you to come across us when you did and see things a lady ought never to see. But me and the boys had every right to stop him from trespassin' and raiding Echo cattle—"

"You deny dragging him behind your horse? Forcibly hauling him off his own land?"

Slade never blinked. "Yes, ma'am, I do. Those are dirty lies."

"And do you also deny trying to kiss me at the Fourth of July dance? Trapping me in the hallway and forcing your unwanted and despicable attentions upon me until Mr. Carleton came to my rescue?"

"What?" Win Malloy lunged around the writing desk, his face white. He gaped at Emma. "Emma, is this true? What are you saying?"

"You heard me, Papa. Mr. Slade was rude and obnoxious to me at the dance. He behaved in a way that you would have found completely unacceptable. In fact, if you'd seen what he did you'd have horse-whipped him!"

"Boss, all I did was steal a kiss." Flushing, Slade twisted his hat in his hand, meeting Win Malloy's frown with a sheepish shrug. "I'd had a bit too much to drink, it's true—and I have to say, your daughter is the most beautiful, most fascinating woman I've ever laid eyes on." Slade hung his head, then lifted it to regard his employer earnestly. "I'm sorry, boss. I reckon I was over-eager in my attentions to Miss Emma. I admit it. But I swear I never meant to insult or frighten her. I've got far too much respect for her."

He stepped forward, his eyes shining with remorse.

"Boss, if you want me to clear out, I will," he vowed. "I sure don't want to make your daughter uncomfortable. I can understand if you don't want me around anymore—"

"I don't," Emma snapped. "You're a liar and a scoundrel, and you would have murdered Tucker Garrettson if I hadn't come along when I did."

"Emma, that's enough." Wearily Win rubbed his hands over his eyes. Then he gave his head a shake. Lord, he needed coffee, and he needed it bad. "I want you to stay on, Slade. Now, Emma," he hurried on as she sucked in her breath and regarded him with a seething fury barely kept in control. "I'm not going to fire a man because he had too much to drink and stole a kiss. Especially if I have Slade's word it will never happen again.''

"I swear on my Mama's grave," the foreman declared.

"And this business about Tucker Garrettson . . . '' Win sighed. "I never thought I'd hear my daughter taking a Garrettson's part, but . . . '' He smiled bleakly at the dark-haired girl regarding him in frozen silence. "You've got a soft heart, honey, and that's a good thing. You don't like to see anyone hurt, even a Garrettson, and that's the woman in you.''

"Papa, listen to me—''

"Enough." Win Malloy held up his hand with finality, his mouth grim. "I've got to get some breakfast in me and get out on the range before the Garrettsons steal the whole damn valley out from under me and every stray they can get their filthy hands on. And Slade has better things to do with his time than stand here jawing all day.'' He nodded dismissal to the foreman, who tipped his hat to Emma and strode from the room.

"You go on upstairs and get some rest," Win told his daughter. "You had a rough night and I'm sure you want to catch up on your sleep. We won't need to talk about all this again. It's finished.''

Finished? Emma thought in stunned bewilderment as her father gave her a perfunctory kiss on the cheek and then left the room.

He may as well have patted me on the head and said: "Go play with your dolls and leave the grown-ups be."

She'd never felt more useless, more ignored, more frustrated.

Or more alone.

Somehow she made it up the stairs to her room as exhaustion crept through her like a slowly spreading poison.

She lay down atop her bed and stared at the ceiling as a meadowlark sang outside her window.

Memories came unbidden. Memories of her night with Tucker. She saw again his bruised face, then she saw him as he'd looked when he'd carried her across the shack and set her down on the bed, watching her through his long-lashed eyes, while lightning split the sky beyond the window.

And finally her mind replayed those rapturous heavenly moments of love and passion when they'd come together with such explosive heat. And tenderness—there'd been such heartbreaking tenderness, Emma thought, wrapping her arms around herself. She'd never expected anything like that from a man as cool, hard-bitten, and cynical as Tucker.

Suddenly, she sat up. *Tenderness . . . love?*

"I've lost my mind," Emma whispered into the hot silence of her bedroom.

Everything was topsy-turvy. She felt as if she were in a strange world where nothing was safe or familiar or as it should be. She was at odds with her father. Angry with him for making light of her complaints against Slade, for taking Slade's word over hers. She had actually helped Jed Garrettson. And she believed Tucker Garrettson's version of events over

Slade's—she *was* taking his part, yes. She had yesterday and again today.

What is happening to me? she wondered despairingly.

She wanted to talk to Tucker. To see him again. God help her, to be held in his arms.

He couldn't make everything better. He was a Garrettson, the bane of her existence.

Or he had been. Until . . .

She didn't know when she had changed. Or what had changed. She only knew that something was different. Everything was different.

When she and Tucker had lain together last night, their world had somehow rocked, shifted. The heavens had danced. And now Emma couldn't stop feeling that she belonged somewhere else than here in her old room at Echo Ranch.

She belonged . . . with Tucker.

But he doesn't want me. He only made love to me so that he could get free of me—free of whatever was between us.

But there *was* something between them, that was undeniable. Was it only passion? Or was there something more, something deeper?

Emma sat up on her bed, her heart thudding in a fearful rhythm.

Was she still in Tucker's thoughts, in his soul, as much as he was in hers?

Closing her eyes, she tried to review what had passed for conversation between them in the shack this morning. The words blurred in her mind. She saw only his eyes, cool and unreadable.

He hadn't touched her, hadn't even tried to kiss her good-bye.

She drew up her knees and buried her face in her hands. Doubt assailed her. And so did despair. There was no chance. None. He was a Garrettson and she was a Malloy.

What the hell chance did they have of anything other than of killing each other?

But even as she told herself this and felt the waves of sorrow washing over her, Emma made a decision.

She needed to see Tucker again, to talk to him.

She didn't know what in the world she would say, but she had to find out if there was any chance for the two of them.

Any chance at all.

Chapter 17

"WHISKY! MORE WHISKY!"

Tucker Garrettson was not surprised to hear those words as he shouldered his way into the Jezebel Saloon. But he was surprised when he saw who had spoken them—and in such a slurred, miserable tone.

Derek Carleton lay half-sprawled across the gleaming wooden bar. His head rested on the somewhat sticky surface. One arm flailed in the air, waving an empty bottle.

"More whisky!" he bellowed.

Scowling, Tucker strode up to the bar. He ignored the easterner and shot a hard glance at Curly, the stout little bartender with the brown handlebar mustache who always wore the same spotless white shirt, red suspenders, black pants, and vest.

"Whisky, Curly."

"Sure thing, Tucker. Kinda early in the day for you though, isn't it, friend?"

Tucker straddled the bar stool, his scowl deepening. "Yeah, well, it's one of those days."

The bartender took one glance at his face and clamped his lips shut. He knew better than to try to talk to any customer with that look of grim desperation on his face. It meant either money trouble or woman trouble—sometimes both.

"Hold your horses, mister," Curly grumbled, as Carleton let out a yell. He plunked a bottle down before him. "Here you go. But don't blame me when you fall off that stool face first."

Tucker paid them scant attention. He was already deep in his own thoughts. Foremost of which was that Curly was right. It was not yet suppertime and here he was in town, in the saloon, preparing to get good and drunk.

Unusual.

So why was he here?

Emma Malloy, that was why.

He gulped back a long swallow of red-eye and felt the edge slipping off his frustration. He sank deeper into his own thoughts, hoping to slide quickly to the level of not knowing or caring about anything. As he lifted the bottle to his lips again and again, he let the chatter and bustle of the saloon, with its wafting tobacco smoke, murmuring card players, gamblers, and saloon girls flow around him without even touching him.

He wanted peace, darkness, oblivion. He didn't want to close his eyes and see Emma Malloy's extraordinary face. He didn't want to suddenly, without reason, hear her light, lovely voice whispering his name, or to have her wildflower perfume haunt him or the memory of her lips singe him.

Damn her. Damn her to hell.

His father had been in fine fettle this morning, riding up to Tall Trees just as Tucker set a foot on the porch steps.

Imagine him having run into Emma and learning from her that there'd been trouble.

But he was more interested in finding out how she was than in addressing the string of questions his father flung at him.

"Just tell me—what did you say to her?" Tucker had demanded. "You yelled at her, didn't you? And upset her."

"Upset her?" Jed had snorted. "Now why would I upset her? It's her damned father I have a bone with, not that slip of a girl." Jed had stomped past him, then paused in the doorway of the house, regarding Tucker narrowly. "And just why are you so all-fired worried? You come home looking like you got run over by a herd of buffalo and all you care about is what I said to the Malloy girl?"

Tucker swatted a fly that landed on his arm, then wiped the sweat from his face with his hat. There were deep weathered creases between his father's eyes and worry all over his blunt, stern features. He knew Jed must have been half-crazed last night when he didn't come home. Not that his father would ever tell him he cared in so many words. That was something that would never happen.

"Emma Malloy helped me out of a tight spot yesterday,'' he said slowly. "If it wasn't for her, I reckon Malloy's men would have killed me."

His father's face blanched. But if Tucker's words stirred emotion from him, he didn't express it in concerned words, or in an embrace. Instead it came out in a torrent of rage.

"Those damned low-down skunk-livered sniveling bastards!"

"You won't get any argument from me about that."

Tucker had started to brush past him then, to head into the house and upstairs, but his father's next words, grated out in a low hoarse tone, stopped him.

"This is all going to be settled real soon, boy. I want Malloy behind bars, and then six feet under. And if the law won't see to it, I will. I will, boy, do you hear me?"

"I hear you, Pop. Now calm down before your heart gives out." Tucker grabbed his sleeve. "Pop, look at me. I'm fine. It'll take more than those low-down buzzards to kill me. And I'm going to see to it that we get justice for Beau—for everything Malloy's done. I told you that."

"I'm tired of waiting."

"So am I. But if you don't take care of yourself, old man, all the justice in the world won't do you a bit of good."

To his surprise, his father had nodded. He'd gone inside, and when Tucker followed him, he'd seen Jed walk into the kitchen, pour himself a steaming cup of Cookie's fresh-made coffee, and sit down in a chair with it, cradling the cup in his hands.

"You see? I'm resting. I'm taking it easy. But when I've finished my coffee, I'm riding out to check the stock."

"Fine."

Tucker started toward the stairs.

"Hey, boy!"

Tucker turned.

"You want some coffee?"

It was asked gruffly, with Jed staring at the cup, not Tucker. But it was one of the few times Tucker could remember his father offering him anything other than a lecture or an argument.

"Later. Think I'm going to clean off in the creek, then see to fixing the corral post. Is Pike all right?"

"He came home," Jed nodded. "I took care of him."

"Thanks."

Now, in the saloon, Tucker recalled that conversation with a mixture of pain and confusion. Obviously his father had been far more worried about him when he hadn't come home than he had let on. He'd been almost—almost solicitous, a word that never really had applied to Jed Garrettson before.

But even his father's unusual behavior hadn't kept his thoughts occupied for long. Dunking himself in the cool creek water, wincing as the icy liquid slid over his bruises, he'd thought of Emma. Dressing in clean work clothes, fastening his belt, tugging on his boots, he thought of Emma. Working on the corral post, hammering and sweating, he thought of Emma. The woman might as well have been kneeling there in the dirt beside him.

She was that close. That real.

But not real enough to touch. Or kiss.

Which is what he really wanted to do.

That was when he knew for certain that instead of getting her out of his blood, their one night of love-making had locked her in. Nothing like this had ever happened before. He had never before wanted any woman the way he wanted her, or thought so endlessly about one, daydreamed about one . . .

Or ached like hell to have one particular woman.

But he ached for Emma.

And that's why, for the first time in all the years since he'd left school and begun working the ranch full-time, he took off early in the afternoon. With the sun still high overhead, he found his father, told him curtly he was going to town and not to expect him back until tomorrow, and had ridden off.

First, I'll get drunk, Tucker promised himself. *So drunk I won't remember Emma Malloy even exists. Then I'm going to find me a woman, a pretty little saloon woman—maybe Lizzie Sue or Wanda—and have some fun. Just plain fun.*

And pray like hell that by the time he woke up tomorrow, this fever Emma had put him in would have cooled off, and he could get back to work without feeling like he was burning up with love for her.

Love.

Now where had that word come from?

Alarmed by the path of his own thoughts, Tucker tipped the bottle and drained it in one desperate gulp.

''Women.'' Through the haze of his own misery, he heard a dejected voice mumble that single word beside him. He recognized it as Carleton's voice. Tucker glanced over, frowning, and saw that the easterner was bent over on the stool, his head in his hands.

"Women!" he groaned again, louder. "To hell with 'em!"

"I'll drink to that," Tucker muttered and reached for the second bottle Curly had set down before him.

"Don't understand 'em. Never will. They can't make up their minds. They . . . oughta just . . . let us tell 'em what to do and we'd all be better off."

"You got that right." Tucker couldn't honestly recall ever having met a woman who would let him tell her what to do, but it seemed to him, as the liquor swirled through his brain like a fuzzy gray cloud, that it would be a big improvement over the normal state of affairs.

He tried to picture Emma Malloy, with her smooth waterfall of dark hair, her assured manner, her ready answer for everything, letting him boss her around, and a raspy laugh shook him. That'd be the day.

"What's so funny, mister? You laughing . . . at me?" Carleton swiveled his head with an effort and fixed Tucker with a stare that was supposed to be intimidating.

Tucker laughed harder, then lifted his bottle in salute. "Naw, Carleton, don't get your britches in a tangle. I'm laughing at us. Men. We don't stand a chance in hell against these women."

"You can say that again." Carleton dragged his stool closer. He almost toppled off, but Tucker grasped his arm and held on, steadying him.

"Th—thanks, my friend. I'd hate to . . . leave Whisper Valley with a broken nose. Already got a broken heart."

Tucker nodded. He turned back to his bottle. He really didn't want to discuss Emma with the man who'd come here to marry her. He peered narrow-eyed around the room, looking for Lizzie Sue or Wanda, but neither of them was in sight.

Carleton clapped him on the shoulder. "Lemme buy you a drink!"

Why not? Why the hell not? Tucker nodded.

"I'm drunk," the other man confided genially as Curly set a glass in front of Tucker and filled it with whisky. "Been drunk since yesterday. I think. The day Emma Malloy sent me packing. Came right in here, yessiree, I did, and started to drink. Trying to get over her, you know. As if I could ever get over her . . . " His voice trailed off sadly.

Poor bastard, Tucker thought, pity welling in him. *I know just how you feel.*

Carleton went on after a series of hiccups. "But you know what . . . I finally figured out—I'm better off without her. She's too . . . " He swigged another belt of whisky, blinking rapidly as he drank, searching for words. "Too independent."

"Independent." Tucker's mouth twisted. "Damn right."

"Oh, she's beautiful all right. And she's graceful," Derek added mistily. "She has a way of coming into a room that draws all eyes to her. Very desirable quality in a woman who's going to help a man entertain for b—business purposes." He let out a lusty, heart-wrenching sigh. "But mostly she's the most beautiful girl I ever did see. You should have seen her in Philadelphia. Night I took her to the Cummings' ball. Oh, she was something."

Tucker closed his eyes as pain curled through his gut. "I reckon she was." The image of Emma at a ball with Carleton, dancing the night away with him gave him the urge to smash the whisky bottle against the bar.

"And that night she wore a dress that was . . . blue-green, I think, a real deep, pretty turquoise. Yes, it matched her eyes almost exactly. Every single man there wanted to dance with her, but I kept her occupied the entire night. Wouldn't let her out of my sight. We drank champagne, we danced. And I made her laugh. I always liked to hear Emma laugh."

Tucker knew then he was going to hit him. He didn't want to hear about Emma laughing with Derek Carleton. *He* wanted to make her laugh. Had he ever once made her laugh?

"Don't tell me any more. I'm warning you," he managed to say and took another swig of whisky, fighting the dangerous mood descending upon him. The liquor went down like fire. A good kind of fire, the kind that usually obliterated all the other pain.

But not this time.

Where the hell were Lizzie Sue and Wanda?

"I knew that night I would marry her. Had it all figured out. Told my father. He was pleased. 'Good choice, son. She'll make you an excellent wife. She'll be an asset in every way.' I was so proud that he . . . liked her. My brother married a girl our father hated.

Cut him out of the will.'' Carleton's voice thickened. ''But Father approved of Emma. Yes, he did. But then . . . who wouldn't?''

Suddenly, he slammed a fist on the bar. His handsome face contorted with rage and frustration, his Adam's apple bobbing.

''But the damned girl turned me down! Ruined everything. *Everything.*''

Curly, drying glasses with a dishrag, spoke up encouragingly. ''So you'll find another girl your father likes.''

''Not like this one. This one had everything, including a cattle ranch. Echo Ranch.'' Carleton rubbed his eyes and stared blearily at the bartender. ''Father and I—we had . . . big plans for that ranch.''

Tucker's head jerked toward him. Carleton's color was high, and his eyes bloodshot. He was swaying on the stool. ''Oh, yeah? What kind of plans?''

''We wanted it to become part of a ranching syndicate . . . we're developing. Good for business. Diversify. We've got railroads, and three factories my brother bought last year. All profitable.'' Carleton grinned. ''Highly profitable. And Echo Ranch was going to become the centerpiece for a ranching syndicate—once Emma and I were married. Her father told me he wasn't interested, but he would have come around . . . once he saw how rich he'd become. We had it all figured out and it was perfect . . . perfect. Win Malloy could have stayed on and run the place, and Emma and I could have lived in Philadelphia and been gloriously happy. I'd have started the syndicate my father wants *and* married the girl of my dreams.''

Carleton's shoulders sagged. His head drooped down into his hands. "But Emma spoiled it all," he muttered, almost in disbelief. "I hate her for that. *Hate* her. Look at me, I spent the whole night drinking, bedding some stupid whore, and now I've missed the stage . . . I think. But who cares? I'm in no hurry to go back and face my father now. Tell him we've lost the finest piece of property in Montana. Except for your ranch, Garrettson," he said suddenly, raising his head.

"Tall Trees, isn't it? You've got an even bigger spread than Malloy—"

"You talk too much, mister." Tucker turned contemptuously away. Good thing Emma hadn't wanted to marry that sniveling little weasel. He'd have had to kill him.

Maybe I should just hit him, Tucker thought. He was in the mood to hit someone, and Carleton was as good as anyone. No, better.

But then he spotted Wanda sashaying down the stairs, and he momentarily forgot about Carleton. He forgot about hitting someone, too. Wanda looked good in her tight, purple gown. She looked real good. He lifted his hand in greeting, and she grinned and came toward him.

Finally. A woman. Someone to help him forget . . .

But as Tucker stood up, feeling as if the floor was tilting sideways on him, Carleton made a grab for his sleeve.

"Hey, wait. What about your ranch? C'mon, Garrettson, want to sell Tall Trees to some very . . . in-

terested investors? We'd make it plenty worth your
while. It's bad enough I have to go back without the
girl I wanted to marry. At least if we could work out a
deal for your ranch my father would—''

"Get your damned hand off me," Tucker
growled.

But Carleton's grip tightened and he continued as
if Tucker hadn't spoken. "You and your father could
even stay on and run the place for us, but . . . ''

Tucker was drunk but not so drunk he couldn't
seize the easterner by his shirt collar and yank him
close so that they were nose to nose.

"Hey, you're cutting off . . . my air . . . ''

"Tell me something, you son-of-a-bitch.'' He
tightened his grip, watching the other man's eyelids
flutter. "Did you ever love her?''

"Wh—who?''

"Emma! Did you *love* her? Yes or no?''

"Sure. But what the hell . . . difference does
that make . . . what matters is that . . . I can't
breathe . . . ''

Tucker shoved him away. Carleton tumbled back,
knocked over a spittoon, and hit the floor with a
groan. He lay sprawled for a moment, too stunned to
fully comprehend what had happened. Then, slowly,
he struggled up to his knees and peered up at the tall,
dark-visaged man standing over him, whose eyes
blazed holy thunder.

"Does that mean . . . you won't sell us your
ranch?''

Tucker started toward him, but Wanda snagged his
arm.

"Honey, you don't want to waste your energy on him, do you?" she crooned. "Curly's going to have a fit if you break up his place. Now why don't you forget all about this fellow and come upstairs with me? I've got something better in mind."

Tucker stood glaring for a moment, trying to remember just why he was so intent on beating the hell out of the pathetic easterner kneeling on the floor. He shrugged then, too light-headed to remember, and allowed himself to be persuaded by Wanda's smile. Gallantly, he offered her his arm.

But he was so drunk by then that he stumbled as they reached the stairs, and she hooked her arm around his waist.

"Careful now, honey. Watch your step. Don't want you to pass out before we have us some fun, do we?"

"I'm not that drunk, Wanda, don't you worry. Wish I was."

Vaguely, Tucker noticed it was getting on toward dusk outside as she led him into a red-curtained room at the back of the upstairs hall. He went across the floor steady enough and yanked the curtains shut.

He wanted to close out the world outside. Everything. The ranch. His father. The feud. Most of all, Emma Malloy.

He turned and grinned at Wanda, with her wild pale curls, buxom figure, and a smile full of voluptuous promise. She laughed and slid into his arms, her hands gliding up to stroke his hair. "You sure are handsome, Tucker. It's been a while since you knocked on my door. I've missed you."

He bent his head and kissed her.

"Umm, nice. Real nice." She reached for the top button of his shirt and opened it. Then the next, her fingers deft and quick, unlike Emma's that night when she'd opened his shirt to apply the salve. "Honey, I don't know what's troubling you, but I'm going to make you forget all about it," she cooed, and her lips clung to his.

Tucker's mouth moved over hers. He willed himself to feel something. Anything. He raised his head, and stared down at her pretty, eager face with its thin curved brows and painted wart on the cheek.

"Can't do this . . . " he muttered.

"Sure you can, honey. You're good at this. Best I ever saw." She giggled and reached toward the buttons of his trousers. "Let me help you get in the mood—"

Tucker shook his head and gripped her wrist. "Wish . . . you could . . . but you're not . . . her . . . "

Then he passed out, toppling over like an aspen struck by lightning. Wanda yelped and snatched at him, managing to break his fall and ease him to the floor.

Breathing hard, she sat there on the floor, cradling his head in her lap. She wondered how on earth she would manage to get him into that bed so he could sleep off whatever was troubling him.

"Poor Tucker. I've never seen you like this before," she mused. "If I didn't know better, honey, I'd think you were in love."

But then Wanda chuckled and brushed a lock of hair back from his brow. Tucker Garrettson—in love?

That was a joke.

All of the girls who worked at the Jezebel had long ago decided one thing between them. Tucker Garrettson was the one man in Whisper Valley who would never get married. No way, no how. He'd rather dance with a rattlesnake than fall in love, give up his freedom, settle down.

He liked women far too much. Liked flirting with them in that low-key, easy-going way he had, liked to have one or more on his lap when he was drinking, another leaning over his shoulder, nibbling his ear, sometimes even when he was playing cards!

He'd never fall in love. Never settle down.

So then . . . who was that "her" he'd mentioned right before he keeled over? Wanda wondered.

Sighing, and pressing a sympathetic kiss to his brow, she decided she must have heard wrong. Because no matter what she *thought* Tucker had said, the facts were the facts.

Everyone knew Tucker Garrettson just wasn't the marrying kind.

Chapter 18

TEMPERATURES AND TENSIONS IN WHISPER VALley ran high during the next week. The town was full of talk about the feuding between the Malloys and the Garrettsons, and nervous whispers abounded about full-scale range war. On more than one occasion shots were fired, but so far no one had been killed.

Sheriff Gill had warned both sides to simmer down and not do anything foolish.

Both sides listened, then ignored his advice. Fury long bottled now flowed over the range, and the men who rode herd on the cattle were stirred by both loyalty to their employers and apprehension over their own fate. If they ran into the enemy and weren't quick enough, alert enough, they could end up dead—as dead as Beau Garrettson.

Anger rolled like a poisonous red dust across the range.

Win Malloy had hired more men to help protect his property, and Emma and Corinne had their hands full as the men worked both day and night shifts, patrolling Echo land. It seemed that there was always a meal to cook, dishes to wash, coffee to make, and chores to do.

Emma was glad of it. She needed to keep busy, to keep her thoughts off Tucker. Every time an image of his face swam into her mind, or she remembered the heat of his touch, or the fire of his lips, she pushed the thoughts away. But they were there—in her heart— and she couldn't banish them from there, no matter how hard she tried.

One night, several weeks later, her father turned in early, Corinne retired to her own room with a cup of tea and the new *Godey's Lady's Book,* and Emma found herself too fidgety to settle down, either with a book or with the white lace kitchen curtains, which needed mending.

Her soul was as restless as the night breeze that flickered the leaves. At last she walked out on to the porch and lifted her face toward the sky.

A wishing star beamed forth out of a glittering black canopy. It was brighter, whiter, more sparkly than all the other stars.

Make a wish.

I wish . . . I wish . . .

She wished she could see Tucker, right this very minute. That he would enfold her in his arms, kiss away her loneliness and doubts, tell her that she was not alone in her foolish feelings for him, that they weren't foolish, that there was something real between them, something deeper even than the anger and mistrust that divided their families, something that wouldn't die no matter how hard they tried to smother it.

She sighed.

The wishing star wouldn't help her. Nothing would help her.

But a friend might. Tara.

Emma hadn't seen Tara for weeks. Shorty and Abigail's wedding was coming up in a few days and she'd doubtless see Tara there, but suddenly she couldn't wait. She needed to confide in someone or she would burst.

Things had been somewhat strained between Emma and her father ever since he'd refused to fire Slade. Oh, he'd tried to make things up to her, to show her he wasn't angry, but Emma was. For the first time in her life, there was a breach between her and Win. It made her feel alone, more alone than she'd felt in her entire life, even when she'd been away in Philadelphia. Then she'd had Aunt Loretta, she'd known that her father was missing her, loving her, just as she missed and loved him. But now . . .

He didn't understand or trust her enough to believe what she said about Slade—and send him packing. That made for a breach between them. And he had no idea—thank heavens—about her involvement with Tucker Garrettson, what was between them, what he meant to her . . .

Emma couldn't deny any longer that he meant something to her—even to herself.

She rode fast through the humid summer night, eager to reach Empire Ranch and find comfort in the company of a friend.

But she slowed Angel to a walk as she neared the ranch, wondering just how much she would say to Tara. She wanted to pour her heart out. Tara had been in love with Beau, so she would understand. And yet . . .

Emma wasn't sure she could speak that word aloud. *Love.*

She was in love with Tucker Garrettson.

It frightened her.

And it would shock Tara, who knew as well as anyone how deep the enmity ran between their families. Ross had been there that fateful, long-ago night when the fabled poker game had taken place. He had been both a witness and a player in the game that had changed the destiny of the Malloys and Garrettsons forever.

Tara, like Emma herself, had been raised on the tale and knew well the seeds of hatred that had been planted that night.

The wind rose around Emma, ruffling her hair, tickling her neck. It made a low, whippy roar as it raced through the hills and the canyons and curled down through the valley. It drowned out the cicadas and the steady even footfalls of Angel's hooves as the mare and her slender rider approached the Empire ranch house in the starlit night.

So it was not surprising that the two people on the porch didn't hear her approach.

They seemed oblivious to everything around them, the old wood railing, the steps which even by the faint starlight were clearly in need of paint, the cat curled at the edge of the porch, its ears twitching.

But Emma saw everything. She took in the railing, the steps, the lazing cat, the glow of lamplight from inside the house, and the tang of tobacco smoke wafting on the air.

But mostly she saw the couple seated together on the old wood bench, their heads close together.

Tucker had his arm around Tara's shoulders. Her head was resting against his chest. As Emma watched, he took his hand and touched her chin, lifting it so that she was gazing into his eyes.

The night reeled. Emma yanked Angel to a halt and clung to the reins, trying to keep from falling as dizzy shock wrapped around her.

Just then an owl swooped down from a tree and across the path, startling Angel. She neighed and half-rose on her hind legs. Without thinking, Emma brought her under control, but the sound and the movement had broken the magical spell of the couple on the porch.

Tara bolted upright and peered into the darkness, her hands at her throat.

Tucker was already on his feet, halfway down the steps, before he recognized Emma's face, pale as the moon, and froze.

Her gaze locked with his for one shattering moment.

And her heart cracked in two.

I believed in him all along. I thought that despite everything, somewhere deep down he cared for me, too, she thought in a flash of agony as she read the shock and dismay and yes, anger, on his face.

As if *he* had a right to be angry.

In that instant, she didn't know what showed in her face and she didn't care. It didn't matter. Nothing mattered.

She was an idiot.

She'd been an idiot all along . . . to think . . .

She wheeled Angel without a word, needing to get away before the explosion of pain inside her burst and shattered her into a million pieces right before them.

"Emma! Damn it, Emma, wait!"

Tucker sounded furious. And then she heard another voice, Tara's voice. High and sweet and clearly distraught.

"Emma, please come back—"

She rode for home as if all the demons of hell were on her heels. She never looked over her shoulder, never slowed. Her hair streamed behind her and the wind blew the tears from her cheeks.

So much for the wishing star.

Chapter 19

TUCKER SWORE BENEATH HIS BREATH AS HE raced through the darkness. The expression on Emma's face when she'd seen him with Tara had cut him like the fangs of a wolf. He'd known instantly what she was thinking, as if he had jumped inside her mind. She'd completely misunderstood the situation.

He and Jed had been invited to the McQuaid ranch for dinner. Ross and Jed were old friends, and he and Tara had grown closer ever since Beau's death. The girl had been a hair's breadth away from marrying into his family, for pete's sake. And Beau's death had torn her up real bad. Tucker felt sorry for her. He also felt a sort of bond with her because they both had loved Beau and then lost him—lost him forever.

But there was nothing more between the two of them. Never had been, never would be.

Only one woman had ever laid claim to his heart, Tucker thought savagely, as he tried to catch up to her. And she was running from him as if for her life.

He'd catch her though. They had to talk. He'd forced himself to stay away from her these past weeks, thinking it might be best for her. But after what she'd just seen, or *thought* she'd seen, her pain burned right through him. If nothing else, he had to make her see that what she was thinking was just plain wrong.

Emma had been on his mind every night and every day since they'd made love. Even when he woke up groggy and sick after that night of drinking, she'd been the first thing in his thoughts.

He'd staggered out of the saloon in time to see Carleton board the stage. The easterner had spotted him while setting a foot on the stagecoach steps and had turned white as milk, scrambling inside the coach with arms and legs flailing, as if he expected Tucker to shoot him.

Tucker hadn't even bothered to watch it roll out of town. He vaguely remembered what had passed between him and the easterner, but it didn't matter. Because Derek Carleton wasn't going to marry Emma Malloy.

The question was—Tucker had tried to brace himself through the pounding of an anvil inside his head. The question *is,* he told himself doggedly, *am I?*

Now as he spurred Pike up the wide tree-rimmed path leading to the Malloy ranch house, he could scarcely believe he was even thinking such a thing.

Beau was the one who had wanted to get married. First to Patricia Stockton, then, years later, to Tara. Beau was the one who'd been the quiet, homebody type. He had been the kind of man who couldn't resist buying candy for any kid he encountered in the mercantile, who'd rather sit by a fire and read ranch ledgers at night than hell-raise in the saloon.

Tucker, on the other hand, had never been able to imagine himself tied to home and hearth—living with just one woman and with a passel of kids scampering around his knees when he came home at night. He'd never been able to imagine his life without the Jezebel Saloon, without poker games, loud tinny piano music, cigars, and a parade of saloon girls all vying for his attentions any time he chose.

But as he bore down on the ranch house that scene flitted before his eyes with very little appeal. All he wanted at this moment was to know the feel of Emma in his arms.

Grimly, he tethered Pike behind some brush and continued toward the house on foot, moving fast. He spotted Emma as she was marching from the stables. When she caught sight of him bearing down on her, she went pale and her eyes grew wide.

He reached her and seized her as she tried to run toward the porch.

"No!" Her fists flailed at him. "Get away from me!"

"Not until you've heard me out."

She kicked, she struggled, but Tucker pinned her up against the door of the stables and she couldn't get away any sooner than she could fly.

"I don't want to hear any more of your lies or your sweet-talk."

"I never lied to you, Emma. Damn it," he exclaimed, his jaw tight, "stop kicking me."

She kicked him again and felt glorious satisfaction when he grunted. "You lied about what would happen if we . . . after we . . . "

"Made love?"

"Shhh!" She went from pallor to adorable bright red. Her eyes lifted to him in the moonlight, bright silvery glimmers reflected in their turquoise depths as she raged at him. He saw that they were no longer filled only with pain, but also with anger.

"If anyone ever found out what a fool I was to listen to you . . . to let you . . . " For a moment her voice cracked, the words tearing from her in a broken whisper. "I'd die—"

"No one's going to die, Malloy, you hear me? Hell, we're going inside. We have to talk."

He shoved her inside the stable and slammed and bolted the door. The moment his back was turned, Emma raced past the stalls to the ladder that led to the hayloft and started up it. She wanted to yank it up after her so he couldn't get to her, but Tucker was too fast. He was right behind her as she tumbled into the loft.

"Cozy." He hoisted himself up alongside her and gave her a grin that made her stomach do a somersault. "Guess it's just the two of us."

"Perhaps you'd like to invite Tara instead." Oh, she hated herself the moment the words were out. She sounded like a petty, jealous shrew. And to make matters worse, there was a catch in her throat which showed him clearly that she was dangerously close to tears.

"I couldn't care less if you did," she added immediately, defiantly, her chin flying up with pride.

To her dismay, Tucker's grin widened. His blue eyes shone in the darkness, to which her eyes were gradually getting accustomed.

"Now who's lying, Sunshine?"

"I'm not your Sunshine!"

"Yes, Emma." He grasped her arms and yanked her forward right into his lap. "You are."

She stared at him. Something about the soft ruefulness of his tone would not let her dismiss the words. They washed over her, igniting a faint, wild hope. What was he saying?

Tucker's face was dark and determined in the meager light that filtered through the single window. "I need to explain about what you saw at the McQuaids."

She swallowed hard. "You don't owe me an explanation."

"Will you shut up and listen or do I have to hogtie you to get your attention?" But his hands were gentle on her hair. To Emma's absolute amazement, he was stroking both of his hands through her curls, and his eyes were rivetted upon hers with amusement, not anger.

"Go ahead, then, if you must," she whispered in a low tone.

He smiled. And inside her, hope soared.

"Tara invited me and my father for supper. That's all there was to it. There's a bond between us . . . because of Beau. We were almost family." His voice was steady, somber. Emma felt her heart going out to him, for despite his control, she knew it hurt him afresh each time he spoke of his brother.

"I understand," she murmured. Because she did. She'd never had a brother or sister, but she could imagine the bond. Tucker must feel as if a part of himself had died.

Without thinking, she lifted a hand to his cheek, then dropped it self-consciously. But not before she saw the flicker of answering warmth in his eyes. It was a warmth that enveloped her, wrapped around her as she longed for his arms to do. Her heart began to beat in a faster rhythm, one that had become all too familiar when Tucker was around.

And then she remembered that there was more to the scenario than Tara inviting him and his father to supper. Engraved in her mind was the image of how cozy they had looked on the porch, side by side on the bench, the way Tucker had lifted her chin, his arm around her . . .

He must have read her thoughts. His voice harshened. "Don't think there was anything more between me and Tara. What you saw was me comforting her. She was all weepy over Beau and I couldn't think of anything to say. I'm not much good in situations like that with women—haven't had a whole lot of practice. All I could think to do was put my arm around her and listen while she went on and on about their plans. She told me more about the two of them than Beau ever did. He always kept his thoughts pretty much to himself—guess it's a Garrettson trait. But I think Tara needed to talk, to lean on me. Then I turned her to face me. I only wanted to tell her that I understood how much she missed him. Because I miss him, too.

And that's it,'' he finished, suddenly shifting his shoulders, as if realizing how much he'd said.

For a man given to a minimal amount of talking, it was a long speech. And Emma believed every word of it.

Or maybe you just want to believe it, she told herself, trying to fight the urge to throw her arms around him and console him over the loss of his brother. *You want to believe everything Tucker Garretson says.*

"So." His hands dropped from her hair. He wasn't touching her now, except with his eyes, which seemed to sear her soul. "Where does that leave us?"

Chapter 20

"Us."

Emma's throat was so dry the word came out in a throaty little gasp. But it sounded almost like a prayer. She was no longer angry, no longer hurt. She was afraid. Breathlessly afraid. After not seeing Tucker for weeks, here he was—in the hayloft with her, stripping bare her needs and emotions just by the way he was gazing at her.

"I didn't know there was an *us.*"

"After what happened that night, you tell me, Sunshine."

Breathless, she clung to sanity while the warmth of his voice calling her "Sunshine" made her melt.

"That night was supposed to put an end to everything between us," she said slowly. "One kiss didn't do it—we found that out in the alley on the Fourth of July. But that night you said . . . you promised . . . "

He raked a hand through his hair. "Reckon I was wrong."

Frustration swept through her. She grabbed the front of his shirt. "You don't have to sound so regretful about it."

Tucker seized her then, so quickly Emma had no chance even to flinch. Suddenly she was being held fiercely, her body rammed hard against his, her midnight hair flying forward over her face.

"I do regret it, damn it!" He shook her, his fingers clamped on her arms. "I never wanted to feel anything like this for any woman—much less you. I don't want ties. I don't want to live inside a fence. I don't think I can."

"Then let me go!" Emma was lost in the mesmerizing blue pull of his eyes. His arms felt so good around her. Too good. It made it difficult to think.

"I definitely think you should let me go!" she insisted, but her voice quavered.

"So do I." His hold tightened, vise-like. "I should *definitely* let you go. Before it's too late."

For a moment they just stared at each other, and he read all the wonder and doubt and fear in her eyes, but beneath all that, shining through it, Tucker saw the longing. Hell, he *felt* the longing, felt it in the way she leaned into him, the way her velvety lips parted as if inviting him in. She wasn't even aware of it. Her heartbeat against his chest was so fast, seemed so vulnerable, that he trembled with the need to be gentle. He was so hungry for her he wanted to throw her down in the hay and bury himself inside of her, but instead he leaned forward and claimed her mouth. But the kiss didn't go as he planned. He'd planned it to be gentle, careful. But ravenous need shot through him during that moment of heated impact and the kiss grew rough and determined, hot as pepper.

And then it *was* too late.

Because her lips opened to him, her body welcomed him, her soul, it seemed to Tucker, reached out to his, and he was lost. Reason was lost.

Passion exploded and he pushed her down upon the loosely scattered hay, lowering himself onto her and grabbing fistfuls of her hair.

"This is . . . crazy . . . Tucker," Emma moaned beneath the onslaught of his lips and hungry hands that were beginning to tear at the buttons of her blouse.

"Uh . . . huh."

Fire licked through her as his tongue burned a path along her throat. Tucker slipped the blouse off her and tossed it aside, and she quivered from head to toe.

Her breasts above the petticoat were creamy and so beautiful in the faintness of starlight. The hunger for her intensified inside him, pulsing through his loins, along every tautly coiled muscle. Deftly, he worked the petticoat off her shoulders and pushed it downward, baring the lovely, rose-tipped mounds of her breasts.

"Beautiful," he rasped against the warmth of her skin.

Emma clutched a fistful of his hair as his hand closed around her breast. Then his tongue licked the hard tip of the other, tasting, teasing. She was sure she'd go mad. She made a low whimpery sound deep in her throat and was lost to the primal seduction of raw sensation.

The knowledge that Tucker wanted her as badly as she wanted him filled her with rapturous triumph. Her nipples hardened and ached deliciously at his touch. Her senses were spinning out of control.

"So damn lovely," he growled, and her heart leaped. Her fingers were in his hair, savoring the thick silk of it, savoring him. When his fingertips brushed her nipple, stroking and rubbing with relentless slowness, delight tingled through her, along with a rising urgency. And heat . . . she was consumed by a honeyed heat that heightened to fire when his tongue twisted around the other nipple, tracing and teasing its rigid rosy peak, driving her wild. The pleasure was exquisite, and with every scrape of his lips, every slow, hot touch, it grew.

A pounding, throbbing need pulsed through her body. Unbearable tension clenched every nerve. She began to tug at his trousers, wanting more, wanting release, wanting him as she had never wanted anything in her life.

"Tucker . . . I want you—I need . . . you so much."

"I want you, too, *need* you . . . too, my sweet, beautiful Sunshine." He'd never thought he would want someone this much. Or need someone with this fevered intensity that overwhelmed everything else, including his own good sense.

Emma. *Emma.* She alone mattered. She was grace, beauty, strength, and spirit. Even her orneriness, her haughtiness, her very stubbornness delighted him as no other woman's most practiced charms ever had.

Tucker kissed her as she'd never been kissed before, kissed her so deeply and powerfully that she shook down to the embers of her soul.

"You have no idea how much I want to hate you," she gasped as his mouth burned into hers.

"I want to hate you, too," he agreed and deepened the kiss before she could reply. A moan of sheer pleasure shivered from her throat. Then another. When his tongue shot between her lips, Emma held him tighter as need sizzled through her and her own tongue engaged his in a sweet, greedy battle that left them both panting for more.

Emma clung to him as if he would disappear in a puff of smoke. Since that night in the line shack, she'd relived the passion that had consumed them over and over in her mind. This was no dream, no frivolous imagining. This was real. Tucker wanted her as much as she wanted him. And he wanted to hate her as much as she wanted to hate him.

They were both in trouble.

But it was glorious trouble.

"We really shouldn't." She tried to sound firm, to be rational, but his hands had driven her body into a mass of thrumming nerves. He was nibbling her ear and tracing its dainty shell with his tongue, and the world was becoming a delicious blur.

"I'll stop if you want me to, Malloy."

Her arms swept tight around him. "Don't you d—dare, Garrettson."

Tucker's laugh rumbled from deep within his chest.

Emma felt a powerful tautness clenching inside her then as he shifted his body and his hand traced its way down her skin. From her breasts it glided down past her hips and her belly, hungrily, knowingly caressing each curve and hollow, sliding downward at last to the vital warmth of her feminine core.

Naked, he crouched above her, exploring, watching her pink-flushed cheeks, the way her eyes smoldered, the breathless parting of her lips. He savored her response as much as the alluring curves and perfume of her body.

Beneath his fingers, Emma felt every sense awakening. Like a flower, she came to blossoming life, quivering with a rich delicate radiance that spiraled beneath his expert hands.

She closed her eyes as the sensations sweeping over her robbed her of all speech. But it wasn't necessary to talk, for Tucker was kissing her again, their mouths melting together as somehow they flung off all the rest of their clothes and rolled together through the sweet, scratchy hay.

She wanted to touch him, too, and pleasure him as he had pleasured her. Reaching out with trembling fingertips, she caressed his manhood and watched as Tucker's eyes became glassy and fevered, as his hot skin began to sweat.

She was starved for him, starved for all of him. She pulled him down atop her, yearning to feel the length of him upon her, yearning to welcome him inside her and find release for the unbearable ache that was tormenting her.

Tucker's heart thrummed against hers as he covered her slender body with his own muscular one. Their touches became quicker, hungrier, their kisses rough and panting. When he called her name, his voice hoarse and scratchy against her lips, Emma wrapped her legs around him and gripped him tight, tighter. Then his body shifted and bracing his hands on either side of her hair, he slid inside her. Her thighs parted for him. A moan flew from her reddened lips.

This time when he slid inside her there was no pain, only an exciting tingling tautness that made Emma whimper with pleasure. Desperate, burning, she clutched him against her as Tucker plunged deeper. Desire became wild, yearning, all-consuming.

He fluttered kisses over her face then covered her mouth with his own in a kiss so seethingly possessive it made her whimper with need. She arched her back and raised her hips to welcome his ever more powerful thrusts, and she felt herself racing with him, clutching him, loving him with all of her being. With each thrust she felt more desperate, more aroused and alive than ever before.

"Tucker," she moaned against his lips. "Please, you're driving me . . . crazy . . . "

His hands tangled in her hair, then caressed her face. "What do you think you're doing to me?" he whispered back. His skin was slick with sweat, his muscles flexing over her body which was writhing with need and desire for him. "Why in hell do you have to be so damned beautiful?"

"I need you . . . so." Emma's legs tightened around him, her fingers dug into his shoulders, as if she could somehow pull him even closer, deeper inside her. "Why do I have to need . . . *you?*"

"Just lucky, I guess, Malloy," he grinned down at her, deepening his thrusts, driving harder within her, faster, until tears of frenzied pleasure spilled from her eyes. "Lucky for us both," he whispered hoarsely. He surveyed her flushed face, her moist, parted lips, and her turquoise eyes which looked glazed with passion and pleasure, and the last of his restraint slipped away. Violent need shook and possessed him and he thrust himself deep into her core.

Emma cried out. The heat and craving she felt for him engulfed her, building and building until there was nothing else—only the two of them and the searing need, the sweating rhythm of their bodies, the beautiful racing harmony of their hearts.

Then, in the darkened barn amidst the sweet-smelling hay, as the night sailed on toward morning and the stars swam in the sky, a cyclone enveloped them.

Afterward, she remembered hoarse whispers and ragged cries and sweet words and raging, blinding need.

Caught up in a spinning vortex, their bodies locked together, wrapping around each other for dear life. And all the while they drank from each other's lips and found themselves consumed by a relentless thirst and a consuming fire. Each touch stoked it hotter, each movement drove them deeper together.

Emma wept softly at the wonder of it. Her head

back, her eyes shining into Tucker's violent blue ones, she sobbed with joy, feeling shattered and whole all at the same time as an explosion tore through them, sealed them, locked them in a fiery blaze that incinerated everything else in the world.

Together their bodies shuddered and bucked and found release—shattering release that left them shaken and spent and filled with unspeakable bliss in each other's arms.

AFTERWARD, SWEAT SHEENED THEIR BODIES. THEY LAY together, entwined, warm and peaceful—until a lone coyote began its melancholy wail from somewhere in the blackness beyond the stable.

The low cry broke the spell.

And as she opened her eyes and brushed a scratchy wisp of hay from her cheek, Emma felt all her rapturous happiness slipping away like a ghost in the night. She sat up, out of the shelter of Tucker's arms, shivering.

"Stay." The lazy warmth of his voice couldn't dissipate the chill seeping through her.

She didn't answer.

"Emma." He sat up, too, and drew her close, wrapping his arms around her. Such strong arms, Emma thought yearningly. So warm, so alive. She wished she *could* stay—here in this loft with him forever.

But deep inside Emma knew that what she and Tucker had here was only a false sense of safety. A false sense of peace.

How could they be safe and peaceful together when there was a range war between their families, a hatred that grew more intense by the day?

Everything would go back to the way it was the moment they climbed down out of this hayloft and stepped outside into the night.

"Tell me what's wrong, Emma."

She could listen to him say her name all night long. Emma quivered as he stroked her shoulders, her hair. He had such gentle hands for a man with his toughness and strength, a man who had beaten Slade to the ground with his bare fists, who had stood up to their teacher, and knocked him down, when Tucker himself was scarcely more than a boy.

"You know what's wrong," she said in a tone so low, so broken he could scarcely hear it. *"This* is all wrong. Us. We're all wrong."

"It feels right to me."

"Me, too," she whispered desperately, tears catching in her throat as she brought her hands up to cradle his face. "But, Tucker, no one else will ever understand—"

"You mean our fathers." Anger ripped through him, such a violent anger that Emma could only stare. "I don't give a damn if they understand. I don't give a damn about the feud. All I know is that my father has wasted his life full of anger and resentment because of that feud. And Beau," Tucker went on savagely, "is dead because of that feud. His life ended, before he could settle down and know the happiness he wanted with Tara McQuaid—all because of that feud. You know what, Emma?"

He caught her bare shoulders and his fingers pressed into the soft flesh. "There are no guarantees in life—none. No guarantees of another sunset or of one more dawn. You have to know what you want, go after it, and not let stupid things like squabbles over land, cattle, or goddamned poker games get in the way."

Tears sparked in her eyes. "Land m—matters. I love this land. Echo Ranch means everything to me!"

"More than love?"

Seeing her falter, Tucker nodded.

"Don't think Tall Trees doesn't matter to me. My sweat and blood is in it, in every inch of soil, every blade of grass, every steer on the range. There's no-where else I'd rather live, nothing else I'd rather do than make it as big, as strong, as prosperous as it can be."

Seeing the determination in his face, Emma felt hope fade.

Then his next words surprised her. "But there has to be a way. A way we can live here together. I saw the feud ruin my father's life and my brother's, and I'll be damned if it's going to ruin mine."

"Do you really think there's a chance—for us? For you and me?"

"If I didn't, Malloy," Tucker said, smoothing her tangle of hair back from her face and then carefully plucking another piece of straw from her hair, "I never would have followed you from McQuaid's."

Silence gripped them as they stared at each other. Emma's heart began to pound. She thought of telling her father: "I'm in love with Tucker Garrettson."

And she wanted to run from the thought—but gazing into the calm determination in Tucker's eyes, she felt her own hope and resolve mounting. Could they do it? Was their love strong enough to break the bonds of hatred?

"You don't want to be fenced in," she reminded him, rubbing her palms across his chest, watching his eyes darken with a banked fire at her touch.

He grinned and caught her hands in both of his. He lifted them to his lips and kissed each one in turn. "Guess it depends on who's doing the fencing."

She leaned in against him then, wrapping her arms around his neck, kissing him with need on her lips and love blazing in her heart. All of her being embraced him as if from his strength, his heart and soul, she could gain courage for what lay ahead.

"I can't imagine my father and yours even in the same room together." She almost chuckled. "Much less sitting down to a meal together, having a civil conversation—"

"Emma, listen to me." Tucker held her close for another moment, wishing like hell he didn't have to say what came next, knowing it could shatter everything between them. But he had to prepare her for what was coming. Tara had told him something else tonight, something he hadn't mentioned to Emma before. That, combined with what he'd already learned from Gill's file, made it clear that Win Malloy would be arrested soon for Beau's murder. Arrested and convicted. And hanged.

They'd never have to worry about their fathers

finding themselves in the same room or trying to engage in civil conversation.

"I've got to warn you about something. Don't think this is easy or what I want. But you have to know."

"Know what?" she asked, pulling back, suddenly wary.

"I know you don't want to believe that your father killed Beau—"

Tensing, she spoke very clearly. "He didn't."

"Sunshine, I think Sheriff Gill has enough evidence to prove that he did."

Jerking away from him as if he were poison, Emma felt all the heat draining from her body. All her tenuous happiness faded to a sickly gray pain. "I don't believe you."

"I'd cut off my arm if I didn't have to tell you this, Emma, but it's true. It's only a matter of days 'til Gill finally gives up hoping he'll magically come up with proof someone else was involved. It's going to happen and soon." Tucker sucked in his breath, feeling his own gut tighten as if he'd been punched. Emma looked ill. She looked like she was going to collapse. He grasped hold of her shoulders and held on tight.

"You have to prepare yourself, Emma." Grimly, he shook his head, wishing things were different, wishing he didn't have to tell her something so terrible, or have to see the agony in her eyes. "Your father is going to be arrested for murder."

"I won't listen to this! You hate my father, you and your father both hate him! You'd make up anything to get him to appear guilty—you'd even frame him!"

"Damn it, Emma, you know that isn't true."

But she wrenched free of him and shaking, began to scramble about in the hay for her clothes.

"Emma, listen—"

"Don't you 'Emma' me." Panting, she struggled back into her clothes, fighting to keep the tears from spilling out. The world was crashing down around her. She felt as if she were trapped at the bottom of a rockslide, being deluged by a thousand boulders, sticks, and stones.

"Just because my heart melts every time you call me that you think you can use it to turn me against my own father," she cried. "Do you really believe you can make me doubt him for even a moment? I won't! He isn't capable of murder. He didn't shoot your brother!"

She flung herself toward the ladder, but Tucker grasped her wrist and yanked her back.

"I'm sorry this hurts you. I'm sorry—"

"Let me go. I don't ever want to see you again, Tucker. It's over—everything between us is over. This time I mean it. You've . . . " Her voice shook, but she quickly got herself under control again and faced him with glittering rage-filled eyes. "You've gone too far. If you can't believe in my father's innocence, then I guess you just don't believe enough in me."

"That's a load of horse manure, Malloy."

Malloy. And he was a Garrettson. They were back to that. They always would be. "There's nothing more for us, Tucker." Her voice was broken. But not as broken as her heart. Still, she kept the tears back somehow. "No future . . . no f—fences. Nothing."

He let her leave, never even coming after her.

As Emma fled through the darkness and up the steps of her home, the tears began.

They continued through all the black empty hours of the night. And even when dawn arrived with its dainty pearl glow, they didn't stop.

Chapter 21

"NOW WHO'S THAT COMING?"

Win Malloy set down his fork and pushed back his chair, striding to the window and frowning out at the approaching rider. He looked as if he expected to see a slew of Jed Garrettson's men converging on the house with guns drawn.

But it was only Tara McQuaid, waving as she caught sight of him in the window. "Look who's come to visit," he exclaimed with pleasure as Emma glanced listlessly up from her plate. "It's Tara. Now isn't this a nice surprise?"

"Maybe she'd like some blueberry pie," Corinne suggested as she began to clear the table.

Emma rose and started toward the door. "I'll ask her."

But she paused as she saw her father and Corinne exchange worried glances.

"What's wrong?"

"Didn't you care for the steak, Emma? You scarcely touched it, or the biscuits." Corinne shook her head over the hefty portion of food remaining on Emma's plate.

"It was fine, Corinne. Everything was fine. I'm just not hungry today."

"Emma."

Her father's voice stopped her as she reached the dining room doorway. "Is something wrong, honey? You haven't seemed yourself lately. If it's still that little disagreement we had over Curt Slade—"

He broke off as Tara called from the porch. "Yoo hoo. Hope I'm not interrupting your supper!"

"Coming!" Emma called, grateful for the excuse to escape, but she did mumble over her shoulder, "I'm not angry anymore, Papa. Everything's fine."

"Well, things don't seem fine," Corinne muttered.

And Win nodded. His brows were knit, his eyes fixed on her the way they used to when she was a child who had scraped her knees but didn't want anyone to know lest stinging ointment be applied.

"Are you sure, honey—" he began, but Emma cut him off, flashing an overbright smile that never reached her eyes.

"Of course I'm sure. Papa, Tara's waiting."

Then she was in the hall, grateful to have escaped their questioning glances and worried looks. But immediately, she braced herself to greet Tara. These days, every moment, every encounter was a trial. Emma couldn't seem to escape the dark cloud which seemed to envelop her.

"I *did* interrupt your supper, didn't I?" Smiling ruefully, Tara shook her head as Emma opened the door for her. "Go ahead and finish. I don't mind waiting."

"No need—we're all finished. Corinne wants to know if you'd like some blueberry pie."

"No, thank you, if I eat another bite today I surely won't fit into the dress I wanted to wear for the wedding tomorrow. I came to ask you what you're wearing, Emma. I can't decide between my pink muslin and my new blue and yellow gingham with the white lace collar." Tara gazed at her searchingly. "You are going to the wedding tomorrow, aren't you?"

"Shorty and Abigail's wedding? Of course."

"I'm glad. You know—I've hardly had a chance to see you lately. But I've been thinking about you."

Emma said nothing as she led Tara through the front hall toward the parlor. "Would you like to see my dress?" she asked at last, and when Tara nodded, she turned toward the stairs.

You must stop behaving so oddly, she told herself as she listened to their footsteps echoing through the quiet ranch house. *You know now that there was nothing the least bit romantic going on between Tara and Tucker. And even if there had been, it should mean nothing to you. You can't have him anyway. And you don't want him—you can't possibly love a man who thinks your father is a cold-blooded murderer.*

The thought that Win might be arrested had been filling her with terror night and day. But every time she began to broach her concerns to her father, he had dismissed them and brushed them off as absurd. She thought of talking to Sheriff Gill herself and trying to learn if he did indeed have evidence, but was afraid that her questions might actually hasten some action on his part.

So she'd kept her heartache and her anxiety all to herself, until now. She knew that if she didn't come out of this shell she'd crawled into soon, and start behaving more like herself, every one who knew her would begin wondering what was so terribly wrong with Emma Malloy.

And the last thing she wanted was more questions.

Tara kept silent until they reached the bedroom. But when Emma brought out her pale sea-green gown she gave a gasp.

"Oh, how lovely." As Emma draped the gown across the bed, Tara's brown eyes skimmed over the sweep of silk, the lace ruching of the fashionably narrow bustle, the scalloped cream-colored lace around the sleeves, and the low neckline. "Did you purchase it in Philadelphia?"

"Yes. I've only worn it once—to the opera with Derek . . . "

She fell silent. Another difficult subject. Her temples throbbed with the effort of making natural conversation, and oh, how she wished she could have loved Derek, instead of Tucker.

"I'm sorry things didn't work out between you and Derek Carleton." Tara sat down beside the dress on the edge of Emma's bed and studied her with concern. She spoke quietly. "From the expression on your face right now, I guess you might have been happier if you'd married him and gone back to Philadelphia after all."

"If only I had." Then she never would have let Tucker Garrettson make love to her. Not once, but *twice*. Her stomach felt queasy just thinking about it.

She sat down abruptly in the chair and returned Tara's gentle gaze. She owed her some explanation. Tara had come all this way, she was trying so hard to be a good friend. But for some reason, Emma had grown accustomed all these weeks to keeping her thoughts all bottled up inside and that made it difficult to begin to share them.

"I didn't love Derek as I should," she sighed. "So I couldn't marry him. And Tara, I would never leave Echo Ranch for good and move far away from my father. Especially with . . . " she grimaced and waved a hand, "all this going on."

Tara nodded.

"I understand, Emma. But it's too bad about Derek, about not loving him and all," she said, and Emma saw the wistfulness in her eyes. "You had so much in Philadelphia. Whisper Valley is beautiful, it's true, but it surely doesn't offer the same advantages. For example, you could never find a dress as gorgeous as this one here."

Yearning filled her voice. Suddenly, Emma felt a stab of sympathy as she saw Tara studying the gown with longing. Yes, Tara would probably love to have dresses like this, to live in Philadelphia. She'd never even left Whisper Valley. All the fripperies and fineries, the amusements, and elegance which Emma had come to take for granted back east must seem like faraway dreams—and must be infinitely alluring. For

Tara, they were all only fanciful imagining, something she might never see or know.

Impulsively, Emma leaned forward, her eyes shining. "Tara, would you like to wear my dress to the wedding tomorrow? It would look wonderful on you."

Tara blinked at her. For a moment her eyes widened, and Emma feared that she had offended her and that what she saw blazing across Tara's face was anger, but the next instant she realized it was shock.

"I c—couldn't." Tara could barely get the words out.

"Of course you could. Why not? I have so many other dresses I could wear—" she broke off, flushing, chagrined that it sounded as if she'd been bragging. Tara's cheeks were crimson.

"I'll let you borrow this dress if one day you let me borrow your darling yellow bonnet with the beads and the feathers. It would be so pretty with my yellow gingham." She smiled winningly. "Come on, do you want to try it on?"

For a moment Emma saw indecision in Tara's eyes, then she shook her head. Her smile was both sweet and sad. "No, Emma, I couldn't. But thank you anyway. It's a generous offer—you're a good friend."

Emma found herself smiling back, grateful for this friend of so many years. "So are you, Tara." A deep sigh escaped her as she rose and began to pace around the room, seized by restlessness. She walked over to the bureau and looked at the small crystal vase on top which contained a bunch of wildflowers she'd picked yesterday out in the foothills. But they reminded her of the wildflowers she'd seen that day with Tucker, when someone had taken a shot at her and he had come near to kissing her in the cool tall grass. She turned quickly away and went instead to the window. But there her gaze was drawn to the south, where Tucker lived with his father at Tall Trees.

Tucker, Tucker, Tucker.

She let out her breath in a frustrated rasp, and spun around, her fingers flying up to massage her aching temples.

"Tara, do you sometimes wish everything could be as easy, as uncomplicated as when we were children?"

Tara studied her consideringly. "Exactly what is so complicated, Emma? Are you talking about Tucker Garrettson?"

Now it was Emma's turn to blush. She felt her cheeks flame, knew they must be brighter than any wild poppy. In fact, she felt warm all over. And slightly dizzy.

But she'd been light-headed for days now. Probably because she wasn't eating much. So, despite the sensation that the floor was tilting beneath her, she managed to keep her voice steady.

"What makes you ask a thing like that?"

"I saw your face that night, Emma. The night you rode over to the ranch and saw me and Tucker together on the porch. You looked as if someone had just punched you in the stomach."

"I was surprised. Surprised to see Tucker there, on your porch. That's all. I mean," she rushed on, "I know that you feel close to him and his father—because of Beau. But it looked like more than that, and I just didn't expect—"

"You were jealous, weren't you? You thought there was something more going on between Tucker and me. Perhaps that he was going to kiss me."

"No . . . yes. I mean, why in heaven's name should I care about that?"

"Emma." There was soft reproof in Tara's voice. She clasped her hands in her lap and offered up a wan smile. "You know how much I loved Beau. I loved him with all my heart." The sigh that came from her then whispered sadly through the bedroom. "Surely you didn't think I could quickly transfer all those feelings to Tucker, did you?"

Emma went to her and knelt beside the bed. "It was foolish of me, Tara. For that one moment, I wasn't sure about anything. It just seemed as if you two were about to . . . "

To kiss. But she was unable to finish the sentence, unable to even bear the thought of Tucker kissing Tara or any other woman.

In the silence that followed, Tara cleared her throat. "Tucker and I are friends, Emma. Good friends. That's all there is to it." Her brown eyes swept over Emma's face with shrewd scrutiny. "But I get the feeling that you and Tucker are more than friends. I *thought* you were enemies, everyone in town thinks you're enemies—but you're not, are you, Emma?"

Reaching out, she clasped Emma's hand. "Please tell me. I can see how troubled you are. Let me help. You can trust me, you know that."

Suddenly the urge to unburden herself was too much. Yes, she could trust Tara. Tara was her oldest friend. And she didn't hate Tucker, as Papa and Corinne did. Tara was the only person she could possibly confide in.

"I do have feelings for Tucker, it's true," she admitted in a rush. "Feelings I shouldn't have. Considering he thinks my father is a murderer," she added darkly. "And that he's going to be arrested any moment, that he deserves to go to jail, maybe even hang! I swear I don't want to care for him, Tara, I've fought against it. But when Derek kissed me, nothing happened, and when Tucker kisses me . . . everything happens."

She swallowed. She'd said enough. More than enough. Yet she felt better for having said it aloud. She searched Tara's face, worried that she might see shock or condemnation. But there was sympathy in her friend's eyes, warmth in her smile.

"Sometimes our feelings just get the better of us, don't they, Emma? None of us is perfect. And I think that despite his being a Garrettson, as you might say," she gave a tiny smile, "Tucker is a good man."

Emma's eyes glowed. "He *is* a good man," she agreed eagerly. "Do you remember how he used to protect Harvey Wells from Mr. Huet? And he protected me from that outlaw during the bank robbery—even though he hated me—or, I *thought* he hated me. And Tucker is as loyal to his father as I am to mine. Loyalty is an admirable quality, isn't it, Tara? And he's gentle, so gentle. But there's a strength in him, too—physical strength and also strength of character—it comes through, it's always come through, though I would never admit it. And—"

She broke off, her hands flying to her burning cheeks. "I sound just like a besotted schoolgirl, don't I?" If it wasn't so utterly pathetic, she might have laughed at herself. Who ever would have thought it?

"You don't know, Tara, you just don't know. In Philadelphia, I had a reputation for being 'The Unflappable Miss Malloy.' Other girls might swoon, or scream, or giggle. Not me. I was always composed, perfectly in control. But listen to me now."

Tara chuckled at her woebegone expression. "People are often different beneath the surface than what they appear to be. It seems to me that beneath your composed surface you're just like every other woman who sets her sights on a man."

"I always prided myself on my good sense, my logic, my competence on a horse and with a gun. I thought I could handle anything. And I guess I can—except I have no idea how to handle a man like Tucker Garrettson." Emma groaned. "But I bet I *could* handle him," she added suddenly, her eyes flashing. "If it weren't for everything else. There's just too much coming between us. He truly thinks my father killed Beau! He's certain of it."

"Have you told Tucker how you feel about him? Does he feel the same way?"

A queasy flutter curled through her stomach. "I'm not sure," Emma said. "Oh, Tara, I'm just not sure about anything!"

From below came Corinne's voice, booming cheerfully up the stairs.

"Girls! Hot coffee! And blueberry pie! Last chance!"

The squeamish sensation heightened. "I don't want anything," Emma said with a shudder, "but I really ought to help Corinne with the dishes. Are you sure you don't want some pie?"

Tara shook her head. "What are you going to do about Tucker?"

She hesitated. What indeed? "I may try to talk to him tomorrow at the wedding. Oh, Tara, you don't know how I wish I could dance with him. But our fathers would probably end up in a gunfight on Main Street if we did!"

"I don't think that's going to happen."

Tara smiled encouragingly as they went downstairs, but Emma couldn't share in her confidence. She had an uneasy feeling about the next day. The Fourth of July dance had been a near disaster, and that was before the range war was in full swing. Now the town was coming together again, this time for a wedding.

Who knew what would happen when the Garrettsons and the Malloys showed up in the same place?

From the porch, she watched Tara ride off after both girls had helped Corinne clean the kitchen, then paused and glanced back before going in the door.

Tara had been intercepted at the end of the corral fence by one of the new ranch hands. Jimmy Joe Pratt, Emma believed it to be, as she squinted into the sunset. He had black hair and nice manners—and had come from Texas, she'd heard.

They talked for a moment, then Tara rode on and Jimmy Joe lifted his hand in farewell.

He swung off the fence and headed toward the bunkhouse, doffing his hat to Emma as he saw her on the porch.

She waved absently in response, thinking about her friend. Perhaps Tara would find a new love soon. She'd heal from losing Beau and start over. She deserved to be happy. And maybe she and Jimmy Joe Pratt—

But here she stopped herself. She wasn't in any position to play Cupid for anyone else. Her own life was as messy as a chicken coop.

She knew she had to sweep and straighten it out before long.

Chapter 22

"MY," CORINNE SAID, "ISN'T IT A FINE DAY for a wedding?"

Entering the church with her father and the housekeeper, Emma was forced to agree. It was a splendid Montana day. The sky was as big and blue as a giant pansy draping the earth. The sun gilded the land, tinging the mountains and hilltops with shimmering fire, dancing golden upon the edges of lush green leaves and wildflowers that were vivid as rainbows.

But she wanted to crawl into a hole, curl up, and die.

She was in no mood for a wedding.

She was in a state of sick panic, unable to smile and nod as the bride came down the aisle of the church, unable to concentrate on the vows being said. She could not join in the murmuring approval of the gathered throng or in the laughter over the new young preacher's stumbling as he said, "I now pronounce you man and woman, I mean, man and wife. You may kiss her, uh, the bride. Abigail."

She could only stare at the back of Tucker Garrettson's head as he sat two rows up and across the aisle.

Jed Garrettson was sitting with the McQuaids. Tara had waved to Emma when she and Win had come in. Though she looked lovely in her pink muslin gown, her brown hair tucked into a pretty chignon atop her head, Tara's eyes had lingered for a moment on the sea-green confection Emma wore.

Don't envy me, Tara, she thought in a daze of misery. *If you only knew what a terrible state my life is in, you would never feel the slightest flicker of envy ever again.*

Happy chatter, good luck wishes, and joviality surged around her, filling the air as everyone congratulated the happy couple and tea and cakes and lemonade were served from long linen-draped tables in the church courtyard.

Two fiddlers began to play and Shorty and Abigail Brown were pushed into the center of the courtyard to dance. All eyes followed them as they waltzed beneath the summer sun, while their friends and families and neighbors applauded. They, however, appeared to see only each other.

"Care to dance, Emma?" Pete Sugar held out his arms.

"You step on her toes, boy, and you'll answer to me," Win joked, smiling broadly as he and Pete shook hands. But one person nearby wasn't smiling. Jed Garrettson, standing near one of the long tables, sent Win a scowl that nearly singed the hair on the back of Emma's neck.

She danced with Pete and with Harvey Wells and Red Peterson. And all the while her eyes searched the throng.

At last she spotted Tucker. He was cornered over near the well, between Mary Lou Kent and Delores Thompson, who wore the ugliest bird's nest hat Emma had ever seen. Suddenly Mabel Barnes tapped her on the arm.

"Just look at that. A big strong man like Tucker Garrettson—and he looks scared to death, now doesn't he?"

Well, not precisely scared to death, but Tucker did look as if he'd rather be nose to nose with a couple of rattlers than with the ladies in question.

Emma felt a sudden surge of love for him, a surge so strong it nearly banished the queasiness in her stomach.

Dare she? Here, in front of everyone? But she had to talk to Tucker. She had to tell him what she'd discovered this morning. What she'd finally realized.

It would take all her courage to do it.

She started forward, gripping her reticule as tightly as she would her gun if she were heading into a battle.

"Excuse me, Mrs. Barnes, there's something I need to do."

With her gaze fastened resolutely on Tucker's tall frame, she started forward.

"Why, then, you just run right along, dear. That's just fine . . ."

Emma heard no more. She was already headed straight toward Tucker and the two chattering young women in their beribboned gowns vying for his attention.

He saw her coming. His eyes lit up at the sight of her. In fact, both young women saw the change in his expression as he stood up straighter, focused on her, his gaze sharp and keen.

They turned their heads simultaneously.

"Why, Emma," Delores exclaimed, in her smooth as cream voice. "How nice to see you. Isn't it nice to see her, Tucker?"

He nodded.

"You look a bit peaked, honey," Mary Lou said, trying hard to sound concerned. "Doesn't she look peaked, Tucker?"

"She looks beautiful."

Tucker said it quietly, simply, but the effect on the other two women was instantaneous. Their jaws dropped.

Neither of them had ever been able to pry so much as a "that's a nice hat" or "pretty dress you're wearing," from him—and here he was telling Emma Malloy that she looked beautiful.

Emma was rendered quite breathless herself. She glanced neither right nor left; her gaze was pinned on Tucker as she summoned her courage and said, "May I speak to you a moment?"

If Delores' and Mary Lou's jaws had dropped before, now they hit the ground.

Even Tucker looked surprised. But he recovered swiftly, reached out and took Emma's arm before anyone else could speak.

"Excuse us, ladies."

Then he was leading her out of the courtyard, around the church, toward a sweeping knoll thick with asters, where a green thicket of trees made for a secluded bower.

Faintly, Emma wondered if Tara or her father or Jed Garrettson had noticed them slipping off together. At the moment she didn't care. The feud was nothing compared to what she had to tell Tucker.

Her hands felt clammy, her stomach roiled as though a thousand tiny bees buzzed inside. Tucker released her arm when they reached the little clearing where several rocks rose up amidst the grass.

With her knees shaky, Emma sat down on one of the rocks and wiped her hands on her skirt. How to begin?

How could she begin to tell him that she was going to bear his child?

Just do it, she told herself. *Tell him straight out.*

But what would he do? Say? No matter what he might have said in the heat of lovemaking Tucker clearly wasn't the type of man to want to settle down. He wouldn't *want* to marry her, but probably he would feel honor-bound to do so. She knew him well enough to know that that would be his way.

Her heart snapped in two at the thought. God, she didn't want that, a loveless marriage, a man who felt trapped, forced to be with her, with their child.

All the fears that had kept her up last night when she'd first realized the implications of her queasiness, her tiredness, the unusual lateness of her monthly cycle, came rushing back.

But if she didn't tell Tucker, what would she do? Her father would kill Tucker if he found out.

Emma had not a doubt of that.

She couldn't tell her father.

There was only one other possible choice. She could go back east. She could talk to Aunt Loretta. Aunt Loretta would help her, and perhaps they could go to Europe until after the baby was born.

Tears burned behind her eyes. How could this have happened? she wondered bitterly.

But she knew well how this had happened. She and Tucker in that line shack, making sweet, beautiful love, love that was wild and tender as a moon-bright summer night.

She didn't regret it—she couldn't regret the ecstasy they'd shared. But she was frightened. Frightened of doing or saying the wrong thing, of the difficulties the future would bring.

"What's wrong?" Tucker asked, studying her in that all-too-piercing way of his. "Reckon it must be something pretty important to make you decide to talk to me again."

"I . . . " But the words froze in her throat. Gazing at him, meeting those searching blue eyes, her heart was full of emotion—of love, tenderness, desire. She loved him too much to drag him to the altar out of some sense of duty. Shorty and Abigail had wed out of love—with a hopeful, happy future before them. If Tucker married her for the sake of their child, there would only be desperation and ultimately bitterness and pain between them. And continued enmity between their families.

"I wanted to tell you that I may follow your advice. The advice you gave me that day when I was riding, when someone shot at me."

His eyes narrowed. "You mean about going back east?"

She nodded.

"You can't do that."

"I can and I might. You can't tell me what to do."

Tucker bit back the fury rising within him. She had him there. What right did he have to tell her anything? None.

But he couldn't imagine her leaving. His gut clenched at the thought and pain stabbed through him like rusty nails. He didn't want to picture Whisper Valley without her.

"You're not going anywhere," he said roughly to cover the emotion seething within him. "Besides, since when do you run away?"

"This isn't about running away. And anyhow, Tucker, it's what you suggested. I'd think you'd be happy I'm doing what you wanted—"

"What about your father? Everything you told me about his needing you?"

She looked down at her hands and swallowed hard. "He'll manage."

It sounded hollow, even to her own ears. And Tucker was no fool. He moved toward her.

"Emma," he said grimly and paused until she looked up at him. He looked so handsome standing there, with the sun glinting off his hair, his mouth set in that firm line she had learned to love, "you're not going anywhere until you give me some straight answers.''

TUCKER HAD TO FIGHT THE ROARING URGE TO SEIZE EMMA in his arms. Hell, she was beautiful. A bit pale today, he noticed, but stunningly beautiful. Her eyes put the sky to shame, and the fragile sweep of her features made her look far too dainty and elegant for this rugged land they both loved.

He'd dreamed of her almost every night since the night they'd made love in the barn. He thought of her every day.

And he tried to convince himself that it would never work between them. Sometimes it helped to remind himself that he wanted to stay a free man. But the Jezebel Saloon and the girls who worked there, and every woman in town, had somehow lost their allure. They were like pale shadows, indistinct and wavery. Emma stood out in his mind in brilliant relief. Slim, lovely Emma with her midnight hair and bewitching eyes, with her mouth that spoke tartly yet tasted sweeter than honeyed wine.

As he stared at her, she licked her lips with her tongue, a nervous gesture. He wished to hell he could read what was going on in her mind. She looked so tense, and yes, unusually pale. Those women had been right about the peaked part, but he'd been too glad to see her to notice.

''Why do you suddenly want to leave town?''

''Maybe I want to get away from you,'' she said

angrily, pushing herself up off the rock. A wave of queasiness assaulted her, but she fought it back.

"What's wrong with you?" he demanded as she swayed beneath the beating sun.

Emma shook her head. "I should go back."

"Not until you level with me."

"You don't want to know, Tucker," she whispered. Her throat closed up, thick with emotion she couldn't express or quell. "Not really."

This took him aback. What the hell did that mean?

He grasped her arms and pulled her against him. "Malloy, I'm warning you. If you don't tell me—"

"No threats, Tucker. Please. Not today."

Before he could say anything further, she summoned up a wan smile. "It was a nice wedding, wasn't it?"

The change of subject stunned him. "Yeah, I guess so. If you like weddings."

"Shorty and Abigail—they both look so happy."

"What does this have to do with you leaving town?"

Tucker obviously wasn't interested in the subject of weddings, or in marital bliss, a small voice inside mocked her. Another inner voice screamed: *Tell him!*

But before she could decide, an outside voice intruded. It was a loud, harsh voice, rough as sun-baked dirt. A voice belonging to Jed Garrettson.

"You might want to get back to the church, son. The party's breaking up, and Wesley Gill just arrived. You're going to want to see this."

Emma's heart leaped into her throat. She didn't

like the excitement and satisfaction she saw in Garrettson's ruddy face. Did this mean . . . ?

She couldn't bear to finish the thought.

Filled with a terrible foreboding, she glanced at Tucker. He was glaring at his father, and Emma noted in alarm that now it was he who had turned pale beneath the bronze of his tan.

"Pop—what are you talking about?"

Jed Garrettson stalked closer. "What are *you* talking about—with *her?*" he demanded, jerking his chin toward Emma.

"None of your damned business. And you ought to see fit to remember that Emma Malloy is a lady and you should take off your hat when you're in the presence of a lady."

"She's a Malloy—"

"Don't give me that, Pop." Tucker's voice was low, dangerously soft. His father met his gaze, saw the steel in it, and shrugged. He doffed his hat.

"Miss Malloy."

"Mr. Garrettson." Emma stared at Jed Garrettson, trying to appear calmer than she felt. But her heart was pounding so hard it was difficult to speak. "What did you mean about Sheriff Gill arriving, and something Tucker will want to see?"

"Go back and look for yourself, girl."

"Pop, damn it!" Tucker swung his father around to face him. "Answer her."

Garrettson flushed at his son's tone. His eyebrows swooped together with disapproval at the notion that his son was taking Emma Malloy's side over his. But he didn't really mind answering the girl. It gave him pleasure to say the words.

"Your old man's finally going to get what's coming to him," Garrettson rasped out, savoring each word with infinite satisfaction.

But if there was equal satisfaction in Tucker's face, Emma never saw it. Without wasting another moment, she whirled around and ran.

She heard the commotion in the church courtyard before she saw anything. Sheriff Gill and Clem were on either side of her father, walking him toward the gate while a low rumble of protest and shock flowed through the few remaining wedding guests. Most had already left, as had the bride and groom. Obviously, Sheriff Gill had not wanted to spoil the festivities. He'd waited until now to place his old friend under arrest. *Kind of him,* Emma thought furiously.

"Stop," she cried, flinging herself before the trio. "Sheriff Gill, how dare you?"

When Gill didn't immediately answer her, she drew herself up very straight and tall.

"I demand that you let my father go this instant. How can you even think about arresting him? You know he had nothing to do with Beau Garrettson's death!"

"I'm afraid I know nothing of the sort, Emma honey," Gill mumbled. His face was ashen and perspiration trailed down his wrinkled old cheeks. But Emma's gaze had shifted to her father, and she moved forward, her lips trembling.

"Papa, don't worry. This is all a terrible mistake.

But we'll fix it. I promise you this will all be straightened out!''

Fury vibrated through Win Malloy. His square, handsome face was red as brick, and his normally genial brown eyes smoldered like lava. His wrath was directed at a point beyond Emma's shoulder, but she knew without looking what, or rather, who it was focused upon.

"Garrettson, I'm going to kill you when I get out of here. This is your doing—it's a set-up and I'll prove it!''

Jed Garrettson snorted derisively.

Emma stepped forward and touched Win's face with shaking fingers. "Papa, of course it's a set-up. Sheriff Gill, why can't you see that?''

"There's proof.'' Gill spoke without enthusiasm. "And it's mighty strong proof, I'm sorry to say.'' With a thick sigh, he nodded at the deputy. "Come on, Clem, we'd best get this over with.''

"Emma,'' her father called over his shoulder as they led him through the gate. "Don't you worry, honey. This will all blow over as soon as I show Gill what a damn fool he's making of himself. . . . ''

His voice dwindled away as Wesley Gill and Clem led him from the courtyard and headed one block up, toward Main Street and the sheriff's office at the far end of town.

Emma could only stare after their retreating figures in dazed horror. When she finally roused herself from the shock and gazed around her, she saw that the previously festive courtyard was nearly deserted. She stared numbly at those who remained, too stricken at first to speak.

Looking shocked, Mabel Barnes and Sue Ellen Gill stood beside Corinne, who had tears streaming down her plump face. A few feet away, Tara was clutching her father's arm, her eyes fixed upon Emma.

And Tucker and Jed Garrettson stood shoulder to shoulder beneath a spreading cottonwood no more than ten feet away.

"Emma, I'm sorry," Tucker said. His face looked taut enough to crack as he started toward her. "We have to . . . ''

"No!" She lifted both hands as if to ward off a blow and he froze. "You stay away from me. Just stay away!"

"You heard what she said, son." Jed nodded with satisfaction. "Let's go home."

But Tucker didn't move. His gaze was locked on Emma's, studying her with an intensity she found unbearable.

"Stay away!" she cried again, agony filling her face, and then she spun away from him and flung herself toward Corinne.

The next thing she knew the housekeeper's soft arms were pillowing her, and she was weeping into Corinne's rounded shoulder.

"There, there, honey. It'll all turn out fine. Let's go on home and talk about what can be done."

"I can't go home, Corinne." Emma stepped back, shaking her head. She dashed the tears away with the back of her hand. "I can't leave Papa now."

"There's nothing to be done for him, child. Not here. Not yet."

Nothing to be done? Emma couldn't accept that. She tried desperately to think, but at that moment a spasm of nausea gripped her and dizziness struck. She sucked in a deep breath, fighting back the sickness. As she tried to steady herself and concentrate, she heard Ross McQuaid clear his throat.

"Win'll need a lawyer for the trial, Emma. I heard of a feller in Butte who is supposed to be damned good at lawyering. I'll take you to meet him if you like."

Her eyes lit. A lawyer—why hadn't she thought of that? She had to collect her wits. "Oh, yes, Mr. McQuaid, I'd be so grateful. May we go today?"

"If you'd like, Emma."

"No, no, that's not a good idea," she decided suddenly, her brain starting to click into gear. "I don't want to speak to the lawyer until I have more information for him. I have to find out about this proof Sheriff Gill claims to have. The lawyer will need to know all about that—"

"Emma." Gently, Tara tapped her arm.

"You can't just go rushing around all upset like this. I know how helpless you must feel, but you need to go home, take in everything that's happened and plan out what to do. My father and I will help you. So will Corinne. But first, let me take you home to Echo Ranch and fix you both some tea. Then we can all talk and figure out what's best to do."

"She's right." Worry clouded Corinne's small, pea-green eyes, and the sun mercilessly outlined every sag and wrinkle in her face. She looked older suddenly and very, very tired. But she glared fiercely at Jed Garrettson and Tucker as she turned on them in rage.

"What are you two still doing here? Gloating? Get on with you!"

Tucker was watching Tara, Emma noticed. His gaze was intent, unwavering. She saw Tara peer over at him and give her head a tiny regretful shake.

"This is all so upsetting," she murmured. "My father and I have always been somewhat caught in the middle between both of our old friends. But now . . . " She sighed. "But now, it's important that the truth come out. For Beau's sake, it has to come out."

"Truth?" Emma's chin flew up. "You mean that Win Malloy never shot Beau Garrettson in the back? That the Garrettsons are the ones causing all the trouble in Whisper Valley and that without them we'd have peace and everyone would get along fine? Is *that* the truth you mean, Tara?"

Jed Garrettson stepped forward furiously and opened his mouth to give the Malloy girl a piece of his mind, but Tucker grasped his arm and yanked him back.

"Not now, Pop." Tucker spoke in a low, firm tone that only just reached Emma's ears. "Leave her alone."

To her surprise, after taking one look at her face, Jed clamped his lips together and stalked away.

Tucker said only two words to her. "Sorry, Sunshine."

And then he was gone, too, his long stride carrying him from the courtyard as Corinne and the Mc-Quaids closed around her in a band of comfort.

But there was no comfort to be had. Her world was falling in upon her. Papa was in jail, and she was having Tucker's baby.

She fought back the urge to weep, swallowed down the bitter frightened tears that filled her throat, and straightened her trembling shoulders.

"Will you come home now?" Tara asked quietly beside her, searching Emma's face with gentle hope. "We know your father is innocent, and we'll help you prove it. Everyone will know the truth—but Emma, it's not going to be easy. We have to think about what can be done. Won't you come home and let us—"

"No." Emma stepped past her, past all of them, her eyes clear and cold. "I'm going to the sheriff's office to have a little chat with Wesley Gill."

Chapter 23

EMMA SAT STIFF AND STRAIGHT IN THE CHAIR opposite Sheriff Gill's desk. "Tell me everything. Every single reason you have—or think you have—for locking my father up when you know he couldn't possibly have done this."

Seated beside her in a straight-backed chair, Win gave a half-hearted chuckle. "Think maybe I should just let Emma be my lawyer, Gill? She'd be a hell of a lot better than most I could find."

But though Wesley Gill tried to offer an answering smile, it was plain to Emma that his heart was heavy. He hated locking Papa up, she realized—and she could almost forgive him.

Now, only a short while later, he'd released Win from the small barren cell and sent Clem home so that the three of them could talk. Simple, straight talk.

They had a right to know the evidence.

Then they could begin disproving it.

Emma was glad Corinne had let Tara and Ross take her home. She had enough to do worrying about

Papa; she didn't need to be worried about Corinne, too. The time had finally come to deal with Beau Garrettson's death. To put the cloud of suspicion behind them, once and for all.

"There's two things," Gill said heavily. "One is this here bandanna. We talked about that, Win, remember? You had no idea how it came to be found near Beau's body."

Emma started. *"What?"*

"That's right, honey." Her father leaned back and sighed. "Wes told me about it the first night you came home. Remember how he rode out to the house? Well, it's true that that bandanna is mine, but I told him then and I'm telling you now that I don't know how the hell it came to be near Dead Dog Tree where Garrettson was found. Obviously someone planted it there to throw suspicion on me. And *that's* the man who should be sitting here right now answering these questions."

Emma stared at the bandanna, her heart sinking. When it was displayed in court, the bandanna would be powerful evidence.

She clenched her hands in her lap and tried to stay calm.

"This only proves that someone is trying to frame my father," she said, but the steadiness of tone she strove for was marred by the catch in her voice. "Go on, Sheriff Gill."

"Here's the second piece of evidence, Win—and Emma. The one I found out about this morning. The one that gave me no choice but to come and find you at the church. And," he said sadly, "to put you under arrest. I sat there for hours staring at it, trying to figure out how to explain it. And I just can't do it. The only way to explain this, Win, is to accept the fact that it was you who killed that young man." He blinked his eyes blearily and went on. "That it was you who set a mighty cruel trap for Beau Garrettson."

"The hell I did!" Win surged to his feet. He was trembling with fury, but Emma reached for his arm and gently, insistently pulled him down again.

"Papa, please, we need to see what it is." But her heart was racing as she watched the sheriff lift a sheet of paper from the folder on his desk and stare at it, as if willing it to be different from the last time he'd looked at it.

"May I see it?" she asked and steeled herself as he handed it over in silence.

Outside the sheriff's office, the boardwalk was quiet. It was Sunday afternoon and people were at home with their families, enjoying the fine day. Here in town, an amber cat lazed beneath the awning of Kent's mercantile, and the summer sun beamed golden over the closed storefronts and lampposts, setting the street dust aglitter.

But inside the sheriff's office the silence was deeper, darker. It thundered in her ears as Emma read the paper in disbelief.

Beau Garrettson—meet me near Dead Dog Tree at sunup. Don't tell anyone about this meeting. I might be interested in selling off some of my land. If you want a chance to bid on it, you'll be there when I say. I'll only make this offer once. If

your father or brother find out about this deal before I'm ready, I'll call it off.
   Win Malloy

"I don't believe this," Emma whispered into the horrible silence that followed. "It's your handwriting, Papa. How can this be?"

Win snatched the note from her. His skin was a sickly green by the time he looked up from the page.

Gill watched him, tight-lipped.

"I swear," Win said hoarsely. "I never wrote this letter. I wasn't the one who set a trap for that boy!"

"I guess you'll have to tell that to a jury, Win." Gill's voice was so low Emma had to strain forward to hear it. "But it doesn't look good. Between that and your bandanna—"

"It's a frame-up!" Emma exclaimed. "Can't you see that, Gill? Someone copied his handwriting, copied it exactly, and left his bandanna out near where Beau was found in order to make him look guilty."

"Now who might that be, Emma?" Wearily, the sheriff sagged back in his chair and picked up a pencil, which he began tapping absently against his desk. "You think Jed Garrettson hates your pa so much he'd kill his own boy just to make it look like Win Malloy did it? Or that Tucker would?"

"Of course I don't think that. But who gave you this note? Someone interested in collecting the reward the Garrettsons offered to anyone with information connecting my father to the murder?"

"No, not in this case. Fact is, no one's been able to collect that reward because no one's offered any information until now. And in this case, the reward wasn't the motive in coming forward—''

"Who was it?" Win demanded.

Gill paused with the pencil clenched in his hand. "Guess I may as well tell you. You'll find out soon enough anyway," he sighed. He glanced from Win to Emma and sighed again. "It was Tara McQuaid."

Tara!

Emma felt as though he'd slapped her. "I don't understand," she said shakily. Unable to sit still a moment longer, she jumped up and began to pace about the office, trying to make sense of everything that was happening today.

"Tara's been going to Tall Trees of late, looking through some of Beau's things—searching, I reckon, for little mementos to keep. You know how women are."

His glance shifted to Emma but she only nodded tersely and made no comment. Gill continued. "Apparently neither Jed nor Tucker had even gone into his room after he died. Didn't want to deal with all of his belongings, I guess—maybe the hurt was too raw. It was hard for Tara at first, too, but lately she's gone over there a few times and tried to face it. Anyway, she found a book of poetry she'd given Beau and brought it home with her as a keepsake. She didn't have the heart to open it. Until last night. Guess she got sentimental about the wedding today—hell, I don't know. All I know is that Tara found this note inside the book and she brought it to me this morning when she came to town for the wedding."

Trying to keep up with all he was saying, Emma

turned to eye the note again. Had Tara found this after she'd come to Echo Ranch last night? She must have. Emma could imagine her, alone in her room, mourning her lost love, opening up the book of poetry . . .

There was only one problem. Her father didn't write that note. Someone else did. Someone who had done a damned good job of copying his handwriting because it was all there—the slant of the t's, the curlicue at the bottom of the D's, the bold strokes he used.

"Tara hated turning this over to me, Win. She was all broken up about it. But she had to—for Beau."

"Damn it, Wes, how many times do I have to say this? I didn't write that letter!"

"What about the bandanna?" Peering out from beneath his scraggly gray brows, the sheriff met his friend's glare.

"All I can tell you is that I didn't drop it at Dead Dog Tree. Hell, I never went there that day."

"I want to believe you, Win, Lord knows I do, but it just isn't easy. This is some strong evidence right here and I can't ignore it."

"Well, I can't *accept* it." Emma came forward and stood beside Win's chair. "If you won't find out who is framing my father, I will."

Gill spread his hands. "I can't stop you, Emma, if you want to try to pretend you're one of those Pinkerton detectives. I wish to heaven I could just ignore all this proof and take your father at his word. I do, Win," he said sorrowfully.

Win sucked in his breath, his eyes cold. He didn't answer.

"But right now . . . I gotta lock you back up. Clem will bring you your supper in a while."

Emma hated saying good-bye to her father. He looked older somehow as she watched him march toward the ugly little cell with its high, barred window. He was too big for that cell. He was a man who relished the huge, grand beauty of all of Montana. He belonged out in the clear, open air, riding the range, free as the eagle that wheeled beneath the great blue sky.

This won't be for long, Papa, she vowed silently, then turned around and quickly left the sheriff's office. She had promised her father she'd go to Butte with Ross to meet that lawyer, but it was too late to start out today. They'd have to go tomorrow.

Still she could head over to the McQuaids on the way home to make arrangements with Ross for the trip.

And she needed to speak to Tara.

Tara was fixing supper when she drove up. Emma saw her face in the window, then she rushed outside, wiping her hands on her apron as Emma climbed down from the seat of the buggy.

Tara's chignon was loose, with brown strands of hair sliding forward over her shoulders. She had flour on her cheek, and her eyes shone with dismay as she stared at Emma.

"Sheriff Gill told you, didn't he? Emma, I'm so sorry. So terribly sorry. I didn't want to bring that note to him, you must believe me—"

"I don't blame you, Tara." Hard as it was to accept, Emma knew Tara was only trying to do the right thing. "Now I know why you said at the church that the truth must come out. But you must know deep down that the truth is still a mystery. My father couldn't have written that note. He'd never do anything like that—any more than your father would."

"I know you believe that, Emma." Tara bit her lip. "No one wants to believe something bad of their own father. But the note and the bandanna—"

"How do you know about the bandanna? Did Sheriff Gill tell you about it?"

Tara nodded dejectedly. "Emma, won't you come in out of the sun? Have supper with us. My father and the hands will be back shortly and I'm frying chicken—there's plenty."

"I'm not hungry."

"You're angry with me. You do blame me." Tara sank down on the porch steps and buried her face in her hands. "I never wanted this, Emma. I'm fond of your father, as fond as I am of you."

"It's all right, Tara." Weariness swept through her. Somehow she managed to put one foot before the other to reach the steps. She sank down beside Tara and squeezed her arm. The girl shuddered and lifted a face that glistened with tears.

"I don't blame you, Tara. But I can't eat supper with you. Not tonight. Will you tell your father that I'd like to go meet that lawyer tomorrow?"

Tara dried her tears on her apron and nodded.

"Thank you. I've got to get home and see how Corinne is doing. And try to think."

"Think?"

"About who could have framed my father. You

don't imagine I'm going to sit by and do nothing, do you? Would *you* sit by if it was your father who was wronged?''

''No, Emma, I wouldn't. I understand completely.'' Tara hugged her arms around herself. ''Believe me, I would do the same as you.''

She reached home without incident. It was one of the few times she'd been out lately without being accompanied by one of the ranch hands, as her father had ordered.

But even a whole battalion of gun-toting cowboys hadn't been able to protect her from the one man who'd posed the most danger, Emma thought as she went into the front hall and leaned against the door. The one man who, just by caressing her hair or giving her a half-mocking smile, or touching his mouth to hers, could shatter her heart.

But she had to somehow forget about Tucker Garrettson and think about who might be framing her father. That was all that mattered now.

The house was lonely without her father's hearty presence, his footsteps, his deep ringing laugh. She and Corinne ate supper in silence, did the dishes in silence, worried in silence.

When they bade each other good night, Corinne tried to sound cheering, but Emma could only manage a faint smile and a weak hug.

She went up to bed early, anticipating that the next day would be long and arduous, but sleep wouldn't come. Even the sweet coolness of the night air wafting through her window couldn't soothe her.

Her father was in jail, instead of home where he belonged.

Tucker was at Tall Trees, with that garrulous father of his, instead of holding her in his arms.

Beau Garrettson's killer was out there—free.

And a tiny child was growing within her, a child that might never know either his father or his grandfather.

But not, Emma vowed desperately, *if I have anything to say about it.*

She had grown up without a mother, and though the bond between her and Win was as strong as could be, Emma knew that she wanted even more than that for her child.

For our child.

Because the baby was Tucker's, too.

She had to find a way to tell him. She would go to Tall Trees tomorrow, before leaving for Butte.

Because she now realized that even if he wouldn't believe in her father's innocence, not until she proved it, Tucker had a right to know the truth about his child.

Chapter 24

RED PETERSON AND JIMMY JOE PRATT INTER-
cepted her as she was riding out early the
next morning beneath a gray sky thick with clouds.

"How about if I ride along with you, Miss
Emma?" Jimmy Joe put a hand on Angel's mane and
gave Emma a quick, easy smile.

"No, thanks, I'll be fine."

Her crisp tone made him nod respectfully and step
back, but Red was not so easily deterred. "Now you
wouldn't be forgetting your father's orders, would
you, Emma?"

"I haven't forgotten. But this is something I have
to do myself."

"Fine, Emma, that's just fine. If you let me ride
along with you, I promise not to trouble you none, I'll
just—"

"Surely there's enough to do on this ranch without your tagging after me," Emma snapped. "Besides, I don't need a chaperone. I'm not afraid of the
Garrettsons or their men."

She spurred Angel forward, leaving both men in a blur of dust. But her conscience pricked at her as the mare's long legs swept over the ground at a fast gallop.

It really wasn't fair to take out her frustration and anxiety on her father's men. They were only trying to help and following his orders. It wasn't their fault that the world was upside down, that she now had to face Tucker Garrettson and tell him that like it or not, he was going to be a father.

A lump of tension lay like bread dough in her chest. But at least so far today the nausea hadn't begun. Probably because she hadn't attempted to eat even a morsel of breakfast. She'd slipped out with only a wave to Corinne and a promise to eat something later.

Yet even as she reached the border of Garrettson land, the invisible boundary south of the creek where Malloy property ended and the vast Tall Trees acreage began, the awful queasiness took hold once more.

Emma didn't know if it was due to her pregnancy or to her nervousness over what she had to say to Tucker, but she swallowed hard and ignored the rolling waves in her stomach. She focused instead on the downward winding trail she was following to Tall Trees.

She was starting Angel across the shallow creek when another rider suddenly veered out of the trees. Curt Slade called out to her and reluctantly she halted.

"Where do you think you're going, Miss Emma?" He pulled his horse up sharply and swept an arm in the direction of the opposite bank. "Straight ahead there is Garrettson land. You looking to have your head shot off?''

She eyed him coldly. ''Where I go is none of your business, Slade.''

''I'm foreman of this ranch, and with your father locked up, I'm in charge. That means—''

''That means nothing. You're no more in charge than my mare is. *I'm* in charge until my father is back where he belongs and don't you forget it.''

Slade bit back an angry retort, though he flushed to the roots of his hair. He reminded himself to go easy. He'd already made mistakes with the girl—hell, he'd gone about things all wrong with her from the beginning. It was true that she was more of a handful than he'd anticipated, but he knew he could tame her once he got the chance. After she was his wife, he could do whatever it took to keep her in line, and then he'd make damn sure that she treated him with respect.

But right now she had to be handled tender as a little kitten.

His day was coming. With Win Malloy out of the picture, Echo Ranch was more dependent on him than ever. If he played his cards right, and he would, the girl would grow dependent on him, too, and Malloy would see his way clear to encouraging her to marry him. The rancher would want to see his daughter settled with a strong man who could protect both her and the ranch in the years to come. And to Slade's way of thinking, now that the easterner had vamoosed, there was no one else as well suited to that position, except that son-of-a-bitch Tucker Garrettson.

It was obvious to him that the girl had a soft spot for Garrettson, even though he was her father's enemy.

But she was loyal enough to the old man that she'd never turn her back on him for Garrettson. And if it ever came to that, which it wouldn't, Slade would just make sure Garrettson was out of the way. *Permanently.*

If Emma hadn't happened by that day of the storm, Garrettson might already have joined his brother in the hereafter. But there was no use thinking about might-have-beens.

He had Emma Malloy in his sights right now, and he was neither drunk as he'd been at the dance nor careless as he'd been the day she'd found him teaching Garrettson a lesson. The time had come to make a better impression on her—especially if she was shortly going to become his wife.

So he gave her his broadest smile. "Beg your pardon, Miss Emma. Didn't mean to rile you. Of course you can do as you please."

Her lovely face remained stony. *Patience,* Slade reminded himself as his temper rose again. He subdued the urge to order her to go back home. *Think of her like a wild filly you want to break. Start with a carrot, and the spurs can come later.*

"Why don't you let me ride along with you then, if you have some business with the Garrettsons? That is, if you *do* have business with them. Or are you planning to rustle up a few head of their cattle to get back at them for your pa being in jail?"

He'd meant it as a joke, trying to pry a smile out

of that statue-like face of hers. All it won him was a glare that could freeze a man's innards.

"Get out of my sight, Slade, before I overrule my father and fire you for good this time. He's not here to save you, and the other men will back me up if need be."

"Like hell they will." He caught himself and tried to look apologetic. "Look, we keep getting off on the wrong foot. But all I want to do is protect Echo Ranch, and take care of you while your father isn't here to do it."

"I'm perfectly capable of taking care of myself. Now I suggest you check the north range. Make sure none of the cattle is trapped in Eagle Canyon."

He hated taking orders from a woman. He remembered his ma, how she'd take the switch to him if he was too pokey getting his chores done for her taste. A dull glint came into his eyes.

"Yes, ma'am." He was no kid now. He'd do as he pleased. And he thought he'd stick around and see what Miss Emma Malloy was up to today. He had a right to know why she was visiting the enemy camp.

"Mornin' then, ma'am," he said crisply, doffing his hat. And turned his horse. But he doubled back after Emma had splashed the mare across the creek and started through the winding trail along the foothills that led to Tall Trees.

We'll just see who's really in charge, little girl, Slade thought as he followed at an easy trot.

Emma had never in her life ridden up the wide, tree-lined path to the Tall Trees ranch house before. Well, only once before, but not this far. She and Tara had come here together after school, but this was as far as Emma had gone, even when Tara had run up to join the others. At school that morning, Tucker had mentioned to Pete Sugar that his father had bought a string of horses in Butte, including a still-wild black stallion. He was going to try his hand at breaking it that afternoon.

All of the other children had heard about it by lunchtime, and later, when the school bell rang, they had swarmed from the schoolhouse to Tall Trees. They crowded around the corral to watch and hoot and whistle while Tucker mounted, remounted, and again remounted the horse. Each time, the glistening stallion reared up on its powerful hind legs and bucked until it threw the boy into the dirt. And each time, that boy had dusted off his pants, set his hat back on his head, and vaulted back into the saddle.

He'd finally broken the stallion to the cheers of all the children, and the approving whoops of the Tall Trees ranch hands. And Emma had squinted far into the distance to see Jed Garrettson standing on the porch steps of his house, his big black Stetson shading his eyes as he watched his son triumph.

She'd turned away then, half-ashamed for even being interested. But she and Tucker had tied for first place at a spelling bee the day before, and she'd been angry over not defeating him. She had hoped he'd be unable to stay on the horse, and as embarrassed by his failure as she'd been by hers.

But he hadn't failed. He'd won.

She'd fought back reluctant admiration for her rival, and the next thing she knew, while turning around with a scowl on her lips, she'd confronted Beau Garrettson.

"I—I just happened by and I heard shouting—"

Beau had cut her short. "I know why you're here. Tucker mentioned something about that spelling bee yesterday. Oh, he wasn't bragging or anything like that," Beau had gone on, cocking his head to study her as Emma flushed with anger. "He was just trying to get a conversation going at the supper table, talking about every single thing that happened at school. It's pretty quiet most nights when we all sit down to eat. That bothers him some, I guess. My pa doesn't talk much. Me either, usually."

"Well, you've got a lot to say now," Emma had replied tartly. "What does the spelling bee have to do with my being here?"

"Easy. You're mad and want to see him get thrown on his butt." Beau had chuckled. "But you don't know Tucker. If you think he could fail, you're wrong. Nothing beats him once he puts his mind to something. My little brother doesn't ever give up."

Now, Emma halted on the same spot where she'd had that brief conversation with Beau Garrettson and wondered that she'd forgotten it for all these years. It was probably the only time she'd ever spoken to Beau. He hadn't said much else, had just nodded at her and ridden on, but he hadn't told Tucker that she'd come to watch. She would have known if he had because Tucker would have been sure to taunt her about it and he never did.

She felt a shiver down her back, and for a moment, it was as if the ghost of Beau Garrettson was there, urging her not to give up either—to find out who had really killed him.

She'd have to, it seemed, if she was going to free her father from the charges. *Tucker isn't the only one who doesn't give up,* she thought resolutely, and sent Angel trotting toward the house.

I guess with us for parents, our child is going to be a stubborn little thing.

That made her smile for the first time in days, and she was smiling still as Jed Garrettson stomped out of the barn just as she rode up.

"What do *you* want?" he demanded.

"And good morning to you, too, Mr. Garrettson." He had his chaps and spurs on and looked ready to ride out for a day's hard work. Thinking of how weak he'd been that morning he'd come looking for Tucker, she wondered how wise it was for him to undertake strenuous ranch work, but quickly reminded herself that Jed Garrettson's health was not her concern.

"I'm looking for your son."

"What the hell do you want with Tucker?"

"That's between him and me."

He stared at her. Gaped was more like it. The bushy brows drew together and then he seemed to be weighing what to say next.

"Hmph. Well, come inside. I'll get him for you."

It was a strange feeling, stepping inside the house. The rooms were big and cool, but a shadowy dimness seemed to cling to the faded gold-flocked paper on the walls and the plain, old-fashioned furniture. Emma had to quell the desire to draw back the heavy green curtains on all the windows, to sweep out the mustiness and let sunshine and laughter in.

There were few feminine touches, and the few that she saw she knew must be remnants from the mother Tucker and Beau had lost so long ago. A lovely glass figurine of a woman playing a harp caught her eye. So graceful, so beautiful. It rested on the mantel beside a photograph, and with a small lurch of her heart, Emma realized that the woman in the photograph must be Tucker's mother.

She was slender and prim, her fair hair piled atop her head, her gloved hands folded on her lap as she sat upon a flowered wing chair. She had a pointed little chin, a dainty upturned nose. Her eyes were quiet. There was a hint of a shy smile at the corners of lips that were long and bow-shaped.

She looked as light and elegant as that figurine, Emma thought. But everything else in the room was heavy, masculine. If ever there had been lace curtains at the windows or pretty throw pillows on the horsehair sofa, they were long gone.

She was drawn to the spinet against the wall, beneath the elk head. It was rosewood, delicate and lovely, and full of dust.

"Did your wife play?" she asked softly.

"She did." His voice was harsh. "No one's touched those keys since she died. I ought to sell the damned thing. There's probably some woman in town who would like it. Don't know why I keep it here."

"You have to keep some memories," Emma said quietly. She turned and studied him and for a moment she saw an expression of pain in his eyes, pain which was quickly covered up by a glower as his eyebrows swooped together.

"Memories aren't worth a damn. You can't snuggle up to 'em on a cold winter's night."

"Sometimes you can. Through photographs or little stories of times spent together. Don't you ever look at your wife's picture? Or talk about her with Tucker?"

"What for? It won't bring her back."

"No, but it can keep her alive, in your heart." Emma thought of all the stories she'd always loved hearing her father tell of her own mother, of their courtship, their struggles to make a go of Echo Ranch. There was one story about Katherine taking all the bed linens to the stream to wash, and a storm had blown up and carried everything away.

"I don't need you poking your nose into my life or my business, young lady. Don't you have enough to worry about, considering your father's going to trial one of these days for murdering my son?"

The words lashed through her. Emma clenched her teeth against their sting.

"Why do you hate him so much?" she cried furiously, advancing toward him with swift steps. "Is it all because you lost a poker game? That wasn't his fault—he beat you fair and square!"

"The hell he did! I don't know where he got that ace but it wasn't from the deck we were playing with!"

"Of course it was! My father never cheated at anything in his life. Anyone in the valley will vouch for him. Ross McQuaid, Wesley Gill, Doc Carson—

all of the ranchers in the Cattleman's Association—
everyone! And if you didn't want to lose part of your
land, you never should have wagered it.''

Garrettson's face was flushed. His hands shook as
he lifted them, as if to ward off her words. Because
deep down, he knew it was true. ''That's enough, little
girl. I reckon it's time you left this house and ride off
of Tall Trees land before I forget you're a lady and
lose my temper.''

Emma wanted nothing more than to ride away
from Tall Trees. But she couldn't. Not yet.

''I won't leave until I see Tucker.''

His lip curled. ''You chasing after my boy? Think
you'll get your claws on the rest of Tall Trees by
trying to rope him in, is that it?''

From somewhere inside she drew upon the icy
haughtiness she'd seen girls in Philadelphia display
when someone they considered their inferior dared to
speak to them. She would not dignify the rantings of
this disagreeable old man with a response.

''Kindly inform Tucker that I am here to see
him—now.''

Jed stared at her, straight and proud as the queen
of Sheba. If he wasn't mad enough to spit, he could
almost admire her spunk. As it was, she'd shaken him
by what she'd said about memories, about his wife.
He'd tried to forget Dorothea all these years and had
been absolutely miserable for it. Maybe he should
have tried to remember instead. But the thought
stirred him up—this outspoken Malloy girl stirred him
up.

The sooner she saw Tucker and got the hell out, the better.

He stalked from the parlor. She heard him calling from the stairs, but there was no answer.

When Garrettson reappeared in the doorway, he was frowning. "Hold on. I'll check the stable."

A few moments later he returned, shaking his head. "Nebrasky says Tucker rode out a while ago. Don't know where he went or when he'll be back."

Disappointment twisted through her, along with a tiny flicker of relief. And a wave of nausea followed.

Suddenly Emma wondered if she'd even have been able to summon the right words to tell Tucker this morning—carrying a child certainly seemed to be draining a good deal of her strength and her energy.

Well, now she had no choice. It would have to wait until tonight at the earliest and possibly tomorrow.

"Will you please tell Tucker I was here? And that I must speak with him?"

How easily she fell into the cool dignity she'd mastered back east. No one, least of all Jed Garrettson, must know how much it was costing her not to let her shoulders sag with disappointment and uncertainty.

"I'll tell him. And by the way," Jed added as she walked toward the door. "I heard from Ross that you're off to Butte today to try to get a lawyer for your pa. Won't do much good—he's guilty as sin and he's going to pay. Sorry to be blunt, little girl, but—"

The nausea clutched at her. Emma grasped at the hall table before her, taking deep breaths.

"Hey there—what's wrong?"

"N—nothing." Emma willed her legs not to give out. She closed her eyes as her stomach roiled and waited for the queasiness to subside.

"Mr. Garrettson," she managed to gasp out between clenched teeth. "You're . . . wrong. Dead wrong. I'm going to prove that my father never hurt Beau."

She paused, taking more deep breaths.

"You're looking mighty green, girl. What in tarnation is the matter with you?"

Emma knew she must be imagining the sharp edge of concern in his voice. Jed Garrettson wouldn't care if she dropped dead on his floor. "I'm f—fine."

The queasiness eased. Emma let go of the table and dragged in another deep breath. "Just tell Tucker I was here."

She left the ranch house without glancing back and didn't see the bitterness of Garrettson's frown, or the flash of shame that suddenly replaced the anger in his eyes as he went to the window and watched her ride away.

Chapter 25

TUCKER STOOD IN GRIM SILENCE AT HIS brother's grave.

He had no idea why he was here. He'd ridden out early without even taking time for breakfast. The sky was cloudy, threatening a downpour. And there was work to be done—fence posts that needed mending before the rain came.

But here he was, beneath a lovely spreading willow, gazing at Beau's tombstone, which rose up hard and gray and cold from the earth.

It was a pretty spot, a deep grassy clearing within sight of the foothills, not far from the river. He could hear the water murmuring. His mother's grave was only a few feet away. He'd placed a bunch of wildflowers on it, as he did each time he came here. But this was the first time he'd been back since Beau was laid to rest.

"I guess I need some answers," he said to no one in particular.

Answers.

He kept seeing Emma's face as she proclaimed her father's innocence. And then he thought of the bandanna, the note.

Win Malloy had shot Beau, he must have.

It was only his feelings for Emma which were causing this nagging feeling of doubt, this wishfulness that it was anyone but him.

It would destroy Emma if her father were to hang. The closeness between them, the love and loyalty was there for all to see. She'd be devastated by the trial, by the hanging. He thought of her pain, and pain sliced through him.

He leaned against the willow, stared at the gravestone, and wished like hell Beau could tell him just what had happened that morning near Dead Dog Tree.

Things had been nagging at him ever since that day someone took a shot at Emma. He'd never figured out who had done that. And then there'd been the Echo Ranch cattle that had been poisoned. He knew damn well he and his father had never given orders for that.

So who had?

Someone trying to stir up further enmity between the two families, to take advantage of it for their own purposes.

Maybe whoever had done those things had also shot Beau. They'd hoped Win Malloy would be blamed, just as the Garrettsons were blamed for the poisoning.

Who would stand to gain by a range war, by having the Garrettsons and Malloys hellbent on destroying each other?

The gravesite was peaceful and quiet. Too quiet.

If he was going to find answers, he'd have to find them somewhere else.

EMMA KNEW SHE SHOULD GO HOME, PUT ON A DECENT dress, and try to prepare herself for the trip to Butte, but on the way back from Tall Trees, she veered toward Empire Ranch.

Ross McQuaid had arranged to call for her at noon, so she had plenty of time. First, there was something else she needed to do.

She had an idea and wanted to talk to Tara about it. It had dawned on her sometime in the middle of the night that if Tara had found one clue among Beau Garrettson's belongings, there might be another one. Only this time, it might lead to the real killer.

Perhaps in riffling through Beau's papers and possessions, Tara had seen something significant, but hadn't recognized it at the time.

I'll have to make it clear to Tara that I don't blame her for turning the note over to Sheriff Gill.

With some prodding, Tara might remember something else, something she'd seen, or something Beau had said or done that might indicate who would have wanted him dead.

Whoever it was had been clever and determined enough not only to plan everything out ahead of time, but also to figure out a way to blame her father. Someone who well knew the tension in Whisper Valley between the two families, who knew the history, someone who had been able to get into the Malloy house without attracting suspicion and steal her father's bandanna. And, she suddenly realized, the person must have also stolen some document with his handwriting on it and then painstakingly copied it.

If she could figure out who that someone was, she would be able to get her father out of jail without the help of any lawyer.

There was no sign of Tara or of Ross when she dismounted in front of the McQuaid home.

"Tara! Mr. McQuaid!"

Only the sighing of the wind as it swept through the empty yard and surrounding pasture land answered her.

Emma glanced at the corral with its sagging posts, at the barn which needed a fresh coat of paint, at the chicken pen where squawking hens raced and flapped their wings.

Not a soul in sight.

She went up the porch steps and rapped on the door. "Tara?"

More silence came from deep inside the house.

Go home. Get ready to meet the lawyer. You'll have a chance to talk to her later.

But something stopped her from turning away and riding for home. She pushed open the door and stepped inside the McQuaid ranch house.

She'd been here many times before, but not recently, not since returning from Philadelphia. The parlor was smaller than that at her own home, but it was cozy and attractive. The sofa was dotted with pretty needlepointed pillows and there were several comfortable chairs grouped around the fireplace. Part of the charm of the room, Emma realized, going in further, was the lovely paintings adorning the walls, not only in the parlor, but in the hall, and the dining room as well. She wandered through, gazing up at them in admiration. They had all been painted by Tara.

Strange, she remembered Tara's fondness for drawing and painting, and how talented she was, but she hadn't known that she was so dedicated. Tara rarely even mentioned her painting. But it was obviously a passion with her.

The paintings on the walls were lovely—dreamy pastels depicting flowers arranged in vases or vivid still lifes of fruit spilling from a basket across a cherry wood table.

In the dining room, a plain wood frame showcased horses cavorting in a meadow. Emma recognized the spot, near the mouth of the creek.

But there were other pictures that were reproductions of famous works. Emma recognized several that she had seen in museums or in books, among them numerous Audubon prints and the artist James Whistler's *Arrangement in Grey and Black No. 1-Portrait of the Artist's Mother*.

Tara's dainty signature with the tiny flourish at the tip of the "T" was visible in the lower right-hand corner of each.

Yet as Emma moved from painting to painting a chill whispered along her shoulder blades. Something about the paintings disturbed her.

Emma stared at the staircase in the center of the hall. She wanted to go up and see Tara's room. She felt drawn there. Surely there was no harm; Tara wouldn't mind if she left a note on her bureau, asking her to try to remember everything she could about the items found among Beau's belongings.

Emma climbed the stairs and went into Tara's room. The easel and paints were lined up beside the narrow bed with its simple yellow quilt. There were paintbrushes and a paint-splattered smock that had once been an apron folded over the back of a chair. There were no paintings on the wall, Emma noted in surprise. None at all. Only faded yellow and white flowered wallpaper, peeling sadly at the edges.

"That's odd." She spoke softly to herself, musing.

Then she saw, sticking out from beneath the bed, what looked to be the edge of a drawing. Reaching down, she pulled it out, and to her surprise saw that there was not only one drawing, but a jumbled stack of them.

The first one was a pen and ink sketch of Beau Garrettson. Emma's heart gave a sorrowful little jump as she recognized the thick brown hair, the strong jaw so like Tucker's, the serious eyes set in the strong, thoughtful face.

It was lovingly drawn, and Emma felt a lump forming in her throat as she studied it.

The next drawing was of the Tall Trees ranch house, at sunset. Gorgeous violet light streaked across the sky, and the gold-tipped mountains loomed gray and purple and black in the distance.

Tara had drawn the home where she planned to live with Beau.

It was so sad.

The third picture made Emma stare.

It was of Dead Dog Tree, with its dead and mangled limbs, the splintered trunk where lightning had struck one year, killing Sam Spenser's dog during a summer storm. This was the site where Beau Garrettson had been shot in the back.

As Emma traced a finger along the page, she saw that this picture was different from the others, startlingly so. It was painted for one thing, not sketched. And it was starker, darker in tone and style. The pencil lines held a bold harshness, the light was an eerie orange glow that permeated the sky. And the spot of blood on the grass . . .

Emma realized that Tara had marked the place where Beau must have fallen with a smear of red paint.

The picture behind it was almost identical. And the one behind that—and the next—except that in each one, the smear of blood grew larger, darker. By the last one, it dominated the entire painting, nearly covering the page.

Emma's blood went cold. She felt ill. She dropped the paintings and they scattered across the floor. But she didn't pause to gather them up, she spun away, suddenly needing to get out of this room, away from this house.

She started toward the door, and just then her eye fell upon a folded sheet of paper lying just beneath the first sketch of Dead Dog Tree and she stopped in her tracks.

Cold fear licked down her spine.

She recognized that green-lined ledger paper, recognized the strong, firm handwriting slanting across the page. She yanked it up and held it between fingers that shook.

It was a page from her father's ledger books, a page listing head of cattle, number of calves, market price, and other pertinent facts, written last autumn, she saw, as she found the date: September 22, 1881.

How on earth did it get here?

The answer shocked her like a pail of ice water poured over her head.

It was here because Tara had stolen it. She had stolen it from Papa's study, from his ranch ledger books so that she could copy his handwriting. So she could make it appear that he had lured Beau to Dead Dog Tree on the morning of his death. . . .

"You shouldn't have come up here, Emma."

Tara's voice sounded sweet and sad.

Emma let out a strangled scream and dropped the ledger sheet. It fluttered to the floor, forgotten, as she stared into the calm velvet brown eyes of the friend she'd known all her life.

Chapter 26

"TARA! YOU—YOU STARTLED ME. I WAS JUST looking for some writing paper so that I could leave you a note."

Her heart thumping, Emma stooped to retrieve the ledger page from the floor, praying Tara hadn't seen what it was. She noticed the back of it for the first time—some kind of map had been scribbled there, with arrows and crude markings. Crumpling it in her hand, she stuffed it into the pocket of her riding skirt and kept talking, trying to sound calm. "I'm so glad you came back before I left."

"Don't play games with me, Emma." Tara smoothed her hair behind her ear and smiled. "I'm too smart for that, you know. You're not glad at all. You're frightened, aren't you?"

When Emma said nothing, Tara's smile deepened. "That's good," she said softly, pleasantly. "You should be. Because now you understand I'm going to have to kill you, too."

Something in that smug, almost distracted tone shot anger through Emma in a white-hot blast.

"I'm not afraid of you. You're the one who should be afraid. You've done terrible things, Tara, and I don't know why, but you're going to be punished for them."

"Do you think so?" Tara tilted her head to one side, consideringly. "I don't. Your father will be punished for them, not me. And of course, now *you* will have to suffer, too. But I'm going to get everything I ever wanted. Everything I ever deserved."

"We'll see about that." Emma started toward the door. "Get out of my way."

But Tara leaped forward as Emma tried to brush past her. She grabbed Emma and shoved her backward. The force of the shove sent Emma toppling into the easel, knocking it over, scattering paints across the floor.

Emma landed on her side, pain throbbing through her elbow.

"This is one time you're not going to win, Miss Emma Malloy. Neither you, nor your father. It's my turn. My turn and my father's turn to have everything we should have had years ago!"

Emma scrambled up. Red paint, like the blood in the painting, dripped across her gray riding skirt.

She forced her gaze away from it and stared instead at Tara's pretty, freckled face. Her eyes looked darker than ever. But she still looked just like Tara, sweet, kind, amiable Tara.

"What kind of a monster are you?" Emma whispered.

Tara laughed. "Remember, I told you that people are not always what they appear? You didn't pay attention. That was your mistake," she chided.

"There must be a reason why you've done these things." Emma slipped her hand into the pocket of her skirt as she talked.

She had her derringer—thank heavens. She would draw it out and force Tara to go with her to Sheriff Gill's office and make her tell the truth.

But first she would know the answer herself.

"Why don't you explain what you meant about your turn to get everything you should have had years ago."

"You already know," Tara reproved her, staying planted where she was so that Emma could not get to the door without passing her. "You must have always known."

Emma shook her head.

"The ranch, the land. It should have been ours."

Blankly, Emma stared at her. "You are quite mad," she said emphatically, and the words sparked an eerie flame of anger in Tara's eyes.

"You think so? Well, my father would have won that poker game if *your* father hadn't cheated. He had the cards to win—a straight flush. He would have been the one to beat Jed Garrettson and acquire all that land—the rich beautiful grazing land and five thousand head of cattle that *your* father turned into Echo Ranch. It should have been *our* empire, Empire Ranch." Tara took a step closer, her cheeks now flushed a bright red. "But your father snuck an ace from his sleeve and laid down a royal flush. And Jed Garrettson lost that land—and so did we.''

Stunned, Emma could only stare. ''No,'' she gasped at last. ''That's wrong, Tara. My father never cheated. Your own father was there—he must have told you what happened. There was no cheating involved!''

''He told me all right. He told me that he saw your father slip the ace into his hand. He only kept quiet because Win was his friend and he didn't want Jed Garrettson to shoot him on the spot!''

''That's a damned lie!''

''It all should have been mine, Emma. Everything that Echo Ranch has become. All the cattle, all the wealth. I should have been the one to go east to school, live in Philadelphia, have fine dresses, meet eligible young men. I should have been able to go to art school, study painting, travel to Europe, and learn from the masters—I might even have become famous. . . . '' Tears sheened her eyes. ''I have a gift, Emma, and the world deserved to share in it.''

In a twinkling, she brightened, smiling so widely her dimples bloomed. ''And they will, after all. You see, after your body is discovered, following a *dreadful* accident, and after your father is hanged for Beau's murder—guess who's going to buy up every inch of Echo Ranch. That's right.'' She beamed as Emma went white. ''Me. I have money now—and a partner who knows how to get more. And since I do all of *my* father's books, he'll believe me when I tell him we can afford it, that we've been making a much more substantial profit than he ever realized.''

She went on with enthusiasm. "So my partner and I are going to buy your ranch together—and he's going to stay on and run it, and I'm going to go east for a while to study." Her tone turned haughty. "You won't have to offer me the loan of your dresses—I'll be able to buy any gown I want. I'm going to become the toast of Europe!"

"I don't understand." Emma studied Tara's rapt face, wondering at how the girl she had known had become the ruthless woman before her. "You killed Beau, didn't you, Tara? But why? How did that figure into your plan?"

"Beau." Tara gave a sad little shudder. "I never planned to kill him, Emma, not at first. I was going to marry him. I cared for him. And, he had something few other men had—except for Tucker, of course."

"Tall Trees." Emma's knees were shaking. She wanted desperately to sit down, but feared making a move and interrupting Tara while she was in the mood to boast about her plans. She had to hear it all.

"Exactly." Tara smiled approvingly. "Tall Trees. My partner and I began some time ago to cause all the trouble we could between the Garrettsons and the Malloys, doing our best to get a range war going. He even jumped your foreman one night and roughed him up with some of his boys, figuring Tucker's father and the Tall Trees men would be blamed. We hoped your pa would either be killed in the course of it all, or he would finally just give up and agree to sell to the Garrettsons, especially if he didn't want you to be in the thick of trouble when you came back. And then, as Mrs. Beau Garrettson, I'd finally have Tall Trees *and*

Echo Ranch. I'd have everything I should have had all along—plus interest.''

A horrible little laugh came from her throat. Emma's mouth went dry.

''But there was one problem,'' Tara added.

''What . . . was that?''

''My partner. He and I fell in love. We hadn't expected that, but it happened. He is much more exciting than Beau was, and he made me see that we could have anything we wanted if we worked together. He didn't mind my marrying Beau—we could still be together whenever we wanted, no one would have to know. You have no idea how thrilling it has been, making all our plans, meeting secretly, fooling everyone.'' Her smile was dreamy. ''The sweet little schoolteacher was not at all what everyone thought she was, you see. But there was one little hitch,'' Tara went on regretfully, her gaze shifting downward to the pen and ink drawing of Beau on the floor. ''Poor Beau caught us together.''

Emma's fingers closed over her derringer. She wasn't ready to slide it out of her pocket, not yet. She wanted to hear what else Tara had to say. The girl was rambling on, her eyes filled with dreams and fantasies—and murder.

''We were making love out there in the foothills one afternoon, and Beau just happened by. It was pure bad luck. He looked so stunned, so hurt, I felt sorry for him. But then he punched my partner—nearly broke his jaw—and told me he wanted nothing more to do with me. He called me names, Emma, that were not very nice at all. Not gentlemanly. He said he wouldn't marry me to save his life.''

Emma felt the air in the room choking her. She needed to get away from Tara, from the ugliness in her foul little soul, from her madness. But not yet. She had to find out all she could, get every bit of information for Sheriff Gill—and for Tucker.

"So you killed him." She said it quietly. "Because he wouldn't marry you? Because he spoiled your plan? Why?"

"Because I couldn't let anyone find out about my partner, about what we were doing. Emma, everyone knows me as the nice, sensible schoolteacher, Ross McQuaid's sweet little daughter. If Beau had decided to tell his father or Tucker what he'd found out about me, how I was cheating on him, it would have ruined me. Besides, he'd spoiled my plan to become part of Tall Trees. I wasn't pleased with him about that.'' She shrugged.

"So I figured out a way that Beau could still be useful to me. It meant killing him, of course, before he could say anything to anyone, and making it look as if your father pulled the trigger.'' She nearly hugged herself with satisfaction. "Of course my partner was the one who actually fired the shot, but I thought of it. All by myself. Brilliant, wasn't it? And it was so easy to steal the neckerchief and your father's ledger page—I was always welcome at your house, wasn't I?'' she asked with a giggle.

The hair at Emma's nape prickled. Such evil. Such cold-blooded horrifying evil. She swallowed hard and forced herself to look into Tara's gloating eyes. "You're forgetting about me," she said quietly. "Did you think I'd just leave Whisper Valley? Sell to you and hightail it out of here? You should have known better, Tara."

"Oh, I didn't forget about you. I thought about you a lot, Emma. I always think about you. About how you've always had everything that should have been mine." Her eyes narrowed. She took a step toward Emma, then stopped herself. She continued speaking, slowly, deliberately. "At first we tried to frighten you—we figured it would make you more likely to want to sell later. My partner shot at you one day when you were out riding." She nodded as Emma gave a start. "He wasn't really aiming to kill you then, just scare you a bit," Tara explained.

She might have been instructing her students in an arithmetic lesson for all the emotion she showed. "And if you thought it was the Garrettsons taking a shot at you, so much the better. But I figured it would only help convince you later, after your father was hanged, that you were better off leaving Whisper Valley."

"I'm not leaving Whisper Valley. And my father isn't going to hang. You are, Tara. Either that, or you're going to prison."

Emma pulled out the derringer and pointed it at Tara's heart. "Get moving. We're going to town. You're going to tell Sheriff Gill everything you just told me."

Tara pursed her lips. "Put the gun away, Emma. I'm not going with you."

"Start moving right now or I'll shoot you in the

arm for starters.'' Emma gestured with the gun. *''Move!''*

She followed at a careful distance as Tara turned and walked toward the door.

Emma followed her all the way downstairs, watching Tara warily. As they headed out onto the porch she saw that the clouds had grown thicker and darker, and it was starting to rain. A gray leaden downpour pattered across the porch and the weed-strewn grass.

She spotted Tara's horse in the corral and jerked the gun that way. ''Come on. Saddle up and then . . .''

She got no farther. As she stepped off the porch, she felt something hard and sharp ram into the center of her back.

''Drop the gun,'' a man's voice ordered.

Fear crashed through her chest. But she managed to hold onto the gun. That voice—it was oddly familiar. But before she had time to try to place it, she heard the click of a safety. Tara had turned around and was smiling joyfully at the man behind her.

''Drop it!'' he commanded again.

Reluctantly, she let the derringer fall into the dirt. Rain spattered her face as she turned her head to see the man behind her.

It was Jimmy Joe Pratt.

And in the same instant, she remembered where she'd heard his voice before. In the bank. It had belonged to the leader of the outlaw gang. The man who had hit her and gotten away.

''Say hello to my partner, Emma.'' Tara spoke as if from a long ways away. But she was right there, picking up the derringer, dropping it into the pocket of her blue serge riding skirt.

Emma glanced from one to the other of them. "You two deserve each other," she said with disgust. But inside she was filled with fear. Not only fear for herself, but for the child she was carrying. Tucker's child.

She had to get away.

"Take her to the camp on Elk Mountain," Tara said quickly. "You'll have to kill her and make it look like an accident."

"That's easy enough, but Tara, listen. I was just in town on Echo Ranch business." He flung a smug grin at Emma who stood sick and silent before him. "And I heard that Carter got himself arrested in Helena by some marshal and he had what was left of his share of the bank loot on him. It's only a matter of time before he spills the beans about where the rest of it is stashed. I'm going to have to dig up the money and get out of Montana—lay low for a while."

"For how long?" Tara cried, then she quickly shook her head. "Never mind. We'll figure it out later—I'll go to the camp with you so we can talk. But Jimmy Joe, my father will be back here any minute to fetch the buggy—he's planning to drive over to Echo Ranch and take Emma to Butte," she added desperately.

"Then we'd better head out. You heard the lady," Pratt gave Emma a shove toward her horse. "Let's go."

"You can't possibly think you'll get away with

this." Emma whirled toward Tara. "Give up now before it gets any worse. No one else has to die—"

"Don't you dare tell me what to do! You stole the life I should have had, you stole my glorious future, and now you want to tell me to give up—to give up everything I worked for! The hell I will!" Her eyes flashed. She reached up and slapped Emma as hard as she could.

"Get her out of here before I forget I want it to look like an accident and kill her right now!" she said angrily.

"Tara!"

This time the voice belonged to Ross McQuaid. Emma watched as Tara spun toward the shed alongside the house. All of the color drained from her face. Her father stood outlined against the doorway, his eyes filled with horror.

"My girl, my sweet, darlin' Tara—what in tarnation is going on?"

Chapter 27

"BOY, I THINK IT'S TIME YOU TOLD ME. WHAT the hell is going on between you and that Malloy girl?"

Striding across the kitchen floor after having downed a mug of steaming coffee, Tucker was headed back out into the gray drizzle, but his father's words stopped him short.

He turned around.

Jed was framed in the door that led from the hall. He had a mug of coffee in one hand, and as Tucker looked at him stone-faced, Jed came forward, set the mug down on the kitchen table so hard that coffee sloshed over, and barked out, "Answer me, son. She came here to see you today. Go figure that. A Malloy coming to this door. I think it's time you told me what's going on between you two."

"Emma was here?" Tucker's voice was sharp. "What did she say? What did she want?"

"Wanted to talk to you. If I didn't know better, I'd think the two of you were sweet on each other. Tell me I'm wrong, boy, I'm begging you, tell me I'm wrong.''

Tucker's eyes gleamed suddenly. ''You've never begged for anything in your life,'' he retorted with rough dismissal.

Jed snorted and then gave a reluctant grin. ''Damn straight. But I'd do more than beg to keep you from getting mixed up with a Malloy. Any more than you already are, that is. She was mighty set on seeing you. Mighty disappointed you weren't here.''

''I went to Echo Ranch this morning to look for her. We missed each other.'' Now why in hell did he tell his father that? He'd gone there straight from Beau's gravesite, thinking that maybe if he and Emma put their heads together, they might come up with something—a clue that could indicate someone else killed Beau, someone other than her father. Even to himself, Tucker was hesitant to admit that Win might be innocent, but for Emma's sake—and Beau's—he could no longer deny the possibility.

But imagine Emma coming here. A warmth licked through him. She was courageous, he'd grant her that. But—the last time he'd seen her, she'd been furious with him, so furious he'd thought she'd never forgive him. What could be so important that she'd suddenly come to Tall Trees to find him?

''Pop, this matters.'' He tried to control the worry stabbing through him. ''Tell me exactly what she said. Do you have any notion why she wanted to talk to me? Was she all right?''

''Seemed all right. Feisty as always. But in that

kind of sweet way she has.'' Jed broke off and forced his lips into a frown.

"Don't start thinking I'm not set against her," he warned hastily. "If she wasn't the daughter of that no-good, yellow-livered, cheating murderer, I might not mind her coming around, but she is, and she's got to be up to something, you mark my words."

Tucker just stared at his father in silent amazement. Emma was incredible. Despite the long-standing enmity between their families, his father sounded half-sweet on her himself.

"Hmph," Jed said suddenly, taking a turn about the kitchen. "Now that you mention it . . . " This time his frown was genuine. "She did look a mite out of sorts."

Tucker tried to control the fear clenching through him. He remembered how pale she'd looked at the wedding, before Gill showed up to arrest Win Malloy. She hadn't seemed well then either. "Damn, could she still be hurting from the time that bastard hit her during the bank hold-up?" he mused aloud, and now it was his fist that slammed against the table.

Jed went to the stove and lifted the coffeepot. He poured more coffee into his mug. "If you ask me, she looked green around the gills. And she was a tad unsteady on her feet." Something about the way Emma Malloy had looked reminded him of something he'd seen before . . . a long time ago. When?

"Damned if I don't know." He slapped his thigh. The words rushed out before he realized what he was saying. "She looked an awful lot like the way your ma looked, when she was carrying Beau and you—"

With a little choke, he broke off.

Stunned, Tucker tried to remember how to breathe. He felt as if someone had rammed him in the stomach with a fence post.

"She looked . . . like *that?*"

Jed nodded. His eyes glinted with fire as he studied his son, awful suspicion dawning. "Don't you tell me . . . you and her . . . you didn't . . . "

From the dazed expression on Tucker's face as he struggled to digest what Jed had described, the older man suddenly knew the truth.

"Damn it, boy! She's pretty enough, but she's a—"

"A Malloy, Pa. I know." Tucker glared at him. "Where was she headed? Did she say?"

"I already knew. Heard it myself from Ross."

"Where?"

"Going to Butte with McQuaid to meet some lawyer about Malloy's trial. Don't know if they're meeting at Echo Ranch or at Ross's place—"

But he was talking to himself. The kitchen door slammed behind Tucker, and his son had sprinted all the way to the corral before Jed could even let out a string of oaths.

Chapter 28

WITH MINGLED HOPE AND TREPIDATION, EMMA watched Ross McQuaid approach them through the drizzle, his jaw frozen in disbelief. Her heart was hammering. Jimmy Joe Pratt still held the gun pressed against the small of her back.

"It's over, Tara," she said quickly. "It's no use. Stop this now, before anyone else gets hurt—"

"Shut up!" Tara shouted.

Quick as lightning, Pratt snaked his gun arm around Emma's throat and yanked her back against his chest, using his free hand to twist her arm behind her as she cried out in pain.

"Hey! You let her go." Appalled, Ross McQuaid sprinted toward him. But Tara jumped into his path.

"Father—go away! This doesn't concern you."

"Doesn't concern me? Tara, what's wrong with you, girl? This is Jimmy Joe Pratt—he works for Win. He's hurting Emma." He swung back and grabbed at Pratt's arm. "Let her go, you son-of-a-bitch."

Pratt kept his stranglehold on Emma, but released

her arm long enough to shove Ross away from him. The older man went sprawling into the dirt.

"Keep away from me, old man," Pratt snarled in a tone that made Emma's blood freeze.

"Father, leave him alone." Frantic and breathless, Tara began helping Ross to his knees. Light rain soaked her hair, her cheeks, and dampened her lace-trimmed white blouse and serge skirt. "He's doing what I ask. He's working with me, with us. Please, I can't explain now."

"Explain what?" Ross asked in a hoarse whisper. He pushed himself to his feet, staring hard at his daughter.

"Tell me what's going on here, Tara. Right now. Emma is your dearest friend. I can't believe you'd stand by and see her hurt—"

"We're the ones who've been hurt, Father. You and I! By the Malloys stealing our land, our cattle. Echo Ranch should have been all ours! And now I'm going to get it back for you, for both of us—"

"No!" Ross began scrubbing at his eyes, as if he could rub out the image before him of Tara's face alight with hate. "You don't know what you're saying."

"You're the one who told me that Win Malloy cheated at that poker game—that otherwise you would have won!"

"Tara, no. *No.*" Ross's face blanched. Raindrops slid from the brim of his hat. "I told you that when you were a little girl. It was only a story. Maybe just the way I wanted things to be. I wanted you to think . . . that if our luck had been different, if things had gone different, we'd have had a big fancy spread like Emma and Win. I didn't mean no harm—it was just a tall tale . . . just a tale . . . ''

His voice trailed off. Tara looked as if he'd told her she was born on the moon. ''I don't believe you.''

''It's true, honey,'' he said brokenly. ''Win won fair and square. I had nothing that hand, nothing. My luck ran bad the whole night. I just liked dreaming about winning a big spread, and so I told you my dream, but it was never true.''

''They killed Beau, Mr. McQuaid.'' Emma choked out the words, feeling as if her legs would collapse at any moment. ''He caught her cheating on him with this outlaw, Pratt, and so Pratt shot him, and Tara made it look like my father—''

''I had to do it!'' Tara cried. ''And I have to kill Emma, too. I've come so close—I've got to have Echo Ranch. Maybe not Tall Trees, but Echo Ranch is going to be mine. Jimmy Joe and I—''

Suddenly she tore her gaze from her father's stricken face. She spun toward the dark-haired outlaw with the pale ice-blue eyes.

''You have to get her out of here. Before someone else shows up. Push her off Elk Mountain—I don't care. I'll meet you there tonight at the camp and we'll go dig up the money together.''

Ross McQuaid moved then. Lumberingly, desperately, he dove for the gun Pratt held, shoving Emma away. She stumbled into the damp earth, scraping her hands and elbows on the scattered pebbles. With an oath, Pratt managed to hold onto the gun, but just barely. Both men tumbled down into the mud as the rain fell.

"Papa—no! Don't! Jimmy Joe, don't hurt him!" In horror, Tara sprang forward, but she wasn't quick enough. One moment the two men were struggling, rolling on the ground, and the next moment, the gunshot exploded like cannon fire.

"No!" Tara screamed into the thin, empty air.

Emma scrambled up to her knees, staring in sick dismay.

Ross McQuaid had jackknifed backward. He lay on his side among the pebbles and weeds. Blood streamed from a gaping wound in his chest.

"I didn't mean to do it," Pratt exclaimed. "Tara, honey, he jumped me—you saw for yourself that he jumped me!" A thin plume of blue smoke drifted up from the gun as Pratt gripped it tight and swung it toward Emma. She had just risen to her feet.

"Don't you move," he shouted. He stalked over to Tara, who stood numbly, staring at her father's prone form. Keeping the gun leveled at Emma, Pratt shook Tara's arm.

"Listen, honey lamb, we've got to get out of here. We've got to get to the money. Let's ride to the camp, get rid of her there, and then at dawn, we'll head out to dig up the money.

"F—father!" Tara pulled away from him and dropped to her knees beside Ross. "Can you hear me?" she whispered.

Ross's chin quivered. With an effort, he managed to open his eyes and stare at his daughter's ashen face.

"Let . . . her go," he whispered hoarsely. "Let . . . Emma go. My . . . fault . . . "

"It's her fault, Papa, not yours. She ruined everything!" Tara rocked back on her heels, wringing her hands. "Now I have to leave. . . . I have to leave you."

"Damn it, woman, let's ride," Pratt yelled.

He pushed Emma toward the barn. There he got rope, tied her hands before her, then dragged her to Angel. By the time he'd hoisted her into the saddle and finished tying her hands to the pommel, Tara was rising from Ross's side.

"I think he's dead," she mumbled. Her gaze fastened on Emma. "It's your fault!"

"Pratt killed him, Tara. Face it. It's your fault—yours and Pratt's. But maybe we can still get a doctor and save him. If we ride to town right now—"

"The only place you're riding to is Elk Mountain. It's going to be your very last ride." Tara spoke coldly now, with flat finality. When she glanced toward Pratt, her expression was eerily calm, filled with purpose.

"You're right, Jimmy Joe. We have to get to the money. Because we can't stay here. Not now. We'll have to start over some place else." She nodded her head, her eyes looking vacant. "We'll buy another ranch. Because she's ruined everything here. But we can still have a ranch, right, Jimmy Joe? A big spread, one that's much better than Echo Ranch, better than Tall Trees!"

"Sure thing, darling."

"And I can still go east to study? And to Europe?

You'll wait for me and run our ranch? Build it up even bigger and better until I come back?''

"Whatever you say, Tara. But damn it, if we don't get out of here, we're not going anywhere except to jail. Come on, girl, let's ride!''

And as the rain streamed like tears over Ross McQuaid's body, Pratt grabbed Angel's reins, and the three of them rode north toward the foothills and Elk Mountain.

THE WIND WHIPPED AT HIS DUSTER AS TUCKER SPURRED Pike up the lane to Empire Ranch. Corinne hadn't wanted to open the door to him, much less answer his questions, but he'd finally gotten her to admit that Emma wasn't at home, that she hadn't seen her all morning.

There was a funny feeling in his gut. A sixth sense of doom.

"Tara!'' As Pike galloped toward the house, Tucker peered ahead through the drizzle. The place looked deserted.

"Ross!'' he called desperately. "Ross! Tara!''

His heart was already sinking because there was no one around. No ranch hands. No sign of Emma's mare. And no answer from inside the house.

Then he saw it.

The unmoving form lying among the weeds no more than twenty feet from the porch.

He vaulted from the saddle and hunkered down beside Ross McQuaid while a lump the size of a fist crammed through his chest.

"Ross." Blood everywhere. "Ross, who did this to you?"

He felt for life. With quickening hope, he found that a faint thread of breath still lingered in McQuaid's bloodied chest.

And then the rancher opened his eyes.

"S—sorry." The old man coughed. Spittle and blood dribbled from the corner of his lip. "My fault. Emma . . ."

"Where's Emma?" A vise of icy fear clamped around Tucker's throat. He leaned closer as sweat broke out on his brow, mingling with the warm summer rain. "Ross, tell me where she is."

"Tara and P—Pratt took her. Left me for d—dead. They'll k—kill her—"

"The hell they will. Ross, *where?* Where did they take Emma?"

"It was Tara." McQuaid was rambling, his eyes rolling in their sockets, his words coming out slurred and with agonizing difficulty. "She and Pratt . . . killed Beau. My sweet Tara . . ."

Shock washed over Tucker. For a moment he couldn't speak. Then the urgency slammed into him, and the deadly, determined fury, and he leaned close over the dying man. "Where did they take Emma, Ross? Ross! Come on, man, you have to tell me! Where is Emma?"

McQuaid drew a shuddering breath. Then his fingers grasped Tucker's hand with the last of his strength.

"Elk Mountain."

For a moment, his bony fingers tightened, as if

grasping onto Tucker's own strength and vitality, trying to draw from them. Then, with a gasping, gurgling hiss that chilled Tucker to the bone, he gave a shudder and his hand went limp.

Tucker sat in the rain for a moment, staring at the lifeless face, making sure the breath was gone.

Then he ran for his horse.

Jed was thundering up the path as he rode out.

"Wait just a damned minute," his father ordered as Tucker reined in with a curse. "I want you to tell me just what you thought you were doing with Miss Emma Malloy—"

"Listen to me, Pop, and listen good." Tucker's voice lashed through the gloom with the ferocity of a bullwhip. There was a terrible desperation in his face.

"Get to town pronto. Tell Sheriff Gill to let Win Malloy go. He didn't kill Beau. I know who did."

"What? Who—"

"There's no time!" Tucker shouted as Pike pranced restlessly and precious seconds ticked by. "Organize a posse to search Elk Mountain. Get Malloy—round up his men and ours—and as many others as you can find. You're looking for Tara McQuaid and Jimmy Joe Pratt. They've got Emma! So make tracks!" He gripped the reins in hands that had never shaken when he'd faced gunfighters, grizzlies, or stampeding cattle. But they shook now as he thought of Emma's danger. And if she *was* carrying their child . . .

"Go!" he commanded his father, then dug in his heels. He rode like a man pursued by every demon in hell and prayed he wouldn't be too late.

Chapter 29

SLADE SQUINTED HIS EYES ALL AROUND THE CANyon, up the trail, into every corner and crevice of the mountainside visible from where he stood.

Where the hell had they gone?

Damn. Here he'd been thinking himself lucky for having followed Emma Malloy today, witnessing everything that had happened at the McQuaid place, and finding himself with a golden opportunity. It was clear that all he had to do was stay on their trail, find out where this camp was, and then sneak up as close as he could get and listen in until Pratt and the McQuaid girl let slip where the bank loot was hidden.

Then he could rescue Emma, kill the pair of them, and go back later for the loot. When Emma told Sheriff Gill about the money, and he or the deputy went in search of it, they'd simply find that someone had beaten them to it.

This was all working out better than he could have planned. It was just what he'd always dreamed of doing: playing the hero, rescuing a beautiful and very rich young woman, *and* acquiring a nice bundle of extra cash, with no one the wiser.

Not only would he have instant prosperity, he'd also get the girl. Emma Malloy couldn't help but be grateful to him after he saved her life. Then there was her father's gratitude. Hell, the stupid town would probably organize a parade in his honor.

It was downright perfect.

Except, damn it all to hell, his luck had just run out.

He'd lost his quarry somewhere between Beaver Point and this canyon. He'd had to follow at too great a distance to keep them from spotting him or hearing his horse's hooves on the trail below, and they must've ducked into some remote pass or ravine somewhere along the way that he hadn't noticed. There were dozens of snaking trails on Elk Mountain, hidden passes, caves, canyons, and ledges—countless places to hide, to make camp, or to ride without being seen from above or below.

Well, Pratt and the McQuaid girl and Emma Malloy were *somewhere*. It might take some time, but he'd track them down.

The rain ebbed to a faint silvery drizzle as he sat there in the silence of a narrow ledge, chewing a wad of tobacco, spitting it over the edge of the canyon wall, trying to think. The sky was clearing; blue spots gleamed through the gray. The sun might even come out this afternoon, hardening the mud. There would be fresh tracks.

So he'd find them, follow them. And watch and

listen. When he was ready, when he knew where the money was hidden, he'd rescue Miss Emma.

A grin split Slade's face as he pictured her tossing her pretty arms around his neck, hugging him in tearful gratitude. And he pictured her father pumping his hand, insisting on giving him a big fat reward for rescuing his little girl.

And then Malloy would decide that it would be a very good thing for his daughter to marry the man who had saved her.

Slade was grinning still as he trotted his horse on up the narrow slit of a trail. Emma and Win Malloy were going to owe him plenty—and he was going to enjoy reaping every bit of the reward.

BENEATH A DOME OF HOT BLUE SKY, THE SUN BEAT DOWN unmercifully.

Emma's hat had slipped off when they'd skidded down a particularly twisting ravine, and it had fallen far down between the narrow walls of a red-rimmed canyon. Now the heat pierced her scalp and baked her skin and the sun glared into her eyes with cruel intensity.

If only the rain would return. She wasn't sure how much more she could take of the sun.

Her lips were stiff, her throat dry as chalk. She thought of Ross McQuaid bleeding to death in the rain, and of Beau sprawled lifeless beside Dead Dog Tree, and a shudder passed through her.

Dead or alive—who would ever find her on Elk Mountain?

Despair mounted as she peered around at the stony sides of the mountain. She tried not to think of her chafed wrists, rubbed raw by the rope that bound them, of the effect this grueling ride beneath the hot sun might be having on the new life she carried within her.

She had to think of something else or she'd lose her mind.

Tucker.

Tucker, I love you. I never even told you.

How foolish they'd been. Why hadn't they realized that time was precious? Love was precious. They'd wasted so much of it arguing, not believing in themselves, in their love, not doing everything they could to make it work.

If only I had another chance . . .

You do, she told herself, blinking back the tears. *You will. It isn't over yet. You must get away. You have to save yourself and the baby—and prove what really happened to Beau.*

She thought of her father imprisoned in a jail cell for a crime he didn't commit. She thought of Jed Garrettson, locked in his own jail, a jail of anger and silence and loneliness, and of Tucker.

Her heart filled with love and anguish as she thought of the man with whom she wanted to spend her future. She knew deep down that she and their baby might not have any future at all.

"We're almost there. Another couple of hours." Tara's voice, smug beside her. Tara stared into her face from beneath the brim of her own hat. And smiled her sweet, quiet smile, but this time it was laced with a malevolent satisfaction that sent chills skittering down Emma's spine.

"For you, Emma, it's going to be the end of the trail."

THEY REACHED A CLEARING ABOVE THE HIGH ROCKS JUST before dusk. It was a desolate spot, at the peak of a jagged canyon. An eagle circled high above the pines. Wildflowers grew stubbornly from between the cracks of rocks. A lizard slithered under some brush. Emma wished she could do the same.

"Let's have supper here." Tara reined in, eyeing a wide patch of grass beneath a tree. "It's still a ways to the camp, and I don't want to risk lighting a fire after dark. Just in case anyone comes looking for her," she added.

"Sure thing, honey lamb. Hey, maybe we should throw her off right here," Pratt suggested, dismounting and glancing over the ledge into the canyon.

"No. Not here." Tara shook her head. She slid off her horse, staring coldly at Emma. "At the camp. I know just the right spot. Where the chasm falls away to the river," she told Pratt, with a small smile. "No one will ever find her."

Pratt grinned at Emma as he cut the rope from her wrists and yanked her down from the saddle. "Bet you'd like a nice long drink of water, Miz Malloy, wouldn't you?" A malicious expression twisted his features when her knees buckled and she fell against him.

"What do you say, honey lamb, should I give Miz Malloy some water?"

"Why? She's going to die anyway." Tara sipped from her canteen, then handed it to Pratt. Her eyes still had that strange look of calm. Unnatural calm. "Tie her up to that tree for now." She spoke as sweetly to Pratt as if she were serving lemonade in her own parlor.

Emma licked her dry lips. "How did you fool us? How did none of us see that there was something so terribly wrong with you?" she whispered hoarsely.

"The only thing wrong with me is that I was deprived of what should have been mine."

"You heard what your father said—he wouldn't have won that game no matter what, and my father never cheated. Ross told you it was only a story—"

"Shut up!" Tara struck her full across the face. "He would have said anything back there to save you. Because he felt sorry for you. But I don't. And I know the truth. No matter what he said today, my father told me the truth when I was a little girl. And now you have to face it—and face what's coming to you."

There was no reasoning with her, Emma realized with dread. She made no sound as Pratt dragged her away. He forced her arms around the trunk of a larch and tied her wrists together.

"That'll hold you."

"People will be looking for me," Emma told him. "They'll be scouring the mountains. And once they find Ross McQuaid's body, every man in the territory will be joining the posse. You should get away now while you can, before you make things worse."

"Think so?" He grinned at her and tilted his head to one side. "Doesn't look like you're in much of a position to be telling people what to do."

"It'll go better for you if you let me go," Emma insisted. "Then you two can just ride—get clear away from here. Find that bank money you stole and—"

"Now listen up." Pratt stepped closer and grabbed her chin. His eyes were mean as a rattle-snake's. "I had enough of your back talk in that bank. You want me to hit you again?"

Emma shook her head, her eyes blurring with the pain his fingers caused as they dug into her flesh.

"Well, then, don't you say another word. Me and Tara have everything under control. Ain't no one go-ing to find you so fast. There's too many places to look. And by the time they do come lookin', you'll be over the side of that chasm and washed clean away down the river," he smirked. "Now as far as that money's concerned, we *are* going to go get it and it's going to buy us a real nice spread, so Tara and I can have that big cattle ranch she's always had a hanker-ing for. No more small places that ain't worth squat. We're going to have a grand place, famous for miles around. The Pratt Homestead. Right, darlin'?"

Tara, pulling jerky out of a pack, glanced up and smiled at him. "The Pratt Homestead," she mur-mured. "Oh, Jimmy Joe, I *do* like the sound of that."

"So there." The outlaw released Emma's chin and gave the rope one cruel final tug. "That there matter's closed."

As dusk came, Emma felt her hope and her

strength fading with the last luminous rays of opal light.

She had slid to the ground, too weary to stand, and was hunkered on her knees against the tree. The bark was rough against her cheek as she leaned against the trunk.

Her one chance would come when they untied her to lead her to her horse. If she was going to get away, that would be the moment.

But she no longer even had her derringer. She had no weapon. Only her wits. And a desperate will to live.

Pratt had shot a squirrel and they had roasted it on a spit for dinner. The tantalizing aroma of meat and beans and the sight of the hardtack biscuits filled her nostrils. Yet it was the water canteens she eyed most longingly. Her throat had never been so parched.

When this is over, she thought, refusing to give in to despair, *I will drink an entire pitcher of water. And then a pitcher of Corinne's lemonade. And then a pitcher of milk . . .*

She closed her eyes and tried to gather whatever strength she had left as twilight descended over Elk Mountain.

FEAR LODGED IN TUCKER'S VERY SOUL AS HE SCOURED THE winding trails of Elk Mountain. The air was still now, cool and calm, with night about to descend. Soon the blue shadows would come, and then the inky blackness of evening, and it would be nearly impossible to find Emma in the dark.

He prayed as he rode, his body tense, his mind tortured with images of her suffering, in pain—or worse.

With eyes that burned from straining to find prints, he scrutinized the rocky ledges and the treacherous ravines that slid and dipped away toward the cold silver shimmer of water far below.

Nothing.

He rode on.

It was almost evening when he spotted the man. A heavyset figure in a black hat crouched among the rocks above him. Tucker drew his gun without conscious thought and urged Pike on up the rocky trail. His gaze remained pinned upon the solitary figure, as he tried to make out who it might be.

The man was watching something or someone, staring fixedly across the narrow chasm of a canyon that separated him from an opposite ledge.

Suddenly, as Tucker closed the distance between them, the glowing sunset rays illuminated the man's profile.

Curt Slade.

Every nerve ending prickled. What the hell was Slade doing up here?

As Tucker spurred his horse forward, Slade turned and began clambering down the rocks. It was then that Tucker saw he was making his way toward his horse, hidden away in a clearing twenty feet below. Tucker swerved onto the path that led to the clearing and spurred Pike forward.

He got there just as Slade scrambled down and started toward his mount.

"Better tell me what you're up to, Slade, and make it quick. I'm in the mood to kill someone tonight and I've got a notion to start with you."

Shock and then fury flashed across the foreman's face.

"Garrettson." It was an oath, spoken as though it burned his tongue.

"Talk." Tucker cocked the safety of his gun. He saw the foreman's gaze shift down to the Colt pointed at his chest, then jerk back up to meet Tucker's eyes.

"I'll be damned if I let you ruin everything," he muttered. "This is my chance. I'm this close."

"This close to what?" Abruptly, his tone sharpened and he swung out of the saddle in one lithe movement. "You son-of-a-bitch, you know where Emma is, don't you? Tell me before I blow your head off."

"Calm down, Garrettson. She's over there. She'll be all right. I'm planning to get her out of there before they kill her. Soon as they let on where that money is hid."

"Money?"

"The bank robbery money. Malloy's ranch hand, Pratt, is one of the outlaws. Seems he's been in cahoots with the McQuaid girl. He's the one who shot your brother."

If Slade hoped to get an instant's advantage by springing this news on Tucker, he was disappointed. The other man's eyes pierced him like a bolt of lightning, but he didn't flinch or show any other sign of emotion.

Slade kept talking, hoping for something to distract the other man so he'd have a chance to draw. "I've been following them, waiting for the right moment. But I figured if I killed Pratt and the girl before they let on where the money is hid, we might never find it. Then it couldn't be returned to the folks in town—"

"You goddamned lying son-of-a-bitch."

Cold lethal fury shot through Tucker. Slade was after the money—not for the town, for himself! He'd seen Emma's danger and could have rescued her long before now. But he wanted the damned money!

Slade saw the murderous rage cross the other man's face and knew in that instant only one of them was going to leave that clearing alive. Greed, hatred, and impatience surged through him.

He'd be damned if he'd let Garrettson stop him now when he was so close to everything he wanted.

"You think you're going to rescue her?" he snarled. "After all I've gone through? I'll see you in hell first!"

And he went for his gun, swift and sure, and fired.

But Tucker was faster. His shot rang out first and Slade spun down into the dirt.

Tucker reached him in three long strides, knelt down, stared at the gasping, contorted face while blood spurted, soaking the earth.

"I would . . . have got her out. I would have—"

The bastard. Tucker's face was like stone. This was too quick for him, too easy. His lip curled in disgust. When Slade's body spasmed, and then went still, Tucker was already turning away. He never glanced back to see the foreman's sightless eyes staring at the darkening sky.

Tucker was already sprinting toward the rocks.

Chapter 30

"WHAT THE HELL WAS THAT?"

Pratt sprang to his feet even before the echo of the gunshots had faded. He scanned the canyon, the rocks, and scrub brush on the opposite ledge, the trail leading up to their clearing.

Nothing.

"It sounded like gunshots," Tara said uneasily.

"Yeah, but who fired them? And from where?"

"Jimmy Joe, do something."

"Like what?"

Tara pointed at Emma. "We have to get rid of her now. She knows too much. Untie her and bring her to the edge of the cliff and push her over. Do it quickly, before something happens—"

Emma had lifted her head at the sound of the shots. Someone was nearby. Perhaps it was someone searching for her, possibly even her own ranch hands, or perhaps just a hunter out shooting game. Whoever it was might come to her aid if they knew she was there.

"Help!" Her scream echoed through the canyon and circled up and up to the eagles gliding over the high rocks above. "Someone help me!"

Pratt bounded toward her and clamped a hand over her mouth. While he held her, Tara cut the rope with a knife.

"You've caused me enough trouble to last a lifetime, Emma Malloy," the girl said furiously. "But now it's all over. I'll be free of you at last."

As Pratt jerked her to her feet, Emma struggled with every vestige of her strength to break free of him, but his wiry arms held her fast.

"No, you don't," he growled as he drew his gun and shoved her away from him. "Now, if you make one more peep, I'll shoot."

He flicked a glance at Tara. "Where do you want her to go over, honey lamb?"

"Right there." Tara darted toward the ledge that overlooked the yawning chasm of the canyon. "I'd wanted to savor the moment," she fretted.

"We'll make it short and sweet. Over there," Pratt ordered Emma, jerking the gun toward the spot where Tara stood. "Pronto."

Emma didn't move.

"I told you to get going." Pratt's shove sent her reeling toward the ledge. She regained her balance and stood there, ten feet from the edge, staring in terror at the dizzying drop.

Jagged rocks and steep granite slopes fell away into a glittering basin. A stream glimmered far below, a twisting silver thread barely visible in the hazy lavender shadows of dusk.

"There is your destiny," Tara pronounced with dreamy pleasure.

Emma's eyes locked upon the other girl's mad, utterly pleasant brown ones. "The hell it is," she muttered and lunged at her.

Her only hope was to use Tara as a shield against Pratt's gun while she got her derringer back from Tara's pocket. The odds were against her, but she didn't have much of a choice, and she'd be damned if she'd go over that ledge without a fight.

But even as she charged at Tara a shot sang out, pinging the dirt only inches from Pratt's boot.

"Nobody move!" Tucker's voice called out across the chasm with the icy blast of a norther.

"Nooo!" Tara's scream was a keening wail of frustration that must have pierced the fringes of the sky. She flung herself at Emma and locked her arms around her with a wild vengeance.

"You're . . . going over!" she screeched and shoved Emma toward the precipice.

Even as Emma fought to free herself, she saw Pratt go for his gun and heard gunshots roaring across the chasm. The acrid stench of gunpowder scorched her nostrils as she dug in her heels and struggled to escape Tara's frenzied hold.

"Tara—freeze or I'll shoot!" Tucker's voice was a slice of thunder. Watching from the opposite ledge, his every muscle clenched with powerlessness. He couldn't shoot—not with Tara and Emma so close together. He couldn't take the chance of hitting Emma.

And he couldn't get to them. Not in time.

He'd reached the spot where Slade had been

watching Pratt's camp, but there was no way of getting across, not without going nearly all the way down the trail and back up the other path to the ledge where they were camped.

"Emma—I need a clear shot!"

But the two women were clasped in a fevered, deadly struggle. Tara suddenly seemed possessed of an ungodly strength. Emma couldn't break free, and Tucker saw her fighting with all she had just to keep from being hurled over the side of the cliff.

He scrambled to the edge of the rocks, digging in a foothold and raising the gun. He'd have to fire and pray that he'd hit Tara and that Emma didn't swerve into range of the bullet at the last instant.

And then, suddenly, with a groan, Emma flung Tara away from her, back into the brambles. A frightening determination glowed in the other girl's eyes, and her laugh was wild, desperate.

"Over, over," she repeated. "You're going over!"

She launched herself at Emma again, even as Tucker fired. The bullet missed, but in her frenzied rush, Tara's foot struck a rock. A choked cry broke from her as she stumbled, slid, and lost her balance. For one heart-stopping instant, she teetered frantically on the edge. With a gasp, acting on pure instinct, Emma reached out, tried to grasp her arm, but touched only empty air.

Tara hurtled downward, her scream echoing horribly as she plummeted straight toward the glinting ribbon below.

Emma never heard her hit bottom. There was a

roaring in her ears. And a weakness in her knees. *Dear God.*

She backed off from the edge, saw Pratt's bullet-ridden body in the dirt, and veered away. She sank down upon a rock, leaned forward with her head in her hands, and tried to blot out Tara's scream, the sight of Pratt, the clamor in her ears.

She didn't know how long she sat there, dazed and numb, rocking back and forth, but suddenly she felt strong arms around her, gathering her close, smelled the familiar masculine scent of leather and tobacco, and heard Tucker saying, "It's all right, Sunshine. You're all right. Everything's going to be fine."

The roaring faded. The dizziness ebbed. She glanced up, smiling tremulously and joyfully into Tucker's eyes. Into his solid, handsome face. Leaned into his shoulder and clung to him with every ounce of strength she had left.

"It's all over, sweet." He held her tighter. "I'm here."

"Stay," she whispered. "Don't leave."

"I won't, Emma. Not ever."

He'd never seen her look this drained, this pale, even though she'd been scorched by the sun. Her beautiful lips were cracked and dry, there were scratches on her arms and bloody streaks on her wrists from a rope. Tucker let her go for a moment and grabbed his canteen. "Drink, Emma. Slow, easy. Not too fast."

As he lowered the canteen, she tilted her head up and closed her eyes.

"It . . . took you long enough," she murmured

and snuggled closer against him. She was rewarded by Tucker's quick gruff laugh.

"Yeah, too damn long." The laughter faded. He couldn't bear to think how close he'd come to losing her. "But you're stuck with me now." His arms tightened, as if somehow they could protect her from any hurt, any pain, any sadness. Ever. "For good," he added, his tone husky.

"Tucker, do you mean that?"

His lips brushed the tip of her sunburnt nose. "I love you, Emma. If you don't start building those fences, I will. So long as we're fenced in together."

She straightened in his arms and stared into his face, joy suffusing hers. "Tucker, I have something to tell you. Something wonderful. I can't wait another minute—"

Suddenly, they heard the sounds of men and horses. "Looks like you'll have to." He released her, sprang up, gun in hand. When he saw Win Malloy, Sheriff Gill, Deputy Clem Tray, and his own father on the trail below, he fired a shot in the air.

"Up here!" he shouted, waving the gun above his head as the men all looked up.

"Emma?" Win Malloy's voice, hoarse and desperate reached them on the clearing. "Is she with you?"

"Yes." Even from that distance, Tucker saw the relief wash across Win Malloy's face. "She's fine," he called.

He turned back to Emma, sat beside her, and encircled her in his arms again. "They'll be here right away."

She spoke wonderingly. "How did my father get out of jail?"

"Before Ross died, he told me that it was Tara and Pratt who killed Beau. I sent word to Gill to set your father free so he could join the search for you."

Tucker smoothed a strand of hair back from her cheek with gentle fingers. Just the sight of Emma's tremulous smile pierced his heart and made him want to kiss her. But she looked like she was ready to break and he scarcely dared to touch her.

"We'll have time to sort everything out after we get you into a nice soft featherbed and let that housekeeper of yours make you tea and soup and whatever else women do when they're fussing over someone."

"You're going to find out about that very soon, Garrettson, because I'm going to be doing a lot of fussing over you," she promised, smiling despite the aching weakness that assailed her.

"Over both of you," she added, with a touch of mischief in her turquoise eyes, and Tucker's heart stopped.

"Both of us?" he asked cautiously, scarcely daring to hope.

Emma touched his hands, clasping them in hers. "We're going to have a baby," she whispered.

The expression of pure joy that lit those hard features made her heart flip. He grabbed her to him, hugged her, and kissed her mouth with gusto, then froze and pulled away.

"I won't break," Emma said softly. "I'm tougher than I look."

"Sure you are, Sunshine. But I'm not taking any

chances, you hear? Not with you and not with our baby.''

Our baby. The words filled them with delight.

As the sounds of the approaching posse reached their ears, and darkness drifted down over the mountain, Tucker and Emma stared into each other's eyes and found everything they had ever looked for.

Chapter 31

THE FOLLOWING DAY TUCKER GARRETTSON rode up to the Malloy ranch in his Sunday best suit, carrying a fistful of wildflowers.

His shirt collar felt too tight, and he ran a finger around it trying to loosen it a notch, then he straightened his shoulders and started up the porch.

Before he could rap on the door, it was opened. Corinne eyed him with frowning speculation. Her hands on her hips, she snapped, "What is it *you* want?"

"I'm here to see—" Tucker broke off in consternation. His voice had cracked like a schoolboy's! He cleared his throat, cursed himself for being so sick with love, and started again.

"Ma'am," he said with cool politeness. "I'm here to see Emma. And Mr. Malloy. And . . ." he added with a dazzling flash of the smile that had charmed saloon women clear across the territory, "you."

"Me?" Suspicion narrowed Corinne's pea-green

little eyes, but she blushed a tad beneath the power of that smile. "What do you want to see me for?"

"To give you these." He thrust the bouquet at her. "To thank you for being so good to Emma—I'm sure you took real good care of her last night when she got home."

"Hmph, I always take good care of her," Corinne huffed, but she edged aside from the door, took a sniff of the bouquet, and almost smiled. "Reckon you can come in. I'll tell Emma you're here."

He stepped inside. He'd never been in the Malloy ranch house before, but he found it every bit as bright and homey as he'd expected. He took a deep breath, swearing he could feel Emma's presence in this high-beamed cheerful house, then suddenly remembered that he'd given her flowers to Corinne.

Damn! He turned and rushed outside again, glancing swiftly around the grounds until he spotted some bluebells and primroses growing over beyond the well. He dashed toward them and began snatching up clumps of them until the sound of soft laughter behind him made him straighten.

"What *are* you doing, Garrettson?"

Turning, he saw the woman he intended to marry. She looked like a dream. Her hair streamed over her shoulders and down her back, loose and lovely and dark as night, and her distinctive turquoise eyes glowed in the sunlight that gilded her face. She wore a buttercup yellow dress edged at the collar with white lace that was delicate as a snowflake, and her hands were clasped demurely before her, at odds with the mischievously amused expression on her adorable face.

Tucker strode toward her. "What does it look like I'm doing, Malloy?" he asked, drinking in the scent of her, the shattering beauty and elegance in every line of her face.

"Are those for me?"

"Who else?"

"Corinne?" She burst out laughing. "She was clutching the bouquet when she came upstairs. I've never seen her eyes sparkle quite like that. You've made yourself a conquest, Garrettson."

"Only one?"

"Two," she whispered, gasping as his arms encircled her. But his embrace was gentle and when he gathered her close against him, it was with tenderness.

"I figured out that I forgot to do something last night—with all the commotion and everything. Your father riding up, and mine, the sheriff, all the questions—"

"You forgot to kiss me." She touched his lips with her fingertips. "I know."

"That, too. But mainly I forgot to propose."

Speechless, Emma gaped up at him. She'd thought she was happier than she'd ever been a moment ago, with Tucker's arms around her, having caught him picking her flowers—imagine Tucker Garrettson picking flowers! But the breathless delight that swept over her now made everything that came before pale in comparison.

"Propose," she repeated dazedly, then opened her eyes wide at him. "Is *that* what this is all about?"

she breathed. "Then, by all means, don't let me stop you—"

"I'll stop you."

Win Malloy's voice made them jump apart. He was standing by the well, but now he strode toward them, eyeing Tucker as if he were a coyote who'd just sneaked into the chicken coop.

"Whatever you're up to, Garrettson, I won't have you manhandling my daughter out here for all the ranch hands to see. State your business. Corinne said you came to see me."

Tucker stuck his thumbs in his pockets and rocked back on his heels, studying Win Malloy coolly from beneath the brim of his hat. "Mostly I came to see Emma," he drawled with a nonchalance that bordered dangerously close to insolence. Emma caught her breath, then hooked her arm through his.

"And I'm so glad you're here," she interjected sweetly. "But you must be thirsty after your ride. Why don't we all go inside and have some lemonade, and then we can chat like civilized human beings. I *hope,*" she added with a meaningful glance at the two most important men in her life.

That was her plan, but as she carried the lemonade into the parlor on a tray, misgivings fluttered within her. So did the queasiness she was becoming accustomed to experiencing.

Tucker ignored the glass of lemonade she handed him, setting it down upon the table before the sofa without a glance. He then took the tray from her and placed it on the table, and then helped Emma to the sofa so solicitously she nearly laughed. She looked over and saw that her father was studying this act of gallantry closely.

"So," Win Malloy began, but at that moment the front door banged open.

Jed Garrettson charged into the hall.

"Garrettson, what the hell do you think you're doing on my property?" Win roared. "It's bad enough that your son—"

"Papa, please!" Emma rushed over and placed herself in front of Jed, who had skidded to a halt. Corinne hurried in from the kitchen at the commotion, a frying pan clutched like a weapon in her hand.

"If Mr. Garrettson wants to come to call, he is welcome here," Emma stated.

"Like hell he is!"

"He is." Emma's tone was firm and calm. But her eyes, fixed upon her father's face, held a glimmer of pleading which Win Malloy could not help but respond to.

"He . . . is." Win grated out between clenched teeth. "But I wish to hell—to heaven . . . " He mopped his brow as sweat gathered and began to drip down to his bushy eyebrows. "That he would have knocked on my front door first!"

As everyone filed back toward the center of the room, including Corinne, who took up a spot near the cherry whatnot with the frying pan still clenched in her hands, Tucker pulled his father aside.

"What the hell are you doing here?" he demanded in an undervoice. Jed's presence could only be trouble. It would be hard enough for him to try to make some kind of peace with Malloy and ask him for his daughter's hand in marriage, but with his own father here—it would be about as easy as eating steak with a spoon.

"I'm here to—" Jed had begun speaking in what for him was a low tone, but as he saw everyone staring at him, he began again, booming out in his usual robust manner. "I'm here to say something to Malloy."

"Say it then," Win growled. He stood behind the sofa, his hands on Emma's shoulders as she sat back against the cushions. She reached up and covered one of his hands with her own.

"I know you didn't kill my boy Beau."

Silence reverberated through the parlor. Emma felt her father's hand stiffen against hers.

"Tucker and Wesley Gill explained it all to me last night after you took Emma home to bed. I do hope you're feeling better today, missy," he said, turning his glance to her.

"Much better, Mr. Garrettson. Thank you for asking." She nodded and gave him a smile full of so much encouraging warmth he dropped his hat and quickly stooped to pick it up.

"Well, you're welcome." He cleared his throat and once again focused his attention on Win Malloy. "So, I reckon—that is, Tucker told me—we both need to apologize to you for accusing you like we did. So . . . this is it. My apology, that is. I'm . . . sorry."

"Papa?" Emma half-turned on the sofa. The yearning expression in her eyes was no match for the anger Win would have liked to hold onto. He let it go. "Apology accepted," he grumbled.

"You have mine, too," Tucker added, and the

smile Emma sent him nearly made his chest hairs melt. He was thankful that he at least managed to hold onto his hat.

"Accepted," Win grated out. But he gave Tucker a slight nod as well, and Emma felt her heart lightening.

"There," she said softly. "Now that wasn't so difficult, was it?"

"There's more." Jed Garrettson squashed the brim of his hat between his fingers. "We sort of figured out that it must have been Tara and that outlaw who were causing all that trouble these past months. They were the ones who poisoned your cattle, Malloy, the ones who were rustling my herd. We're going to check the brands on some of McQuaid's stock and see if they've been changed. Poor Ross didn't have any notion what was going on."

"No, he didn't." Emma glanced from Jed to her father. "He was so shocked, so devastated when he heard what Tara was admitting to doing. He tried to stop her, to save me. That's how he got shot."

"He was a good friend," Win said heavily. "I'll miss him. But Tara . . . " He shook his head. "I just don't understand what was wrong with that girl."

"It must have been Pratt who shot at you that day," Tucker said suddenly, and Win Malloy started.

"Shot at you, Emma? When?"

She explained. And added that Pratt *had* been responsible. All because Tara had wanted to frighten her into leaving Montana so that she and the outlaw could buy Echo Ranch.

''Who'd have thought that sweet little thing could be so full of evil?'' Jed exclaimed.

Win Malloy squared his shoulders and walked toward him. ''Garrettson, guess if you're man enough to apologize, then so am I. I'm sorry I accused you of being behind all the trouble. Guess it really wasn't your men raiding our cattle, jumping Slade and roughing him up—'' He swung toward Tucker. ''Which brings me to another thing. What in hell happened to Slade? Heard from Clem that they found his corpse on Elk Mountain. That you shot him.''

''Only wish I could have horsewhipped him first.'' Tucker's expression was grim. ''He'd been following Emma and Tara and Pratt. He knew Emma was in trouble, told me he planned to rescue her, but not until after those two let slip where the bank money was hidden.''

''What?'' Both Win and Jed shouted simultaneously, and Corinne's jaw dropped. She snapped it shut and stared hard at Tucker.

''You mean to tell me he was more concerned about the money than saving Emma from those vermin?''

''That sounds exactly like Slade to me.'' Emma answered for him. ''He wasn't the man you thought he was, Papa. There was another side to him. Just as there was to Tara.''

''Slade was ready to kill me before he'd let me get to Emma first and ruin his plan,'' Tucker added, his eyes narrowed. The sunlight glinted on his sandy hair as he took a seat beside Emma and held her hand. ''So I had no choice but to kill him first.''

"Thank you." Emma gazed into his eyes and for a moment they were the only two people in the room. "I owe you my life—more than once."

"You owe me a hell of a lot more than that, Sunshine," Tucker said softly, and her heart rejoiced at the gentle upward curve of his lips.

"Well, I'm tickled that Slade's dead," Corinne piped up, nodding with satisfaction. "But it's too bad for everyone in town that we'll never know where Pratt hid all that money he stole—"

"Wait!" Sudden inspiration swept over Emma. "I bet I know." She sprang off the sofa and hurried up the stairs, returning a moment later with a crumpled sheet of ledger paper. "We can give this to Sheriff Gill later. It's proof that Tara copied my father's handwriting. But on the other side—look, Tucker! It's a map."

He took the note from her and examined it. When he glanced up, his eyes rested admiringly upon her eager face. "Looks like this could be what we need. It shows a spot three miles west of Bear Paw Canyon. Looks like the money's hidden in a hollowed out tree stump."

"Let's see." Win snatched the map and studied it, a satisfied smile breaking out on his face.

"Maybe you ought to join the Pinkerton Agency," Tucker told Emma, and she laughed.

"Maybe I will, unless I get a better offer."

Corinne spoke up then, having missed nothing that passed between the lean, handsome cowboy with the devastating smile and her darling Emma. She'd never seen the girl glow as she was today, despite the ordeal of yesterday. She was radiant as a dewdrop.

"Seems to me it's time we let these young people have a moment alone," she began, but Emma interrupted her.

"Not just yet." She rose from the sofa and turned to face her father and Jed. To her amusement, they suddenly looked as wary and as guilty as recalcitrant schoolboys.

"It's time we settled this feud once and for all," she announced, and there was no mistaking the firm outward thrust of her chin, a sure sign that they had a better chance of catching a mountain lion in a butterfly net than of swaying her from what she had in mind.

"Papa, I want you to shake Mr. Garrettson's hand."

"Emma, don't start this. Isn't it enough I let the man in my house? Don't expect me to—"

"I do expect you to do just that. Too much mistrust, grief, pain, and death has come from this feud already—from other people trying to use it to their own advantage. We must end it—now. Today. So that the future can be better," she added and the gentleness of her tone as she spoke these last words pierced Win Malloy's heart.

Late last night, as he and Corinne had hovered over her while she lay in her bed, she had told them about the baby. And that was what Win Malloy thought about in that moment when she spoke of the future. *The baby.* His future grandchild, who also would be the grandchild of this man who had been his enemy for sixteen years.

Every word Emma said was true. The feud had caused more pain than it had a right to. And there was another generation to think of now.

"Papa?"

He peered over at Jed and remembered the man he had played poker with years before. They'd been friends once, friendly rivals, at least. Until that one night.

"Only if he'll admit that I wasn't cheating!"

"Pop." Tucker advanced on his father, frowning. "Your turn. Face up to what needs to be done."

Jed Garrettson had seen how Win responded to his daughter's every word and glance. The love and devotion that was so obvious between them had struck him on more than one occasion, but never more so than today. He looked at his own son, his remaining son, with new eyes. And there he saw it: the same quiet yearning, hoping that Emma's eyes had shown, was mirrored there in the gaze that Tucker was directing upon him now.

Suddenly he was awash in emotions that had been buried for so long, squashed down so deep, that their surfacing made him sway on his feet. Tucker grasped his arm to steady him, and Emma rushed forward.

"Do you need your tonic?" she asked in her soft, direct way, and Jed shook his head. It wasn't his heart that ailed him—well, it was—but not in the way that any tonic could help. Except one.

He glanced from Emma's lovely, anxious face to his son's lean, strong, concerned one and felt a rush of love and tenderness such as he hadn't felt in a long, long time. And he knew what he had to do. For Tucker. And for the sweet, beautiful girl Tucker loved.

"The truth is," Jed met Win Malloy's frowning gaze head-on. "I know damn well you won fair and square. Guess I knew it all along. I was drunk that night and I never should have wagered my land, and it was my own damn fault I lost it." He took a deep breath and stuck out his hand.

"What do you say we end this feud now, Malloy? For the sake of our children?"

Win met Garrettson's eyes. He didn't have to look in Emma's to know what she was feeling right now: hope, eagerness, and at the same time, uncertainty.

"For the sake of our children," Win said hoarsely and grasped Jed's outstretched fingers. They shook hands vigorously and broke apart, each a little stunned at what had just occurred.

It was Corinne, grinning with relief, who burst out, "Not to mention the sake of your grandchildren."

Everyone turned and stared at her. She turned beet red. "Oh. Goodness, Emma, please forgive me. Me and my loose tongue. Dang if it didn't just slip out."

"I told Papa and Corinne about the baby last night," Emma explained quickly to Tucker, studying his face for a sign of anger because she had told the secret before everything was worked out between them. "They couldn't understand why I didn't want to eat much despite not having eaten all day and . . . ''

"It's all right." He caught her to him in a hug and

his grin filled her with relief. "I told my father last night, too."

"That's right, missy, he did." Jed Garrettson stalked forward and clapped his son on the back. "So when are you two getting married?" he demanded. "And where? I say it should be at Tall Trees. Our parlor is a mite bigger than this one here," he added, sweeping a critical glance over it, "and you women-folk can brighten it up all you want with flowers and all, and I think your ma would like to have you married there, Tucker. Yep, I do."

"Well, I think these two young people should tie the knot right here." Win was equally emphatic. He turned and pointed toward the hall. "Emma can come down those stairs in her mama's wedding dress, and Corinne will cook a feast like you've never seen, and it's only right that my little girl get married in her very own home."

"Well, it won't be her home for long. They're going to come and live at Tall Trees after the wedding. I've got me a hankering to liven up that house, and it's only right that my grandson grow up on the property that's going to belong to him one day—"

"Echo Ranch will be his one day, too," Win countered. "I mean hers. Sure as shooting that baby's going to be a girl."

"Girl? You're loco, Malloy. Loco." Jed snorted contemptuously. There was fire in his eyes. "Anyone can see you don't know a cow chip from a hayseed. This little missy here is sick the very same way my wife was sick and she had two sons. These two children of ours are having a *boy*."

"Don't you tell me what they're having, you ignorant old sourpuss! My gut says it's a girl, and she's going to be as beautiful as her mother and—"

"Hold on!" Corinne banged the frying pan against the arm of the sofa with a resounding thwack that brought startled silence to the room.

"Has this young man even proposed to Emma yet?" she demanded.

Jed and Win both turned toward Emma and Tucker.

"Not yet." Tucker's jaw was tight. "But if you'd let me get a word in edgewise—"

"Hell, son, what are you waiting for? Go ahead now—get it over with and don't be shy. Any fool can see you're in love with the gal."

"This is no way for a man to propose to my daughter." Win frowned. "They have a right to a little privacy and Emma deserves—"

"Emma deserves to speak for herself." Her laughter floated like a summer breeze through the room. "And I say 'yes.' "

"I haven't asked you yet," Tucker growled, silently cursing the two garrulous old men who'd spoiled his plan for flowers and a proposal on bended knee, for a formal request to Emma's father for her hand in marriage.

"Sunshine." He tilted her chin up and tried to frown, but couldn't help chuckling. "Don't you think you should wait until I ask you?"

"I'm not much good at waiting, and I've already done enough of it, but if you like, Garrettson," she grinned saucily up at him, "go ahead and ask."

"Here? With them?"

"As long as neither of them answers."

"You heard my daughter, young man."

"Son, if you don't make an honest woman out of this little lady soon, I'll—"

"Everyone just hold your horses." Tucker glanced down and saw the flowers he'd inadvertently crushed in his hand. He set them on the table, then snatched them back up and thrust them at Emma. "Here. These are for you."

"Why, thank you, Tucker." Her eyes danced, and he wasn't sure if he wanted to spank her or kiss her. But Emma's comeuppance would wait. Not much longer, but it would wait.

"Glad you like them. Now . . . " He went down on one knee. Win Malloy and his father and the housekeeper were inspecting his every move. He swore under his breath and wiped sweat from his brow. Good thing no one from the Jezebel Saloon could see him now. They'd never believe it.

"Now," he went on, with desperate purpose, "I'd like to ask you, Emma . . . "

"Dearest Emma," she said softly, and her finger stroked lightly along his cheek. His razor blue eyes pierced her laughing ones, and suddenly Tucker forgot about everyone watching them, forgot about every saloon woman who'd teased him about not being a marrying man, forgot about everything except how much he loved her, and how close he'd come to losing her. And how their baby would make them a family.

He seized her hand and kissed her cool palm. There was a huskiness in his voice as he said, for her ears only, "Dearest Emma—you are my sunshine. I need you. I love you. I think I've loved you since that first kiss all those years ago. There's been an emptiness inside of me until you came back, one I didn't even know I had. If you don't consent to marry me, I'm going to up and die. And if you do, I'll be the happiest hombre who ever lived. So," he finished, and felt a flash of pride and joy and triumph at the shimmering tears in her beautiful eyes. "Emma Malloy, will you marry me?"

"Yes, I will." Emma gave a shriek as Tucker yanked her onto his knee and his mouth covered hers with a sudden heat that made the room spin. When she could breathe again, and speak, he settled her on the sofa and sat beside her, cupping her face in his hands.

"Tell me again," he urged, chuckling deep in his throat. "It's the least you could do after such a fancy proposal."

"Yes, Tucker Garrettson, I will marry you," she obliged, with love radiating from her eyes. Her hands threaded through his hair, her lips inched closer to his. When she was only a breath away she dimly heard exclamations of congratulations and hand-clapping, but she couldn't take her eyes off the incredibly dear and handsome face of her fiancé.

"I will marry you," she whispered again, her lips against his, "and I'll love you 'til the day I die and I'll make you and our child—our children very happy."

"And so will I," he vowed with every fiber of his being.

And that is exactly what they did.